HOUSE OF SPELLS AND SECRETS

Also available by Ivy Cassidy (writing as Melissa Bourbon)

The Lola Cruz Mysteries

Fa-La-La-La-Lola

Lola Baby

Drop Dead Lola

What Lola Wants

Bare-Naked Lola

Hasta La Vista, Lola

Living the Vida Lola

The Magical Dressmaking Mysteries

Hem Fatale

Bobbin for Answers

Bodice of Evidence

A Seamless Murder

A Killing Notion

A Custom-Fit Crime

Deadly Patterns

A Fitting End

Pleating for Mercy

The Book Magic Mysteries

Shadows on the Page

The Open Door Bookshop

Long Forgotten Stories

The Bibliomancer's Daughter

Between the Lines

The Legends Series

The Final Victim

The Final Prey

The Spellbound Series

Storiebook Charm

The Foxy Ladies Mysteries

God Rest Ye Murdered Gentleman

Love, Lies, and Lousy Exes

Writing as Winnie Archer

The Bread Shop Mysteries

Bread Over Troubled Water

A Murder Yule Regret

Death Gone A-Rye

Dough or Die

Flour in the Attic

The Walking Bread

Crust No One

Kneaded to Death

HOUSE OF SPELLS AND SECRETS

A Novel

IVY CASSIDY

alcove press

Published in the United States by Alcove Press, an imprint of The Quick Brown Fox & Company LLC.

Alcove Press and its logo are trademarks of The Quick Brown Fox & Company LLC.

Library of Congress Catalog-in-Publication data available upon request.

ISBN (hardcover): 979-8-89242-420-2
ISBN (paperback): 979-8-89242-421-9
ISBN (ebook): 979-8-89242-422-6

Cover design by Colin Verdi

Printed in the United States.

www.alcovepress.com

Alcove Press
34 West 27th St., 10th Floor
New York, NY 10001

First Edition: March 2026

The authorized representative in the EU for product safety and compliance is eucomply OÜPärnu mnt 139b-14, 11317 Tallinn, Estonia, hello@eucompliancepartner.com, +33757690241

10 9 8 7 6 5 4 3 2 1

For my dad,
who is always in my heart—
and now, forever inked on my arm.
I carry you with me in every word.

And for my mom,
my first and forever best friend.
Your love grounds me, always.

Prologue

Paddy, 1839

The swallows came to roost under the eaves of the house on the Chesapeake Bay the day Paddy Early mortared the last brick and hung the last shingle. They'd followed him all the way from Ireland. Some people thought they were his protectors, but he knew better. They were loyal not to him but to his mother, Biddy. She called herself a Silverborn—one who remembered. One who heard memories.

She was bewitched, and he'd betrayed her.

The swallows were going to be the bane of his new existence in America. He was three thousand miles from his home, but he knew that no matter how far he traveled, he would never escape his mother or her magic. He stared up at the house he'd built with its steep A-line roof. Stared at the mud nests the birds had already built, at the bird with the red feathers, and for a moment, he was transported back to the three-room cottage in Feakle, County Clare. The swallows' nests there were identical. They conjured up the memory of the last time he'd seen his mother. Biddy had watched him as he'd walked down the lane.

"You can never escape who you are, Paddy, and you can't escape me," she said. "The magic, it will always find you."

She'd spoken calmly, as if she'd expected his disloyalty. He'd shifted the parcel tucked under his arm, the object wrapped in one of her quilts. The quilt had been given to her in trade for some healing ointment or cure. That's how things worked in Biddy's life. It was how the goats and pigs came to graze in her yard, how the stack of knitted blankets in the bedrooms grew, and why the cupboards overflowed with whiskey. Their house had become a social hall where townsfolk came to drink and play cards. It had also been a target for the tenant landlords and Catholic priests who thought Biddy was a heretic.

Who thought he was one too. Guilt by association.

The bundle he held pulsed with energy. He thought it would fade the farther away he got from Biddy, but the opposite happened. It grew stronger until his arms quivered.

He ignored it as best he could because leaving Ireland meant an end to his suffering. No more taunting about Biddy being a changeling or about her talking to the fairies.

No more accusations of witchcraft.

No more because he had left, and he had taken the thing that was her lifeblood. During the entire crossing from Belfast to Baltimore, the wrapped parcel had felt heavy, like an anchor that would take him to the bottom of the sea if he let it. Onboard the *Glenmore*, he'd heard his mother's voice calling to him from the sky, through the clouds and the billowing sails. His first thought was that she had transformed herself into a swallow and was following the ship. Over and over, his gaze shot upward, and over and over, he spotted Biddy's swallows. He heard her say his name. He heard Siobhan ó Dálaigh too. And he saw one swallow turn and glide away from the ship, back the way it had come. Reporting to Biddy, no doubt. He closed his eyes against their warnings, telling him he shouldn't leave. He ignored the omen that he would pay for his betrayal.

Oh, but he held no loyalty to Biddy, and he certainly held none to Siobhan. He had loved her as much as a twenty-year-old man can love. But he loved the idea of freedom more. Siobhan had run after him, begging him to stay, the dust of the road swirling around her feet. He'd stopped once. Turned to look at her. But it was Biddy, standing still as a stone on the road behind Siobhan, who drew his attention. She didn't look angry or hurt at his thievery. He'd faltered for a moment when she'd shaken her head. Even from where he'd stood, he could see the expression on her face. Disappointment, plain and simple.

Biddy had ruined his life with her potions and spells, curses and cures. He'd thought taking the one thing she cared about most would be the end of her, but he still felt her presence like an aura, always pressing down on him.

Now he stood on the threshold of the house he'd built on the little island in the Chesapeake Bay, the Flemish bond making the brick structure sturdy and immovable. He raked his fingers through his hair, yanking loose the knots, strands of auburn coming free in his hand. Overnight, a vine he had not planted had grown alongside the house. A winter creeper. He'd have to keep an eye on it, cut it back or it would take over.

Overhead, the swallows warbled and chirped, but he ignored them. He was done with Biddy. She was an ocean away. Here in America, he would take his mother's magic and make it his own.

He lifted his arm and waved them away. "Go 'ome," he hollered. Without warning, his mind hurtled back to that last moment with Biddy when he'd turned his back on her. Her voice had come after him, spiraling from her mouth straight into his ear. He still wasn't sure if she'd actually spoken or if he'd only heard the words in his head. "De swallows, dey are de keepers now."

Chapter One

Rowan, 1971

The Connors girls had always been called witches.

Not the cauldron-stirring kind, but the kind people whispered about. The kind who made the air shift when they entered a room. Who left something behind after they'd gone.

"You have a gift," their mother used to say, tucking Rowan's hair behind her ear like it was a blessing. "A charm. Something older than you can imagine."

People called it intuition. A knowing. But Rowan had always known better. There was magic in their blood. In all of them.

She'd seen it clearly in her sisters.

They were triplets, born within nine minutes of each other. Caraline was the oldest, born on the thirty-first of December in the waning minutes of 1950. Saoirse had come on the cusp of midnight, and Rowan had been delivered mere minutes later.

True to being the firstborn, Caraline's magic was louder and warmer. It thrived in her cooking, when she folded it into dough and steeped it in broth. Rowan didn't know how hibiscus rolls could soften an argument, or why rosemary bread helped someone remember things that had long ago started to fade, but somehow they did. Caraline called it comfort, but Rowan knew it was enchantment.

Saoirse could coax flowers to bloom out of season and lure herbs to grow even in the heaviest clay soil. Her teas did more than soothe. Rowan had seen them ease fevers, quiet grief, and silence nightmares. Saoirse didn't call it magic, but Rowan had always felt it in the way a room calmed when she entered. She carried stillness like a cloak.

And then there was Rowan. She didn't brew curative tinctures or bake healing breads. Her magic, such as it was, served no purpose. It didn't look like theirs.

In fact, it didn't look like anything.

Her eyes, green like clover and threaded with gold, drew stares she couldn't explain. And her hair, with a single streak of impossible red, practically glowed in the moonlight. She tried to hide it, oh, how she tried. She used bleach to turn it Marilyn Monroe blonde, but it didn't work. She dyed it every shade of brown, then black, thinking she could bury the flame. But it never lasted. The ruby streak always returned, a mark she couldn't shake.

People always looked at her a second too long, as if they could sense something inexplicable about her. Sometimes she even felt it too. But most of the time she felt like the odd one out with her sisters.

Saoirse had a head of red hair and her eyes were dark like pine needles. Unlike Rowan, she didn't long for friends. All she needed were her plants, herbs, and whatever flower she held at any given moment, plus the apothecary she always created wherever they lived. And, of course, the swallows, which she *could* make behave.

Caraline's hair was the color of midnight, which set off the flecks of amber in her eyes. She was the opposite of both Rowan and Saoirse. Friendships with women she could do without, but the attention she got from men? That practically fed her soul. At every new place they went, Caraline had herself a new beau within days.

And Rowan had her red streak.

But it wasn't just her hair. It wasn't just her eyes. Worse were the unexpected tastes that bloomed on her tongue whenever she was around people. Her magic stirred, and it was as if she could taste their emotions and who they were, deep down inside. Bridget called it "clear tasting." Bridget, not Mom, because she'd always insisted. "I'm too young to be called Mom." She'd say it with a wink, like it was a joke they were all in on.

Rowan's first taste came when she was six. Molly Jameson had swiped a brownie from Rowan's lunchbox—one of Bridget's best, rich with dark chocolate and a pinch of sea salt. She shoved it into her mouth with a smug, greedy grin.

That's when Rowan's magic flared. Hot, musty bitterness spread across her tongue, sour and sharp, like spoiled milk and old pennies. It wasn't the brownie at all. She understood that the tastes she experienced were an expression of who Molly was inside: Mean. Petty. Rotten at the edges.

And that's when Rowan knew that people might lie, but her magic never would.

Clear tasting didn't have anything to do with food. It was tasting *people.* Their hidden selves. The truths they carried but never spoke aloud. Most of the time, it was like standing in a candy shop surrounded by sweetness, only to bite down and find something spoiled and rancid beneath the sugar.

Happy people tasted like bright citrus or warm honey. Angry people left a bitter film, like burnt coffee. But the worst were the cruel ones. While they wore smiles, their hearts were dark and they tasted of decay and ash.

There was no comfort in a gift like that. No peace. Only the constant hum of other people's emotions, sour and sweet, sharp and searing, pressing against her senses until she couldn't breathe.

Her only reprieve was with her family. With her sisters the onslaught of tastes didn't come, and with Bridget it was always subtle.

Rowan learned to avoid crowded rooms, to steer clear of groups of people, especially those who were sick, and to keep her eyes on the ground. Her sisters wove their gifts into kindness, healing, and warmth. But Rowan's magic was hard to deal with. It was relentless and impossible to escape.

Not even Bridget understood. She only whispered, "Keep your gifts contained." But how did you contain something that lived in your blood, in your senses, in the fire-colored streak of hair that refused to disappear?

They made a covenant with Bridget to keep their magic a secret between them, renewing the pact every year on December thirty-first at midnight, the moment that straddled Caraline's and Saoirse's birthday and Rowan's on January first. Their magic belonged only to them. Thank God she had her sisters. She didn't think she'd survive without them.

But the truth was, her sisters had gifts that mattered, and Rowan had a burden. "It's a curse," she complained to her mother when she was young. "I hate it!"

"That's the thing about magic," her mother said. "It doesn't always show itself when you want it to. Sometimes, it waits for the right moment. Someday you will understand it. You'll learn what it means and how to use it."

"I doubt it," Rowan had muttered under her breath.

"Do you know what our greatest gifts are?" Bridget asked her after a particularly bad day when Rowan was thirteen years old. She had spent the day hiding from the kids who made fun of the crimson streak in her hair, trying to swallow the horrid tastes that assaulted her tastebuds.

She felt herself deflate at her mother's question. "There's another one?"

They'd sat side by side on the steps of the front porch. Bridget bumped her arm against Rowan's, smiling at her. "There is. And we all carry them with us. It's our names. I named you after my favorite tree. The rowan tree. It has white flowers in the spring, red berries in the fall, and the leaves turn yellow in autumn. It's so delicate looking, but really it's hardy and strong." She smiled, bumping Rowan again. "It's a tree of power, where magic will flower. That's you."

After her mother told her about the tree, Rowan liked her name a little bit more. Still, she envied Caraline with her normal name—despite the Irish spelling. "I knew the moment I laid eyes on her that your sister would be a free spirit, like me. Difficult to tie down. That's what Caraline means, and it fits her."

That was true. Caraline ran around barefoot in fields of flowers and snuck through windows into the deep of night. Even as a preteen, she had this haunting look about her, like a brooding princess who refused to be trapped in a tower.

"And Saoirse?" Rowan had asked. No one knew how to pronounce it, but her sister didn't mind. She just said, "Seer-sha" to people who struggled to make the sounds work and carried on with whatever she'd been doing.

"Ah, Saoirse. Her name means liberty. That girl is, and always will be, true to herself. She sees the world differently. She has the freedom inside her to always be herself—nothing more, nothing less. She's going to be powerful one day once she learns how to lean into it."

Powerful? Saoirse? Rowan was skeptical about that. Saoirse only liked plants. She could grow anything she wanted. All she had to do was think about it, touch the soil, and a seed sprouted then and there. "What, like Jack and the Beanstalk? I want to climb to the clouds!"

Bridget laughed, but Rowan detected a hint of melancholy which Bridget always seemed to carry with her. "We can't always go where we want to," she said cryptically.

Rowan moved on, picking at a jagged cuticle. "What they do is cool. My magic is just . . ." She wanted to say it was lame. A burden. And it had no purpose.

"I feel it in you, *a leanbh*," she said, calling Rowan by her favorite Irish endearment. "Your magic is stronger than either of your sisters."

"No, it's not! All I have is this—" she tugged at her red streak. "And the terrible tastes." Rowan felt tears prick her eyelids "How is any of that stronger than healing people, even Caraline who doesn't hardly try?"

"You have to trust me," Bridget said. "You will grow into your gifts and your name. You, Rowan, are important. You will always protect them because it's who you are."

Rowan had eyed her mother. "Protect them from what?" she'd asked, but Bridget just looked past her as if she were lost in a memory, and Rowan let it go.

The sisters knew they were three parts of a whole. They had an immutable bond—because of their magic or because they were triplets, Rowan didn't know. They were her lifeblood. An invisible thread wove them together, body and soul. She could feel Saoirse's vexation when a potion fizzled out. She felt the heat of the stove's flame against her own skin as Caraline leaned over a boiling pot. And her sisters suffered right alongside Rowan when her frustration bubbled over and the air around her turned stifling. When something was off with one, they all felt it.

And Bridget had been right. As they'd grown older, Rowan slipped into the role of protector and leader. Saoirse was always too distracted with her flowers and potions to be in charge of anything, and Caraline was always flitting off doing who knows what.

As adults, they had their own dreams, but they were still interconnected. Caraline wanted to run a café with a bake shop. Saoirse wanted to make lotions and curatives and put them for sale in a corner of Caraline's shop, and Rowan would be the one behind the scenes, doing everything else. As long as she wasn't around people, she'd be just fine. Which was work because her magic wasn't centered on anything specific like her sisters' was.

But they had to settle down somewhere first, and even now, at twenty-seven, their mother had been adamant that it wasn't the right time or place. "We'll know when it's right," she told them. "Be patient."

But now their mother was gone. Bridget Connors had died, and everything felt wrong. She had been the sun to their orbiting planets, and now the sisters were adrift, spinning away with nothing to ground them. Saoirse's way of dealing with the sudden separation was to grow a plant that bloomed with creamy white flowers, had stems like bamboo, and whose leaves looked like the head of a pointy-ended shovel. She used it to brew a special tea and made them sit together in the little house they shared in Arkansas, sipping it.

Twice Caraline got up to leave, and twice Rowan convinced her to stay.

"It's knotweed," Saoirse said, and Caraline pulled a face.

"You're making us drink tea made from weeds?"

Saoirse didn't take offense. She pushed her black-framed glasses up the bridge of her nose but kept her gaze on the teapot. She gave a mirthless closed-lip smile and said, "We're all spinning, don't you feel it? This will bind us together. It'll help us be strong." And it did. Saoirse, who always roamed, looking for flora, stayed put. Caraline wandered a little less than normal. But Rowan felt like the delicate thread woven around them, keeping them more connected, could break at any moment.

Still, with every passing day since Bridget's death, more and more shadows lurked. Rowan saw them wherever she went. The swallows had grown restless, and Saoirse warned that they'd leave soon. Icy fingertips crawled over her spine despite the unseasonably warm fall weather. Something dark and ominous hovered overhead like a cloud heavy with rain.

Maybe it was the idea of facing her mother's things in her room and the life she'd lived with them. Rowan had been avoiding going in there, but finally she couldn't shake the idea that something in Bridget's room would help them move forward and deal with their grief. She turned the knob and crossed the threshold. Bridget, like her daughters, didn't have many belongings. It was far easier to move from town to town when you didn't have much to take with you.

Rowan looked through the closet first, but it held only clothes, bell-bottoms and peasant blouses, and a few dresses. She ran her hand along the single shelf, but it only bumped up against an empty purse and a photo album from their childhood. She dropped to her knees and peered under the bed. Nothing but dust bunnies. She spun around, catching her breath at the lingering scent of lemon from the leaves of the melissa balm plant on the windowsill. It was her mother's favorite, and Saoirse kept it thriving, always blooming with little white flowers, and always scenting the air around her with the bright sharpness of citrus.

"What am I looking for?" Rowan muttered, barely audible.

She heard footsteps coming down the hall, then she saw Caraline. "You're looking for the answer to a question you haven't asked yet."

Rowan almost snorted at her sister's response. Hearing each other's whispered words was a game they'd played as children. They'd been nine, living in Missouri. The woods behind their rented house were wild that summer, buzzing with bees, tangled with green. Their favorite place was the old oak tree. That's where Rowan invented the game. No rules—just a promise to always tell each other the truth, even if they didn't speak it aloud. Somehow, it worked. Whispered thoughts drifted through the air, and suddenly they just knew each other's fears and wishes and hidden truths. They played that game a hundred times that summer, learning to speak to the wind and hear each other without uttering a single syllable. They never told anyone else, not even their mother. These were their secrets.

Now Caraline leaned against the doorjamb. She didn't ask what Rowan was doing in their mother's room. She just arched a brow and leaned forward. "So? What are you looking for?"

"For something to tell us where to go," Rowan said, the answer coming without thinking.

That's when she saw it—a familiar red container no bigger than a shoebox, tucked on the lower shelf of the nightstand. Echoes of memories played in her mind: Bridget, Rowan, and her sisters walking, the box tucked firmly under Bridget's arm. Bridget shooing Rowan away when she came in to find her mother sitting cross-legged on her bed, the contents of the box strewn in front of her. The box sitting on Bridget's dresser one minute, gone the next.

"Earth to Row," Caraline snapped her fingers in front of Rowan's face, bringing her back to the present.

Without answering, Rowan walked to the nightstand and pulled the box out. She and Caraline stared at it. "Should we open it?" Caraline whispered.

"Open what?" They turned, this time seeing Saoirse at the door. Saoirse's gaze shifted to the bed. "Oh, Bridget's secret box."

They sat cross-legged on the bed, the box in the middle, and Rowan lifted the lid. Inside were mementos. Locks of hair. Letters to Santa the sisters had written throughout the years. Keepsakes. The only thing unrelated to the sisters was an old photograph with a note clipped to the top. Rowan reached for it. Flipped it over. *Swallow Hall, Chesapeake Bay, 1937* was written on the back. A destination, Rowan thought, a snap of energy crackling through her. The note said simply, *Take me home, leanaí. The truth is there. Find it.*

Now, nearly two months after Bridget's death, in the waning light of a fall afternoon, the Connors sisters stood on the sidewalk in downtown New Bethel, a small town on the shores of the Chesapeake Bay. Deep in the marrow of her bones, Rowan knew everything was about to change.

Chapter Two

As Rowan and her sisters walked down the sidewalk, people stared openly, their mouths agape. They whispered behind the backs of their hands as if they'd never seen three young women pass through their town. The door to the vestibule of the Disciples of Christ Tabernacle with its brown shingles and cupola, slowly closed, as if to keep the Connors sisters out.

A tentacle of niggling doubt crept through Rowan. Maybe coming to Chesapeake Bay *had* been a mistake. They'd never been on the East Coast. From the way people stared at them, they weren't welcome. But Rowan heard Bridget's voice in her head. *Trust yourself. Trust your instincts. You will keep them safe.*

Trusting herself didn't come easily, not when she always felt she was lacking, but she'd suggested they come here, and Caraline and Saoirse had agreed. She breathed in the salt air, tamping down her worry.

Caraline peered down the street, her face pinched. "Are we really sure about this?"

Despite her doubt, deep down Rowan knew there was no other choice. They weren't going back to Arkansas. They had no roots anywhere they'd lived, so what was there to go back to? "We're sure. If Bridget kept the photo, it had to be important, right? She told us to take her home. This has to be where she came from."

"I guess so," Caraline said, doubt in her voice, and Saoirse nodded.

"Good. Let's go." Rowan started walking, her utilitarian heather gray satchel slung across her body, a small hard-shell silver suitcase, which had been a thrift shop find in a small town somewhere in the Midwest, bouncing along behind her. Past the tabernacle, the street gave way to a row of shops painted in different vibrant colors, brackets extending from each, signs swinging in the fall breeze. Chesapeake Camera Hut, based on the signage, sold vintage and new cameras, and also developed film. A small movie theater featured *The French Connection* and *Play Misty for Me* on the marquee.

The town had a definite nautical flair, with a crab house boasting The Best Crab on the Eastern Seashore!, Moody's Saltwater Kitchen, a sign in the window touting the Oyster Festival in November, and eighteenth- and nineteenth-century row houses and Victorians in varying states of repair. In the distance, they could see boats moored at a small marina.

Caraline caught up to Rowan. She looked around, taking it all in. "Toto, we're not in Kansas anymore," she muttered under her breath.

New Bethel wasn't Kansas or Arkansas. But it also wasn't Texas, Oklahoma, or Missouri, which were just a few of the places they'd lived. They had been perpetually on the move, always in the old Nash her mother had driven until it died—but tied together like the four-strand braids Bridget had loved to weave their hair into. "We're interlocked and always together," she'd often said.

Until now.

Bridget had died so suddenly that it felt as if every molecule of air had been sucked out of Rowan's body, and she was still struggling to reinflate her lungs. Her mother's absence was a gaping hole in her heart that would never be filled. They came from nowhere and lived a nomadic lifestyle Bridget had embraced wholeheartedly. They had each other and that had been enough. But now Bridget was dead, which meant Rowan and her sisters were truly alone. Her ashes, safely tucked away in her satchel, made Rowan feel like Atlas carrying the world on his shoulders.

She felt the weight of people's stares on her back as she and her sisters came to a crossroads on High Street. Caraline looked around, then threw her arms up. "How are we supposed to know which way to go?"

Rowan had no idea. She'd gotten them this far, based on the tightly formed letters written on the back of the photograph. *Swallow Hall, Chesapeake Bay, 1937.* That had led them here, to Maryland. To New Bethel.

"We need a map," she decided, and she made an abrupt turn into Chester's Dime Store. Less than a minute later, she was back, empty-handed.

Caraline rolled her eyes. "What, they don't sell maps here?"

"The man asked where I was going," Rowan said. "I told him, and he said we don't need a map." What Rowan didn't tell her sisters about was the strange way the man looked at her when she first walked in, and how he said, "You're an Early, aren't you?" She'd given him a puzzled look. "Your last name. It's Early."

She shook her head. "No. It's Connors."

"Can't be. You've gotta be an Early."

"Sorry, nope," she said, swallowing the brackish taste of his annoyance filling her mouth.

The man pinched his brows. Shook his head. He stared at her, but finally shrugged. "My mistake."

She swung her arm wide to indicate her sisters standing outside the shop. "We're heading to Swallow Hall."

"Swallow Hall? Then you *are* . . ." He trailed off, his tone making it clear there was something he didn't understand about that.

She put her hands on her hips and blinked. "Yes. Swallow Hall."

He pulled back, creating thick folds in his neck, and he pushed a sharp breath through his nose. "Okay, then," he said, and he pointed south. "Go on to the end of High Street and turn right when you get to the woods. There's a road that'll take you to the footbridge and onto Bird Island."

As Rowan told her sisters about the woods, the swallows appeared. As if by magic, the random pattern of their flight took on order. They formed the two lines of an arrow's point, shifted direction, and glided toward them in formation.

Caraline dipped her chin and let her brown-tinted sunglasses slip down the bridge of her nose. She peered over the top of them at the birds. "Geez, are they going to attack us?"

"Of course not." Saoirse lifted one arm and flicked her wrist like she was flicking away an annoying fly. A moment later, as if they'd seen the movement and understood its meaning, the flock shifted direction, angling up and heading in the very direction the man at Chester's Dime Store had told Rowan to go.

"They're leading Bridget home," Saoirse murmured, more to herself than to them, but Rowan heard the whispered words.

The taste of salt coated her tongue. "I think they are."

A single swallow broke away from the flock, its wings slicing through the air with a sudden, determined grace. It didn't rejoin the others. Instead, it circled back, gliding low, skimming the wind as if to guide them.

As Saoirse grabbed her suitcase, heavy with all the apothecary goods she'd refused to leave behind, a pale yellow station wagon rumbled slowly along the road, its long, sloping hood like the bow of a ship cutting through still water. The engine purred as it stopped in the road, idling. The driver leaned forward, one arm draped lazily over the steering wheel, his gaze tracking them with quiet curiosity. Rowan didn't have a clear view of him, but she could tell he was handsome in that classic, almost too-perfect way, like a Hollywood star. She couldn't pinpoint his age from here, but he was older than the sisters. There was a relaxed confidence about him, but it didn't put her at ease. If anything, it unsettled her, because he was exactly the kind of guy Caraline would fall for.

Caraline lifted her hand in a flirty wave. The driver's smile widened, slow and easy.

"Great," Rowan muttered under her breath, feeling the familiar, restless hum beneath her skin, the quiet spark that always seemed to stir when she was anxious. A faint prickle danced along her fingertips, a tingling heat she forced herself to ignore. "We're not even there yet, and you've already caught some guy's attention."

"You know it," Caraline replied through her smile, because, of course, she'd heard Rowan's whispered words.

The lone swallow swooped low over the station wagon, then darted up, vanishing into the trees. The movement caught the man's attention and his gaze flickered, leaving Caraline and following the bird. A moment later, he drove on, the engine's rumble fading into the distance.

"Come on," Saoirse called, already halfway up the path. "We're wasting daylight."

Rowan glanced up at the darkening sky. Saoirse was right. The sun had started its descent, daylight waning. She stepped around Caraline and onto the woodsy lane. The narrow strip of land they walked on was like a snake slithering through the woods, more trail than road. Trees, their leaves fiery red, blazing orange, and golden yellow, created a canopy above them. The leaves that had already fallen crunched beneath their boots. In the shade of the trees, the temperature dropped a solid ten degrees. A shiver wound through Rowan. Her lightweight sweater and jeans weren't enough to keep her warm in the late hours of the day. Caraline, in a gauzy skirt and cropped tee, looked even more chilled. The third week of September in Arkansas had been warm with only a hint of fall in the air. Here on the Eastern Seaboard, a decided bite of cold laced the air. Only Saoirse in her bell-bottomed jeans, long-sleeved corduroy shirt, and crocheted vest looked unfazed by the change in weather.

After a few more minutes, Caraline pulled up short and peered around, muttering to herself. "Where the hell are we?"

Literally speaking, their destination was nothing more than a spit of an island near the Chester River on the Chesapeake Bay, but Caraline knew that, so Rowan kept quiet. They walked on, each lost in their thoughts. Rowan knew Saoirse was cataloging the vegetation to see what was new to her and what she'd need to learn about. Knowing her sister, she was probably already concocting new fragrances for her curative soaps and oils.

Caraline looked around, skepticism etched on her face. Still, she examined the flora, most likely figuring out what was edible and what was not.

Rowan didn't care about the plants along the path. Her temple pulsed with energy, and she could feel the fiery strands of her crimson hair spark with energy. Their roots burned hot against her skin. She kept her eyes straight ahead as she walked, stopping when the peaked roofline of a monstrous gabled house came into view. The mass of swallows that had flown ahead of them the entire trip led them down this path and now they circled above the roof, trilling their song.

"Wow," Saoirse said almost reverently just as Caraline gave a low whistle that sounded like minor notes descending on a piano's keyboard in a haunting melody.

Rowan understood Caraline's unease. She even felt a twinge of it herself, but she started walking again and her sisters fell into step beside her. A few minutes later, the woods gave way to a narrow, arched bridge connecting the woods to what had to be Bird

Island. On the other side stood the house that belonged to the gables. It canted left like a sunflower seeking light. It looked old, with crumbling bricks and fractured walls. A hundred years, at least, Rowan thought, and full of history and long-forgotten memories. No one had bothered to bring it into the twentieth century. A brassy uncertainty about what lay ahead was palpable. She swallowed, but before she could chase away the metallic taste, it evaporated, replaced by the subtle sweetness of cornflower. Hope.

"That thing should be condemned," Caraline muttered, gesturing to the house that looked destined to sink below the waters of the bay.

Rowan looked at Saoirse and saw her lips curve up into a smile. Where Caraline saw something on the verge of uninhabitable and Rowan saw a century of stories written between the cracks, Saoirse's view looked to be sugarcoated. It was clear she saw potential the others didn't.

Saoirse's gaze drifted back to the flora and the woods. She left her suitcase and stepped off into a thicket of shrubs. As she knelt before one, examining the leaves, Rowan pulled the worn black-and-white photograph from the front pouch of her bag. She looked at the picture for the hundredth time. It was a little girl in a checkered dress, white socks with dark buckled shoes, and a bonnet that was like an awning around her face. In the photo, the girl craned her neck and stared at the house behind them. Or maybe at the mass of swallows perched along the eaves of the crooked house.

Saoirse returned to the path as Rowan's gaze strayed up to the sky and to the circling birds—Saoirse's swallows, they called them, because of her connection to them—then back to the photo. Swallows, she knew, lived four to eight years, so of course they weren't the same ones. But were Saoirse's swallows related to the ones in the photograph? Their offspring's offspring, generations removed? She flipped the photo over, lifting the paper-clipped note so she could read the inscription yet again. *Swallow Hall, Chesapeake Bay, 1937.*

Rowan felt Caraline's arm brush hers as she moved closer and peered at the photo. "That's the same house as"—she pointed to the monstrosity in front of them—"*that*?"

Doubt clawed at Rowan. She studied the house in the picture and then the one across the bridge. Caraline was right. They didn't look the same. The three- or maybe four-story house in front of them barely resembled the image in the thirty-four-year-old photo. The gardens and plants in living color across the bridge were overgrown with the branches of a vine climbing up the sides of the house like tentacles. The house itself stood askew as if one side of the island was hoisted up higher than the other, making everything off-kilter. The windows, too, were odd. Some were positioned sideways, while others sat at an angle. An outdoor staircase started at the top floor and ended at the one below, pressed to the wall like a wobbly fire escape on a city building.

The house in the picture had similar features. The brick siding looked the same, though not yet in disrepair, as did the front door. The 1937 version of the home was a smaller, newer rendering of the one across the bridge. Certainty slipped through Rowan. They *were* the same house, she was sure of it, and yet they were so utterly different. She suddenly felt like Alice and the bridge was the rabbit hole. The house felt like it belonged in a twisted version of Wonderland. "It's the same house," she whispered.

Rowan tasted the coolness of the dark cloud that suddenly blocked out the sun. It zapped the residual warmth from her body, and she shivered. She had a fleeting thought that coming here might be a mistake. Maybe Caraline was right. If Bridget had wanted them to see this place, she would have taken them herself.

She looked up at the swallows again. They seemed suspended in the sky above, held in place by the ominously darkening sky. Another icy claw moved over her. A gust of wind picked up, the faint sound of someone speaking muted by the rustling leaves. She spun around, looking for whoever was there, but they were alone at the edge of the woods. She heard it again, more clearly this time, and coming from across the bridge. *"Welcome home."*

The words echoed, the sound ricocheting between the trees, over the narrow strip of water separating the island from the mainland. The ground shifted under their feet. Rowan stared. It looked like the house was sinking into the cold waters of the Chesapeake Bay, but that couldn't be. Could it?

She shut her eyes and counted to three, and when she opened them again, she started. Something moved just to the side of the house. She peered but saw only growing darkness spilling from the trees, marking the earth beneath with long murky streaks. Maybe she had imagined it, but then the shadow shifted, barely visible but definitely there. Rowan's mouth suddenly filled with the sharp tang of iron—acidic and vinegary. She lifted her arm. Pointed. "Did you see that? Tell me you saw that."

Saoirse and Caraline followed the line of her arm and looked at the copse of trees. "See what?" Caraline asked.

Rowan started at the dark shape darting through the woods. "There!"

Saoirse took a few steps forward. Peered. "Is it an animal?"

A visible shiver wound through Caraline. She wrapped her arms around herself. "I don't want to stay here."

Rowan searched the darkness for a sign of movement. The leaves of a tree rustled and the swallows emerged from the woods, circling back toward the house. Whatever else had moved through the woods was gone.

A movement in one of the upstairs windows of the house caught Rowan's attention, and she felt the weight of someone's eyes on them. She turned her back on the monstrosity. "There are secrets here," she said as quietly as possible for fear her voice would carry on the wind, straight into the shadowy crevices of Swallow Hall.

Saoirse's glasses had slipped down to the edge of her nose. She pushed them back into place, looking toward Rowan but not directly at her. She whispered back. "Of course there are."

"I don't want to deal with secrets," Caraline blurted, not bothering to keep her voice low. She flung one arm straight up. "Are we voting? Because if we're voting, I say we leave. Right now."

"We came halfway across the country." Saoirse reached around Rowan to pat her satchel. "We brought Bridget here. We can't leave until we know what the truth is."

"Of course we can," Caraline said. "Bridget never mentioned this place. She never brought us here. That should tell us something."

It was true. Bridget had never been open with them about her past. Whenever Rowan had asked who their father was—and she was the only one who did ask because Caraline chose not to think about the fact that they had a father, at least not in any concrete way, and Saoirse's mind simply never went there—Bridget merely took Rowan's hand in hers and squeezed. "It's just us, *a leanbh*," she said.

"The note said to bring her back here. We have to find the perfect place for her ashes," Rowan said. Plus, there was the photograph, their only other clue to their mother's past.

As if reading her mind, Caraline continued. "That picture doesn't mean anything. We don't even know if it's her."

They'd pondered that question, but no amount of talk could give them an answer. The photo was black-and-white. There was no way to know if the girl had the red hair Bridget had. And with the bonnet creating a canopy around her head and her face turned toward the house, they couldn't make out enough details to say if it was their mother or not.

In 1937, Bridget would have been ten years old, so the year fit, and it was all they had to go on. None of them knew anything about who they were or where they came from. All they had was this photo and the message. That, in and of itself, was enough to make the photo hugely important because Bridget had no mementos from her childhood. No letters. No baby book. Nothing. Just this single picture. Rowan felt sure that whoever lived at Swallow Hall could answer their questions. She did not doubt that this was where they needed to be.

Without warning, the taste of blackberries bloomed on her tongue. She looked at her sisters. They were the only people her ability didn't work with. Even with Bridget, she'd often tasted the sour bite of green apples or the saltiness of the sea.

"Are you just going to stand there gawking?"

From the way they each jumped, synchronously, it was as if the voice shot at them like a bullet, flying across the footbridge and right into their hearts. In the dim light, Rowan saw a figure. A real figure this time, not the shadow of a ghost or a nebulous shape behind a dark window. Blackberries. She didn't take time to think. She just moved. She grabbed her suitcase, adjusted her satchel, and started over the arched bridge. A moment later, she heard Saoirse dragging her suitcase over the wooden slats, and the reluctant, heavy footsteps of Caraline trailing behind.

The house was a short walk from the east side of the bridge—maybe thirty yards or so. Rowan stopped when she reached the stone walkway, the light from the porch spilling out enough to illuminate the woman. She had steel-colored hair in a long braid slung over one shoulder. Rowan peered at her, looking for some familiarity—in her body, in her posture, in her face. But there was nothing. With her wide-legged pants, long knitted sweater over a T-shirt, head scarf tied in a knot under her braid, she was the epitome of an aging hippie. As Rowan's gaze slipped to the shiny black stone hanging from a black leather cord around her neck, the woman wrapped her hand around the pendant. "It's obsidian."

"It's beautiful," Rowan said. The closer Rowan got to the woman and the house, the stronger the taste of blackberries became. She thought of what she knew about blackberries. Saoirse had once told her they were part of the rose family. They flowered, leafed, and had thorns. Was this woman before them complicated in the same way? Was that why Rowan's mouth filled with a strange mixture of sweet, tart, and tang?

Bridget had always said she had no family, no home—so what was this place?

The woman didn't budge, and her expression remained wary as she peered at the three of them and their suitcases, likely nothing more than dark figures from where she stood. "I don't take in strangers," she said, preemptively turning them away.

Before any of them could respond, the swallows appeared overhead, circling the house. The woman startled, staring up at them for a beat, then, as Rowan moved into the edges of the porch light, the woman stared at her. Her face had paled. Her mouth tightened. "Who are you?"

Caraline elbowed past Rowan. "Who are *you*?" she demanded.

The woman's eyes passed over Caraline. She stared for a long few seconds. Sometimes Rowan looked at her sister and felt a jolt of déjà vu as if she were looking at Bridget's ghost. Is that what this woman saw in Caraline? Was it recognition?

Finally, the woman spoke, answering Caraline's question. "I, my dear, am the Keeper of Swallow Hall."

Rowan let those words roll around in her head.

Saoirse stepped forward, standing shoulder to shoulder with Rowan. "We think our mother knew this place," she said, looking upward toward the swallows who had slipped into the ancient-looking mud nests built into the eaves of the house.

"Your mother . . ." the woman repeated slowly, her gaze flicking to Caraline again.

"Maybe. We don't know," Rowan said, swallowing the lump in her throat that always appeared whenever Bridget was mentioned aloud. "She, uh, died recently and we found something. A photo—"

The woman reached her hand out, grasping the thick trunk of the espalier tree canopying the porch as if to hold her steady. Her voice choked. "Bridget . . . died?"

The skin on Rowan's nose pricked with tiny needles. She looked at her sisters and then back at this woman, so clearly shaken. They hadn't given Bridget's name. Tears suddenly pooled in her eyes, on the cusp of crashing through the barrier she kept in place. She blinked them away. "You knew her?"

The woman—the Keeper of Swallow Hall, as she'd called herself—stared at them, unseeing. "Bridget is dead," she murmured, a statement, not a question.

Saoirse pressed the back of her hand against her nose. Her eyes turned glassy, but Rowan knew she wouldn't cry now. She might later, in the privacy of her room, but not now. Not here. None of them would.

The woman blinked. Found the swallows again. "How?"

"She drowned," Caraline blurted, although the truth was more complicated than that. The police had told them that Bridget had tripped, hitting her head against the cement edge of a fountain, falling into the water. The impact had knocked her out and she'd drowned. Rowan still couldn't get her head around how it had happened. Bridget was one of those people who skipped through puddles, who swam just to feel the slickness of the water on her skin, who was always hyperaware of her surroundings. She shouldn't have tripped. She shouldn't have drowned.

But she did.

The woman released the doorframe. She stood motionless, as if Medusa herself had looked straight in her eyes and turned her to stone. After a long moment, she seemed to come back to the present. "You are triplets," she said, and then she spoke sharply. "How old are you?"

"Twenty-seven," Rowan answered.

The woman nodded, as if her suspicion had been confirmed. "And your names?"

Rowan released the breath she'd been holding. She wanted answers, and so far all she had were more questions. "I'm Rowan," she said. "These are my sisters, Caraline and Saoirse."

"Irish names," the woman said, and then she muttered to herself just loud enough for them to hear, "The shamrock, the triskele, and the Triple Goddess. Powerful Celtic symbols. Oh Bridget, *a leanbh*."

Rowan stared at the woman. Beside her, she felt Caraline and Saoirse both tense. *A leanbh.* It was the endearment Bridget had always used, said with the same lilt. Suddenly Rowan felt as if she knew the truth—knew who this woman was—but was it really possible? Surely their mother would not have kept such a monumental secret from them. But this woman's very presence had created a cocoon of warmth around her. The taste of blackberries was still there, but the chill was gone. The ever-present ache in her heart was a tiny bit less overwhelming. The air around her grew warmer. Somewhere inside, a long, aching moan sounded.

The woman exhaled a long, laden breath. She stepped back, giving them room to pass. "Come in," she said, beckoning them forward. "Welcome to Swallow Hall."

Chapter Three

Rowan and her sisters sat in awkward silence, in the strangest room, in the strangest house they had ever seen. It harkened back to a different era. The higgledy-piggledy photos elbowing for space on the walls were in sepia and black-and-white. The windows hung in a disorderly fashion, some crooked, some sideways. The ceilings vaulted up much higher than seemed reasonable. One chandelier and three ancient candelabras hung on rusted chains from the wrinkled ceiling.

"My name is Everly," said the woman as they'd entered the house. She'd waved a hand around, gesturing broadly. "This is the gathering room." She placed her palm on her chest as if to steady her frenetic heartbeat. When she spoke again, her voice was wistful. "Your mother—Bridget—grew up here. I've missed her all these years."

Caraline scoffed under her breath. "Well, she never mentioned you, so . . ."

Rowan shot daggers at her sister. Antagonizing this woman wasn't going to help them.

"No, I guess she wouldn't have. Still, she led you back home. Back to me."

Rowan's thoughts spun like a kaleidoscopic top in her mind, the array of colors and memories colliding in a dizzying whirl.

How could this be home when she and her sisters had never set foot here? And yet, the house seemed to breathe, its old timbers creaking with a rhythm that echoed in Rowan's chest. The warm air tingled against her skin, almost electric, and the trees outside whispered with a voice just beyond hearing.

There was a familiarity to the house. To the island. Beneath them, the earth vibrated, sending a faint, shimmering energy pulsing through her. It prickled against her fingertips, hummed in her ears, and stirred the air around her.

She couldn't explain it, but she felt as if the island knew her. Recognized her, maybe. But that was impossible.

Everly smiled, and the sweet, tart, tangy sensation of blackberries finally faded away. When Rowan had first laid eyes on her, she'd looked tense. The moment she'd heard Bridget had died, her grief became palpable. She'd aged ten years before their eyes. But now, the more they talked, the younger she looked, the wrinkles smoothing out, and the bone-weariness that had been radiating out from her fading. "As I'm sure you've guessed, Bridget—your mother—was my daughter. She grew up here on Bird Island. In Swallow Hall."

Rowan's head felt fuzzy, a strange pressure building just behind her eyes, like the air was suddenly too thick to breathe. It didn't make any sense. How could Bridget have kept something so monumental from them, and for so many years? Why had she told them they had no family?

That hum returned, prickling at her fingertips as the room seemed to shift, shadows stretching and then snapping back as if the walls themselves were holding their breath. The old, dark beams above them creaked, and Rowan could have sworn she heard a low, groaning whisper. Somewhere, a window rattled, its glass shivering in the frame.

The house seemed to be listening. Rowan's pulse quickened, a new kind of magic skittering beneath her skin, a restless, sparking energy. The faint scent of damp earth grew stronger, and for a moment, she thought she saw a muslin curtain framing one of the crooked windows flutter in the still air.

She forced herself to breathe, to hold her tingling palms against her sides. It was impossible, wasn't it? It had to be. It was her imagination hard at work. But she couldn't shake the weight of the room. It leaned in around her, pressing against her senses.

Rowan pushed through the heavy air, leaning forward. "Why didn't she tell us about you?" She flung her arms wide, her arms encompassing the vast room they were in. "About this place?"

Everly's gaze traveled from the three of them to the windows to the stairs, finally landing back on the sisters. "There are secrets here," she said ominously, as if that was an answer. It was exactly what Rowan had thought the moment she laid eyes on the house.

Caraline gave a scornful laugh. "You're saying that's why she left? Because of the secrets?"

"Secrets need protecting," Everly said cryptically.

"What do you mean?" Rowan asked, but Everly seemed to slip into a memory, her face placid with it. "*It's the only way. Trust me*," she said quietly. She blinked. Looked back at them. "I didn't think she would be gone forever. As to why she kept it from *you*? That, I can't say."

Caraline pinched her eyes. "You were her mother. How could you not know?"

Caraline wasn't afraid of confrontation, but neither, it seemed, was Everly. She met Caraline's challenge. "Did *you* tell Bridget everything?" Caraline's steady gaze faltered, and Everly barked out a satisfied laugh. "No, I didn't think so. You said Bridget kept this place a secret. She kept me a secret from you. Correct?"

Caraline shrugged. "Yeah?"

Everly looked at each of them in turn. She shook her head and let out a mournful sigh. "She had her reasons."

"She lied to us." The words slipped out, barely louder than a whisper, but they felt heavy, sinking like a stone in Rowan's chest. "All these years, she lied to us about everything. She said we didn't have a family. Definitely not a grandmother. No history."

The faint sound of the birds trilling drifted inside. Saoirse shifted in her chair. A spattering of the white petals she'd plucked from a flower fell into her lap as she spoke. "The swallows led her away."

A gust of wind suddenly shook the house. The chain of the chandelier above them creaked. It began to swing, gently at first, then rapidly. Frenetically. A loud cracking sound came from the ceiling. Rowan lurched back in her chair. Caraline jumped up with a yelp. Saoirse sat perfectly still.

Rowan stared at the light fixture. She hadn't imagined any of it. This house—Swallow Hall—was more than it seemed. She turned to Everly. To her grandmother. Everly's lips were pressed tightly together. Very calmly, she patted the air. From the bowels of the house, Rowan heard what sounded like a relieved sigh. The swinging of the chandelier slowed. Stopped.

"Holy shit!" Caraline sat and yanked her legs up, crouching on the seat as if a cockroach was scurrying across the floor. She spun her head back and forth, looking at the walls of the house. Saoirse stayed calm. She gathered up her flower petals, the forgotten stem discarded on the floor.

Upstairs, another door slammed, once, twice, then over and over, the booming crash of it like something physical ricocheting off the walls. More joined in. The hands of the multiple clocks scattered around the room spun backward, rewinding themselves, and the phone sitting on the table started up with an intermittent jangle, its handset bouncing, the knotted cord jumping with each shrill ring. The candelabras began to swing again as if a gale was blowing through the room.

Rowan pressed her palms to the sides of her face, the heat of her cheeks seeping into them. "What. Is. Happening?"

Everly ran her hand down her thick braid, pulling it back over one shoulder so it hung like a rope. A sound—like a haunting cry—reverberated from behind the walls.

Rowan's gaze snapped to the hearth. Flickering flames danced to life for the briefest second, the mortar between the bricks fracturing, picture frames along the mantle trembling on their edges. The wood at the ends of the mantle seemed to slope downward—almost . . . sorrowfully. But it was impossible.

She steadied her breath, reaching out without thinking, fingers grazing the wall beside her. She felt the wrinkles in the damp wallpaper, the coolness of the plaster beneath it.

Finally, everything stilled. The photos settled. The mantle straightened. The hearth silenced.

Rowan blinked, pulse slowing, and when she turned, Everly was watching her, the weight of her grandmother's gaze sharp and searching. A melancholy smile played on Everly's lips, the expression haunting, as if the final piece of a puzzle their grandmother had spent a lifetime trying to complete had finally slipped into place.

Chapter Four

Rowan felt the preternatural pulsing all around her and a deep longing for something unknown pooled in the pit of her stomach. She wanted to be settled. Rooted somewhere. To discover the depth of the magic Bridget had seen in her. And now here they all were on a sinking island a thousand miles away from what Rowan already saw as their old lives. Everly had welcomed them home. Only it wasn't their home, and this was about as far from grounded and settled as she could be. And yet, it felt right.

Everly disappeared for a moment, returning with a tray of cheese, crackers, and sliced fruit, along with three glasses of water. "It's not much, I'm afraid. I wasn't expecting company," she said.

Rowan's hunger settled as she nibbled on the snacks, fatigue threading through her limbs now that the adrenaline of arriving at Swallow Hall was fading. The house seemed to breathe around them, quietly watching.

"You must be tired," Everly said at last, her voice gentle but firm. "We do have rooms waiting—one for each of you. Settle in. We'll talk again tomorrow."

There was a finality in her words. No room for argument, which was okay with Rowan. She needed to process. To think about everything that had happened since they'd set foot on Bird Island.

"I'll be outside," Everly said. Rowan waited to see if she'd add, "In case you need me," but she didn't, and without another word, Everly rose and walked to the front door. It swung open just before she reached it, as though sensing her approach, and closed with a soft click behind her.

"This place," Saoirse said, a touch of awe in her voice.

Caraline pressed her fingertips to her temples. "What the hell just happened?"

None of them could answer. Every nerve in Rowan's body was firing. She touched her hairline where the roots of her crimson streak sizzled. Magic flickered around in her mind like a firefly. She registered the taste of pine, rosemary, and sage. She thought of Saoirse and the swallows. Of her curatives. She thought of Caraline and the impact the food she made had on anyone who tasted it. Bridget had told her she'd grow into her power. It had always felt so far away, like it wasn't really real, and yet, here, she felt the possibility of it.

Rowan studied the house, marveling at its features. At the cadence of its heartbeat. Magic. Here it was all around them. None of them knew *why* they possessed magic. They didn't know where it came from, but maybe Everly could answer that question for them.

Rowan glanced at her sisters as they stood in the quiet, shadowed hallway. The house pressed close, its walls seeming to lean in, just slightly. Rowan's gaze drifted to the staircase, soft, muted light spilling down from a crooked window on the second floor. "I guess we . . . find our rooms?" she said.

Saoirse took a slow breath. "They're already waiting for us. That's what she said."

Caraline gave a half-hearted humorless laugh. "We need to stay together."

"Good idea," Rowan said, and Saoirse nodded.

Rowan, Saoirse, and Caraline were a trio bound by something deeper than blood. They moved together, stepping onto the carpeted stairs, but it didn't feel like climbing. It felt like floating. Their feet barely seemed to touch the steps, as though an invisible breeze was lifting them, carrying them upward. The air was soft around them, nothing more than a quiet, gentle whisper against their cheeks.

Caraline's expression remained tense. Saoirse closed her eyes, her breath slowing, a sense of calm slipping over her. Only Rowan's eyes searched the house as if it would give her some clue as to what was happening, and where the magic came from. She wanted to talk about it more, but not now. They all needed time and space to think about Everly. About Swallow Hall. To grieve their mother in this place where she'd grown up, and to wonder why she'd kept it a secret from them.

They paused at the top of the stairs, a low hum settling between them, that invisible thread vibrating as it wove their breaths together. Here, within the whispering walls of Swallow Hall, their connection felt stronger. It drummed with heightened energy. Whatever lay ahead, they'd face it together.

The air around them stirred, sounding like the soft sigh of wind. It swirled between them, and then it pulled apart, pushing them each in a different direction.

To the left, a door swung open with a quiet whoosh. A gentle gust nudged Saoirse forward. She stepped into the room, her eyes wide with wonder at the pale green walls and delicate wallpaper with a faded floral pattern. As Saoirse meandered, Rowan leaned closer, her gaze snagging on the wallpaper's edges. They were slightly curled, browned with age, but as she watched, those worn edges twitched. Impossible, but Rowan shook the word away because it clearly *wasn't* impossible. It was happening before her very eyes. The edges pressed themselves flat against the wall. The faint yellow of the old adhesive darkened and refreshed. It was as if it was aging backward.

Rowan's pulse fluttered. Magic lived here, in the walls, in the very air they breathed. This house—Swallow Hall—was *alive.*

Saoirse brushed her fingers over the faded floral fabric of the quilt on the bed. Instantly, it seemed to brighten, the pattern gaining depth and color. At the window, a small table cradled an assortment of flowers and houseplants in terra-cotta pots. Each one was different. Slightly wild, with leaves reaching and tangling together. Rowan saw Saoirse's shoulders relax, her fingers trailing over a fern's fronds, over the leaves of the melissa balm, just like the one Bridget had always loved. Everly hadn't known they were coming, so she hadn't decorated this room for Saoirse. Deep down, Rowan knew it was the house itself responding to the three of them being here. It knew *exactly* what Saoirse needed, what would make her feel settled.

Rowan turned at the creak of a second door opening, this one from across the hall. The breeze stirred again, brushing past Rowan and billowing around Caraline. Her sister hesitated, a flicker of distrust flashing in her eyes. But then, as if she'd resigned herself to give into the magic, Caraline glided forward and into a room decorated with peach walls, wrapping the room in warmth. "Oh God, really? Peach?"

It had never been one of her favorite colors, so the house had gotten *that* wrong. The color was slightly patchy in places, but as Caroline moved around the room and Rowan stood there watching, those patches softened, the hues blending until the paint looked fresh and new. The wandering cracks in the ceiling's plaster shimmered faintly, the lines growing fainter before her eyes until they evaporated into nothing. The plush white comforter on the bed was fresh and clean. The joints of the bed frame groaned softly as Caraline leaned against it. She jumped away, eyes wide, but then it quieted, stilled, its old wood settling. She exhaled.

Stepped toward it and let her palm rest on the comforter, pressing down like she was testing its softness.

"It's . . . nice," she murmured, her voice barely carrying. "Better than I thought it would be." Rowan smiled in relief. Caraline's uncertainty about this place was settling, softening, if only slightly.

Finally, it was Rowan's turn. The air gathered around her like a cashmere blanket, pulling her away from her sisters' rooms. It guided her up a narrow, steep staircase she hadn't noticed before. The tired wood creaked beneath her feet. The banister's worn surface was marred with tiny nicks and scratches. To her it looked like a map of time reflecting the generations of people who'd lived here. As she climbed the stairs, the nicks and scrapes began to smooth. "No," she said. "Stop!" Those marks were from generations of her *family's* hands. They connected her to her history. She didn't want them to vanish.

The stairs creaked and groaned, the boards lifting beneath her feet. "I don't want you to erase them," Rowan hurried on, directing the words up into the air. "They're your history. *Our* history."

The wood beneath her palm warmed and the stairway quieted. Rowan's heart thrummed in her temples. She had talked to the house . . . and the house had listened.

At the top of the stairs, a door stood open, leading into a room painted in soft periwinkle blue. The ceiling sloped sharply, the room nestled beneath the eaves. She'd half expected the attic room to be barren, but it was lovely. A quilt spread across the bed in a burst of color. Coral, navy, and white patches were sewn together with delicate, careful stitches. The quilt's edges were frayed, but she waited. Watched. The fabric riffled, then drew together, the loose threads reweaving themselves.

"Amazing," she muttered. After seeing the magic in her sisters' rooms, she'd expected something similar in hers, but it was still awe-inspiring. Moonlight slipped through two off-centered windows. It spilled silvery light across the planks of the wood floor, which remained lovingly scuffed.

Rowan moved to one of the windows. The panes were lightly fogged with salt spray. The glass cleared slightly, and her gaze was drawn to the vast, shadowed waters of the Chesapeake Bay beyond. She knew its dark expanse flowed into the Atlantic somewhere in the far distance. She turned again, absorbing the feel of the room. It was warm, not with the stuffiness she expected from an attic, but with a soft, comforting heat. A trace of sweetness lingered in the air, a taste on her tongue. It was a cross between blueberry and grape. Peace settled over her, heavy and soothing. It was a feeling she didn't quite understand, and one she hadn't felt since her mother died. She breathed in, letting it fill her cells.

Like her sisters had, she touched the quilt. Beneath her fingers she felt a subtle cadence. It wasn't just the house that was alive, but everything in it. The house *knew* them—knew what they needed.

"Saoirse?" Rowan called softly, the walls gently absorbing her voice. "Cara?"

"I'm here," came the faint reply, a note of wonderment lacing Saoirse's voice.

"I'm fine," Caraline added, her tone lighter, almost amused. "Turns out, a little peach isn't so bad. In fact, I . . . I kinda like it."

Rowan stood corrected. The house *had* known. They couldn't see each other, but they didn't need to. That almost undetectable vibration was still there, linking them with a quiet, steady beat. They were together, even in separate rooms, even in the depths of a house that might actually know them as well as they knew themselves. Caraline's peach walls flashed in her mind. Maybe *better* than they knew themselves.

Rowan unpacked, cleaned up, then curled onto the bed, resting her cheek against the cool sheets. The scent of the quilt wafted above her, smelling faintly of lavender and something sweeter—an earthy, floral scent she couldn't quite name. As her eyes drifted shut, her thoughts turned to questions. Why had Bridget left? What secrets were waiting within these walls?

One feeling, however, settled above the rest, like cream rising to the surface. It was contentment. A quiet, unexpected sense of belonging.

For the first time in a long while, Rowan didn't feel like she was trying to fit somewhere she didn't belong. Swallow Hall wasn't just magical or strange—it was something more. It felt like it was reaching out to them, offering more than a solution. Maybe, just maybe, this place could be theirs. A home.

Chapter Five

Rowan couldn't sleep. Her heartbeat echoed the creaks and cracks of the house, all the questions she carried pulsing through her mind. She was exhausted, but the air around her thrummed with energy and seeped through her skin, keeping her wide awake. Finally, she gave up. She rose and scooped up the knitted shawl draped over an old wooden rocking chair in the corner. She wrapped it around her shoulders and went to the window.

Outside, the light of the waning crescent moon cast a pale glow over the bay, its light stretching across the dark water in a shimmering, silvery path of light and shadow. She caught a movement on the beach and her breath snagged, remembering the form from earlier, the one she'd felt more than seen moving through the woods. The weight of being watched. The shadows were everywhere on this tiny island. She waited. But the shape below didn't disappear. It moved across the sand, stepping into a sliver of light that caught silver strands of hair. Her breath steadied.

Everly.

Her grandmother couldn't sleep either. Rowan moved without thinking. She wanted answers. She wrapped the shawl tighter as she crept from her room. As she tiptoed down the attic staircase trying to avoid the groan of the floor under her feet, she thought she heard a faint whisper—*Go. Go. Go.*—but it stopped and she wondered if she had imagined it.

A wide strip of carpet ran down the center of the wood staircase that led from the second story to the main floor. As Rowan placed her foot on the first step, she felt the carpet pull and heard a low popping sound followed by the sharp pings of tiny pin-nails hitting the wood. She yelped as the belt of carpet pulled free of the wood frame, stretching across the edges of the stairs like a flying carpet. She found her balance as she listened to the cadence of the magic alive in the walls of Swallow Hall. She walked slowly . . . tentatively . . . so she wouldn't topple down. At the bottom, she released the breath she'd been holding and crossed through the gathering room where she and her sisters had sat with Everly. In the dim light, she thought the room looked a little bit tidier than it had earlier. A few of the crooked windows appeared straighter. The walls seemed brighter and taller as if someone had yanked up socks that had been pooling around their ankles. The bubbles and creases in the wallpaper had smoothed out. The house had thrown back its head and stood, shoulders back and spine straight.

And hadn't the ribbon of carpet leading to the front door been a dull brown? Because now it was deep red. Rowan rubbed her eyes. The front door swung open as she approached, just as it had for Everly. She stepped onto the listing porch and ducked beneath the arching branches of the espalier tree, its twisted limbs carefully trained to fan out against a weathered trellis. The thick, crisscrossed vines clung to the branches. Even in the dark, she could see their glossy leaves tangled with clusters of tiny, pale blossoms. Above her, in the eaves of the house, she heard the faint collective breaths of the swallows in their mud nests.

Rowan walked to the south end of Swallow Hall, catching a glimpse of an uneven stone path that curved around the house, past glass walls, and into the shadowed woods. Most of the cloud cover from that afternoon had blown away and a few minutes later she emerged from the fiery canopy of trees. Night had brought a drop in the temperature. The blanket of warmth she'd felt since stepping into Swallow Hall had vanished, the light shawl around her shoulders not enough to ward off the chill. A shiver raised goosebumps on her skin. She braced herself against the breeze as she headed toward the beach.

The sky shimmered a deep amethyst, the fractured light of the moon illuminating the inky bay water. It lapped against the shore, the tide high on the beach. She'd never been around bodies of water like this. Bridget had kept them in the middle of the country, landlocked. No ocean. No lakes. This was Rowan's first time standing before such a vast stretch of water, and it stole her breath away.

Everly seemed to sense her presence. She turned, whisking away her tears and ushering Rowan forward. She spoke in a quavering voice. "There's nothing like the bay at night."

It was true. It stretched endlessly, a gleaming, silver-blue expanse that seemed to swallow the horizon. How impossibly small Rowan felt compared to the vastness of it.

They stood side by side, watching as moonlight cast silver slivers of light across the dark water, breaking into rippling shadows. Rowan's breath caught when she thought she heard a forlorn whisper—Bridget's name—carried on the breeze, drifting out to sea.

Everly turned and held her arm out, and Rowan realized the chill had left her. That feeling of warmth she'd felt inside the house seeped through her skin again as she slipped into Everly's embrace. After a few minutes, Rowan broke the silence. "When did you first come here?"

"To Bird Island? Oh, I was born here," Everly said. "Bridget was too. You and your sisters—you're the first of the Early family in America *not* to be born in Swallow Hall."

"Early," she said, the name tumbling in her mind. The man at the dime store had asked if she was an Early and had seemed so puzzled when she'd said she wasn't. Now she knew why. She *was* an Early.

"Paddy—Patrick—Early— he would be your great-great-great-grandfather—"

"That's a lot of greats," Rowan said.

"It is. He was from Ireland. He landed in Baltimore and made his way here." She glanced over her shoulder. "He built Swallow Hall in 1839. Then he married an Irish girl . . . Maeve Cleite."

"My great-great-great-grandmother."

She nodded. "The Earlys have been here ever since."

More than a hundred and twenty-five years ago. Rowan took a moment to process this.

"Maeve was a beauty," Everly said. "Bridget's red hair, and Saoirse's . . . that streak in yours . . . it comes from her."

Rowan had an entire family history she knew nothing about. Her grief over losing her mother commingled with the ire from the secrets she'd kept bubbled up. "Our last name . . . Connors."

Everly tilted her head to one side. "Yes, that *is* interesting."

Rowan frowned. "Why?"

"Bridget left the name Early behind, but she gave you and your sisters a family name in its place . . . the surname of our oldest ancestor." She swung her arm out to encompass the island and the house. "She kept you connected to me. To this place. To the past."

Rowan tried to make sense of what Everly was saying. Bridget had kept things from her daughters, yet she'd yoked them to this island and her past at the same time.

Everly suddenly turned to face her. "How did you find me? Find Bird Island? You mentioned a photo . . . ?"

Rowan glanced back at the hulking house, so different than the one in the picture. "We found it after Bridget died. She kept it so we knew it had to mean something to her. It led us here."

"What photograph? Where is it?" Everly asked, her brows raised, an accordion of wrinkles across her forehead.

Rowan pointed toward the attic windows. "It's there. Inside. It's of her—or a girl, at least—standing in front of this house." She gave a little laugh. "A much smaller, more normal version of it, anyway. On the back, it says: *Swallow Hall, Chesapeake Bay, 1937*."

Everly turned back toward the bay, falling quiet. She seemed lost in a memory the same way Bridget often had been. "I remember that day," she said, breaking the silence. "Bridget loved that bonnet. She said it made her feel like a pioneer woman in the Wild West."

"The photo was the only thing we found from her childhood. The only thing with any history. That picture and a message."

Everly's head snapped up. "What message?"

Rowan told her, mulling the words over. *Take me home, leanaí. The truth is there. Find it.* "What my sisters and I don't understand, though, is why she'd send us here when she'd kept us away from it for so long. She left this place for a reason. If the truth she was talking about drove her away, why would she want us to come back?"

"That is a good question, *a leanbh.* Did something happen?"

Rowan considered the question. Bridget had always been looking over her shoulder, always peering into crowds. She seemed to be searching for someone who was never there. That was why they'd always been on the move, never staying in one place for long. They'd been in Fayetteville for more than six months, and they all wanted to settle into the college town and just live for a while. But . . . Rowan remembered something. "A few days before she died, I heard her on the phone. She was making a reservation for a motel somewhere. That's what she did when she was ready to leave wherever we were."

"All these years and she was still running." A shadow crossed Everly's face. She looked toward the sky. "Who were you running from, *a leanbh?*"

Rowan knew the question wasn't for her. She watched as a series of thoughts passed over Everly's face. Finally, her grandmother turned to her. "When your mother was young, she loved it here. She used to say she'd never leave, but fate has a way of pulling you toward places you never planned to go." Her gaze followed the dark, graceful form of a heron gliding silently across the moonlit water. She released a heavy sigh. "So many lost years."

A thought rose in Rowan's consciousness. What if the truth they were supposed to find wasn't about Bridget and why she ran away? What if it was about *them*? *Their* history. Bridget had never talked about their father. Who was he? *Where* was he? She blurted the question out before she'd consciously formed it. "Do you know who our father is?"

Everly looked back to the water. She gave a barely perceptible shake of her head. "I didn't know she was pregnant."

They stood side by side, both staring out at the inky water. It was possible Everly hadn't known who Bridget had been seeing as a seventeen-year-old, who could have gotten her pregnant, but as Rowan took a sidelong look at her grandmother, she wondered how much trust she could put in what this woman told her. Rowan and her sisters didn't know her, but they'd known Bridget. They'd loved Bridget and trusted her, even if she had kept secrets from them. And she'd run away from Bird Island, Swallow Hall, and Everly Early.

Everly said she didn't know why, but that was another thing Rowan wasn't sure she could believe. She turned and walked slowly down the beach, feeling the sand push between her toes. With each step away from Everly, the chill grew stronger, the warm cocoon evaporating. Had Bridget felt the cold when she'd left here, or had she needed to escape the cloistered island so badly that the chill didn't matter?

"This place," Rowan said. "The house. I've never seen anything like it. It's . . ." She trailed off, not knowing how to put it into words.

"It is special," Everly finished for her. "Magical."

"Yes."

"Its history is in your blood," Everly said. Rowan frowned. What did that mean? Before she could ask, a yawn slipped out. The corner of Everly's mouth lifted in another small smile. "We'll talk more tomorrow, *a leanbh*. You need sleep."

It was a dismissal. Rowan turned to go back to the house, craving the warmth of the attic bed, but she stopped when she saw a large circle rimmed by gathered stones sitting at the edge of the woods. "What's that?" she asked, moving toward it.

Everly came up behind her. "That is a moon circle. It is from Lughnasadh." Rowan looked at her blankly and Everly explained, "The first harvest."

The center of the circle was filled with a light dusting of fallen leaves, but the mixture of dirt and sand visible beneath looked compressed. "What's it for?" Rowan asked, her mind conjuring up covens and naked women dancing in the moonlight.

"Bridget didn't teach you, did she?" It was a rhetorical question she said more to herself than to Rowan. She sighed, looking at Rowan with doleful eyes. "You cast a circle and bring in ceremonial tools . . . a candle and a loaf of bread. You thank Mother Earth for the richness of the soil, the goodness infused in it, and the blessings it brings. Lughnasadh marks the beginning of the descent into the darkness of winter. It's almost the autumn equinox—the second harvest. Mabon, as it is called now, marks the time when the length of days and nights are equal. The sun shines over the equator. The two hemispheres receive equal amounts of light and darkness. It is a moment in time when the world is in balance."

Rowan stood transfixed as she listened to Everly. This was how Bridget grew up, celebrating pagan rituals and festivals. Rowan felt like a sponge, porous and ready to absorb every bit of information Everly had to share about this part of her life because here, on Bird Island, she and her sisters could embrace their magic. They didn't have to keep it contained. "What do you do for . . . what did you call it? Mabon?" she asked.

"We will celebrate leaving summer in the past, and we embrace autumn as the world prepares for the coming winter."

Rowan wrapped her arms around herself. The taste of blackberries was back and feelings of hope and peace, both things she'd experienced since arriving, bloomed larger inside of her.

Everly had said "we."

She expected Rowan and her sisters to stay on the island.

It wasn't until Rowan was back inside that something Everly said really registered. She'd spoken to the sky, as if Bridget was there, and said, *Who are you running from?* She hadn't said *Why* were you running, or *What* made you run. She'd said *Who.* What made her think Bridget had been running away from a person? Who could it have been? And what had that person done to drive their mother from her home?

Chapter Six

The sinister idea that, throughout Rowan's life, Bridget had been on the run from someone had taken root in Rowan's mind. She had dragged her three girls from state to state, always making it an adventure, preventing other people from getting too close and learning about their magic. The idea that she had constantly been on the run from someone shook Rowan. Surely not their father?

She started down the stairs the next morning bleary-eyed. She heard Caraline's angry voice before she saw her sister, one hand reaching for the doorknob. "What the actual hell?" She gripped it with both hands and shook it. "Open up, goddammit!"

Rowan rushed to Caraline's side. "What are you doing?"

Caraline spun around, her eyes red-rimmed with frustration. "I just want to take a walk outside, but this door won't open." She flung her head around, looking this way and that. "Stupid house."

Something creaked and groaned from the depths of Swallow Hall. It clearly hadn't liked that. Another moan echoed from below, and realization hit her. "I think it's worried that you want to leave." Rowan whispered into the air so the house couldn't hear. "Like Bridget."

Caraline stared. "So, what, if I did want to leave it wouldn't let me? God, no wonder Bridget split if both Everly and the house wanted to keep her trapped."

Rowan tried to pull Caraline away from the door. "She didn't leave because she was trapped. You know she was most likely pregnant with us when she left."

Caraline flung her raven hair behind her shoulders and snorted. "That's not news, Row. We've done the math. Everly was probably the kind of mother who wouldn't understand pregnancy out of wedlock. That's a pretty good reason to leave if you ask me."

Rowan didn't agree. "I don't think Everly knew. She didn't kick Bridget out."

Caraline folded her arms over her chest, her head waggling derisively. "And how do you know that?"

"Because she told us. She said she never wanted Bridget to leave. She said she wished she hadn't left."

Caraline laughed. "She says that now, but back then? Unmarried and pregnant?"

"I believe her," Rowan said. Not because Everly was her grandmother, but because she knew there had to be more to the story. Bridget wasn't the type of person to hold a grudge. She wouldn't have abandoned her mother and her home unless she felt like she had no other choice. Was being seventeen and pregnant in 1944 enough of a reason? Rowan didn't think so. *She'd been running from someone. That* was enough of a reason. But was that the truth Bridget wanted them to find on Bird Island? Another disconcerting thought slammed into her. Could whoever Bridget had been running from be after them now? Were *they* in some sort of danger? Had Bridget assumed the girls would find the photo if she died? Was that why she'd left the message, thinking that Bird Island and Swallow Hall would keep them safe?

The idea slipped away when Caraline said, "Well, I don't. People don't always show you who they really are. They show you what they want you to see. I don't have on rose-colored glasses."

"Don't you, though? You fall for a new guy every other week—"

"Exactly. And I break up with them because I know they're usually too good to be true. Better that *I* leave first."

Rowan felt the warmth of being near her grandmother. The sweet taste of violets and blackberries and grapes. "Bridget didn't leave because of Everly."

Caraline flailed her arm around again. "You can't know that, Row. Everyone has something to hide. And what the hell is the story with this place? The Keeper of Swallow Hall? What does that even mean?"

"We *just* got here. We're just seeing the magic in this house. Give her time. This is all just as much a shock to her as it is to us."

Caraline turned and paced, spinning back to face Rowan. "So you don't think Everly knew Bridget was pregnant with us."

A challenge, not a question. "No."

"So why *did* she leave then, huh? Why'd she go off when she was seventeen to raise triplets on her own?"

Because she was on the run from someone, Rowan thought, but she couldn't blurt that out. She could hear her sister's response in her head. *You're basing it on the fact that Everly said "who" and not "why"?*

"That's the thing, Caraline. Bridget is the one who kept things from us. Don't you see that? She kept us from the only family we have. From a home. Maybe she had a good reason, and if she did, I want to know what it was. She had secrets, Cara, but she also kept that picture. It led us here. Don't you want to know why?" Rowan took a breath before saying the most logical explanation, her ace in the hole. "What if the truth we're supposed to find is about our father?"

For the first time since they started this conversation, Caraline faltered. Her voice dropped low. "Do you think that's it?"

A sudden screech sliced through the morning. Saoirse! Rowan and Caraline spun around trying to discern where the sound had come from.

Rowan cocked her head, listening. Which direction? She hollered her sister's name. "Where are you?"

They heard the echoey sound of footsteps pounding the floor, then Saoirse calling, "The kitchen!"

All they'd seen of the house the night before had been the gathering room and their bedrooms. Rowan spun around again, this time trying to remember where Everly had come from with the tray of snacks last night. She couldn't place a direction, though. Doors and hallways sprouted from every side of the main living space, but none screamed *This way to the kitchen!*

She picked a direction and raced through the gathering room. She heard Caraline behind her, the locked door forgotten. They started down a hallway that ended with a closed door. Rowan opened it, plowing into . . . a wall. Caraline careened into her back. "What the . . . ?"

Rowan didn't have time to think. They backtracked and took another hallway. This one opened wide and spilled them into a kitchen that looked ancient. An enormous fireplace made from old bricks stood against the far wall. A rectangular table made of equally old dark wood stood in the center of the room. Worn wood countertops wrapped around the perimeter of the space, and open shelving lined the walls, every nook and cranny filled with bowls and plates, cups, and tin canisters. Double-hung windows faced south and framed a view of the dense woods, with a glimpse of the beach peeking through on the left.

Rowan couldn't absorb it all because Saoirse stood in an arched opening on the opposite side of the room. "You have to see this!" she blurted, then turned on her heel and scurried away.

Rowan's worry evaporated. Whatever the screech was about, it wasn't bad. She and Caraline hurried after her. "What is it?" Rowan called, but then she saw it: a vestibule that linked the house to the outbuilding she'd seen the night before, and in it were plants. Dozens and dozens of plants. She hadn't realized the outbuilding—like a sunroom—was connected to the house, and it was a piece of heaven for Saoirse. This was the apothecary to end all apothecaries—a glass-walled sanctuary most definitely infused with magic. The dappled morning light poured through the deceptively tall glass walls and ceiling. Every branch and leaf seemed to stretch toward the light, searching for its warmth and light.

The space itself was an airy rectangle, bursting with greenery. On the two shorter, angled walls were multitiered potting tables, each layer crowded with voluminous herbs, delicate blossoms, and trailing vines that cascaded over the edges.

The longer glass wall had a counter-height table that ran its full length. Clay pots, glass beakers, and neatly labeled tins cluttered the top. Even the outside seemed to want in, with the leaves still clinging to the trees outside brushing against the glass.

On the opposite side was a brick wall lined with open shelves from floor to ceiling. Rowan tracked jars of every shape and size on the shelves. They were filled with dried herbs, amber and emerald oils, crushed petals, powdered roots, and mystery mixtures just waiting for Saoirse to use them.

Possibility. It was the only word that came to mind. This apothecary held a world of possibilities for Saoirse. With everything at her fingertips, her sister could spend a lifetime crafting healing potions, infusing them into soaps, lotions, and balms.

Saoirse stood in the center of the room, arms wide. She whirled around. "Isn't it perfect?" she squealed, pushing her glasses up. She wrapped her arms around herself. "I was just wandering around and it's like a magnet pulled me to this room. *My* room."

It *was* perfect, Rowan agreed. Abso*lute*ly perfect. Saoirse spent the next ten minutes showing them around, pointing to a jar filled with dried lavender, another with fragrant rosemary, and still others with obscure plants Rowan had never heard of. She talked them through an entire shelf of propagations. Her suitcase sat open in the corner, all the things she hadn't been able to leave behind practically exploding from it. "If you need me, I'll be in here," she said once she'd rattled off the name of every flower, every herb, every oil that filled every shelf.

They might never see her because she might never actually leave this room. Rowan turned, but Caraline wasn't there anymore. She panicked for a split second until she realized her sister had retreated to the kitchen for a closer look. Rowan found her standing in a small pantry room, gazing at its contents, her hand on top of her head as if she couldn't believe what she was seeing. "Cara?"

Caraline slowly turned, her eyes wide. "It's a secret room," she said reverently, as if she'd just stumbled upon a treasure chest buried beneath the floorboards. Her fingers trembled against the ornate doorknob etched with a design she couldn't make out, and she stepped back so Rowan could see the narrow, hidden space beyond the pantry. A room within a room. Shelves lined the walls, crowded with ancient books, faded ribbons, and delicate porcelain trinkets. A small, dust-covered mirror reflected the faint, golden glow of the hallway light, illuminating the space far more than it logically should have.

"It's more than a closet," Rowan said, stepping closer. She scanned the shelves. "It's like a time capsule."

Caraline leaned in, her fingers brushing against a weathered leather journal with brittle pages. "It's like a piece of someone's life . . . forgotten but waiting to be found."

She pulled out the ancient leather-bound book held together with cording. She undid the tie and flipped through the first pages.

"What is *this*?"

They both spun to see Everly walking toward them, the shock of her voice hanging in the air between them. A knit shawl almost identical to the one Rowan had worn the night before was draped around her shoulders.

Caraline stepped back so Everly could see the hidden room. "I was looking for the pantry," Caraline said. "I thought this might be it." She gestured to the pantry door. "But when I opened it, something felt . . . off."

Everly's eyes narrowed as she peered past the pantry with its flours and sugars and jars of stewed tomatoes and into the space beyond. "I've been here my whole life and I've never seen that . . ." She trailed off, rolling her hand in the air so Caraline would carry on.

"The shelves seemed a little too deep, and the air felt cooler, like a draft was coming from . . . somewhere. So I pushed aside a few old spice jars, and my fingers brushed something hard." She pointed to a hidden latch. "I twisted it, and the back panel swung open and . . . voilà! A tiny room."

Rowan picked out a few more details. Old recipe cards lay scattered across a weathered wooden table, their ink faded but still legible. It smelled faintly of lavender and cloves, like it had been sealed away for years.

Everly's shock faded, replaced by an astonished smile. She looked at Caraline. "This was waiting for *you*."

Caraline's gaze darted from Everly to the hidden room beyond the pantry. Rowan could feel her sister's chest tighten, see a thousand emotions surging all at once—disbelief, awe, a spark of joy. "Me?" Caraline whispered, her voice trembling. "But I . . . how . . . ?"

"It just *is,*" Everly said cryptically. "Swallow Hall reveals things when they need to be revealed. This was a sealed room. It was forgotten, but now it's remembered. The house showed it to *you* so it's yours now."

Caraline stepped forward, her fingers brushing over the time-worn recipe cards, the glass jars, the tiny vials glinting in the faint light. "Mine . . ." she repeated, softer now, wonder filling her voice. She held up the book so Everly could see it. "It says it belongs to Erin Early."

Everly's eyes softened. "Erin Early was my grandmother. Those are all her recipes."

Rowan felt a buzz flitter through her, felt the electric charge shooting through her sister. Caraline flipped through the first few loose pages. "Potato soup. Soda bread. Hand pies. Dublin Coddle—"

"What's Dublin Coddle?" Rowan asked.

Caraline skimmed the recipe, her brow furrowing. "It's sort of like a stew, I think? Potatoes, onions, bacon, sausages, and beer slow-cooked together. But look." She pointed to another section of ingredients. "These are things I've never heard of."

Her finger traced the delicate, faded script:

Briarroot Bulbs
Pishogue Peppercorns
Midsummer Honeycomb

"What even are these?" Caraline said quietly, her gaze darting to the shelves around her. Her fingers hovered over a glass jar filled with something that looked like tiny, silver-flecked seeds.

Realization hit Rowan. "It's a spell disguised as a stew." She leaned closer, her own curiosity sparking. "Maybe it's a charm. Or a blessing. Or—" That word, Pishogue, sounded ominous. "Maybe a warning."

Caraline cocked one brow. She reached for the briarroot bulbs. "Whatever it is, I want to try making it."

Everly pulled her thick braid from underneath the shawl, dropping it so it hung down her back. "My granny used to say how she'd make Dublin Coddle before she went to bed so her da—Paddy, who built this house—would have something warm to eat when he stumbled home from the pub." Everly's brows formed a V. "I know my great-granda was a bit of a drunk. Took an axe to this house many times, in fits of madness. Hard to imagine why Maeve—my great-grandmother—put up with him. She tried to keep him calm."

Caraline closed the recipe book and wrapped her arms around it, holding it close like she didn't want to let it go. She looked around the kitchen, talking to the room as if it had ears. "I still don't like it here." The house groaned. Caraline looked past Rowan at a random wall. "Okay, yes, the peach color in the bedroom was a nice touch, and this room, but I don't know if I'm staying."

From upstairs, a door slammed. Caraline jumped, then threw up her hand as if that proved something. "I get it! You don't want me here either."

"Nonsense," Everly said. "It showed you the hidden room. This is where you belong."

Caraline retreated a step. "No, this is definitely *not* where I belong."

"You do. You *do* belong at Swallow Hall. I let your mother go. We won't make that mistake with you."

Rowan stared at Everly. Who was *we*? Everly and the house?

Caraline sputtered. "I could leave if I wanted to." She hesitated for a second, then strode out of the kitchen.

"Wait!" Rowan called, scurrying behind her. But Caraline didn't break stride. Back at the front door, she put the book down and grasped the knob. She rattled it, but like before, the door didn't budge. She bent to take a closer look and growled.

Rowan knew from experience that challenging her sister could just make her double down. She'd leave out of spite, just because Everly said she couldn't. So she stayed quiet.

"This old house has a mind of its own," Everly said from behind them. "Like I said, it doesn't want you to leave."

"So it's gonna keep me prisoner? Where's the key?" Caraline straightened up and held her hand out as if the key would materialize out of thin air and float right into her waiting hand.

"None of the doors have locks," Everly said.

"But it's locked."

"I'm sure you'll find that it is not."

Caraline just looked at her. And then turned, grabbed the doorknob again, and yanked. This time it turned with ease and the door flew open. The unexpected force knocked her off her feet and sent her flying back and right toward Rowan. Rowan used her arms to brace herself. Somehow, she managed to keep them both upright.

A second later the front door slammed shut again. Caraline looked around before settling her stare on Everly. "How did you do that?"

"How did I do what?" Everly asked, a bit too innocently.

"Lock the door. Unlock the door. Make it close!" Caraline clawed her way free of Rowan's grasp. Once again, she grabbed the knob on the front door, and once again it opened with ease. Caraline whipped her arm into motion, flinging the door closed with a bang. She hurried to the next door in the hallway. It opened, no problem. A closet. She moved to the next one in the hallway, grabbed the knob, and turned. It didn't budge, not one centimeter.

Caraline let out a frustrated screech. As if in response, the walls in the front hallway seemed to quiver and the sound of laughter echoed around them.

Caraline darted her gaze every which way. "Really? It's mocking me?" She moved on to a different door. Another closet. She circled past the hall leading to the kitchen and back to where Everly and Rowan stood. She flung her arm out, pointing to the door that still didn't open. "So what's in there?"

"That was your mother's favorite room," Everly said evenly.

Caraline frowned. "So now you don't go in there? What, is it like a shrine?"

Rowan watched Everly, half expecting her to be irritated by Caraline's attitude, but she didn't react. Her gaze was steely, just like it had been when she'd first laid eyes on the three girls—trespassers on her island. "Houses hold on to things. Every flaw, every scuff mark, every hole your ancestors put in the walls tells a story, just as surely as the lines on our faces. A house like Swallow Hall goes back generations. It tells the stories of those who came before. So, no, the room is not a shrine. The house is not a mausoleum. It's a memory. Swallow Hall holds the echoes of the past."

As Rowan's gaze drifted to the door, a chill crept along her spine. Whatever echo her mother left behind, Swallow Hall was still holding it. She wondered how long it would take for the house to tell her.

Chapter Seven

Rowan stared out the window as Caraline clanked around in the kitchen. Everly's words rolled through her mind. *Swallow Hall is a memory. It holds echoes of the past.*

"Row."

When she'd pressed for more, the older woman simply shook her head, her braid swinging stiffly behind her. "We'll get there, my dear," she said, and she'd walked away.

"Rowan!"

She startled and looked up. Caraline stood facing her, a wide scarf holding her hair back, her hands jammed on her hips. "What's going on with you?"

Had she asked that already? "Nothing," she said.

Her sister shook her head. "You've got that deep in thought expression," she said, making air quotes to emphasize *deep in thought*. "I know you. Everly's getting to you with her cryptic words, isn't she? And now you think this house has Bridget's memories."

For someone else, the accuracy of Caraline's assessment might have been astounding. For Rowan, it was par for the course. "Don't you?" she asked.

Caraline lifted one shoulder and pulled a face as she walked toward the hidden pantry room. "Maybe, but so what?"

"I want to know more about her childhood. About who she was . . . before."

Caraline disappeared for a few seconds then came back, her arms laden with jars. Rowan winced as she plunked them onto the wooden counter. "You're going to break those."

Caraline waved away the concern. "This glass is, like, an inch thick. It would take more than that to shatter it." She perched on a stool at the counter and started sorting through it all, grouping the jars into some kind of order that only she understood.

"I want to find our father," Rowan said, more quietly this time.

Caraline stopped her sorting and looked at her. "I know you do. I guess . . . I guess I do too, but aren't you worried he doesn't want to know us? I mean, if Bridget thought he did, why would she have taken us from him?" Caraline's gaze bore into her. "Or, Row, he might know about us and not even care."

She was right. Maybe he'd known all along that he had children, and he'd chosen to stay away. If that was the case and if their mom knew it, then the truth Bridget wanted them to find was something else altogether. And if that was the case, Rowan was at a complete loss. What other secrets had Bridget kept from them? Her thoughts were a jumbled mess of threads knotted together. She needed to pick them apart, one by one. "Will you help me?"

Caraline sighed. "I'm not so sure this is what Bridget wanted. I think she would have told us about this place and Everly if she'd wanted us to know. And she would have told us about our father."

That meant no, but Rowan wasn't ready to give up. "What if New Bethel is the right place and this is the right time?"

Caraline put down the jar she'd been holding and looked at her. "You mean for the café."

"Think about it." She pointed toward the apothecary. "Saoirse can make anything she wants to in there. We can find a spot and open the café. You can bake. I can do . . . everything else."

It was the perfect solution, because if Caraline ever left, the sisters would be split apart, their connection broken, and Rowan couldn't even imagine that. The thought of it burned her throat. She knew they wouldn't stay together forever. The time would come when they had to make choices and live their own lives. But that day was not here, not now. And if they could make their childhood dream come true, then they could have both: each other *and* their own lives.

"You're going to love it here," Rowan said. "Eventually."

Caraline tucked a wayward strand of her inky hair back under her scarf. "I don't know about that, but a café is . . . an interesting idea."

Rowan's relief was palpable, if Caraline was considering it, it meant she had time to figure out who their father was—assuming *that* was the truth Bridget had been referring to. She didn't know where to start, but she'd figure it out, because unlike Saoirse and Caraline, she didn't have an apothecary or kitchen to occupy her. She had nothing but time.

* * *

Despite the unanswered questions coursing through her, with every breath Rowan took at Swallow Hall, the weight of Bridget's death grew a bit lighter. She felt her mother all around her. It was as if the house emitted Bridget's essence so it could seep into Rowan's skin and ease her pain. If only it could tell her what truth Bridget wanted them to find.

When Everly announced she was going into town, Rowan joined her. She watched her grandmother's every move, trying to get a read on her. Everly strode through the woods with purpose. "You need to be watchful." She was on alert, her eyes darting around as if she thought a dark figure like the one Rowan had seen when they arrived might jump out from between the trees.

It felt like a warning. "Why?"

"People fear what they don't understand, and there are people who—"

She broke off, leaving the words hanging there. "People who . . . ?" Rowan prompted.

Everly drew in her lips, pressing them together as her expression clouded. Finally, she turned to look at Rowan. "If the wrong sort of person gets ahold of something they shouldn't . . . well, it's like Pandora's box. You can't stop the evils once they've taken hold. Power in the wrong hands . . . it will have grave consequences. Not all magic is good, and you can't always detect it. You need to remember that, my dear."

Rowan took a step back, a pall of bitter cold enveloping her. She knew Everly wasn't making some vast generalization about the dangers of dark magic. No, she was talking about something specific.

"It's about the magic," Everly said as she glanced back at Swallow Hall. "It's always been about the magic. It keeps most people away."

"They know, then, the people in town?" Rowan asked.

Everly didn't answer. She kept her attention on the house. A better question Rowan thought—the one she should have asked—was how could people *not* know? It was impossible not to see the strangeness of Swallow Hall, how it was sinking, how it had changed from the house it was when Paddy Early built it to what it was now. "Are they afraid of you?"

Finally, Everly shifted her gaze back to Rowan. "They?"

Rowan swept her arm out in the direction of New Bethel. "The people in town? Your neighbors?"

Everly shifted the basket she carried to her other arm. She gave a one-shouldered shrug. "I suppose they are. Some people, anyway."

A lump formed in Rowan's throat. She'd hoped being here would let her escape the taunts and judgments she'd grown up with. *Witch. Witch. Witch.*

They walked in silence "What was Bridget like when she was little?"

A moment passed before Everly answered. "She was sweet. Full of curiosity. She flitted around like a firefly. Knew every tree. Every stone. I couldn't keep track of her most days."

"And when she was older? A teenager?"

"She was a lot like Caraline, truth be told. Free spirited. Not a care in the world. Until . . ."

A knot formed in the pit of Rowan's stomach. "Until what? Did something happen?"

When Everly didn't speak, Rowan thought she was going to ignore the question. But then she looked squarely at Rowan. "Not some*thing*. Some*one*."

The intensity with which she looked at Rowan sent a shiver skittering over her. *Who, not why. The truth is there. Find it.*

Everly stopped in front of an ancient tree, walking around it, the pads of her fingers skimming the trunk, tracing something carved into the wood. It was half of a heart, the initial B in the top left and another letter, carved too shallowly to be clear, below it. "She did this not long before she left."

"Whose initial?" Rowan asked, brushing her fingers over the faded lines. The mark was old, but there was something restless beneath it, almost as if the tree itself held tight to the memory.

"There was a man . . ." Everly started, but her words drifted off, tangled in the wind.

"Her boyfriend?"

Everly shook her head and started walking again, her steps slower now. "No . . . not exactly." The words stretched, laden with hesitation. "But she . . . she was captivated by him. It was like . . . like he had this hold on her."

Rowan's pulse flickered. "Like she was bewitched?"

"Maybe." Everly exhaled, her hand trailing along the nearby branches. "Or maybe it was him that couldn't let *her* go. There was something about him . . . I hoped the infatuation would pass, that she'd come back . . . She never did, though. Once she met him, she had one foot out the door." Her voice thinned with quiet regret. "And then she left. Said she had no choice."

"She was that in love with him?" Rowan tried to picture Bridget giving up this place and her family for a man, but it didn't sit right. Her mother had always been too independent. Too careful.

Everly's eyes darkened, her gaze fixed on the ground ahead. "She never said it was love." Her voice was low and threaded with uncertainty. "I don't know what it was. But whatever bound them . . . it wasn't simple."

Rowan had been holding her breath as she listened. As they approached the edge of the woods, she finally exhaled. Who was the man who'd transfixed her mother so? And if Bridget had left with him, what happened? Why hadn't they stayed together?

Everly's pace quickened as they turned onto the sidewalk in New Bethel. Rowan felt the weight of people's gazes on them as they walked through downtown. How many of them had known Bridget?

They strode with staunch purpose past the same colorful businesses the sisters had passed the day before. It wasn't until they turned into an old neighborhood, then onto another street filled with a hodgepodge of old houses, that Everly spoke again. "I don't know if he is your father, this man," she said, speaking as if she'd read Rowan's mind. Maybe she had. Rowan had no clue what her grandmother's magic was. "What I know is that my daughter left because of him. He took her from here. He took her from *me*."

Everly's voice was thick with old anguish. She'd lost her daughter completely—and after all this time, it was clear she still didn't understand why.

What a different life Rowan and her sisters might've had if Bridget had stayed at Swallow Hall. It was impossible to imagine.

"He never came back either?" Rowan asked. He certainly hadn't been part of their lives—or maybe he had, before they were old enough to remember.

Everly shook her head. "I never saw him again."

"Last night you said something about Bridget running from someone," Rowan said.

Everly's gaze darkened, drifting toward the tangled trees. "I did." Her voice faltered, weighted down and conflicted. "I still wonder." She shook her head, her words uneven. "She left with him . . . but I've always thought . . ."

"What?" Rowan pressed.

"She left with him, but that doesn't mean she wasn't running."

A thin thread of salt and copper, the unmistakable bitterness of doubt, coiled in Rowan's mouth, settling on her tongue. Everly was holding on to uncertainty, a fracture in the story she couldn't explain.

"If he was our father, maybe she thought leaving with him was the right thing to do," Rowan said, but something about that idea didn't sit right.

"Maybe," Everly said, but the doubt Rowan tasted turned raw and sharp, curling under her teeth. Everly was holding pieces of the truth, but they didn't fit neatly.

"She never told you why she really left," Rowan said quietly.

Everly shook her head once, eyes distant. "No." Her voice cracked, low and bitter. "She never did."

A breath stretched between them, full of the secrets Bridget had held close to the breast.

"I don't know why she never stopped moving," Everly added. She looked at Rowan. "You lived with her. She was running . . . all that time, she *was* running, wasn't she?"

Rowan nodded. The truth hovered just out of reach, but deep down in the marrow of her bones, Rowan knew that finding out why Bridget had left Bird Island all those years ago would lead her to it.

They walked in silence after that, each lost in their own thoughts. The narrow street curved ahead, and a shotgun house came into view. It had a sagging roofline, its paint peeled in strips, and the shutters were crooked in the same way some of the windows at Swallow Hall were, but here it was neglect, not magic, pulling the house apart.

Rowan pointed at the dilapidated house. "What happened to that place?"

"It was abandoned years ago and fell into ruin," Everly said. "Houses are like memories—they can be forgotten, neglected, even crushed. But that doesn't mean they're gone altogether. Sometimes all they need is a little care to wake them up again. To remember."

Rowan's gaze drifted to the decrepit house, to the tangled vines creeping up one side, to the shattered windows, their glass clouded with dust and webs. She was amazed it was still standing. Like Swallow Hall, it listed to one side, but while the house on the island seemed to have an invisible string attached to the roof, pulling it up toward the sky, this house looked like it was fighting—and losing—the pull of gravity that was trying to make it topple to the ground.

"So even that house has a story waiting to be told, or maybe . . . waiting to be finished?" It seemed hard to believe. Too far gone.

"Even that house," Everly said.

The past, it seemed, was buried everywhere in New Bethel, sometimes in plain sight.

They stopped in front of the house next door, which appeared to be in much better shape. It was an ancient red brick with bushy, leafy plants surrounding it. Splashes of little white flowers scented the air. Mint. Two wide chimneys flanked either side of the structure, and a set of wood steps led to a small porch at the front door, which sat squarely at the center of the house. On either side were windows framed by worn red shutters. Directly above were perfectly aligned second-story windows. The spaces where shutters might have been looked naked, whitewashed bricks framing them instead. Three small dormers emerged from the peaked roof like three eyes that kept constant watch of the street and its inhabitants. The house was a symmetrical rectangle with a shingled roof. It sat close to the street, a narrow sidewalk of red cement pavers butting up to the dead grass which was the extent of the front yard.

"Who lives here?" she asked.

"His name is Kyle Floyd." Everly let the handle of her market basket slide down her arm, grasping it with one hand as she rifled through the contents. A moment later she pulled a small jar of some sort of red oil and a mason jar filled with a dingy-looking fluid from the basket. "He has chronic pain from scars—an injury from a long time ago—so I make him a soothing oil with St. John's wort. He likes my special reishi ginger tea too. I brew it for him every other week."

"Reishi?"

"The polypore fungus."

Rowan's upper lip curled. "Fungus?"

Everly shook her head, and Rowan could almost hear her commenting about how this was another thing Bridget had not taught them. "The good kind. A mushroom from the *Ganoderma tsugae* family. It clings to the sides of the hemlock—"

"Hemlock, as in *hemlock*?" Rowan stared. Was Everly giving this man poisonous tea?

"No relation. There are hemlock trees in the woods. The mushrooms grow on the trunks."

"Do you eat them? The mushrooms?"

"No, no, my dear. They're too woody. I slice them, dry them, then steep them to make teas, extracts, and tinctures. They have very strong medicinal properties."

Ohh. The apothecary suddenly made sense. The house hadn't created it for Saoirse, it was Everly's. Rowan eyed the pale liquid with a grimace. "How does it taste?"

"Quite good, actually. I cut the bitterness with honey, which allows space to appreciate the lovely notes of umami. Beautiful. Come on, now."

"Do you always make deliveries? They never come to you?" Rowan asked.

"One or two do. Simon Moody comes by every few weeks. Macy Davis does sometimes. Mr. Floyd here came once, but it was too hard on him and, well, it's just easier this way."

Rowan walked slowly behind her, the air becoming stifling. The earthy roots of all that citrusy mint threatened to overpower her senses, but the dirt quelled it, keeping it buried.

Everly started up the porch steps, stopping to break off a sprig of the mint that crept onto the porch. "For his tea," she explained before Rowan could even ask. Everly rapped her knuckles on the door and before she'd dropped her arm back to her side, it swung open and a man stood there, hunched, his spotted hand clutching the handle of a cane. "You're late," he said gruffly, lifting his stoney gaze to Everly.

Rowan drew in a sharp breath, then bit her lip to keep her face placid. Everly hadn't prepared her for the man's physical disfigurement. He wore a brown leather patch over one eye and a map of scars crisscrossed the entirety of his face. One arm seemed to work fine, holding on to his cane. The other hung limply by his side. The small jar of St. John's wort oil hardly seemed enough given the expanse of scarring.

Everly wasn't fazed. She flashed him a mollifying smile and handed him the herb she'd picked. "My tea is worth waiting for, now, isn't it, Kyle?"

He grumbled as he shuffled back. "You can put it in the kitchen. Money's there."

Everly's long braid swung gently behind her as she strode past him. As she disappeared into the depths of the house, the man shifted his gaze to Rowan. His thin-lipped mouth opened slightly, his one good eye narrowing. "You look like her," he said, his gravelly voice making it sound like an accusation.

Rowan managed a smile as she tried to push out the thick air that settled in her lungs. "Do I?"

Everly reappeared with a small white envelope in one hand. "She ought to, Kyle. She's my granddaughter."

He grunted. "That right? So where's she been all these years? Square dancin' and pickin' apple blossoms, too high 'n' mighty to come on home to her poor granny." He spoke to Everly as if Rowan wasn't standing right there, which was fine with her. Her breathing had grown shallow. The stuffiness of the house made her head burn.

"Now, now, Mr. Floyd," Everly said lightly. "You're chirping nonsense."

Another low guttural sound escaped his throat. "Just call me a mockingbird," he jeered. "Humph."

Everly frowned. "I don't think anyone would compare you to that joyful bird."

Kyle Floyd's dark eyes clouded. He gritted his teeth and seemed to brace himself against a sudden burst of pain.

At the same moment, a heaviness pressed down on Rowan. She felt as if she was under ten fathoms of water, the pressure of it crushing her lungs. Her mouth started to fill with a woody, bitter taste, commingling with the sharp coolness of menthol. She clutched the railing and moved away from the house—away from Kyle Floyd and his terrible injuries, from his pain. The pressure in her body abated with each step.

She felt his eye pierce her back as he spoke through the rattling globs in his throat. "Looks like your girl needs some of your tea."

"You worry about yourself, Kyle," Everly said brusquely. "See you next time."

Rowan heard the door close firmly behind them with a thud. She felt Everly's fingertips on her arm. "Rowan, my dear, are you okay?"

Rowan stepped into the street. Sucked in a deep breath. Walked farther from the red brick house. She pushed out an exhalation. "I don't know . . ."

Everly was by her side, her hand on her back, guiding her up the street. "What happened?" she said. "Tell me."

Rowan's eyes pricked and turned glassy. "I . . . I couldn't breathe. It was like I could feel his pain." She drew in a deep breath, letting it fill her lungs before expelling the remnant of heaviness lingering there.

Everly repositioned her basket on her forearm. "Have you felt that before?"

Slowly, Rowan nodded. Too often. Which was why friendships had always been so elusive to her. Her body seemed to absorb others' physical sensations. Pain was the worst.

"But you're okay now?"

"A little shaky," Rowan said.

"Take deep breaths," Everly instructed, then she inhaled, nodding at Rowan to do the same.

Rowan did, drawing the air into her gut, releasing it slowly. Together, they breathed until Rowan's body calmed. Everly watched her intently, as if Rowan were a page of a book full of words she hadn't quite deciphered yet. For a moment, her expression shifted, but if Everly understood what had just happened, she kept it to herself.

She hoisted her basket higher on her arm and started walking again, guiding Rowan alongside, but something was different now. Rowan's boots crunched over fallen leaves, the ground beneath her feet almost humming, faint but insistent. It prickled at the edges of her awareness. It was as if her magic was heightened, pulling at something buried deep inside. The marshmallow clouds against the vibrant blue sky looked impossibly close. The briny air tingled on her lips, salt settling on her tongue. Even the swallows' delicate trills seemed to spiral around her.

Everly glanced over, a slight furrow in her brow. "You're quiet, my dear."

Rowan's gaze lingered on the wildflowers nodding in the breeze. Each petal was bright and alive. She wasn't sure if she could explain it. "It's just . . . everything feels so . . . real. Like it was black and white and now it's all in technicolor." She felt like Dorothy seeing Munchkinland in blazing color for the first time.

Everly's lips curved in a subtle, knowing smile, her gaze turning to the whispering trees. "Sometimes a place has a way of waking you up, making you notice the things you didn't even know were there. It seems Swallow Hall has awakened your magic."

Rowan nodded slowly, her heart quickening. She dawdled for a few minutes, finally catching up when Everly stopped and summoned her. They made a loop through one of the residential areas of town. Everly flipped through a small notebook she kept tucked in her basket. They stopped two more times. At each house, Everly delivered a mason jar of tea, and at each house, the pressure built around Rowan. She stayed on the sidewalk, keeping it from overwhelming her as it had at Kyle Floyd's.

Finally, with the deliveries finished, they turned onto High Street. Everly walked at a brisk pace. They passed a dry cleaner, a doughnut shop, and a real estate office. They passed a few station wagons and sedans parallel parked on the street. An old Mercury with a beige ragtop was parked in front of a quaint house that had been converted into a seafood restaurant. A wooden sign swung in the afternoon breeze: Moody's Saltwater Kitchen. In the yard, a man whacked a hammer against a piece of siding. He looked to Rowan to be somewhere in his fifties, solid and healthy. He picked up another plank, held it in place, and with quick precision, pounded nails into it. As he reached for another piece of wood, he spotted them and raised a hand in greeting. "Afternoon, Ms. Everly."

It didn't look like Everly wanted to stop, but she did, treating him with half a smile. "Moody," she said.

He looked at Rowan, his smile fading. He tilted his head to one side, considering her. "Who's this?"

Rowan closed her eyes, holding her breath, waiting for the onslaught of tastes to erupt in her mouth.

"Rowan?" A hand squeezed her shoulder and she jolted back to the moment. Everly looked at her, concerned. "Did it happen again?"

Rowan couldn't even count the times Bridget had tried to help her control the sensory overload she experienced around other people. "Try to keep it in check, *a leanbh,*" Bridget had often coached her. "It's going to take practice, but you can do it. Take deep breaths. One. Two. Three. That's it. Now release. One. Two. Three."

Again and again, Rowan had tried, but her mouth continued to fill with the taste of colors and the feel of shapes, with bitterness, or salt, or something so sour it puckered her lips. No amount of deep breaths helped create a barrier between her and the unspoken feelings of the people around her. Eventually, it was just easier to be alone and stick only to the people who didn't affect her—which meant Bridget, Saoirse, and Caraline.

"Rowan?"

She'd prepared herself for the same onslaught that had happened at Kyle Floyd's and at the other houses they'd made deliveries to, but she breathed in and out—one, two, three. The flatness of loss commingled with the briny air settled on her tongue. She tasted the sharp edges of this man Moody's sorrow, dulled by time but ever-present. She stepped backward, putting more space between them. As the sensations dimmed, she blew out a relieved breath. Slowly shook her head. Gave a slight smile. "I think I'm okay."

Everly nodded and spoke quietly. "That's good. You can manage this." Her gaze lingered on Rowan for another moment before she gave one short nod. "Rowan, this is Simon Moody—"

"Just Moody," he said.

She recognized the name. Everly had mentioned it earlier. He was one of the few clients who sometimes came to Bird Island. "Moody, this is Rowan. She's . . . one of Bridget's girls."

Moody set his hammer on the makeshift workbench he'd created by placing a sheet of plywood across two sawhorses. He folded his arms over his chest, rocking back on his heels. "One of Bridget's girls," he repeated. "Well, nice to meet you," he said to Rowan, but the words lacked sincerity. He looked at Everly. "I heard your granddaughters were here. And Bridget?"

At this question, the coolness of water Rowan associated with her mother sluiced over her tastebuds. Once again, she drew in a deep breath, counting to three as she exhaled, and the sensation of liquid in her mouth passed. Everly hesitated, keeping an eye on her. "Bridget—" she shook her head like she was clearing out the debris that was clogging her thoughts, "—died recently."

He frowned and his jaw pulsed, silent as he processed the information. He raked his fingers through his hair, coating the strands with the sawdust that had clung to his skin. "I'm really sorry to hear that."

He opened his mouth to speak again, to ask what had happened to Bridget, Rowan suspected, but stopped when Everly swallowed hard. "Yes. Well." As she wrapped one arm around Rowan, a different taste danced over Rowan's tongue . . . the mustiness of regret. It faded when her grandmother said, "It brought these girls home to me."

From inside the restaurant, a telephone rang. Moody looked over his shoulder, waiting as if whoever was calling might change their mind and hang up, but the sharp insistent jangle continued. He sighed. "I better get that," he said to Everly, and with a quick nod at Rowan, he jogged inside to answer the phone.

"He knew Bridget," Rowan asked as she and Everly continued toward town.

Everly nodded. "Everyone knew Bridget. New Bethel is a small town, and back then—when your mother was younger—Swallow Hall wasn't quite so . . . contrary."

"What do you mean, contrary?" Rowan asked.

"Your mother was quite connected to the house. When she left, that's when things changed."

Rowan wanted more, but they were walking past the Disciples of Christ Tabernacle. Everly's lips drew into a terse line. She looked around her, seemingly aware of everyone and everything, as if she anticipated trouble and was ready to deal with it. Above them the white clouds turned dark and gloomy.

When Rowan had walked this way with her sisters, people had thrown them curious glances and lingering looks. But walking this way with Everly was different. She didn't just feel seen, she felt watched. Most people gave them a wide berth, their faces turning away, and the typical bustle of a town seemed muted. Only the steady rhythm of their footsteps tapping against the sidewalk registered like a quiet, measured echo in Rowan's mind.

Then a breeze stirred, brisk, whispering through the air. It was followed by a faint, almost inaudible murmur meant just for her.

"Cill . . . ian."

Rowan's head snapped around. She scanned the street, eyes darting from one face to another. A shadow slipped into the entrance of a shop—a figure in a dark coat—but they were too far away, too indistinct. Just another stranger, not someone who'd whispered in her ear.

Her gaze shot to Everly. Her grandmother's shoulders were rigid, tension coiled tight beneath the fabric of her shawl. But she kept walking, her pace steady, her gaze fixed ahead.

Rowan's skin prickled, and a chill laced her spine. Everly didn't say so, but Rowan felt sure she had heard it too. Apparently, it was something they were not going to talk about.

Across the street, two women slowed, both dressed in black, their heads bent together like crows, beak to beak. Their eyes skimmed over Rowan and followed Everly. Rowan slowed and watched them, and an uneasy feeling enveloped her. She scurried to catch up with Everly. "Who are they?"

Everly strode on. "Nobody worth your time."

"But who are they?" Rowan pressed.

Everly sighed. "Louise Janson and Lorna McNicol. Daughters of the Disciples of Christ." She said the words with disdain. "Laughable because they are the farthest things from Christian a person can be."

Rowan's mouth tingled with the pungent sourness of a lemon or a particularly tart piece of grapefruit. She smacked her lips to chase it away as she looked over her shoulder catching a last glimpse of the women before they turned a corner and disappeared from her sight. "They don't like you?"

"Not even a little bit. But I don't like them, either," Everly said curtly. "They're the type that would burn you at the stake for witchcraft. Steer clear."

Rowan watched Everly from the corner of her eye. She didn't know what to make of her grandmother. She was a force, and yet the longer she was away from Bird Island and Swallow Hall, the more tense and alert she became. A minute later they were across the street from Chester's Dime Store where she could see the shape of a person behind the window. She felt eyes follow them but she shook away the anxious feeling that slipped through her. Ahead, two elderly women made their way down the walkway of another old red brick house, this one bearing a sign in the front that read *New Bethel Historic Society*. One of the women had dark gray hair the color of steel wool. The other had a snowy bob. They stopped when they reached the sidewalk. One of them raised a hand in greeting. "Ahoy there, Everly."

"Macy. Esther," Everly said, slowing her pace.

Both women looked at Rowan. The darker-haired one had discerning brown eyes rimmed with green. "Macy Davis," she said jovially. She flicked her wrist toward the other woman. "This is my cousin, Esther Canvey. And you are . . . ?"

"Ladies, this is my granddaughter," Everly said before Rowan could answer.

Esther's bright blue eyes flew open wide. "Heavens! Is that right? You have a granddaughter?"

Everly smiled, but Rowan could see it didn't reach her eyes. "I know you already heard, Esther. No need to play pretend."

Esther arched a thin charcoal brow managing to look both sheepish at being caught out and puffed up like a preening bird at the same time. "Right you are." She pointed at the dime store. "Matthew said he met a young woman who looked like an Early."

Rowan raised her hand. "That'd be me. I tried to buy a map to find Swallow Hall."

Esther's eyes sparkled from under her translucent eyelashes. "No need for one of those around here. We're a friendly bunch. Just ask anyone for directions. We'll be glad to help."

Rowan thought that was debatable. Those Daughters of the Disciples of Christ hadn't looked very friendly or helpful.

At that moment, a dark cloud slid across the sky, casting a long shadow over the street. Everly peered up. "Looks like rain. We best be going," she said. She brushed Rowan's sleeve, propelling her around Esther and Macy. "Ladies," she said with a nod.

"Good day to you, Everly," one of them said. The other followed with, "Nice to meet you, Rowan."

"Is it really supposed to rain?" Rowan asked as the clouds blew away, and the sky cleared. She peered at the expanse of bright blue above.

"Doesn't look like it, not anymore," Everly said, tightly. "So many busybodies in New Bethel. I don't have the patience for them."

Rowan considered that. It almost sounded as if Everly had summoned up a darkening sky as an excuse to leave. How deep did her grandmother's magic run?

Once again, she looked over her shoulder. Esther and Macy hadn't budged. They waved when they saw her turn.

As they walked, Rowan shook away the heaviness of being in New Bethel. She'd convinced Caraline that this was the right place and the right time for their dreams, but maybe she was wrong.

It wasn't until they were well into the woods that Everly's shoulders relaxed and the pungent flavors that had lingered in Rowan's mouth finally faded.

Chapter Eight

Rowan had started to ask Everly about the house three times, but three times she stopped herself. One thing she'd learned about her grandmother right away was that she told you only what she wanted to—no more, no less. She'd already said the house was special, but she hadn't elaborated. Rowan peered up at the uneven walls. At the cockeyed windows. At the wallpaper that seemed alive, as if the vines embossed on it were growing, just like the winter creeper along the house.

Rowan had to find out more about the island, the house, her mother's time here and why she'd left. She needed to know the truth.

Saoirse had barricaded herself in the apothecary and Caraline had taken over the kitchen. That left Rowan to roam the island on her own looking for signs of where Bridget had once been. Had she sat on that rock, staring into the bay? Had she walked along this pathway, through the woods? Touched her toe in the same water? Had she left some clue for her future daughters to discover?

She didn't find the answers to her questions. Instead, she found new questions, because it wasn't just the house that had magic coursing through it. The island did, too. Why had the earth turned to mudflat at the water's edge? Why did the water spread into shallow pools as she approached, receding after she walked past? When she turned to look back the way she'd come, a new cluster of dark and foreboding clouds hovered overhead.

Magic. That single word spiraled in her mind. They all had magic coursing through their blood, but what about Bridget? Rowan had never seen her mother do anything magical. Is that part of why she'd left Swallow Hall? Maybe she'd been like Rowan, unsure how to exist with magic all around her, and the man she'd left with had given her an opportunity.

The ethereal glowing light of the fireflies flickered all around. She closed her eyes against the gusty breeze and thought of her mother's remains sitting in a ceramic container in her room. "Is this what you want, Bridget?" Rowan said aloud. The wind carried her voice away, and then, like a boomerang, it brought it back carrying that name again, slow and stretched out. *Cill . . . ian.*

Rowan started back toward the house, the water lapping ahead of her, receding behind her. As if Rowan herself was the invisible force pushing and pulling the fresh water to and from the shoreline.

The lightning bugs swarmed around her and then suddenly scattered, flying toward the woods. Their bright green glow turned bluish-white from afar. Blue ghosts, Rowan thought. Her gaze followed them, catching a glimpse of a dark form slipping into the shadows of the woods.

Her heart thudded in her chest. She thought about following the fireflies—about chasing whoever lurked in the shadows—but her feet wouldn't move. They stayed rooted to the damp ground, every nerve beneath her skin sparking like live wires. She stared into the darkness, holding her breath, but when she looked again, everything was still. The fireflies were gone, their soft, flashing glow swallowed by the mist.

Slowly, Rowan exhaled, the tension in her muscles easing just enough for her to turn away from the woods. But instead of dissipating, her unease pressed against her. What was she so afraid of?

Her gaze drifted to the darkened windows of the house and she shuddered. The taste of bitterness filled her mouth, mixed with something sweet. The blackberries again, or maybe brown sugar? She couldn't put her finger on it. It was a flavor that grew on her tongue, familiar but elusive, like a half-remembered dream. The magic woven through this place was a tangle of secrets wrapped around memories, spells threaded into shadows. But she didn't know what they could be.

Her thoughts hovered at the edges of her mind. She couldn't escape the feeling that the house was watching her—waiting for her to understand.

A thin layer of fog had drifted in, curling around the house like one of Saturn's rings. The temperature had dropped in the time she'd been outside, the crisp air now biting against her cheeks. Even with her sweater pulled tight around her, a shiver scuttled across her skin, prickling the fine hairs on her arms.

She quickened her pace, wrapping her arms around herself, trying to trap what little warmth she had left. But as she hurried on, the wind seemed to sigh, its chilly breath hushed, just beyond the reach of hearing. She strained to listen, but she heard only the faint rustle of leaves and the silence of the fog. It had been a trick of the wind, she told herself. Just her imagination.

Where should she look next for answers about Bridget's past? Who should she talk to?

Who? Who? Who? the wind whispered, each word a chilling echo. Not *what* had made Bridget leave, but *who.*

"I don't know, but I'm going to find out," Rowan whispered back, her breath misting in the cold air.

With her next step, she caught a sudden, frantic burst of movement next to her. She jumped back. A sharp, startled scream escaped her throat as something small and quick darted between her legs. It was nothing but a blur of gray fur vanishing behind a hulking tree trunk.

Rowan's gaze snapped to the towering hemlock, its rough trunk sprouting shelves of reishi mushrooms, their wide, flat caps fanning out like the pages of an ancient book. She let out a nervous laugh. Just a mouse. Or a vole. Nothing more. But the tension in her shoulders didn't ease, and she found herself scanning the mist, listening for that voice, watching for that shadow.

That's when she saw it. A nose peeking out from behind the tree. A thin white line bisected the brown and black markings on its face. Not a rodent at all. Rowan crouched down and extended her hand to lure the dog from hiding. Slowly, it emerged, its black and white splotches making it look more bovine than canine. "Well, hello there," she said, wriggling her fingers. "What are you doing way out here on your own?"

The dog looked up at her and a deep feeling of loneliness started in Rowan's core, emanating out like a pulsing light, spilling onto her tongue, filling her mouth. She flipped her hand, beckoning the dog from its hiding place, moving glacially slow so she wouldn't spook it. As it inched out, tail half wagging, the emotion shifted, taking on a layer of excitement. The further the dog came out, the stronger the feeling became. Once it stood in front of her, it tilted its head back and yelped, clear and with some intention—although Rowan had no idea what it was trying to say. She looked around in case the dog's owner—the shadow she'd seen?—had crossed onto Bird Island chasing after their dog, but the private island in the Chesapeake Bay was deserted.

Except for this dog. It—Rowan ducked her head to get a look at the pup's undercarriage and registered that it was a *she*—looked up at her expectantly. Beneath the dingy white of her coat, her ribs were visible. "Poor baby. I bet you're hungry. Do you want to come to the house with me?"

The dog yelped again, launching its four legs off the ground with the effort, her head moving in an abrupt nod at the same time. Rowan laughed. "I'll take that as a yes." She stood up and started to walk, patting the side of her leg so the dog would follow. She trotted alongside as if she'd always been glued to Rowan's side. Rowan looked down at her. At the green-brown speckles in her blue eyes—unusual for a dog, weren't they? "Your eyes are hazel," she said, and just like that, the dog had a name. Hazel. She stayed on Rowan's heels until they got to the back Dutch door leading into the kitchen, the top half with its four windowpanes closed against the autumn chill. Rowan stopped and squatted down to get as close to the dog's level as possible. Hazel's stubby legs kept her low to the ground. She couldn't have weighed more than nine or ten pounds. "Listen, I don't know how Everly will feel about you. You'd best be on good behavior."

This time Hazel's yelp was quieter, as if she understood her position as Rowan's guest was tenuous. Once they were inside the kitchen, Rowan shut the door behind her, instantly cutting off the whistling of the wind. The quiet inside, though, was just as disconcerting.

As if in response to the mere thought, the walls of the house groaned and Hazel jumped back, her tail down between her hind legs. She barked, this time short and high-pitched. The house creaked like it was shifting on its foundation. And then, as quickly as it had started, it fell silent.

Caraline looked up from where she stood at the counter, a bowl cradled in one arm, a wooden spoon in the other. Her gaze skittered over the walls. "What was that?"

She wore a half apron and her jet-black hair was pulled back into a ponytail. She spotted Hazel and dipped her chin. "And what is *that*?"

"No idea, and *this* is Hazel."

"Is there an address or phone number?"

"Nope. Nothing."

Caraline narrowed her eyes. "Then how do you know her name is Hazel?"

"Because I named her," Rowan said.

Caraline's frown deepened. "You're keeping her? What do you think our persnickety grandmother is going to say about that?"

"What will I say about what?" Everly said as she strode into the kitchen holding a steaming mug of tea. Impeccable timing, Rowan thought. Everly spotted the dog. "Aha. About *her* I take it."

Rowan words rushed out. "She found me and she doesn't have tags so I thought—"

"You thought you could keep her." For a few seconds, Rowan thought Everly was going to say no and throw the dog out on her cute, floppy ears, but a smile cracked open on her face. "It's been a long time since we've had a dog around here. You girls are breathing new life into this place."

Caraline pulled a face and turned her back on Everly, but Rowan took the opening. "I want to explore the house a bit. Is that . . . okay?"

Every's eyes narrowed almost imperceptibly. "It's not *me* you need to ask," she said, pressing her open palm to her chest.

Rowan pulled back, puzzled. "Then who—"

She broke off when the floor suddenly slid out from under her like a rolling wave breaking under a boat, sending the vessel careening down into nothingness. It undulated and she stumbled. Oh God, was this an earthquake? Did they have those in Maryland? She grabbed for the back of a chair at the table for support, but it jumped from the rollicking, doing nothing to steady her. Hazel barked. Bottles and jars on the open shelves jumped and clattered. One slid off, shattering on the floor. Caraline spun around just as Saoirse reached into the kitchen from the hallway connected to the apothecary, arms stretched out to touch either side of the threshold.

"What the hell? Why? Why?!" Caraline demanded as the rocking went on and on. Her face was pale. She gripped the kitchen counter to brace herself.

Saoirse didn't say anything. She let go of the wall and slammed her hands over her ears, the noise disturbing for her. She kept her eyes on the floor, focused on the broken shards of glass scattered there. Rowan hurried over to her and lightly touched Saoirse's shoulder with hers. Just a soft, quick bump. Saoirse blinked, eyes still cast downward. Nodded slightly.

Another jar fell, this one in the pantry. Pickled carrots slid across the tiles, the short orange pieces spreading and reconfiguring like magnified cells under the lens of a microscope. The briny liquid ran in every direction.

Rowan stared as Everly raised her free hand and pressed it against the wall. She breathed in and out, slowly, again and again, muttering something under her breath, just as she had when the cascading emotions had threatened to overwhelm Rowan in town. Just like her mom had from the time she was a child.

Rowan scooped Hazel up into her arms and held her close until the shaking floor finally stilled and Hazel's trembling eased. The jars and bottles stopped clattering against one another. Rowan heard her sisters' thoughts, each of them asking what had just happened. Why had the house moved like that?

Before they could voice the question aloud, Everly lowered her hands to her sides and met each of their gazes, one by one. She ended with Rowan and her lips formed an uneven line. "It's time."

Caraline huffed. "It's time for what?"

Everly exhaled a heavy breath. "It's time we talk about Swallow Hall."

"Like why the hell it just felt like we were in a huge earthquake?" Caraline demanded.

Everly moved to the kitchen window, her fingers wrapped around her mug which, miraculously, had not spilled a drop.

Rowan sat at the kitchen table, Hazel in her lap. She leaned forward, her gaze fixed on her grandmother's profile. Caraline leaned against the counter, her arms crossed, watching with wary curiosity. Saoirse came to sit beside Rowan.

Everly waved one hand around, gesturing to encompass the entire space. "You asked about exploring the house. You need to understand that it's in turmoil. But there's more." Everly's voice was low and steady, the warmth of it a contrast to the chill seeping in from outside. "Swallow Hall is more than just wood and brick and stone. It's a living thing, a keeper of memories, a place where magic has always flowed. As long as it has stood, someone has been charged with caring for it, for understanding it. That person is the Keeper."

Rowan's fingers spread through Hazel's short hair. "You said you were the Keeper."

"I am, by default."

Caraline peered at her. "What does that mean? A 'Keeper' of what? The physical house? Cutting back the winter creeper, like you said?"

Everly turned, her gaze sweeping over all three of them. "Yes, but not just that. It's about the house's history. The Keeper is meant to protect this place, to know its stories. The spells cast here, the secrets it keeps, the whispers beneath its eaves."

"Like a . . . a historian?" Saoirse asked, wide-eyed.

"More than that," Everly said, a faint smile touching her lips. "A historian preserves the past, but a Keeper is *part* of it. You see, ideally, the house chooses its Keeper, always someone with magic of their own, someone who can hear its whispers, sense its needs. Someone who can mend the frayed threads of its magic." Her smile took on a mix of pride and sadness. "It remembers. It feels. It protects, and it punishes. But only a Keeper can truly speak to it."

"You speak to it? Like, it hears you?" Caraline asked. The usual sharpness of her voice when she spoke to Everly had tempered.

"To a degree," Everly said, turning back to the window, her gaze shifting to the mist-shrouded woods. "Your mother did too."

The kitchen went still.

Saoirse leaned in closer to Rowan without realizing it. Caraline's arms dropped from her chest. Even Hazel shifted in Rowan's lap, her ears twitching at the sudden hush that fell over the room.

Everly's gaze fixed on something beyond the kitchen window, where the woods met the creeping edge of fog. "She had the gift for listening. For sensing what the house needed. She understood what it was to live in a place that remembers."

"But she left," Caraline said. "If she had that connection . . . why walk away?"

Everly exhaled slowly, her hands tightening around her mug. "That's a question with more than one answer. I'm still trying to understand." Her eyes clouded with memory. "I don't think she knew what would happen when she left. Bridget's absence . . . it nearly shattered the whole place. She wasn't the Keeper yet, but she was meant to be. The house . . . it loved her. It recognized her, the way it only does with the strongest of us. She was a Silverborn," she added quietly, her gaze drifting over them.

"My magic—" She continued, shaking her head sadly. "It was never enough to hold this place together." Her fingers tapped the porcelain of her mug as if grounding herself. "When Bridget left, everything shifted. Cracks appeared, spells faltered. The house lost hope of another Keeper, and I wasn't sure we'd survive the fracture."

"The default Keeper," Saoirse said.

Everly nodded. "Yes."

Rowan's fingers trailed gently over Hazel's back. "It's been waiting for her to come back."

Everly looked at her, thoughtful. "We both were, but now we know that's not possible."

"It's been better though, right?" Saoirse said. "Our rooms, and the windows . . ."

"It has," Everly said. She gestured to the shards of glass spewed across the floor. "But not consistently, as you can see."

"So what now?" Caraline asked.

Outside, a branch scraped against the roof, sharp and grating. The walls gave a faint groan, floorboards creaking. If felt to Rowan as if the house itself was listening.

"I've done what I can to keep hope alive over the years," Everly said, "but the house doesn't listen to me the way it once did. And now we know Bridget can never come home."

The faintest vibration rippled beneath their feet, the house shifting, unsettled.

Everly straightened, her voice steadying. She looked intently at each of them in turn. "But here you all are, and now, my dear girls, what was forgotten must be remembered."

The house emitted a long, splintering sigh, as though it agreed, and had been waiting for this very moment since Bridget left nearly thirty years ago.

Chapter Nine

On the morning of the autumn equinox, Saoirse emerged from her apothecary, her eyes bleary, yet glowing, carrying three vials of oils. "For Mabon," she told Everly. "They will protect us." Protect them from what, Rowan didn't know and Saoirse didn't elaborate. Everly, though, nodded. She seemed to understand.

Moments later Caraline appeared cradling a tray loaded down with fruits she'd spent the last few days drying, ale she'd brewed, and an array of bread she'd baked in Everly's ancient oven. "For the feast," she said, her tone fiery. Looking past her, Rowan knew why. She was a tornado in the kitchen, and now that everything was prepared, she had to deal with the aftermath.

The day before, Rowan found a stash of crystals and gems tucked in the back corner of the closet in her attic room, along with leather and hemp cording, delicate clasps, tweezers and pointed chain-nose pliers, cutters, and a slew of other unfamiliar things. She'd spent hours learning how to use the tools, which came intuitively, finally creating a beautiful, if simple, necklace. After more hours, she'd made her second, her third, and her fourth. One for each of the Early women. When Rowan had held each crystal in the palm of her hand, she knew who it belonged to, as surely as if they'd sung to her, and she knew they'd serve a purpose for each of them. She presented a necklace to each of her sisters—carnelian for Saoirse to help with her insomnia, yellow agate for Caraline to help her stay calm and work through the fiery walls she put up, and yellow topaz for Everly to wear alongside the black stone pendant she never took off, a buffer against danger. For herself, she'd used the purple amethyst, the feeling of serenity washing over her when she slipped it around her neck.

When it was dusk, they gathered everything they needed for Mabon. Caraline grumbled under her breath, cranky from the late night finishing her baking. Clearly the necklace Rowan had made for her wasn't helping her stay calm.

Everly's announcement that it was time to go to the moon circle had filled Rowan with foreboding. So her necklace also wasn't bringing her peace. Evidently working with crystals was not part of her magical gift.

The last hints of twilight began fading into the night, and the full harvest moon, amber and glowing, hung low and heavy in the sky. It seemed suspended, casting long shadows through the trees as Rowan, Saoirse, and Caraline followed Everly down a narrow path to the beach.

To the west, the woods were alive with sound, leaves rustling like whispered spells, crickets singing in steady rhythm, the glow of the fireflies blinking on and off. Rowan felt the air shift as they approached the moon circle. It was warmer and charged with energy. As she stepped over the rocks and into the sacred space, a feeling of belonging washed over her. At the same time, it felt like stepping into a space that didn't quite belong to the rest of the world.

The moon circle was outlined by stones, and just beyond, ancient stumps covered in moss and lichen created a barrier between the beach and the woods. Everly had already prepared the shallow firepit. Logs were neatly stacked, herbs and dried apple slices tucked among them.

Everly moved with purpose, the hem of her cloak sweeping the earth. Once in the circle, she turned to her granddaughters. "Mabon is balance," she said. "Light and dark in equal measure. We give thanks, and we prepare to let go. Tonight, we honor the turning of the wheel, and what it asks of us."

Rowan's throat tightened. Something about the ritual—about being there with her sisters, surrounded by trees and starlight—made her feel vulnerable and open, yet complete at the same time.

Caraline shifted, clearly uncertain. "We've never done this before."

"Maybe not like this," Everly said gently, "but the magic is in you. You've done it in ways you don't even know. This is just . . . remembering."

She handed them each a small bundle of dried herbs—mugwort, rosemary, lavender, bay, sage, and a pinch of marigold. "Hold on to these until the fire's lit. Think about what you're grateful for. And what you're ready to release."

Saoirse closed her eyes immediately, clutching hers with both hands. Rowan felt the textures of the bundle, a combination of soft and brittle. Aromatic. Caraline turned hers over, studying it.

Everly struck a match and lit the fire. The flames caught quickly, dancing higher and higher as the herbs nestled in between the logs began to crackle and smoke. "Speak what you're ready to leave behind," she directed them, "then toss it in."

They hesitated, but finally Saoirse stepped closer to the fire. "I'm releasing uncertainty and doubt. I'm releasing the idea that I have to know everything before I begin." Her voice trembled, but her hands didn't. She tossed the bundle of herbs into the fire and watched it crackle and catch, finally stepping back when it disintegrated in the flames.

Caraline shot a glance at Rowan before taking a deep breath, then moving forward. "I guess . . . fear," she said. "Of belonging?

Or maybe of *not* belonging? Of not knowing what to do?" She threw the little harvest parcel in, and the fire sparked, flared. She stared at it until it, too, vanished.

It was Rowan's turn, but she hung back, staring at the flames. They shifted and shimmered. Her gaze was pulled to the house. It sat utterly still and silent, but Rowan got the distinct feeling it was listening. "I let go of holding everything in and keeping people out," she said at last. "Of carrying everyone else's emotions like they're mine." She tossed the bundle in, and a burst of lavender smoke ribboned upward, the fragrance quickly fading away.

Everly smiled at each of them, her eyes catching the firelight. "You girls," she started, her words catching in her throat. "You're each so beautiful. So powerful." She paused, letting the sentiment hang in the air until it seemed the words actually pulled apart and floated away. Only then did she step forward, her bundle clutched gently in her weathered hands. She closed her eyes for a breath, then said something too softly to hear.

"Hey, that's not fair. You heard ours. What did you release?" Caraline demanded.

Everly opened her eyes, the flames from the fire dancing in them. "You're right," she said. She cleared her throat. "I release the weight of waiting and of watching," she said after a moment, her voice low but clear. "Of knowing and not speaking. Of protecting with silence when I should have searched for the truth."

The firelight flickered across her face as she tossed her bundle into the flames. It crackled, sending up a stream of golden sparks and the sharp, bittersweet scent of rosemary and bay.

"I release the guilt," she added more softly, "of letting your mother leave without stopping her. And I release the hope that she'd come back."

The flames danced, flaring high for a moment before calming again. The circle felt hushed, reverent.

Everly didn't wipe away the tear that slid down her cheek. She let it fall, then smiled at her granddaughters, her quiet relief palpable. Rowan felt her release. Everly had finally laid something down after carrying it for far too long.

The fire blazed brighter for a moment, then settled into a steady glow. The moon hung above them, watching just like Swallow Hall was.

They stood in silence, the four of them, bound not just by blood but by something older, something awakened in the heart of the circle.

And when the wind stirred again, Rowan swore she heard it whisper: "You are not alone."

* * *

Everly sat back in her Adirondack chair, crossing one leg over the other, her cape encasing her like a queen. "Let me start at the beginning."

And she did. She began by telling them about Biddy Early, their oldest ancestor. "She was the last woman tried for witchcraft in Ireland. She was never convicted, though. There was no proof."

"Since when did they need proof to burn a woman at the stake?" Caraline muttered.

Everly ignored Caraline's grousing. "Biddy had a son. Paddy. As a young man, he left his mother and Ireland behind. The legend goes that a flight of swallows led by a red-breasted bird followed Paddy from Ireland to America. When he built this house in 1839, the swallows roosted here."

"So that's why it's called Bird Island and Swallow Hall," Saoirse said. She'd pinched half the dried lavender buds from the sprig she held, all of which were now spread across her lap, the scent permeating the air.

"They migrated twice a year, but always came back to the house Paddy built. That was true until your mother left Swallow Hall. The birds left with her. They returned with you."

"What happened to Paddy?"

"He went mad—"

Caraline threw up her hands and scoffed. "Because the house probably played games with him too."

"He died in 1868. I've never found his grave, if it's here at all. His wife, Maeve, and his daughter, Erin—they were the first Keepers of Swallow Hall."

"Erin, your grandmother," Rowan said.

Everly nodded.

The air around them grew still. Saoirse asked the question buzzing through Rowan's mind. "What does it actually mean, to be a Keeper?"

"You've seen the magic here—"

"It's a little hard to miss a house with upside-down windows and doors that lead nowhere," Caraline grumbled.

"Some people say the house is enchanted," Everly said. "Others—like the Daughters of the Disciples of Christ—say it is cursed."

"Which is it?" Caraline said.

"That's not an easy question to answer," Everly said. "Local lore says that the minute Paddy finished building the house, the island started sinking into the bay. The water at the shoreline began turning to mudflat. When Paddy died, it slowed. Maeve, and then Erin, kept it in check just by being here."

The temperature outside had dropped ten degrees. Rowan's fingers turned a mottled blue. She rubbed them together, then held her palms toward the fire. "How exactly is the house alive?" she asked. "What's its purpose?

Everly watched the flames flicker and stretch toward the night sky. Finally, she said, "What I know to be true and what I believe are two different things. All the knowledge I have is from the Keepers who came before me."

"What do you know to be true?" Saoirse asked.

The slamming of a door reverberated from deep inside the house. The wind blew and Rowan swore she heard it whistling *Now. Now. Now.*

Everly leaned forward, propping her forearms on her knees. Her cape billowed around her like the wings of a raven. "The house holds Biddy's magic."

The declaration settled over them. "But how?" Saoirse asked.

"Biddy's magic is strongest in the women in her line," Everly explained. "From what I understand, Paddy felt cheated by his mother. That's why he left Ireland."

Rowan closed her eyes for a long few seconds as she tried to reframe what she knew about her mother and sisters. Their magic was one thing. It had always floated around, untethered, not connected to anything. But now, according to Everly, it was connected to an ancestor. To a witch. To Biddy Early, who'd passed her magic to them.

The wind whispered again, straight into her ears: *The Silverborn.*

Saoirse dropped her gaze to the bits of lavender on her lap. She swept them into a small pile with her fingertips, scooping them into the palm of her hand. "But you said *Paddy* built the house."

Rowan picked up on the thread. "Right. And if the magic flows strongest through the women and he felt cheated, then it didn't flow through him, right?"

Caraline finished their collective thought, circling back to the question Rowan had asked a few minutes ago. "So how, exactly, is the house magical?"

Everly exhaled a deep, almost frustrated sigh. "Maeve believed his very possession of what he stole from Biddy released a protection spell."

"Protection from what?" Rowan asked. "What did he steal?"

Everly's jaw tightened. "Biddy's book. Her shadows. Her work. He took it before he left Ireland. Before this place ever existed."

"Where is it?" Saoirse asked at the same time Caraline said, "What's in it?"

"Maeve wrote that she saw it but only briefly. No one knows exactly what it holds. Or where it is." She looked up at the house, its lights ablaze, the air rippling around it as if it were a mirage in the desert.

"What else did Maeve say?" Rowan asked.

"Maeve met Paddy after the house was already built. She came from nothing. She had no family. Her whole life became her daughter, Erin, and taking on the role of a true Keeper. She spent her life protecting the house from Paddy. She knew that, in the wrong hands, the magic of our oldest ancestor would wreak havoc. Every spell has both a dark and a light side. Biddy used her power for good. All the Keepers that have come before me are protectors. But black magic . . . the dark art of sorcery . . . it is destructive. Used by the wrong people, Biddy's magic might be merely pernicious at first, but ultimately, it will be ruinous. The magic infected Paddy. He built the house, but he also tried to destroy it."

"You think he hid the book when he built the house," Saoirse said, rubbing bits of lavender together between the pads of her fingers.

"Pft." Caraline shook her head. "What, then forgot where he put it?"

"I agree with you," Everly said to Caraline. "If he hid it when he built the house, surely he'd remember where it was. But he didn't seem to, and Maeve always said his attempts to find it made no sense. With each blow, the house responded by building a staircase to nowhere, or an upside-down window, like you said, Caraline. Or a door with a gaping hole behind it."

Understanding lit Caraline's face. "It didn't want him to find it again."

"Swallow Hall has kept the book hidden within its hollows for more than a century. No one—not even the Keepers—has ever seen it."

Bridget's determination to leave here and never come back slid into Rowan's mind. "Who else knows about the magic? Who else knows Paddy took something from his mother?" Rowan asked. *Who, not why.*

Everly pressed her hand to her forehead. "I wish I knew."

Rowan's hair whipped around her face from a sudden gust of wind. She could see her stripe of crimson hair glowing. Feel the roots sizzling at her temple. The thwack of the tree branches against the house echoed in her head. Everly had answered the biggest question she had—the one Bridget could—or would—never answer: Where their magic came from. They were the descendants of an Irish witch. But so many more questions had surfaced.

"With each of Paddy's attempts to reclaim the book he stole from his mother, the house reacted and the island sank a bit more into the bay," Everly said. "His passing brought a period of calm, but it was riled up again years later, and it's stayed that way. My mother did her best. I did too. Bridget could keep a lot of the magic at bay. But when she left, the unsettled chaos came back full force, and then some."

Everly sank back, her skin pale, her face tired. Telling the tale had drained her. Yet she seemed lighter as if releasing the story had peeled back another layer of the weight she'd been carrying all these years. To Rowan, it almost looked as if her body floated above her chair, just slightly, the wings of her cape lifting her. Everly was no longer alone, bearing the burden of keeping the house safe on her own, because she and Saoirse and Caraline had come to Bird Island.

Rowan turned to look at the house with its lights blazing through the windows—lights that hadn't been on when they'd come down to the moon circle—its crooked shutters, and the mud nests under the eaves. All these years it had been protecting the book of shadows Paddy had taken from Biddy. But who was it keeping it safe from?

When Everly spoke again, her voice was quiet. Reverent. "I wage war against the winter creeper so it doesn't completely engulf the house. I leave the swallows' mud nests be. I welcome the fireflies knowing they'll help us one day."

Rowan started, then swung to face the woods. The fireflies. The shadow slipping through the trees. Were the lightning bugs enchanted too? Had they been trying to help her? Warn her about a threat lurking in the darkness?

She felt Everly's gaze tethered to her for a long moment. When she turned to meet it, Everly gave a slight nod as if she knew what Rowan had seen. Knew the fireflies had been there. A shiver crawled over her skin as Everly's eyes darkened. When she spoke, her words carried the weight of something far older than any of them. "If the darkness comes, only two paths remain." Her voice lowered, heavy with the certainty of what she was sharing with them. "The house will turn on itself before it lets Biddy's book fall into the wrong hands. The island will sink, and what it protects will be lost to the sea, forgotten forever."

She paused, letting her gaze settle on each of them in turn. "Or worse—the book will survive. And it will find its way to someone it was never meant for."

The ominousness of Everly's words sent a chill threading down Rowan's spine, coiling low in her stomach, tightening like a fist. This wasn't just about the house crumbling or the island weathering storms. It was so much bigger and older than she could have imagined. The secrets were buried in the very bones of this place.

They'd been so focused on the strange happenings in Swallow Hall to think about why it was happening in the first place.

Everly's words changed everything. Biddy's book wasn't lost. It was being protected because someone wanted it.

A thought occurred to her. Maybe the truth Bridget wanted them to find wasn't about their father at all. What if it was about finding who else wanted Biddy's book? What if it was all about what the house was protecting . . . about helping Everly keep Swallow Hall and its secrets safe? And making sure the book never fell into the wrong hands.

It wouldn't be easy, but if discovering the truth could bring peace to Swallow Hall, she had to try.

"Who else knows Paddy stole his mother's book? Who are the wrong hands?" Rowan asked.

Everly nodded at her, ready to answer the question. "What I learned from the Keepers before me is that before Paddy left Ireland, he'd been married and had the makings of another family. It's another bloodline where Biddy's magic lives, but Paddy held a darkness in his soul, and his leaving unleashed a bitterness in his descendants that turned that bloodline dark. Swallow Hall is not safe from the bitter magic he left behind. Without a Keeper to either help protect the book or defeat those who search for it, the house will lose control. I try never to leave for more than a few hours."

"So we're trapped here?" Caraline said, dismay lacing her voice.

Everly turned on her. Her voice snapped like a jolt of electricity. "You see it as trapped, *a leanbh*, but being an Early comes with responsibility. If, once you fully understand, you choose to leave—"

"Like Bridget did," Caraline challenged.

Everly kept on, her eyes locked on Caraline. "Yes, your mother knew her responsibility. She left, but," she swept her arm wide, gesturing to the three of them, "it didn't change anything. You are here now, fulfilling your destiny and hers." She continued, speaking slowly, the warning heavy in her tone. The air crackled with her emotions, and a sonorous moan came from the direction of Swallow Hall. "If you leave here, that is your choice. But before you do, you must feel the strength of Swallow Hall, as well as its weakness and vulnerability. You must know what will happen in your absence before you choose to go. Bridget didn't understand. You cannot make the same mistake."

"We come from Paddy's blood," Saoirse said.

That fact struck Rowan head on. Saoirse was right. They had Paddy's darkness in them.

"It's true, but you also have Maeve's. She created the balance. She protected what was Biddy's."

Rowan turned over the idea of Biddy's power in the wrong hands. Manipulation. Dark rituals. Curses and hexes. Corruption. Oh God, necromancy. Was that really a thing? What kind of domination could Biddy's magic bring? It would be disastrous, that much was clear.

Everly looked at the three of them, her gaze focused and heavy. "Know this, *leanaí*. I am the Keeper, but I am not like Bridget was. I alone cannot protect Swallow Hall and guard Biddy's legacy. My magic is not strong enough. I am not Silverborn."

It was the second time Everly had used that word, and hadn't Rowan heard it in the wind? Her brow creased as she frowned. "What does that mean? Silverborn?"

Everly's gaze stayed on the house, lights still ablaze, the walls vibrating. "They are the ones the house chooses. Biddy's blood flows through all of us, but the Silverborn . . ." Her eyes drifted to each of them, lingering briefly on Rowan before quickly sliding away. "They're different. They hear the island. They taste truth. The house bends for them."

The wind shifted, cool against Rowan's skin. The faintest tang of salt bloomed on her tongue, sharp and metallic. She swallowed hard, saying nothing, but the house already felt different to her.

Chapter Ten

The New Bethel Co-op smelled like dried thyme, wool soap, and citrus. It was no wonder it was Everly's favorite shop. It had the kind of clean, earthy scent Rowan usually found comforting. But today, something about it felt *off,* like the rosemary and lemon balm were trying too hard. Or maybe it was simply that everything felt off after their grandmother's dark warnings and the realization that Swallow Hall held the magic of Biddy Early.

Inside, the soft light streaming through the windows painted everything in pale gold. It should have been a peaceful scene, but Rowan couldn't tamp down her trepidation. She spotted Caraline standing near the squash bins, the handle of one of Everly's woven baskets looped over her arm, cheeks pink, smiling in that coquettish way she had.

Rowan's stomach tightened. Her sister was alone, but that was a smile she reserved for men. Attractive men she was interested in knowing better. Rowan moved closer. "You left the house without telling anyone."

Caraline jumped, a look of apology flashing over her face, there and gone in a split second. She jabbed her free hand on her hip, her chin ticking up defiantly. "I left a note."

"You didn't."

"Well, I thought about it." She shrugged. "Guess I didn't need to since you found me."

It was true. The sisters were threads woven into a tapestry. They would always be pulled back together. The invisible tug had led Rowan straight to Caraline. She knew her sister hadn't left for good, but it was completely true to form for her to go off on her own in search of company.

Rowan's attention shifted as the bell above the door jingled behind her. The air in the room wavered—cool one moment, warm the next—as if the space itself hadn't quite settled. A low pressure formed in her chest, weighty and familiar, like the hum before a storm. But then the sharp, green scent of citrus filled the space, clean and crisp, and the feeling ebbed away like it had never been there at all.

A man's voice followed, smooth and easy. "Hey, beautiful, I'm back."

By the time Rowan looked up, he was already beside Caraline, tall and lean. His dark hair was swept neatly to the side, his clothes unremarkable. It was as if the room had softened around him, reshaped itself to make him fit. She understood why Caraline was smitten. She felt a faint prickle beneath her skin too, and the taste of chocolate on her tongue.

"Hey there," Caraline said, her smile broadening. She looked at him, completely forgetting Rowan was standing right there.

Despite the man's good looks, Rowan wanted to press her face into her palm. No, no, no. This was not the time for Caraline to find romance. They had other things to do, and a man would distract her sister from their goal, which had expanded to helping Everly protect Swallow Hall. She knew she couldn't stop her sister, though, so she cleared her throat.

Caraline jumped. "Oh!" She rolled her hand out, gesturing toward Rowan. "This is my sister."

The man put his hands in his pockets and nodded to her, his smile still in place. "I'm Warren. Warren Lansing."

Rowan narrowed her eyes. The name meant nothing. But the way he said it—like it should—irked her.

Caraline gave a soft laugh. "Well, Warren Lansing. I'm glad you came back. I was just thinking how squash soup sounds perfect right about now. You should join us for din—"

"Cara," Rowan said sharply, cutting her off. "Everly might not want to have a guest."

But Caraline waved away Rowan's concern. She looked at Warren, her palm against her chest. "I'm inviting you. It'll be fine."

"Everly?" Warren asked.

"Our . . . grandmother," Rowan said, the word still catching in her throat. She wasn't entirely used to saying it so casually yet.

"The witch." A new voice spoke up from behind them.

Rowan turned to the woman who'd spoken. She was replenishing the Golden Delicious apple bin, wearing a sage green apron with New Bethel Co-op embroidered on the bib. She stood wide-eyed, staring at them. She clapped her hand over her mouth. "Whoops . . . did I say that out loud?"

Warren looked from the woman—Beth, her name tag read—to Rowan then to Caraline. "Sorry, did you say witch?"

Beth cleared her throat. "It's just what people call her. You know, because she makes tinctures and teas for people. And if you see the house . . ."

"She makes *homeopathic* teas," Rowan interrupted. "That doesn't make her a witch." She didn't say that being a descendant of Biddy Early definitely *did*.

Beth's cheeks tinted pink. She dipped her chin and went back to her apples.

Rowan tamped down the churning in her stomach, turning her attention from the shopgirl to Warren. "You haven't heard of Everly?" she asked, because everyone seemed to know the Early family.

Warren rocked back on his heels. "Mm, maybe in passing? I'm here visiting family. Just learning my way around. Thought I'd see what the Co-op had brewing."

Caraline cocked her head and grinned. "Apparently, me."

Rowan frowned. "You always introduce yourself over produce?"

Warren smiled. "Only when the company's good."

This guy was too smooth. Too practiced. And that scent. It was lemon mixed with chocolate and something else Rowan couldn't put her finger on. Whatever it was, Rowan knew this guy's motives were not pure. This guy was the love 'em and leave 'em type, and that was definitely not what Caraline needed right now. Caraline seemed to feel differently because she cleared her throat and spoke again, her voice bright. "So, dinner tonight?"

Rowan wanted to shake some sense into her. This was a town full of people they didn't know and that seemed to be hot and cold about Everly. Inviting people over and letting them see the monstrosity that was Swallow Hall was not a good idea.

"Maybe another night," Rowan said before Warren could accept the invitation.

His smile faltered, but he pulled it back into place. "Sure, another night. I'll let you two finish your shopping. Caraline, maybe I'll see you tomorrow?"

She'd flashed a death-stare at Rowan, but quickly masked that, smiling again as she turned to Warren. "Definitely."

Once he was gone, the bell jingling softly behind him and the scent of citrus fading, Rowan spun to face Caraline. "Seriously?"

Caraline had watched Warren go, but now, she turned to glare at Rowan. "What?"

"You don't even know him!"

Caraline cocked her head again. "That's the point. I want to *get* to know him." She leaned closer, dropping her voice to a coy whisper. "He's *cute*."

"Yeah," Rowan muttered. "He's *too* cute." But out of sight, out of mind. With him gone, Caraline finished her shopping and the sisters returned to Bird Island.

* * *

The next afternoon, Caraline was gone again. The very fact that the house was protecting something meant danger lurked, and then there was the danger of a love affair and a broken heart. She couldn't find the end of the thread that usually linked them together. Rowan sighed. She was going to have to trust Caraline.

She heard the distressed warble of a single swallow. After nearly two weeks on the island, she knew that sound—could isolate it in her mind just as surely as she could hear the lapping water on the island's shore at high tide when the moon was full. According to Everly, the swallows had been Bridget's constant companions growing up, disappearing the day she left the island. Rowan could hear the silence that had to have come with their absence.

Her feet felt heavy as she walked slowly down the stairs of Swallow Hall following the sound of the swallow's song. Hazel stuck to her side. The bones of the original house that Paddy Early had built still existed here somewhere, but in the one hundred and thirty-two years since he'd built it, the structure had become something else entirely. It had multiplied, growing in breadth as well as height. Rowan had spent her free time since they'd been here peering into closets, prying up loose floorboards, and climbing into hidden spaces. She'd dug and searched for signs of Bridget—and for Biddy Early's book—clues she might have left behind, only finding crooked walls and endless hallways, cockeyed banisters and an upside-down staircase. It was a carnival funhouse.

She'd started talking to the house, whispering to it in the dark when she was alone in her attic room, because, why not? The house had a pulse that Rowan could feel deep in her core. Sometimes she thought she saw the vines in the wallpaper growing. Changing, like the winter creeper outside grew at lightning speed. "Do you hear it too?" she asked the house now about the swallow's anguish.

The front door swung open, creaking on its hinges as if it were saying, *Yes, yes, yes.*

Without breaking stride, Rowan walked outside under the awning of the flowers and canopied branches of the espalier. Hazel trotted after her. A light layer of dead leaves crunched underfoot. She caught a glimpse of Saoirse by the side of the house, a basket over her arm just like Everly carried hers, clipped flowers gathered in it.

The gnarled branches of the trees, fiery with their autumn leaves, arched over the narrow walkway leading to the footbridge, which started about thirty yards from the house. Sunlight pressed through the blazing canopy, scattering flickering shards of gold across the path. The arched bridge that stretched from the island to the mainland was wide enough for several people to walk side by side but no more. The long-hooded paneled station wagons couldn't make it across, nor could the muscle cars that growled along the streets of New Bethel. No cars came to Bird Island.

Rowan headed toward the bridge, following the swallow's song, stopping for a minute to survey the sky. A few dark clouds dotted the otherwise blue expanse. A red-breasted swallow swooped toward her. Did they normally have red feathers? She didn't think so. And it was odd that it was alone, wasn't it? A good omen or a bad one?

The hair on Hazel's back suddenly stood up. She let out a sharp bark just as Caraline appeared at the other end of the footbridge. Rowan's breath caught in her throat. With her dark hair and bohemian style, her sister looked so much like their mother. She didn't usually sense her sisters' emotions, but a flurry of sensations cascaded over, crashing together like turbulent rollers formed at the bottom of a steep waterfall. They filled her mouth with the sticky sweetness of figs and lemon and peaches in the summertime. With the added layer of thick fog encasing a valley. She swallowed hard, clearing it all away.

Rowan hurried to meet her when she stepped from the bridge to the island. "Where were you?"

From the way Caraline's cheeks flushed, Rowan knew the answer, and she wanted to throttle her sister. "Oh no, you didn't."

Caraline flushed and nodded, a smile curving her lips up. "I did."

"You went to meet that guy?"

"Warren," Caraline said dreamily. "His name. Is Warren."

Rowan rolled her eyes.

Hazel barked again, not at Caraline, but at the woods. Rowan crouched to pick her up. The puppy nuzzled her snout in the crook of her arm. "It's okay, girl."

Caraline spun around, her smile disappearing. She wrapped her arms around herself. "Do you feel that?"

"What?" Rowan asked, but she was instantly on alert.

"I think I *saw* someone in the woods. It felt like someone was watching me."

Rowan's insides clenched. She followed the direction of her sister's gaze. "Just now?"

"A little while ago, yeah. Warren walked me to the woods, but I didn't let him come any farther." She shot a look at Rowan. "You're welcome."

Thank God. How could they ever explain the house to a stranger? "Thank you," she said.

Hazel leaped from Rowan's arms, her body jumping forward as she barked, her tail straightening. Rowan scanned the area, looking for dark, lurking shadow but everything was calm. No fireflies blinked their presence . . . or warning. "Did you see who it was?"

Caraline balked. "Like I'd know? It was a ghost, there and then gone." The swallow that had been hovering swooped low. Its warbled song broke the quiet. Caraline glowered at it, tracking its flight. "And that! It followed me. Like a damn chaperone."

At this, Rowan looked up to the sky again. And then she gasped and drew in a breath before hollering at the top of her lungs, "Saoirse!"

A minute later Saoirse appeared, her basket now bursting with flora Rowan didn't think grew here. She didn't need to tell Saoirse her concern. Her sister noticed it right away. The flight of swallows had left their mud nests and had joined the single red-breasted swallow, but they hadn't slipped into any kind of organized formation. The only way to describe their frenetic circling was chaos.

Saoirse pressed her basket against her stomach. "Something's wrong." As she spoke, the sky darkened.

Behind them, the house emitted a loud moan, as if Saoirse's words had spoken directly to it. Rowan spun around and gasped. The structure swayed perilously on its foundation and beneath their feet, the earth rocked. All at once, everything changed. The sound of the water lapping at the shoreline echoed, growing louder than it should have been. The wind became a gale, picking up particles of dirt and sand, whipping it all around with ferocity. The island itself lurched and plummeted, causing them all to lose their footing. Rowan's feet hit the earth again, which was decidedly lower than it had been a moment before.

She wanted to go to the house, to help it. To stop the pain it seemed to be in. They heard Everly yelling, "To the footbridge! Hurry!" She rounded the side of the house, running toward them and the narrow bridge that spanned the distance between the island and the mainland. Around her, dirt and pebbles spun, circling the house like a gathering tornado.

Debris shot toward them, sand particles pinging against Rowan's skin like pellets shot from a gun. Everly's gaze was focused on something beyond them, but she yelled again, "To the footbridge!"

Rowan grabbed Caroline's arm and pulled her. Together, they raced back over the bridge. The thud of their footsteps crashed in her head and mixed with the cacophony of the swallows' discordant song. Alarm shot through her. Finally, they pulled to a stop, staring at the sky and the mayhem of the birds.

"Saoirse, move," Everly yelled.

Rowan spun to see her sister still rooted in place. Bits of earth pummeled her, but Saoirse's gaze was intent on the swallows overhead. Everly had stopped next to her, one arm crooked and covering her face against the turmoil. She moved her other arm behind Saoirse to guide her forward. "Don't!" Rowan yelled. Saoirse did not like to be touched. Caraline and Rowan had learned never to do it, and they'd become their sister's protectors, stopping others when they seemed inclined to touch her in some way.

Everly froze, her arm hovering inches from Saoirse's back. She looked at Rowan, who shook her head. Drop it, she willed, hoping Everly understood, because they needed to deal with whatever was happening to the house—whatever had freaked Everly out—which meant Saoirse needed to remain not only calm but connected to the swallows.

Everly dropped her arm, urging Saoirse forward. "Come on, *a leanbh*. Cross the bridge."

Saoirse didn't seem to hear. She didn't blink. Just kept watch on the swallows.

When Saoirse didn't move, Everly's brows drew together. She turned her back on all of them and faced the house. Faced the maelstrom. "*Stad a chur le*," she yelled, slapping her open palm against the air, then repeated, "*Stad a chur le*. Just. Stop."

Everly repeated it over and over and over. Seconds passed, then minutes. At long last, the keening, hollow and low, finally began to still.

The air did not. It whipped up into a renewed frenzy, taking form, looking like the wind in a painting circling in gusty, visible drifts in the sky. It roused Saoirse from her trance, propelling her forward—not toward Rowan and Caraline on the other side of the bridge, but toward Swallow Hall.

"Saoirse!" Rowan raced back across the bridge, crooking her arm in front of her face to block the pummeling wind. She leaped down and careened past Everly, catching up to her sister. "Stop! What are you doing? You can't go in—"

"It's okay now. It's over," Everly said, and as she spoke, the swallows fell into a loose formation and glided back to their mud nests. Just as suddenly, the air became still, every bit of earth and pebble and sand falling to the ground as if released from a spell.

Caraline had crossed the bridge and joined them. "What . . . the hell . . . just happened?" she ground out.

Everly spoke, her voice quiet. Haunting. "There is darkness lurking in the shadows."

At Everly's words, the house reacted. Vines crept up the side of the house, tendrils slithering up the bricks like snakes. The house itself shifted, windows warping, walls tilting. A spiral staircase clung to the exterior now, when it hadn't been there a moment before.

"When Bridget left . . . with no Keeper to take my place . . . I thought it was over. It felt like whole place would buckle in on itself, that the island might disappear entirely." Everly's gaze drifted to the walls, her expression tight. "The house wept for her. It still does."

Rowan conjured up an image of the streaks on the walls. Tears that had puckered and bubbled the wallpaper and the wallboard underneath. Swallow Hall had cried in anguish.

"But this is different," Everly said. "There is new energy pulsing. It has responded to all of your presence, my *spéirmhná*."

Rowan and Caraline stared at Everly. Saoirse pulled petals from one of the flowers in her basket. "*Speir*-what now?" Caraline asked, one brow cocked.

Everly gazed up at the monstrosity of a house before turning back to them. "Biddy Early was a wise woman. A healer. You girls are healers too," Everly said to Caraline and Saoirse. Now Bridget, she was a—"

She broke off, but Caraline leaned forward. "She was a what?"

A small smile danced over Everly's face. "She could *see* things."

"No she couldn't," Caraline said.

The girls had their gifts, but Bridget never seemed to. Or did she? A memory surfaced in Rowan of the three of them, maybe five years old, in the bathtub. Bridget had rubbed shampoo between her hands, and one by one, she'd scrubbed their heads, using her fingernails to lightly scratch their scalps. And then she'd suddenly frozen, turning as still as a statue, her eyes glazing over.

Caraline and Saoirse had seemed oblivious to the vacant look on their mother's face, but Rowan had tasted something dark and foreboding. She hadn't been able to make sense of the feeling at the time, but it happened again when the girls were older and they'd been swimming at the community pool. That time Rowan could define the feeling. Dread had filled her mouth like a dark shadow, covering every cell until she had to swim away, putting distance between her and her mother.

"Like a fortune teller?" Saoirse asked Everly, and the memory popped like a bath bubble.

The echo of the past slipped over Everly's face. "In a way, yes."

"What about Rowan?" Caraline asked.

Everly turned to Rowan. "You sense the energy in things. You taste shapes and sounds, and even colors. *You* are the memory keeper." She flipped her braid over her shoulder, tucking wayward strands of her hair behind her ears. She took Rowan's hand in hers. "You are what is called a physical empath."

Rowan deflated. She knew this. It was a fancier way to say she was a clear taster. "That's like a sixth sense, not magic."

Everly considered her. "There are many kinds of magic, *a leanbh*."

Maybe, but some were definitely better than others. She said as much to her grandmother.

"Why are you putting a value on it?" Everly asked.

"Because being a physical empath, if that's what I am, doesn't help people like Saoirse's alchemy or Caraline's food do. I'm not a healer like they are, or like Biddy was."

"Not everything your sisters make helps others. Sometimes soap is just soap and soup is just soup. Have faith. There are depths to your magic you haven't discovered yet."

That's what Bridget had always said, but Rowan shook her head. "I don't see how tasting emotions and energy can help anyone."

But Everly wasn't deterred. "It's perception. If you perceive something about someone else, you can understand them. And once you have information, you can choose what to do with it."

Caraline scoffed. "Did you get that from a fortune cookie?"

Everly ignored her. "On our little island and in Swallow Hall, your truest self will come out . . . if you let it."

Caraline waved her hand dismissively. "I'm already my truest self."

Everly turned to her as if she could see right into the depths of her soul. "Are you though, my dear?" she asked, and before Caraline could respond, Everly looked back to Rowan. "You, my dear, will grow into your magic. When you're ready, it will happen. You are all healers in your own way. As was your mother. As am I. As are all the women who came after Biddy. We are *spéirmhná*." She looked at each of them in turn, her gaze lingering for an extra beat on Rowan. "We are Sky Girls."

Sky Girls. The words turned over each other in Rowan's head. *Sky Girls.*

"The women from Biddy Early's line are all *spéirmhná*," Everly continued. "*We* are all Sky Girls. Biddy is in us. In our blood. In our bones. I have done my duty. And done my best to keep Swallow Hall safe. But *mo ghrá* . . . my loves . . . I won't be here forever. A Sky Girl must become the true Keeper. As a Silverborn, it was your mother's fate, but she ran from it," Everly said quietly. "She managed to escape it, but you can't ever truly escape your destiny."

In front of them, the house creaked, the walls shifting the way they always did when the air grew heavy with memory. "She left," Rowan whispered, the words sticking to her tongue. "She left all of this."

Everly didn't answer right away. Her eyes drifted toward the third story, the walls bending like the house was listening.

"She was young," Everly said softly. "She thought she could change her stars."

"She was Silverborn," Rowan countered. "The house . . . it loved her. You said so. Why would she run from it? Not for a man, surely?"

Everly's gaze met hers, steady, tired. "Love doesn't always feel safe. Because when this house wakes for you—when the island chooses you—it can be more than you're prepared for." Her voice faltered, just for a breath. "I don't know what was in her heart. Maybe she thought leaving would *stop* it from unraveling. But the house . . . it never lets go. And I . . . I have never been strong enough."

Rowan looked at the warped walls, the whispering shadows, the creeping vines that clawed up the bricks. Her chest ached with questions, but only one mattered right now.

They all stared at Everly. At the house. At the bay and the disappearing shoreline. A thousand needles pricked Rowan's skin. She didn't know if she loved Swallow Hall, or if it loved her, but it had become *part* of her, and she couldn't bear the anguish. The pain. The ache that lived inside the walls. The book Paddy had taken was at the root. If Rowan could help Swallow Hall protect it, she would. She knew Saoirse would be by her side, and when push came to shove, Caraline would too.

"Will the book always remain hidden?" Rowan asked.

"I don't know," Everly said. She met Rowan's gaze. "But you understand, don't you?"

Slowly, Rowan nodded and the taste of bitter chocolate filled her mouth.

"Your mother outran her fate, but in doing so, she unwittingly passed that responsibility on to the next generation. To *you*, her daughters. One of you is Silverborn. Which means that one of you, my Sky Girls, will be the next *true* Keeper of Swallow Hall."

Chapter Eleven

Since being at Swallow Hall, sleep had evaded Rowan. She'd fought it, staying in bed, tossing and turning, but to no avail. Usually, she had found things to be easier at night when there weren't other people around to cloud her emotions, when it was just her. At night, she had felt as if she lived a second life, one where she was the only inhabitant and her emotions were her own. Not so at Swallow Hall. Here, the blue-gray sense of melancholy centered deep in the back of her throat. It was as if the ever-present gloom emanating from the bowels of the house seeped into her, and at night, there were no distractions to keep her from focusing on it.

A slice of moonlight glowed through the attic window, throwing beams of diffused light across the room. She let out a heavy sigh. It was no use trying to fall back asleep. It didn't happen on a normal night, and tonight was anything but. Everly's proclamation had been reverberating in Rowan's mind. *One of you, my Sky Girls, will be the next* true *Keeper of Swallow Hall.*

She worked one leg out of the cocoon of her quilt to test the air. Heat was supposed to rise, but it seemed to slide right past the attic room. A sharp chill bit her skin. She sat up and pulled on a long pair of tube socks, tucking the pant legs of her pajamas into them. She wrapped herself up in the knitted shawl she'd claimed as her own and left the warmth of her bed. At the window, she peered through the murky haze hanging low like a blanket over the island. The island was so isolated. The house was lonely too. For almost thirty years, it had only had Everly here. No wonder it had reacted when Rowan and her sisters arrived. They filled the space with voices. With energy. With echoes of Bridget.

The low sounds of the house matched the whisper of her slow breaths and the faint *da-thunk* of her heartbeat. She swore she could hear both reverberating from somewhere in the depths of the house.

Caraline's relentless reminder that their mother had left Bird Island and Swallow Hall never to return had planted a seed of doubt in Rowan, but deep down she felt there had to be something more to their mother's leaving. She wondered what else Everly knew about it. Bridget had loved her daughters fiercely, with a sense of protection that rivaled Swallow Hall's. She pushed Caraline's skepticism aside, breaking the threads of doubt knitted together inside of her.

Bridget wouldn't have left her mother, her home, her *life* . . . without good reason.

"Why did you go?" Rowan asked the question to her mother aloud—softly—but her voice reverberated in the stillness of the night.

A whisper came back to her, silent in her head. *The answer is underfoot where the floorboards creak.*

Her heart climbed to her throat, her skin pricking with anticipation. She blinked. Pinched herself. Had she imagined it, or had she just communicated with the house?

She left Hazel sound asleep on the bed and padded to the top of the stairwell where she stood with her arms holding her shawl tight. Would the house guide her, just as it had led Saoirse to the sunroom and Caraline to the hidden pantry and Erin Early's recipes? She'd been waiting for it to lead her somewhere . . . to help her find her magic and her purpose. Was this the moment? She looked around, speaking to the whole house. "Tell me where to look," she whispered.

She listened for any sign that the house had registered her voice, but all she heard was her own steady breathing. She turned in a slow circle, imagining herself as a planchette, the house a Ouija board, and the invisible force of Biddy Early moving her in the right direction.

She felt nothing but the ripple of the radiator as it kicked on from inside her room, warm air blowing through the metal slats. Downstairs, the hands of the clocks ticked a cacophonous symphony as they moved asynchronously. As she descended both sets of stairs, her heartbeat began to match the discordant ticks. She paused at the bottom step and looked around. Everything was the same as it had been when she'd gone up to bed—cockeyed and janky. Her gaze strayed to the locked door Everly had said nobody entered, and her imagination ran wild. Was it a shrine to the Sky Girls of the past? A room with a bubbling cauldron their grandmother kept under lock and key? This is where she wanted to explore, a place that might hold answers.

Like someone's fingers lightly pushing the planchette, she turned toward the door, telling herself the house wanted her to see inside the room. In truth, she felt an opposing force trying to block her forward movement. But Rowan was nothing if not persistent, and with Everly asleep, now was the time to see what was hiding behind the heavy wooden door.

She put her hand on the knob, turned, and pushed. The door shuddered but stayed closed, almost shoving against her. The force of it shot through Rowan like a jolt of electricity. She jerked her hand away as if the knob itself was charged. It forced her backward and she fell with a harsh thud.

Pushing up onto her forearms, she watched as the frenetic rattling slowed. Stopped. Once again, all was silent. She frowned. So it wasn't just Everly forbidding entrance to that room. Did the house not want her to go in either, or was it a game . . . an enticement it offered knowing she'd be too tempted to let it go?

Was that where it kept Biddy's book hidden?

She stood and brushed herself off, picking up her shawl where it had fallen and wrapped it around her shoulders again. She walked the perimeter of the gathering room. Maybe there was another secret door like the hidden pantry in the kitchen. When she was about to pass the staircase again and head to the kitchen, something stopped her in her tracks. It was as if a hand had gathered up the fabric of her pajamas and held tight. She lifted her foot to take a step forward only to careen backward.

Rowan managed to right herself. She gave a sharp hiss. "What? What do you want me to do?"

In response, the front door flew open. As the chilly air blew in, Rowan's skin alighted in goosebumps. Pale moonlight cut through the mist, lighting a path for her to follow. "You want me to go outside?" she whispered.

The door moved with a creak. *Hurry. Hurry. Hurry.*

Wariness crept over her, but she pushed it aside. She had to trust someone—or something. *Trust the house,* she told herself.

Her subconscious replied. *But Bridget left Swallow Hall.*

But she brought us back, she countered.

She thrust aside the doubt and her unease and went where the house led her, the breeze guiding across the stone walkway and toward the footbridge. Sinister shadows danced all around spreading her trepidation like an angry hive of bees.

"Trust the house," she murmured.

Her steps slowed until she came to a stop. A movement in the middle of the footbridge caught her eye. The heavy mist softened the hard lines of the tree trunks crowding into the woods, as well as the path beyond leading to the island. Only the tops of the trees with their blood-red and amber leaves reaching into the sky were visible.

No invisible force tried to stop her as she moved toward the bridge. Her jaw clenched tighter with each step. Her already pounding heartbeat quickened. "Hello?" she called, wanting to kick herself. Was she like one of those too-stupid-to-live characters in a B movie who raced headlong into a precarious situation at the first sign of trouble without a second thought?

Maybe. Yes, maybe, but the house had brought her here, hadn't it? Despite her misgivings, she wanted to know why because if she was going to trust the house, she had to do it completely.

At the bridge, she laid her hand on the railing and tried to see through the haze. The mist swirled in the moonlight, so thick it muffled the sounds of the night. The shape of something caught her eye, slumped on the wooden planks halfway across the footbridge. A feeling of foreboding slid over her like a cloak. Whatever it was would lead to trouble. She moved toward it slowly, each step deliberate.

On the bridge, the fog thinned, vanishing like hot breath disappearing on glass.

Rowan inched closer. Her breath caught when she saw it was Everly's shawl—the one she wore every night when she walked the property. It lay pooled on the damp wood.

Rowan bent to pick it up. As she lifted the fabric, something dropped from its folds and landed with a dull thud. It slid, catching between two warped boards. She knelt, recognizing it immediately. It was Everly's obsidian pendant, knotted with the yellow topaz necklace Rowan had given her before Mabon. A slice of moonlight broke through the thinning fog, shining across the center of the bridge. She could see that the knot and clasp were both broken, as if the necklaces had been wrenched from Everly's neck. The moment Rowan's fingers closed around the tangled leather, she was hit by a rush of tastes crowding her mouth—metal and salt, stone and ash, sharp like the tang of rain on old iron. And underneath all of that, she tasted the bitter bite of fear. It was dread, running cold and deep.

Rowan's mouth went dry. Whatever had happened here, it had happened fast. She felt it in her bones.

Rowan stood, her fist clenched tightly around the stones. Worry lodged in the depths of her body as the planks and pilings of the bridge groaned softly beneath her feet. "Everly?" Her voice bounced through the shadows, ricocheting off the tree trunks.

She was met with an eerie silence.

"Everly?" she tried again, turning slowly, peering through the mist. Inside, her blood thrummed uneasily. She'd only known her grandmother a short period, but during that time, she'd never seen her without the black pendant on, and she'd kept the topaz with it since Rowan had given it to her. Worry rippled through her. Surely Everly hadn't run away like Bridget, seizing the opportunity to escape her fate. She dismissed the idea as soon as it entered her mind. The shawl and necklaces, along with the overwhelming taste in her mouth, were proof enough for her that something had happened here and that Everly was in danger. She would never abandon her duty as the Keeper of Swallow Hall.

She left the footbridge, her grandmother's shawl draped over her arm, holding the pendants tightly in her palm. She wanted to check Everly's bedroom, hoping her worry was unfounded and that she'd find her fast asleep. She hurried toward the house. A faint movement from the woods made her skin prickle. She blinked and it was gone. Her grandmother's ominous words came back to her. *Without a Keeper, the house will destroy itself. The island will sink. What it protects will be gone forever.*

Rowan's blood ran cold. If Everly was gone, it would be up to Rowan and her sisters to help Swallow Hall keep its secrets safe. The bigger question at the moment, though, was what had happened to her grandmother?

Chapter Twelve

Rowan hurried back inside, an insistent breeze helping her move faster, faster, faster. She plowed through the door, up the stairs, straight to Everly's room. Empty.

She raised the alarm, waking Saoirse and Caraline. They stumbled groggily out of bed, and she pulled them onto the second floor landing. "I can't find Everly," she said.

Saoirse had grabbed her glasses from the bedside table. Now she unfolded the arms and slipped them on. "What do you mean?"

"I mean, I found her shawl and her pendants on the footbridge. But she wasn't with them."

Caraline rubbed the sleep from her eyes and yawned. "She's probably just out for a walk," she said as she gathered her hair in one hand to contain it.

"Not in the middle of the night," Rowan said. "I felt something."

Saoirse tilted her head, looking toward Rowan but not quite at her. "What kind of something?"

Rowan hesitated, searching for the right words. "Like a warning. The front door opened and the air changed. It pushed me like it *wanted* me to know something was wrong."

Caraline opened her mouth to respond, but Rowan wasn't finished.

"And when I touched her necklace . . ." She swallowed hard, the memory still vibrating on her skin. "I tasted something."

"What was it?" Caraline asked. She'd finished winding her hair into a messy bun. All the sleepiness was gone from her face.

"Like copper and stone. Like old rainwater and bitter tea. It was fear. Not mine. *Hers*. She's in trouble," Rowan said. "I think she left those things for us to find, like breadcrumbs."

Saoirse's fingers clenched around the stair rail. Caraline's eyes flashed. Rowan looked at them both. "We have to find her."

Somewhere downstairs, the wind moaned against the front door, as if in agreement.

A few minutes later, Saoirse sat cross-legged in one of the velvet chairs on one side of the fireplace. "Should we call the police?" she asked, but skepticism laced her voice. None of them wanted the police on Bird Island or near Swallow Hall where they might have to explain the weirdness of the house or the fact that the island was sinking.

Caraline leaned against the wall. For the first time, Rowan registered what her sister was wearing: a pair of men's boxer shorts and a ribbed tank top. Surely not Warren's? "Maybe she's out making one of her deliveries."

Rowan gaze met Caraline's. "To who? The ogre under the bridge? She doesn't make deliveries in the middle of the night. Plus the shawl, and her stones. Those pendants were *ripped from her neck*."

Through the walls, Rowan heard the swallows squawking. Hazel whimpered from the kitchen. "I'll take her out," Saoirse said, standing and disappearing into the kitchen. Seconds later, she burst back in, the dog at her heels. Her hair was wind-whipped, her eyes wide. "The ground outside. The water . . . the tide," she started, panting. "It's rising."

Instantly, Rowan felt the clutch of nerves in the pit of her stomach. She and Caraline stared.

Saoirse's skin had turned pallid. The scent of salt water and sea air, thick and briny, wafted in from outside.

The chandelier swung suddenly. It lurched hard enough to knock one of the hanging crystals loose. It flew off the fixture, falling, shattering when it made impact on a sliver of hardwood visible through the overlapping rugs.

Rowan searched the room. The windows were closed. They were crooked and there was a new one, but they were all sealed tight.

Caroline jumped, linking arms with Rowan. Saoirse stood, moving next to them, her arms by her side. Without talking, they moved in unison, like synchronized swimmers, their steps unsteady but determined. Beneath their feet, the floorboards swelled. It was as if the island had absorbed too much of the bay water, and now the house was taking it in, unable to hold it.

Before their eyes, doors that usually stayed open now swung shut.

A painting of an early rendition of Swallow Hall crashed to the ground, its glass cracking down the center.

And through every window, Rowan could see the water level rising.

The island was growing smaller before their eyes, as if the bay was reclaiming it.

"What is happening?" Caraline whispered, voice barely audible over the sudden hush in the air.

Outside, the wind sounded like mournful cries, and inside, the walls trembled in distress. "It's because of Everly. Because she's . . . gone."

Deep in her bones, Rowan knew it was a cry for help. They needed to step in. To keep the house calm. To be the Keepers until Everly was back.

"Tell it that." Caraline clutched her arm, and Rowan knew her sister had heard every one of her thoughts.

"We're here," Rowan said, then louder, "We're listening."

As if in response, a low moan reverberated through the walls. Beneath their feet, the ground shifted. It was listing left, then right, as if the island wasn't sure whether to rise or sink.

They stayed together, searching the house and what they could of the island and the woods beyond, but there was no sign of Everly.

Back inside, the air thickened, humming with tension. Floorboards creaked beneath unseen weight. Picture frames rattled on the mantle, the glass trembling, and for a heartbeat, Rowan thought she heard the house breathing, strained and uneven. It was a warning that darkness had come, and it was asking for help.

Their instincts kicked in, old knowledge surfacing in them. They spent the day in protection mode. Rowan lit rosemary and thyme at every threshold, the herbs crackling softly, their smoke curling through the doorways like protective veils. Caraline retreated to the kitchen, working lemon and blueberries into a sticky dough—sharp bite of citrus meant to steady the house's pulse and to clear the air, if only for a while. Saoirse circled each room, scattering salt and lavender along the sills, tracing quiet lines of protection along every window.

They hadn't been taught these things, but the knowing lived inside them, passed down through generations of Biddy's magic.

The house had called for help, and they answered the only way they knew how.

But by late morning, the sky had gone a strange gray-purple and the tide still pressed in. The mirrors hanging on the walls had fogged over with the soft opacity of hot breath.

Still, the water kept rising, swallowing more and more of the island. Rowan didn't understand. They were here. They'd stepped in as Keepers in Everly's absence.

But the tide refused to pull back.

Everly had said she wasn't a *true* Keeper. She'd claimed that one of the sisters would be the next Keeper, and that one of them was Silverborn, but for nearly thirty years, Everly had been the only thread holding Swallow Hall together. Without her, the house was unraveling, frantic and lost, reaching for what it couldn't find. It had lost Bridget. It didn't want to lose Everly too.

Rowan pressed her palm to the wall. The wood pulsed beneath her touch, alive with magic. "We'll find her," she said quietly, the words curling into the walls, into the bones of the house itself. "We'll bring her home."

The floor creaked softly underfoot, and for just a breath, it settled.

* * *

Rowan didn't remember going back to bed, but she awakened under her quilt at daybreak, sunlight sluicing into the attic room. Splashes of coral and amber and azure streaked across the sky. The distress of the day before, Everly's shawl and pendants on the footbridge and of her missing, and the bay water encroaching on the island rushed into her mind, and she was instantly alert. She hurriedly dressed in a pair of jeans, a flannel shirt, one of Everly's warm coats, and a pair of her grandmother's hiking boots. Hazel stayed by her side and together they went down the stairs and out the kitchen door, the cold like a punch to the gut. Her warm breath turned to mist as she exhaled. She walked past the outside of the sunroom and through the garden.

She rounded the corner and stopped dead in her tracks. The night before, the shoreline had risen beyond the moon circle. Now water lapped past its perimeter. The leaves of the trees had been a picture-perfect fall landscape. Now the branches were bare, reaching into the sky like the bony fingers of skeletons. In a matter of hours, the island had transformed. The rising water was swallowing the land, and the trees had thrown off the last vestiges of fall all at once, some of the leaves floating in shallow pools of bay water, the rest laying still, forgotten, and forlorn. The ground was on fire, vibrant autumn hues carpeting the earth. She looked across the bay into the distance where trees still held their fall colors, only a few leaves fluttering and wafting to the ground. Rowan's stomach twisted into knots. Every element of the island, like the house, was responding to Everly's disappearance. If only the trees could tell her what they'd seen.

Rowan searched the woods again, but there was no sign of Everly. She trudged down the path, one foot sinking into the mounds of leaves and the soft soil until she hauled it up and took the next step. Progress was slower than trudging through a snowstorm with fresh powder. Hazel plowed through in front of her, sinking then resurfacing, carving a semblance of a path, eventually circling back around to the side of the house.

She climbed the steps back to the kitchen, Hazel on her heels. Caraline was awake and at the stove, stirring whatever she had stewing in the heavy cast-iron pot. The house had gone still, as if it were sleeping now, exhausted from the day before.

Rowan longed for a distraction—to cook, like Caraline was doing, or toil in the apothecary as Saoirse probably was. Those things were inherently part of her sisters, but she didn't have anything like that. She'd hoped being on Bird Island, in Swallow Hall, and learning more about their family's legacy would have helped her uncover her gift. Now, without Everly, that hope was fading.

"Still nothing?"

Rowan had muttered to herself enough during the search that her words had seeped right into her sisters' heads. "None."

"Maybe she has a secret lover," Caraline said, but the attempt at levity didn't hit. They had to accept that something bad had happened to Everly, but they felt helpless. Caraline tried again. "Maybe that guy, what's his name? Kyle Floyd? Or maybe the guy from the dime store. Oh!" She snapped her fingers and dropped her voice to a loud whisper. "Maybe she's a werewolf."

"No, Mr. Floyd is definitely not someone *anyone* would get romantic with, least of all Everly. I doubt she's even dated. How could she when the house goes crazy every time she leaves? And a werewolf is a bit of a stretch."

"Is it, though? I would have said an enchanted house was a stretch before we saw this place," Caraline countered.

Rowan looked through the window at the mass of birds perched on the branches of the barren trees silhouetted against the sky. Everything was off.

Vertical lines suddenly carved between Caraline's brows as she pinched them together. "You don't think she's lying dead somewhere?"

"Not on the island. There is no sign of her," Rowan said, but the idea that Everly could be injured somewhere away from the island, unable to call for help, had flitted in and out of her mind, but if she'd been hurt somewhere else, surely someone would have called.

No, the most likely possibility was that she had been taken. But why, and by whom?

She left Caraline in the kitchen. As she always did when she passed by the locked room, she grabbed hold of the handle. She turned the knob, expecting it to be locked, but this time it moved. Just barely, but she'd definitely felt it. Was Everly inside?

She tried again and it wriggled under her hand. She gave it one more try, gripping it with both hands and directing all her energy into them. She turned and pushed. It opened.

She felt her chest tightening again . . . tasted the saltiness of her anxiety . . . but she took another deep breath and stepped over the threshold.

It was like a library with built-in bookshelves lining two of the walls, all of the shelves themselves situated at odd angles. Looking at them from where she stood at the door, they created a diagonal zigzag effect, like ramps. The books on each shelf had slid down to the lowest point, tipping each respective shelf a little bit more. It was as if an earthquake had knocked the shelves loose and no one had ever fixed them.

Dust motes hung suspended in the air, caught by streams of light shining through clerestory windows placed horizontally close to the ceiling. She frowned. Had she never noticed them from the outside? She closed her eyes and pictured the exterior of Swallow Hall. No, it wasn't that she hadn't seen the clerestory windows. It was that they weren't there . . . at least not from the outside. But here they were bringing in light when it was still overcast and raining outside.

There was a single overstuffed armchair big enough to curl up in, a round occasional table by its side. An antique secretary stood sentry against one wall.

But there was no Everly. Once her grandmother was found, Rowan would come back to this room, to breathe in the air of her mother's favorite space. She backed out, quietly closing the door behind her.

Room after room yielded nothing that gave Rowan any ideas as to where Everly was or what might have happened to her. The living room walls were damp to the touch. It could be bay water seeping into the wood, but deep down, Rowan knew the house was weeping for Everly as it had for Bridget.

She ran her fingertips over spaces she thought might reveal hidden cupboards like the pantry in the kitchen.

Nothing.

She peeked in every corner searching for a secret, tucked away.

Nothing.

She opened every drawer and cabinet hoping for a journal or notepad or something else that would tell her more about her grandmother.

Nothing.

"What now?" Rowan muttered because she was at a loss. She started upstairs to regroup, trying to avoid the squeaky parts of the stairs. It turned out that was an impossible feat. Every time she used the stairs, the creaks and groans changed places, always muffled under the carpet runner. Except . . . the fourth step always squeaked in the center, didn't it? And was it getting louder, or was she imagining that?

She stood on the step above it and stepped down with one foot, testing. She pressed on the left side, then on the right. No sound. She stepped down, dead center, and it popped beneath her weight.

She skipped that step, moving up and down the others. Every time, the groans came from different places. But each time she stepped on the fourth step, it only creaked in the middle. A memory rushed into her consciousness. She'd been in the attic, talking to her mother, asking her why she left. A whispered response had slid into her head. *The answer is underfoot where the floorboards creak.*

She perched on the step below and pried up the carpet, the pin nails popping out as it came loose. She gathered them up and set them aside, then slid her hand under the carpet, feeling the wood beneath her fingertips. It was rough and worn after more than a century of use. She bent to peer into the dark space, wishing she had a flashlight. That's when a cloud that had been blocking the sun moved and a ray of light shone through the skylight. A skylight that hadn't been there a minute ago.

"Thank you," Rowan said.

She went back to the fourth step. The light was enough to see a cutout in the wood. She ran her fingertips around the perimeter of it. She could barely feel the thin crack. If she hadn't seen it with the light from the window, she'd never have known it was there. She managed to dig her fingernails into the crevasse, but that didn't give her enough leverage to lift it. She jumped up and ran up to her room, digging through her things until she found what she was looking for—a metal nail file with a pointed tip. Back at the step, she held up the loose carpet and found the minuscule gap in the wood. Seconds later and with the help of the nail file, she'd pried the wood up.

Removing it revealed a cavity. She reached her hand in, holding her breath, hoping there weren't spiders holed up there. No creepy crawlies attacked her. She felt the cool smoothness of a tidy stack of papers. She grabbed the small pile and pulled it out. Not papers. Envelopes. She set them aside for the moment and felt around in the space for anything else that might be hidden there. Her fingers touched something shoved against the side of the cubby. She pulled it out and stared. An old Kodak camera with what looked like the bellows from an accordion, but worn and brittle from age. Had it been Bridget's? Or Everly's?

She handled it carefully, turning it over in her hands. She couldn't tell if there was film inside. She'd take it to that camera shop in town, but later. Right now, she set it aside and stuck her hand back in the hollow of the stairs. This time, her fingers touched something cold and hard. She dragged it to the opening, using both hands to carefully lift it out. The heavy object was a bowl about six inches in diameter, carved from stone. Obsidian, she thought, touching Everly's pendant again. It could have come from the same piece of crystallized rock.

Sitting in the cavity of the bowl was a small dark bottle. She held it up to the light, tilting it. There was liquid inside, viscous and slow-moving like Saoirse's essential oils. She uncorked the bottle and held it to her nose. No scent. She replaced the cork and returned it to the bowl. The bowl was like a mortar, minus the pestle. Was it used for crushing herbs? She felt around the space under the floorboard in case the pestle had fallen out, but the cubby was empty.

When she found Everly, safe and sound, she'd ask her about the bowl. She replaced the wood, patted down the carpet, and returned the pin nails to where they belonged. She'd need to find a hammer—

A quiet suction sounded, then another, and another. It was as if a strong magnet was underneath, the force pulling the pin nails back into place one by one.

Of course she *didn't* need a hammer because the house was helping her. She smiled. "Thank you," she said again. The house whispered, and this time it sounded like it said, *Sky Girl.*

* * *

Rowan put the camera and bowl on her dresser behind the ceramic container that held Bridget's ashes. She rested her hand on the belly of it, letting it linger for a few seconds. "Soon," she said to her mother. They'd find the perfect place to spread her ashes after they found Everly.

She wasn't sure what to do next in that search, so she took a moment, sitting on her bedroom floor, the envelopes she'd found in a neat stack in front of her. They were all letters addressed to Bridget.

She felt a zingy charge of electricity. This had to be what divers felt when they discovered treasure from a sunken pirate ship. But opening the letters was another story. She drew in a steadying breath, trying to tame her beating heart. Seeing Bridget's name brought a taste of longing to Rowan's mouth. She'd never imagined that her mother could have concealed so much from her daughters. It seemed as if there were more secrets than truths. Maybe these missives held the answers as to why she'd left Swallow Hall.

There were five letters in all, not exactly a treasure trove, but Rowan would take what she could get. None were postmarked. They hadn't gone through the mail, but the paper of the first three envelopes was soft. Worn. These had been well handled, each letter read many times over. The last two were crisp, the corners still pointy, the edges still sharp.

She tried to discern some order to them, but without postmarks, there were no dates. She kept them in the order she'd found them, starting at the top. She slipped the first letter out and unfolded the plain sheet of paper. It was a single line of writing. The ink was splotched from moisture that had made the ink run and then dried making them look like inkblots in a Rorschach text.

B—

I need to see you.

—S

Instantly, Rowan's head filled with cotton that made her thoughts fuzzy around the edges. Who was S?

She moved to the next letter.

B—

Meet me at the bridge tonight. Please.

—S

This letter was dated. Seeing it made a lump lodge in Rowan's throat. May 12, 1944. Seven months from the birthday she shared with her sisters.

She set the first two letters aside with their envelopes and pulled the next one out. The paper felt soft in Rowan's hands. She imagined Bridget holding it. Crying over it. Crumbling it, then flattening it out again in regret.

B—

I put my first letters to you in the hollow of the ash tree where that red-breasted swallow roosts, hoping you'd find them. They're gone now so I guess you did. I came to Swallow Hall today, but you didn't answer the door. Bridget, tell me what's happening.

—S

Another thought came to Rowan. These could be from their— She stopped the thought in its tracks. Tried to stop herself from thinking the word that crowded her throat, but she couldn't. Could these letters be from their *father*? Had he been bad news? Abusive? A dull ache started at the base of her head. Something had driven Bridget away from her mother and her home. Maybe it was love, but what if it was to escape from an untenable situation? And if that was true, did she want to know? It would be easier to believe her father was a decent person who didn't know she and her sisters existed.

As she read the next letter, the ache spread its tendrils, clawing into her head until spasms erupted.

B—

I saw you today in the woods talking to him and everything suddenly made sense. He's the reason you won't see me, isn't he? I never thought you could betray me, but there you both were, right in front of me.

I tried to reach you before you crossed the bridge to Bird Island, but I was too late. By the time I got there, you were gone and I couldn't get across. You always said the island and house were alive. I felt it today. It was like some invisible wall had been erected and I couldn't pass. It's probably just as well. Why can't you see Cillian for what he is? B, be careful. I still love you.

—S

Rowan pressed her fingertips to her temples. The ache in the pit of her stomach was sharp and overwhelming. Her mouth was dry with the fetid taste of black, withering rose petals. This man thought Bridget had betrayed him. That was so unlike the mother Rowan had known. Then again, she'd been just a girl in 1944. She had grown into a woman with the responsibility of motherhood. Who she'd been back then and who she'd become might have been two completely different people. She searched her memories for the mother she'd known. She remembered her leading the girls on a scavenger hunt in the park, a mother with her ducklings, the swallows overhead. Bridget had lived for her daughters. As long as they were all together, she was happy.

Rowan set the letter aside and picked up the final one, slowly sliding it from the envelope. Once free, the tri-folded page unfolded. It was less worn than the others, as if it had been read only once before being tucked away into the hole in the stairs.

B—

I don't even know why I'm writing this except that I have to get the words out of my head so they stop spinning because . . . because you're already gone. I saw you leave with him. It doesn't surprise me. You've always been a free spirit. I knew you'd never stay put. Then I saw . . . you're pregnant. And now you're gone. B, you broke my heart.

—S

For a long time, Rowan stared at the five letters. Reread them over and over and over. Fought the tears.

The mother Rowan knew wouldn't have abandoned Everly. She wouldn't have betrayed her boyfriend—a man who clearly loved her—without a word, even if she'd fallen in love with someone else.

And yet she had done both of those things.

She had her reasons.

Her hands shook as she folded the letters, replacing them in their envelopes. Two thoughts formed. The first was whether or not Bridget had seen the last letter. In it, S said he saw her leave with the other man. That meant she wouldn't have been here at Swallow Hall to find the letter. That's why it was pristine compared to the other four, which looked to have been read a hundred times each. Had Everly found it? Had she hidden it away with the ones Bridget had left behind?

The second was the other man's name. She'd heard it twice before, both times whispered on the wind, for her ears only.

Cillian.

The man who might well be their father.

Chapter Thirteen

Rowan knew a stranger was on Bird Island. She tasted mint and vanilla, but it was the hint of lemon mixed with spicy chocolate on her tongue that brought back their first meeting at the Co-op. She stood at one of the second-floor windows facing west just out of sight and watched as Warren Lansing started across the footbridge, then paused and looked up, staring at the house. She'd expected him to look incredulous. Instead, he curled the fingers of one hand and scraped them across his scalp.

Seeing Swallow Hall for the first time was disconcerting at best. For someone who didn't know magic existed, it was more like a scary, decaying house from a horror movie. She thought Warren Lansing, who Caraline hardly knew, might turn around and run, but he didn't. He started walking again, making it across the footbridge and stepping onto the stone path that led to the front door.

Rowan didn't want him here, but she also knew that was for her own selfish reasons. They needed to find Everly, that was their first priority, rather than a potential boyfriend hanging around. But Caraline would be thrilled for the distraction and preoccupied with him.

The faint sense of metal was gone, only the freshness of citrus remaining as Rowan moved to the top of the stairs. "Caraline!"

The sound of pots clanging from the kitchen amplified. It was the house telling her where her sister was, in case she hadn't guessed. Rowan hurried down the stairs so Caraline could be the one to meet Warren at the door, but the knock came just as she took the last step.

"Caraline!" she hollered again, but she didn't want Warren just standing out there under the canopy of the espalier tree, its boughs thick and woody overhead while the sprawling branches of the winter creeper skulked up the side of the house. She sensed its movements. Its sudden growth. For all she knew, the winter creeper would creep right over him, making him disappear.

As she flung the door open, she uttered, "*Stad a chur le*" preemptively. It was something she'd picked up from Everly. It was Irish, meaning stop, and she hoped the vine listened. Explaining the oddities of the house was going to be hard enough without the added difficulty of the vine growing before his very eyes.

Warren stood on the porch, one foot resting casually against the old stone flooring, a canvas backpack slung across his back. He smiled when he saw her, all warm edges and harmless charm. He wore a black T-shirt under a bomber jacket, his dark hair swept to the right, his eyebrows slashed above graphite eyes. He plucked a lemon balm leaf from the plant growing by the steps, smelling it, then taking a nibble. The faint scent of citrus and mint drifted in the air, clean and sharp enough to cut through the salt and earth of the island.

His features taken separately were nothing to write home about, but when put together, they arranged into something darkly appealing—the kind of face you remembered, like the air around him shimmered just enough to soften the flaws, to pull you in.

"Rowan," he said, remembering her name.

He offered her his sly, one-sided smile, the quintessential bad boy, which Caraline would eat up.

Rowan nodded at him, eyeing him curiously as he plucked a stalk off the lemon balm plant.

"I'm addicted to this stuff," he said with a chuckle. "Better than smoking, right?"

She had to agree. If he was a former smoker replacing one addiction with another, well . . . there were worse things to be dependent on. His attention shifted to over her shoulder and his smile grew. "There you are, gorgeous."

From behind her, Caraline screeched. She elbowed past Rowan. He slipped his arm around her, both of them wearing stupid grins.

"Mm, lemon and chocolate," she muttered as she leaned into him.

Warren answered by gesturing wide and saying with trepidation, "Weird place. Your grandmother really lives here?"

Caraline frowned, but nodded. Good girl, Rowan thought, willing her to keep their family business to herself. Rowan backed away and headed to the apothecary. No matter what time of day or night it was, the sunroom—Saoirse's apothecary—was always bright with warm yellow light. Even since Everly had gone missing, Saoirse spent most of her time there, leaving only when Caraline called her to come eat or to venture to the garden or pantry to gather ingredients for some new concoction. This was how she coped with life, and especially with Everly being gone. Rowan didn't know how her sister could stand it, self-isolating in that one room nearly around the clock. But this time, when she walked in, it was gloomy despite the open windows and the blue sky. She was instantly hit by a sharp chill in the air.

"What are you—" she started but stopped when she heard the faint hiss of kerosene flowing into the portable stove Saoirse was hunched over. She wore rubber kitchen gloves, long sleeves, and goggles. She'd pulled her hair into a ponytail, and she slowly stirred the concoction in the pot with a sturdy wooden spoon.

Rowan knew from the getup and the old brass stove that her sister was making soap. Rosemary and lavender, based on the array of both spread out on the center table.

Before Rowan could speak, Saoirse held up one hand. "One minute."

"Mm," Rowan said. She knew better than to press Saoirse when she was working. Her sister was single-minded. Multitasking wasn't how she operated, so she needed to finish whatever it was she doing before she could give her attention to something else. Rowan also knew that throwing herself into whatever she had brewing was Saoirse's way of coping with stress, and Everly's disappearance had definitely caused them all a lot of worry.

Whenever Rowan was in the sunroom for too long, she felt a tightening in her chest. Cotton in her mouth. She felt boxed in to the point she couldn't breathe. She needed to be outside, which is why she'd decided she'd be the one to check on the swallow's mud nests and cut back the winter creeper, two of the things Everly had told them that were the job of the Keeper. Both Caraline and Saoirse could have done the tasks, but Rowan would be the one reminding them. Better to simply do them herself.

At precisely one minute, Saoirse looked toward Rowan, not quite meeting her eyes. "Quick. I'm almost at trace," she said, meaning the point of no return when the soap mixture of oils and lye reached a stable emulsified consistency where the two wouldn't separate again.

"Guess who just showed up?" Rowan said.

Saoirse's gaze drifted to the glass portion of the ceiling. She thought for about three seconds before shaking her head. "Caraline's man."

It had been more of a rhetorical question, because of course Saoirse had heard Rowan's thoughts. "Yes! That guy she met at the Co-op."

Saoirse's gaze landed somewhere in the vicinity of Rowan's face. "He's *here*?"

"Just waltzed right up to the door."

"Not surprising. She's got a way of bewitching anyone she sets her sights on."

"I guess." Maybe Saoirse was right. Their sister went through men like they were sticks of Doublemint gum. Still, this felt different. Caraline seemed unusually smitten. "What are you working on?" Rowan asked.

"Lavender salt soap. I found Everly's notebook in her basket," she said as she continued to stir the oils and lye in the pot. "It has some of her recipes and her delivery schedule—who gets what and when. This is my second batch. I added peppermint oil to the first one. This one has frankincense. Better for breathing. I also made a batch of her reishi ginger tea." She pointed to two mason jars on one of the shelves and three squares of soap tied with a thin strand of twine. "The soap with the peppermint goes to—" She stood on her tiptoes to peer at the open page of a small notebook propped against the wall where she worked. "—Macy Davis. The peppermint should help her headaches."

It made sense that Saoirse would focus on something practical. She had an inability to function in chaotic, unpredictable social situations—especially with strangers. Too many people, too many variables, too much unspoken expectation. It overwhelmed her, short-circuited her ability to think clearly.

When they were kids, she'd freeze when their mother had taken them to the park, or she'd disappear into the shadows at school. As she got older, she learned to mask it a little—counting herbs at the apothecary table, losing herself in patterns and tasks, learning about every flower under the sun, avoiding eye contact. But the wiring underneath never changed.

It was simply how Saoirse functioned in the world, and Rowan and Caraline accepted that.

"Does Everly put peppermint in it when she makes it?" Rowan asked, going back to the soap for Macy Davis. When Saoirse shook her head, she asked, "Do you think you should change what she does? What if she doesn't like peppermint?"

Saoirse kept stirring the soap in the pot. "Alchemy is an art, Rowan. It's personal, and this is the way I do it. I can use Everly's base recipes, but I have to make them my own. I have to create in a way that makes sense to me." She turned off the heat and added a series of ingredients she'd already prepped and portioned out, including tiny lavender buds and mineral salt. Rowan clasped her hands together and watched while Saoirse finished mixing the cold press soap and carefully poured it into the tin molds she'd prepared. She no longer offered to help Saoirse with any of her alchemy. On the rare occasion her sister wanted or needed help, she asked for it.

The phone rang, loud and shrill, breaking Saoirse's concentration. She jerked, a glob of the viscous mixture landing on the counter rather than in the mold. "No, no, no!"

"I'll get it," Rowan said, and she sprinted to the kitchen, snatching the handset from its wall cradle before the next ring started.

"Where's my 'shrooms?" a man's voice rasped.

Rowan frowned. "What?"

"My 'shrooms! My 'shrooms! Everly was supposed to bring me my 'shroom tea this morning. I need my 'shrooms!"

Rowan recognized the voice. "Ah, Mr. Floyd, I'm so sorry. She was supposed to come today?"

"That she was. First thing. She ain't never missed a day. Not once. I need that 'shroom tea she makes. It's the only thing that helps my pain."

"It's just, Everly isn't here, Mr. Flo—"

"Bah!" he rasped again. "I don't give a flying fig about excuses. I just need my tea. You're that granddaughter, right? You've been here. *You* bring it."

Rowan stretched the phone cord long, pulling it taut so she could see the shelf where Everly stored her week's deliveries. There was nothing there, so Everly hadn't had time to prepare her tea before she'd vanished. "I don't have—" she started, but broke off when Saoirse called, "Yes, you do!"

She turned and saw Saoirse pointing again to the mason jars. Right. Saoirse had brewed it. A fist of anticipation exploded in Rowan's gut. She *could* make Everly's deliveries. Maybe someone in town had seen Everly. Maybe one of the people Everly delivered things to could tell her something.

Mr. Floyd's wet cough accosted Rowan's ear. "Hey there, missy? Did you hear me? You still there?"

Rowan pulled the phone away and grimaced before nodding. "I'm still here."

"And? You gonna bring me my tea?"

"Yes, sir, I will," she said. "I'll come right now."

Chapter Fourteen

Crossing the footbridge felt like entering a parallel universe, one where the leaves still clung to the trees and where dappled sunlight found its way through those leaves, dotting the ground with a magical sprinkling of light. The air was cool but didn't have the bite that existed on the island where an invisible bubble enclosed it, giving it weather patterns and seasons that were ruled by the emotions of the house rather than the sun, the moon, and the spinning of the planet.

She felt like Red Riding Hood walking through the woods with her hooded shawl and basket of potions. She watched for lurking shadows as she walked. For signs of Everly, of a struggle, of any clue she might have missed. Because she was more and more certain that there was a Big Bad Wolf they didn't know about. She worried that it was someone who knew about the magic. About Swallow Hall. About what it protected.

"Ahoy!"

Rowan nearly jumped out of her boots at the intrusion of the booming voice. She clutched her basket tighter and peered through the mottled light at a male figure taking form. Moving closer.

"Ahoy!" he said again, this time with a lift of one arm.

"Hi," Rowan said, offering a faint smile. She stopped, keeping plenty of distance between them.

He kept moving forward, though, until they were just a few feet apart, her looking like a girl from a fairy tale, and him looking nothing like the Big Bad Wolf. He was slim and tall with wire-framed glasses and flyaway blond hair that caught the sunlight in wild strands. She placed him in his early fifties. His chin jutted slightly, long and oddly pronounced, and when he smiled at her, his lower teeth fit neatly over his uppers in a way that made his grin look almost too wide.

Rowan braced herself, expecting the usual sharp rush of tastes to coat her tongue, but only the faintest trace of yellow trout lily surfaced. Bright. Wild. Inherently joyful. Still . . . something in the air around him shimmered at the edges, the way heat rises off asphalt. It passed as quickly as it came, gone before she could question it.

"You must be one of Everly's granddaughters," he exclaimed, his grin brightening further. "What a treat to run into you. Such a treat! You are all the talk of the town."

Were they? Everly didn't seem to have many friends in New Bethel. Given this, Rowan imagined being the talk of the town wasn't necessarily a good thing. "I'm Rowan."

"Oh! Yes! Rowan!" the man said, every word ending with an excited exclamation point. Caraline would be suspicious of him on principle. "I'm Pastor Janson. Wylie Janson." He started to stick his hand out toward her but noticed both of hers holding tightly to her basket and dropped it again. "How are you settling in now that you're here with Everly? She looked absolutely thrilled when I saw her—"

"When was that?" Rowan cut in. She cleared her throat and took a breath to keep the anxiousness out of her voice. "Um, I mean when did you see her last?"

"Let's see, it was last week sometime. She was doing a few deliveries," he practically bellowed. He looked at her basket. Changed the subject. "Are you making them for her?"

Rowan lifted it up. "Yes. Just helping out."

"That's unusual." He puffed his lips out in consternation. "Is Everly sick?"

Rowan's instinct was to look down or look away like Saoirse did, but she forced herself to meet his gaze. "No, she's not sick. Just busy doing . . . other stuff."

His brows pinched, carving a small dent between them. The happiness of the trout lily faded to something else. Her mouth turned dry and she tasted licorice or . . . fennel. Pastor Wylie Janson's expression had gone from joyful to concerned. He flipped his wrist and glanced at his watch. "Strange. I would have said I could set my clock to Everly's routine."

He was the second person to say that. If Everly usually strode down High Street at a certain time, her absence would be noticed, which didn't bode well for keeping it a secret. "So I've heard. Um, Pastor . . ."

She hesitated. What had he said his name was?

He filled in the blank. "Janson, but folks call me Pastor Wylie."

"Right. Paster Wylie. I was just wondering, do you know if Everly has friends outside of New Bethel? Or *in* New Bethel, for that matter?"

He cocked his head to one side, considering her. "Why do you ask?"

She didn't know why, but she'd felt it was important to keep Everly's absence private. But now she debated with herself. Should she tell him? He was a man of God, after all. If there was anyone she could trust, it would be him. She looked over her shoulder. Scanned the woods all around. Turned back to him. He seemed sincere and . . . well . . . *pastorly.* "It's just—"

His whole body leaned toward her. "It's just what, child?" he asked, pulling out his preacher language.

She felt the heat of the obsidian and topaz under her sweater, flat against her chest. Instantly she changed her mind. She couldn't tell this stranger that Everly had disappeared in the middle of the night. Instead, she concocted a plausible scenario. "I thought I heard her mention she was going to visit someone, but she, um, forgot to leave a note." She made her expression sheepish. "I think she's not used to having people around all the time."

"So you're cramping her style, eh?" The pastor chuckled, his concern tempered. "I don't know Everly well enough to say if she has friends somewhere else. What I can say is that *I've* never seen her leave New Bethel. That doesn't mean she hasn't, only that I've never known it to happen."

Everly herself had told them she never left Swallow Hall for more than a few hours, so that tracked.

"She's been on her own for a long time. I wouldn't worry. She'll be back soon enough."

She forced a smile and nodded. "I'm sure you're right."

The pastor peered into her basket. "Ah, let me guess. Kyle Floyd?"

She nodded. "Two bottles of his ginger reishi tea for his pain."

"Poor man. He's had those scars for decades now."

Indeed. Rowan had felt the man's pain. She'd *tasted* it, but she kept that to herself.

The pastor continued. "But if it helps Everly keep the lights on. And she has a gift for—"

He broke off. Bit his upper lip with those protruding teeth, but she pressed. "For?"

"Some folks around here think your grandmother is . . ."

Rowan could fill in the blank with a variety of words. A healer. A medicine woman. A hippie. A *witch*. If that's what people thought, they were on the money. "She's good with herbs," she said quickly. "She has a . . . knack."

"That she does. I've been trying to get my wife to pay her a visit for . . . ah, never mind . . ." He trailed off again, clearly thinking it better that he not reveal to a perfect stranger what his wife's ailments were.

Rowan looked over her shoulder toward the house. "Are you, uh, going to Swallow Hall?" she asked, because why else would he be on this particular path? No reason that she could think of.

"No. I like to wander in the woods. The happiest man is he who learns from nature the lesson of worship."

"Thoreau?" she ventured.

"Close," he said, grinning. "Ralph Waldo Emerson."

He looked past her, toward the island with its crazy house and sinking land. Rowan couldn't read his expression. Curiosity? Wariness?

The thread of suspicion spread its tentacles inside her. The figure in the dark she had been seeing. Could it have been him? Sometimes the Big Bad Wolf hid beneath lamb's clothes, smiling wide and harmless. She studied him now—the wispy blond hair, the eager grin, the faint shimmer in the air that still clung to him like the aftertaste of a forgotten spell.

Was there a darker side to Pastor Wylie Janson that he kept well hidden? One he kept tucked neatly behind bright eyes and joyful words?

Then again, he said he'd wanted his wife to see Everly, so he knew she could heal. She held up her basket. "I better be going. Mr. Floyd needs his tea."

Pastor Wylie's face turned serious. "That he does, that he does." He turned and walked with her until they were on the sidewalk on High Street. "Give Everly my best when you see her," he said, not a trace of concern in his voice.

"I will," Rowan said.

As they parted ways and she watched him walk in the direction of the tabernacle, her tastebuds let go of the licorice and fennel that had lingered, but she held on to the misgivings. He was a pastor, so she wanted to trust him. But she'd met him in the woods across from Bird Island—a strange place for casual encounters.

By sheer proximity, Pastor Wylie was the most likely suspect. That was what unsettled her the most—the possibility that his easy smile and joyful words were just a cover, hiding something she wasn't meant to see. Because in her experience, wickedness didn't always scream in your face. Sometimes it wore a joyful mask and came dressed in warmth and charm.

She headed straight to Mr. Floyd's street. She spotted the house from a hundred yards away, recognizing it right away because it was next to the splintered one with the broken windows and the cockeyed door. And because it was hard to forget. It was a relic of old red bricks and worn-out shutters, discordant with the abundance of blooming lavender and mint. The house looked like it was sprouting from the center of the leggy flowers and the invasive herb. Swallow Hall was wonky, but it was loved. That was evident in the way Everly touched the walls with gentle care; with the way she managed the winter creeper; from the reverence with which she spoke to it using her Irish phrases to calm it down. Rowan would lay money down that Kyle Floyd didn't do any of those things. The place and the one next door were neglected, plain and simple. If the Floyd house could, she'd wager it would swallow him up whole and be done with him. And the neighbor's house too, for good measure.

The closer she came to the red brick structure and Kyle Floyd's pain, the heavier the air felt, its neglect spreading its tendrils beyond the premises, unfurling the bite of bitterness in her mouth. Rowan dragged in a labored breath, but this time, instead of feeling crushed under water, she willed herself to be calm. She heard Bridget's voice, then Everly's. *Breathe in. Breathe out.* The brightness of mint rose to the surface, displacing the metallic discontent. At the moment, she was glad she wasn't a healer. She didn't know how she'd be able to help people like Kyle Floyd—people laden with injuries and maladies—if she could only focus on controlling the emotions her body absorbed in their presence. She came to a standstill on the sidewalk. "Mr. Floyd?"

When he didn't come, she called again, louder this time. "Mr. Floyd."

The front door banged open, and he stood there leaning heavily on his cane. "Took you long enough, girlie," he rasped. He looked much the same as he had the first time she'd seen him with his liver-spotted hands, eye patch, and map of scars intersecting each other on his face.

Rowan closed her eyes for a beat and drew in a deep breath. "Sorry about that. But I'm here now." She set her basket down and took out the two mason jars of tea, holding them in front of her.

"What'd'ya expecting me to do? Hobble on down there and get 'em from ya?"

She chided herself. Of course he couldn't do that. She was going to have to go closer. Into the house even to put the jars in the kitchen like Everly had, and collect the money he owed. She surged forward, making her feet move up the short path, up the few steps to the small porch. He didn't move out of the way so she turned sideways and shimmied past him, stepping into the house. Being so close to him displaced the mint on her tastebuds with the pungent anger his pain imbued him with. It pressed down on her. Her breath turned shallow.

He thumped his cane on the floor as he turned. "In the kitchen with that."

Rowan scurried down the short hall. The kitchen was surprisingly tidy. Empty mason jars were lined up on one of the Formica counters. The appliances were old but clean. She put the jars on the table and hurried back to the front.

He lifted his cane and flung it horizontally as she passed him. It landed with a thunk on an envelope sitting on the entry table.

He gave a quick flick of his wrist, sending it into the air. It flew at Rowan, the corner grazing her cheek before it fluttered to the ground. Mr. Floyd pointed his cane at it. "Give that to Everly."

She bent to grab it, waving it at him as she raced out the door and into the fresh air.

She scooped up the market basket and hurried away, dragging in deep breaths, leaving the taste of Kyle Floyd's pain behind.

Rowan traveled the same path she'd gone with Everly, battling down the intrusive smacks of salt or sweet, lemon or hibiscus as she dropped off each curative. At each stop, someone said, "Where's Everly?" or "That's Everly's basket."

Her lie became a little bit easier each time she uttered it. "She had something she had to take care of. I'm doing her deliveries for her." Every time she asked when the last time they saw Everly was, the answer was always at her last delivery. The whole trip, aside from helping Everly's clients, had been unfruitful and disappointing. She'd learned nothing that could help her.

Finally, she was back on High Street with Macy Davis's headache soap left to deliver. The effort of controlling the bombardment of emotions had worn her down. She stopped on the sidewalk in front of Moody's Saltwater Kitchen to steady herself and regain her sense of equilibrium. Through the windows, she saw people at tables, talking, and laughing their way through lunch. How strange it was that her life had turned upside down, that Everly had vanished, and here were people living theirs, perfectly content. They existed side by side but knew nothing about one another's troubles, and likely never would.

The door to the restaurant opened and the owner stepped out. Instead of the work clothes he'd been wearing the first time she'd met him, he wore khaki pants and a black button-down shirt. He strode down the steps toward a discarded newspaper next to the walkway. He spotted her, his brows lifting with recognition. "Bridget's daughter."

"And you're Mr. Moody." The taste of self-reproach mixed with enduring anger coated her tastebuds. She hadn't experienced it the first time. Maybe Everly had been a buffer. Now she felt it full force. This man had unresolved pain, and his emotions ran deep. Rowan stepped back to put more distance between them.

"Just Moody." Like everyone else, he noted the basket she carried and the question settled on his face. "Where's Everly?"

The lie slipped off her tongue. "She was busy today. I'm doing her deliveries for her."

He studied her. "I've never known her to be too busy for her clients."

She had no response to that, and an awkward silence fell between them. She said the only thing that came to mind. "You knew my mother?"

"I . . . did." He hesitated, as if he wasn't sure what to say next. Finally, he said, "You sound like her."

"Do I?" She liked hearing that, knowing that something discernible from Bridget lived in her.

He paused, as if lost in a memory. "I was . . . surprised . . . when she up and left. I think everyone was. Then again, Bridget always did have a stubborn streak. She was as independent as they come. A free spirit. She was too big for a small town like New Bethel."

All Rowan could do was nod and swallow down the taste of loss coating her tongue. Bridget had had an entire life filled with people Rowan, Saoirse, and Caraline knew nothing about.

"I was sorry to hear she died," Moody said. He paused and Rowan felt the weight of his thoughts. He cleared his throat before speaking again. "If you don't mind my asking, how did it happen?"

Rowan looked past him. Her nostrils flared as she breathed in, tamping down the sudden onslaught of emotions surfacing. "She . . . drowned."

He drew back, surprised. "Really? I remember her being such a good swimmer," he said, clearly trying to connect the dots.

"She . . . she wasn't swimming when it happened."

Another oppressive pause fell between them. "Then how . . ."

"They said she tripped. Fell and hit her head on the edge of a cement fountain. That she was unconscious when her head slipped under water."

"They said?" Moody repeated.

Rowan pressed her lips together. She didn't want to talk about it with this stranger. A family exited the restaurant, saving her from having to answer his question.

He stepped aside as a group of five left the restaurant, filing down the walkway. Rowan tasted the faintest bit of something warm and golden—like fresh bread and sunlight on clean sheets. Joy. Simple, unburdened joy. The kind that didn't question itself.

The man nodded at Rowan and the woman smiled. The kids skipped along behind their parents, their laughter trailing behind them like a song fading in the wind.

A few moments later, an older couple passed by, arms linked, faces creased from a lifetime of emotions. She moved out of the way so they could follow the walkway to the restaurant's entrance. As they passed her, the tastes in her mouth shifted to chamomile and woodsmoke. They intensified, slow and steady, and she felt a quiet kind of contentment.

It was refreshing for a moment, but then a lump formed in her throat. Not every emotion tasted like warning. Some were soft and gentle. These weren't things she'd experienced very often. She just didn't trust that they'd last. She thought about her mother being gone and about Everly missing, and in the blink of an eye, all that soft gentleness evaporated.

As Moody greeted his customers, Rowan slipped away. She hadn't gone far when she felt the weight of someone's eyes on her. It was heavy. Just the way Caraline had described. It felt as if she was being watched.

She turned and saw Moody still looking at her. Pastor Wylie was one possibility, but he certainly wasn't the only one. Could it have been Moody lurking in the darkness? She turned again just as he stepped back inside and shut the door behind him. As she walked on, the feeling of someone's eyes on her turned fuzzy, finally dissipating, but the worry remained. She'd gotten the sense from Everly that the owner of Moody's Saltwater Kitchen was one of the good ones, a New Bethel resident who didn't want to string her up like a Salem witch. But Rowan wasn't so sure. She couldn't shake the feeling that there was something dark buried deep within him. Something Everly hadn't sensed.

She looked for Everly, her eyes scanning every corner and shop, but there was no sign of her. Ahead, the Disciples of Christ Tabernacle looked just as drab as it had every other time she'd walked by it, the mud-colored shingles looking like weights that were trying to crush the building. The joy she'd sensed in Pastor Wylie didn't extend to his church. She was about to walk past but stopped. Made a split-second decision and turned back. She paused at the top of the steps. The rough texture of the wrought iron handle felt solid in her hand. According to the banner, this town and this church had been here since 1871. The history on the East Coast was so different than the West, with the Oregon Trail and the Gold Rush. Rowan felt the energy of all the people who had touched this iron, and who had walked through these doors in the past two hundred years seep into her.

"Can we help you?"

She released the door handle and moisture came back to her dry mouth. She turned. At the bottom of the steps stood the two birdlike women Rowan and Everly had seen on their first walk through town. Once again, they were dressed in black, their long skirts dusting the ground. Give them bonnets and they might have been straight out of the seventeen hundreds. These women didn't look like they belonged in 1971. She tried to remember the names Everly had given. Lorraine . . . no, no. But something similar. She snapped when it came to her. Lorna McNicol and Louise . . . Janson. Janson as in the pastor's wife? That took her aback. They didn't look like two puzzle pieces that fit perfectly together.

"You're Everly Early's granddaughter," the McNicol woman said, frowning.

The pastor's wife added, "You look like an Early."

It didn't come across as a compliment.

Rowan tamped down her unease and swallowed the odd combination of bitter and honey filling her mouth. Everly had told her she did not like these women, and that the feeling was mutual. Had they snapped and taken Everly to finally be rid of her? It sounded farfetched, but so did being a descendant of an Irish witch, so . . . "I'm Rowan."

They introduced themselves as sisters. Lorna McNicol said, "We are Daughters of the Disciples of Christ."

Rowan could see the resemblance between the women but with the hard planes of her face, her sharp features and thin lips, Louise had a much harsher look about her. Lorna's face was softer. Rounder. "What does that mean, Daughters of the Disciples of Christ?"

Louise hissed something at her sister before answering Rowan's question. "We are direct descendants of Cormac MacCantilly. He built this church."

Rowan felt her eyebrows reach for her hairline. "Ohh. Kind of like the descendants of the Mayflower?"

Lorna huffed out a sigh. "Much smaller, obviously. The Mayflower came earlier, in 1620, and those 102 souls have descendants spread far and wide. Cormac MacCantilly came to America for a better life. He founded this town and this church. Sadly, there are only a handful of his proud descendants left—"

"—of which we are two," Louise finished.

Rowan rolled her head in a roundabout nod.

Louise glared at her. "You and your sisters best not cause trouble in this town like your mother did."

If Rowan had been drinking something, she would have sputtered then spewed it out, right into their faces. "You . . . you knew my mother?"

"We know everyone in these parts," Louise said, as if the answer was obvious.

What Louise had said a moment ago registered. Rowan had only known about the problems Bridget had caused at Swallow Hall, not in New Bethel. "What kind of trouble did she cause?"

The sisters looked at each other and some sort of silent communique happened, just like it happened with Rowan, Saoirse, and Caraline.

Louise spoke first. "A local man disappeared around the same time your mother did. He left his job, his house . . . his *life*. All for that girl who *lured* him away."

It was clear to Rowan that "that girl' meant Bridget.

"Some people *have* said they've seen him back here," Lorna added, but Louise scoffed. "Rubbish. No one ever saw him." She pulled her fingers in, then splayed them out. "Poof, he was just gone."

Icy fingers clawed Rowan's skull. Because of the letters she found, she could guess the name of the man, but she asked anyway. "What was his name?"

Louise moved closer to Rowan, her bird nose leading the way. "His name was Cillian Tully."

She said it hoarsely, as if the man was a ghost who haunted the town rather than someone who'd been in love and had run off. Rowan schooled her expression so they wouldn't see that she'd heard the name before—not uttered by a person, but by the wind and by Swallow Hall.

Lorna looked at her, the tone of her voice belying the softness of her face. "Like Louise said. You three best not cause any trouble around here."

It felt like a warning and that old sense of being a square peg in a round hole leached back into her thoughts. There was an awkward silence. Rowan cleared her throat to break it. "I better go," she said, holding up the basket. "One more delivery."

"Where *is* your grandmother?" Lorna asked, looking around as if Everly might suddenly appear.

The crazy idea that these harsh women who apparently hated Everly could have taken her and stashed her somewhere in the church shot to Rowan's mind. She disregarded it and the thought was gone just as fast. "I wanted to help out today," she said, changing her story. Even if she didn't think they had anything to do with Everly's disappearance, she didn't want to give them any hint that something was amiss.

She scurried down the steps and with a quick wave, she left the two Daughters of the Disciples of Christ behind, their eyes on her back like hot beams of light. In her mind, Rowan heard the provoking chant her classmates had often hurled at her and her sisters, advancing on them with make-believe pitchforks and wicked faces.

Witch. Witch. You can't play.
Witch. Witch. Go away.

The echo of the taunt curled around her like smoke, thick and suffocating. Rowan clenched her jaw, pushing her shoulders back as she walked. She wasn't that girl anymore—she was strong. Her mother had called her powerful. Still, some ghosts clung tight, never fully willing to let go.

Chapter Fifteen

As Rowan walked toward her last stop, she passed Chesapeake Camera Hut. That's where she could bring the old Kodak she'd found. Next time, after Everly was back at Swallow Hall, safe and sound.

At Chester's Dime Store, she waved at the man behind the counter. Matthew, she remembered. When he smiled and waved back, a touch of warmth radiated out from her core. The town of New Bethel certainly didn't feel like home, but it was becoming familiar and there were a few people who seemed friendly enough. She crossed the street at a diagonal, heading to the New Bethel Historic Society in the old red brick house that sat at the end of the street before it turned to woods.

Her basket had grown light with only the lavender peppermint salt soap remaining. As she rapped her knuckles on the heavy wood door, it swung inward on creaky hinges. She thought she heard the faint sound of talking but hesitated, not sure if she should step in or wait. "Hello? Ms. Davis?"

"Hello! Hello!" The voices came first, followed by the women Rowan had briefly met during her first trip to town with Everly. They walked side by side, both grinning broadly. The one with the dark iron-gray hair and the brown eyes with an outer circle of vibrant green was Macy Davis, she remembered, and the one with the azure eyes and snowy white hair was Esther Canvey.

"Heavens, would you look at that?" Esther said, turning to Macy. "It's Rowan Early!"

"Oh, it's Connors, actually. I hope I'm not bothering you." She let her basket slide down her forearm, breathing easily when only the mustiness of old books filled her mouth. "I'm making Everly's deliveries today."

Macy gasped, and Esther's eyes skittered around, surprised. "You're making her deliveries?" Macy repeated.

"Well, since my sisters and I are here, we're giving her a little break."

"Well deserved, well deserved," Macy said, and then she moved on. "You have my soap, then?"

"Yes," Rowan said, plucking the stack of square bars from the basket. "My sister made it this time. I hope that's okay."

Macy's smile dimmed. "But Everly makes my soap. It's the only thing that helps with my headaches. It's a special recipe."

Rowan had worried about this. She hoped the new formula would be okay, at least until Everly was back. She hesitated before adding, "Saoirse added peppermint. She says that'll help."

Now Macy frowned. "Peppermint, you say?" She took the soap, turning the bars over in her hands. Gingerly, as if they might contain some poison, she lifted them to her nose and breathed in the scent. Her brows lifted in surprise. "They are lovely. Different than Everly's, but lovely. I suppose I can give them a try."

"Saoirse's like Everly with her essential oils and her . . . talent for making soaps and things," Rowan said.

Macy and Esther exchanged a look, and Esther smiled. "By that, you mean absolutely magical."

Rowan's face froze. Surely she didn't mean *actual* magic. Everly wouldn't have shared her witchery. She couldn't see her divulging Early family history to any of the New Bethel biddies.

"Rowan, dear, are you alright? You look pale."

Rowan tamped down her unease. It was just a figure of speech.

"Rowan?"

She blinked and came back to the moment. "Sorry. I'm fine." She wanted to ask Macy and Esther about Everly's habits. Ask if they'd seen her, but she hesitated.

"Oh, heavens!" Esther exclaimed. "How rude of us not to invite you in. Come, come. I'll make us some tea."

Rowan wanted to get back to Bird Island and Swallow Hall, to figure out what to do next, but she was parched after walking all over town and tea sounded good. "If you're sure," she said.

Esther had already disappeared into the house. Macy held the door open and beckoned Rowan in, shutting out the cold once she was inside. "Positive," Macy said. "You look a little peaked. A cup of tea will do you good."

Inside, Macy gestured for Rowan to sit in one of the overstuffed chairs. She'd worn a pair of Caraline's bell-bottom jeans today and as she crossed her legs, she felt the stark contrast of them with the fussy room and the dowdy dresses Macy and Esther wore.

Esther returned with a delicate tea service on a tray, setting it on the sideboard. She poured it into dainty china cups. With the cup in one hand, gently holding its tiny handle, and the saucer in the other, Rowan felt like a little girl playing dress-up—minus the dress.

The house was a museum with what looked like artifacts from early settlers. Macy pointed out a well loved Bible and a heavy iron key, rusted with age; a shelf of books that looked to be hundreds of years old; a brass sextant and an old maritime clock.

Rowan asked about the collection, and Macy said, "The founder of New Bethel came aboard the Bowditch from Liverpool to New York. We're lucky enough to have some of the items he brought with him—"

"They're probably not from *that* immigrant ship, though," Esther chimed in.

Macy gave a nonchalant shrug. "Well, of course, the captain of the Bowditch wouldn't just give up the ship's sextant and clock, but we know they came from a ship of the same era. Anyway, they were amongst Cormac MacCantilly's possessions and donated to the town, so it's a good story—"

"If not fully accurate—"

"But we like to think it's close. The Bible belonged to him too—"

"Cormac was our great-great-grandfather. He founded the Disciples in 1849. That was just a few years after your ancestor, Paddy Early, came to Maryland and built Swallow Hall," Esther said.

"You're sisters?" Rowan asked noting how they spoke, glancing at one another in the same way that Rowan, Saoirse, and Caraline did, and like Lorna McNicol and Louise Janson had—a silent transmission of information passing between people who knew each other inside and out.

"Cousins," they said at the same time. They looked at each other, eyes twinkling, and giggled, both of them exclaiming, "Jinx!"

Their easy manner and closeness reminded Rowan of the way she and her sisters finished each other's sentences and how they thought alike in so many ways. She'd always wondered if they'd grow apart as they got older, fell in love, and had families of their own. Seeing Esther and Macy gave her hope that none of that had to separate them.

The name Cormac MacCantilly echoed in her brain. "Louise Janson and Lorna McNicol . . ." She looked over her shoulder and gestured in the general direction of the church. "They mentioned that name, Cormac . . ."

"Well now, of course they did," Esther said. "We come from the same line. Different generation, of course."

"Our great-nieces," Macy said.

The thought that Louise Janson had knocked Everly out and dragged her into a dungeon of the church resurfaced. It felt ridiculous, but still . . . "They, um, don't seem to like Everly much."

Esther grimaced. "Lorna's not so bad, but Louise doesn't like many people. How she ended up with that charming Pastor Wylie is a question for the ages."

"I say she was a project for him," Macy said.

"If you're right, he definitely failed. She's as ornery now as she ever was."

There didn't seem to be any love lost between Esther, Macy, and their great-niece.

Rowan put her hand over her cup when Esther offered to top it off. "No thanks. I need to get back," she said.

"Of course, dear."

"I was wondering . . ."

She stopped, thinking about what she could ask to help her find Everly. The elderly women waited, looking at her expectantly. "Yes?" Macy prompted.

"It's just. I don't really *know* Ever—my grandmother. We didn't know we *had* a grandmother until we came here. You've known her for a long time. I was wondering if—"

"Ah," Macy broke in. "You were wondering if we could tell you anything about her." She chuckled. Glanced at Esther. "We *have* known her for a long time, that's true. I would say she's a bit of a mystery. She's always been very private. She loves that house of hers. Been in your family since the day it was built."

"That house, Swallow Hall, it's . . . *unusual*, isn't it?" Esther commented.

"Some folks say it's haunted." Macy dropped her voice, speaking with gravitas. "And that the Earlys are *witches*."

Rowan choked on her tea. She coughed, clearing her throat. "O-oh-oh," she stuttered.

"People are hard to understand sometimes," Esther said. "They need to explain the unexplainable—"

"And Swallow Hall is most assuredly unexplainable. The way it's changed over the years. Everly says all the Earlys have added on to the house, and that she's done some of it herself, but I don't know . . ." Macy trailed off, making it clear that people didn't believe that story. That *she* didn't believe it.

In her head, Rowan heard the explanation Macy hadn't spoken aloud. Magic.

Rowan knew the truth, but there was no way she was going to say it. *No, Everly didn't actually do any of it. The house did it all on its own because yes, in fact, Swallow Hall is cursed or enchanted, or whatever you want to call it, and Everly is, in fact, a witch.* Rowan just scoffed as lightheartedly as she could.

"A story behind the inexplicable makes it easier to accept," Esther said, slowly blinking her deep blue eyes and sounding like a wise old owl.

"But *magic*?" The idea of it in and of itself was hard to understand as a reality. Rowan lived with it and didn't have a clue how or why it worked. It simply was. But maybe it was easier for ordinary people who *didn't* have magic running through their veins to create inexplicable explanations.

"*Especially* magic," Macy said. "It's what the Greeks did, after all, assigning a god or goddess as the puppet master behind things they couldn't explain."

Esther stood and clasped the teapot, refilling Rowan's cup despite her earlier refusal, then Macy's, and finally her own. Macy considered the umber liquid in her cup. "Bridget never brought you here."

It wasn't a question, so Rowan didn't respond, but Esther's eyes went wide and she pushed. "Heavens. Why ever not?"

It was the very question Rowan had asked since the beginning, and the one she'd likely never get the answer to. "I wish I knew," she said.

Esther tsk'd. "Such a shame."

To this Rowan agreed.

"What made you come to New Bethel now?" Macy asked.

Rowan couldn't tell anyone about the photo and cryptic message from Bridget, least of all women Everly said were gossips. Instead, she told yet another lie. "We wanted to meet our grandmother."

Macy nodded vigorously. "Of course, of course. I imagine Everly's thrilled to have you here.

Rowan lifted her teacup to her lips. Everly was thrilled . . . but now she was gone.

"Your family goes back a long way," Macy said, filling the silence.

"I guess it does, but I don't know much about the Earlys," Rowan said. Other than the story of Biddy Early, but she kept that to herself too.

"History is a beautiful thing. So enlightening, yet so full of secrets. What brought *your* great-great-great-grandfather here? Was he after the American dream? Did he achieve it?" Macy gestured at Rowan. "Look at you and your sisters. At your mother, God rest her soul, and Everly. All successful women, so by my estimation, Paddy succeeded."

Rowan hadn't thought of it like that. She'd been so focused on Everly as the Keeper of Swallow Hall and the house Paddy had built and the trouble he'd caused to wonder why he'd come to America in the first place, to Maryland, to this town and island.

"Everly told us the history of Swallow Hall, but not much about why Paddy left Ireland."

Esther and Macy locked eyes for a second, another imperceptible thread of communication passing between them. "Funny you should say that," Esther said, turning back to her. "We always wondered what brought him here. What would make someone take the risk of traveling across the ocean, leaving their home country, mother, and family behind?" She chuckled. "It's not like they had cruise ships back then."

"We wondered the same thing about our ancestors—" Macy said.

"So, of course, we researched—" Esther finished. She looked earnestly at Rowan. "There isn't much about your family's history. He went mad, you know, Paddy did. That was before our time, of course, but folks around here have always told the stories."

"What stories?" Rowan asked.

"About Swallow Hall," Macy said.

"What about it?" Rowan asked, wondering what they'd found out about the Earlys.

"It should be on the historic registry," Macy said. "We've tried to get Everly to fill out the forms, goodness, half a dozen times? Maybe more—"

"Definitely more," Esther said.

Macy tilted her head in agreement. "Definitely more."

"We finally did it for her," Esther said.

"It's up to the state at this point," Macy said.

"They have everything they need—"

"And we expect a letter at some point." Macy clasped her hands together. "I can't wait to bring the acceptance letter to show Everly."

"We hope the state will allocate some resources to help preserve Bird Island—"

They both exhaled heavy sighs. Macy leaned forward like she was imparting a secret. "It's sinking, you know."

Rowan shifted her gaze back and forth between the cousins. She felt like she was watching a tennis match between Chris Evert and Billie Jean King at the U.S. Open, only with verbal volleys. She conjured up an image of the island's marshy higher ground and how the earth turned to a mudflat closer to the water. Everly had talked about that. Was it common knowledge?

"No one knows how or why," Esther said. "It shouldn't be happening. The polar ice caps and glaciers are intact—"

"Greenland's ice sheets too."

"We've done our research. There's no rhyme or reason for it, but it's happening nonetheless. A real conundrum with no logical explanation."

"It defies reason," Macy said with a tinge of wonder.

Now that she'd found the island, Rowan didn't want anything to happen to it. And though she couldn't say this to Esther or Macy, she didn't for one single minute think that ice sheets or glaciers had anything to do with it. No, it was the magic of the house reacting to its losses. To Paddy's destruction, to Bridget's abandonment, and now to losing Everly. And if Everly was gone for good, who knew what Bird Island and Swallow Hall would do? "Does Everly know you applied for the historic designation?"

"It'll be a surprise!" Macy exclaimed.

That was an understatement. Rowan didn't think Everly would want to have the house designated as historic because that would only draw attention to all its strangeness and people might start asking questions. Right now, Everly lived privately, with few visitors and little risk of anyone of significance asking questions. Rowan wanted to help her keep it that way. "But if Everly didn't want to fill out the paperwork, maybe she doesn't want it designated," she said, careful not to accuse them of butting in.

"Nonsense!" Macy said.

Esther lowered her teacup. "It was built by her ancestor. That history must be preserved."

Macy sat up straighter, preening. "We have a display about Paddy Early. Come."

Both women set their teacups down, stood, and strode from the room. Rowan left her cup and saucer on the sideboard and hurried after them. In the room opposite the parlor, artifacts of New Bethel's history were artfully displayed in glass cases sitting atop trestles. Against the wall were more items connected to the town. Esther and Macy had walked side by side, splitting apart only when they reached one of the displays, falling into place on either side of it. Macy tapped her fingertips on the glass. "These are things Everly gave us—"

"She gave us a box about twenty years ago now. A straight donation—"

"Things that belonged to Patrick Early," Macy finished.

Rowan clutched Everly's obsidian pendant as she studied the array of items. A tin cup. A silver brooch with gilded gold filigree. A cotton panel that looked like a remnant of a lightweight shawl or some other piece of clothing. Her eye snagged on an open letter, the ink faded but legible. "Can I see that?" she asked.

Esther's expression clouded. "No, no, dear. Things like that are susceptible to the elements of time, you know. We don't allow them to be handled."

She understood. She did, but this had something to do with her great-great-great-grandfather. She bent closer, peering through the glass to read. The writing slanted heavily to the right, the lines straight, the letters mashed together, time erasing some of the letters, the language old and hard to understand. She read slowly, trying to make out the words.

Paddy me lad,

'Tis me greatest hope dat you arrived safely in america and you have de good book in 'and. If you wahnder how I know, you need only look to de sky . . . to de swallows—dat did come wit' ya on yer voyage. Dey are harbengers o' de troehth. Me keepers. Dey'll stay wit you and all who come 'ence.

While I do mooehrn all you have taken frahm me, laddie, you saved me. Naht yooehr intention, I reckahn, boeht 'tis de truhth fahr how cooehld I be convected wit' naht a shred o' proof? No cuhrses ahr cures. Ahnly juhgs o' wheskey and de wahven blankets fell me walls, and pegs roam de couehntry-side. Nahne o' dese are true—staments o' dat fahr whech I was accused.

Paddy, me lad, you ded save me. Dis is de light you brooehght me. Siobhan is wit cheld. I fear a peshahgue because you left her. I am believin' you ded naht know dis when you went, boeht Paddy, I 'ave -kried. I 'ave seen dat she is Pandahra herself, yooehr seed de bohx dat wance ahpened'll naht be closed again, and so I moehst protect what is mine. You ohpened de door when you left. Dis is de dark. Look fahr de swallow wit de red feathers . . . de first speirbhean. De first keeper. Throoehgh her, o ruadhain'll shine de light again.

It was signed simply, *Mam*.

A chill crept over her skin, leaving Rowan cold. "It's from Biddy to Paddy?" she said, wanting confirmation but not needing it. Her mind exploded with questions. "Who's Siobhan?" she asked, blurting out the first one she could grab hold of.

Esther nodded. "This letter is a hundred and thirty-two years old. Siobhan, we know, was in Ireland. But there is no way to know who she was."

Rowan thought about the implications of Biddy's words and what Everly had said about Paddy's other bloodline. "Everly said Paddy was married and left his pregnant wife behind. That must be Siobhan?"

"It's possible," Esther said.

Macy tapped her finger on the glass. "Oh, yes. Quite possible."

"What do you think she means that he saved her? That Paddy saved his mother?"

The two elderly women shared another laden look. Macy finally answered. "Your great-great-great—"

"—great—" Esther threw in.

"Four greats—grandmother. People in Ireland thought she was a witch."

"Everly mentioned something about that," Rowan said, omitting the part about it being true.

"Yes, well, those were different times. She was accused of using witchcraft—"

"The Witchcraft Act of 1586—"

"The what?" Rowan asked.

"A law against *witchcraft and sorcerie*," Macy said, invisible quotation marks around the words. "Accusing someone of witchcraft under that act, centuries later in the 1860s? Not typical, but fear drove people to do unconscionable things. Trying Biddy Early was one of them."

Rowan went back to the letter. *While I do mooehrn all you have taken frahm me, laddie, you saved me.* It had to be the book Everly told them about. "*You have de good book in 'and*?" She murmured aloud.

"It's the Bible, of course," Esther said.

Or not, but Rowan didn't say that. "Could there have been something in the . . . Bible . . . that might have *proved* to the courts that she was a witch?"

Esther looked at her, a deep frown on her face. "Only if you *believe* in witches."

Rowan forced a laugh. "Right, but it was never about actual witchcraft. Like you said, it was fear."

Macy looked like she was considering Rowan's question. Finally, she shook her head. "She wasn't really a witch, so nothing could have convicted her."

Tell that to the Salem witches who'd lost their lives, Rowan thought. But she nodded, brushing away what Esther and Macy considered to be an outlandish idea.

As Rowan walked back toward Swallow Hall, the letter stayed with her. The one thing she couldn't shake was the line when Biddy had told her son she'd *kried*. Had she meant cried? The misspelling bugged her, and the fact that she saw Siobhan as Pandora. At first, she thought Biddy's grief must have been all-consuming, but she realized something when she thought back to the next part of that sentence, and the lines following.

> *I 'ave -kried. I have seen dat she is Pandahra herself, yooehr seed de bohx dat wance ahpened'll naht be closed again, and so I moehst protect what is mine.*

I have seen. Was seeing the future something Biddy could do? She thought back to the next line of the letter.

> *You ohpened de door when you left. Dis is de dark. Look fahr de swallow wit de red feathers . . . de first speirbhean. De first keeper. Throoehgh 'er, o ruadhain'll shine de light again.*

The truth in that line hit her. Everly and Bridget. Rowan and her sisters. They all had Paddy's blood coursing through them, but they weren't dark. Everly had said it was because they also had Maeve's. She thought through the line again:

Look fahr de swallow wit de red feathers . . . de first speirbhean. de first keeper. Throoehgh her, o ruadhain'll shine de light again.

That had to be it. Biddy had sent Maeve! Her scalp sizzled where her streak of red hair grew. Maeve had been the red-breasted swallow.

Biddy Early had seen something about Siobhan and the future, and the darkness that loomed. And she had sent the swallow—Maeve—to be the light.

Chapter Sixteen

Rowan needed to clear her head. Not only about trying to find Everly but about Cillian Tully and the Early family. By the time she was back on the island, the clouds had slid into place in front of the sun, turning everything gray. They had threatened rain several times since Rowan, Saoirse, and Caraline had come to Bird Island. Now Rowan peered at the darkening sky. It looked like the clouds might finally follow through. She spotted rusty garden sheers halfway buried in the fallen leaves. She looked from them to the abundance of the winter creeper deepening its grip on the house.

With the rain coming, she needed to work fast, but taking care of the house with Everly's instructions would at least make her feel like she was doing *something*. She set the market basket aside and plucked the garden shears from their hiding place. She positioned the blades on either side of one of the branches of the winter creeper crisscrossing in front of the door, and snapped the shears shut. Again and again, she attacked the vine, clipping back the growth. It had doubled in size overnight, twining around the espalier tree, blocking the entrance to the house. If she didn't cut it back, it would take over the entire front of Swallow Hall.

She'd pruned enough of the vine to be able to get in and out the front door, but if she left it now she felt sure it would just grow back. Everly's words came back to her: *I wage war against the winter creeper. I leave the swallow's mud nests be. I follow the fireflies.*

She couldn't leave the job half done. She had to do in Everly's absence what her grandmother couldn't. She had to wage war too.

She attacked the overgrown vine with renewed energy, careful not to step on any of the frogs that had migrated to a puddle near the porch. Hazel rounded the corner of the house, seeing her first, then the frogs. She barked at them, chasing them away as Rowan worked. Branches piled on the ground around her, higher and higher and higher. Sweat beaded on her forehead as she worked, but the effort didn't distract her from the questions circling in her mind, spinning round and round like a tornado. She had to prioritize. She tucked the letter from Biddy to Paddy into the corner of her mind, focusing instead on the more pressing question of what had happened to Everly. Maybe it was time to call the authorities and report her missing.

By the time she was done pruning, the rain had come. It started lightly, but as she dealt with the piles of clippings, raking them to the north side of the house and leaving them on the edge of the woods, it turned into a downpour. She watched as the front door creaked open, almost like it was sucking in a deep breath now that the vines had been cleared. Hazel darted into the house to stay dry. The door closed after her.

Rowan was hungry, thirsty, and a bit lightheaded. And she was drenched. She headed back toward the house, the water in her sneakers squishing as she stepped into a shallow puddle. She lifted her foot and shook it to dislodge the little frog that had situated itself smack in the middle of the top of her shoe but it didn't budge. "Come on, little guy. You gotta go."

It moved, breathing, but didn't leave its place. Witches had familiars. She'd realized that's what Saoirse's swallows probably were. Surely hers weren't frogs. That was so much less appealing than a flock of birds gliding effortlessly through the air.

The rain stopped as suddenly as it had begun and two other frogs appeared by her feet. Then two more. "Is that it? Are you little demon spirits in frog bodies?" she said to them. She crouched, waving her hand to shoo them away, plucking the one from her shoe, and setting it on the other side of the puddle.

The water had grown eerily still. As smooth as glass. She saw her reflection in it, luminescent, as clearly as if she were looking into a mirror. Before her eyes, though, her likeness turned cloudy and then, slowly, an image began to form. Bridget.

Rowan blinked and shook her head. She opened her eyes, expecting to see her own face staring back at her. But it was her mother's still, just as she remembered her on that last day, a little clearer, but fuzzy around the edges. Bridget's mouth moved, but no sound came out. Rowan squeezed her eyes shut. Kept herself steady with the fingers of one hand perched on the ground next to her. Slowly, she opened her eyes again and gasped, because now the reflection in the water played like a grainy scene from a movie. Her mother was walking and a dark, looming figure came up behind her. They pushed her and held her down.

The shock of it made her lurch back. She scrambled onto all fours, crawling back to the puddle. The frog was there now, sitting smack in the middle. The image of Bridget was gone. Erased by the ripples radiating outward.

A wave of nausea rocked her. She took deep breaths until it passed, then stood, stopping to let the dizziness pass. Had she really seen that, or had she been hallucinating? Had the exertion of cutting back the winter creeper made her that woozy?

She backed away, telling herself it was her imagination. She wanted to pretend that whole thing hadn't happened, but as she approached the front door of Swallow Hall and it swung open for her, she knew that it had. She shivered, goosebumps coating her arms, her teeth chattering. She had seen someone push Bridget. Hold her head in the water.

In the foyer, she leaned against the wall trying to make sense of it all. It had always seemed strange that their mother had drowned. Something about it had never felt right. But was it really possible? Had someone *killed* Bridget?

* * *

Rowan tried not to think about what she'd seen in the puddle of water because she didn't know if it was real or not. She was worried about Everly. Exhausted. Hungry. Unsteady on her feet. Together these things could have made her imagine something that wasn't really there.

She showered and then went to find her sisters. Caraline stood at the stove in front of a soup pot, stirring its contents with a heavy wooden spoon. A witch with her cauldron, Rowan thought. "What are you making?"

"Potato soup. Erin's recipe. We have to eat," she said, then she raised one eyebrow at Rowan.

Rowan answered the unasked question by shaking her head. She hadn't discovered anything new, and they were no closer to finding Everly.

"Something heavy is on her mind," Warren commented.

Rowan jumped. She hadn't known he was still here, hadn't seen him sitting at the table, and hadn't tasted any of his emotions or heard Caraline's thoughts. Everything was murky. On the other side of the table were beautifully wrapped bundles of dried plants. Warren followed her gaze. He held up a cellophane packet filled with seeds so tiny they looked more like ash and dust than anything living. "These are orchid seeds. Caraline said your other sister has a green thumb." Then he pointed to the dried flowers. "And I didn't want to show up here empty-handed. These are for your grandmother. It's foxglove and valerian," he said. "I thought she might want to try them for her tinctures."

"You can meet her next time," Caraline said, catching Rowan's eye and nodding. There *would* be a next time. Everly would be back.

Warren tilted his head, looking from Caraline to Rowan. "She okay?"

Rowan waved the question away. "Yeah, of course."

His smile dimmed just a little. The house creaked. It wasn't loud, just a soft sound, like pressure shifting deep in the bones of the walls.

"Everly's going to really appreciate the thought," Caraline said, smiling.

That smile didn't reach her eyes, but Warren grinned big, unaware of the inner turmoil she was going through. "Ready soon?"

An alarm went off in Rowan's head. "Ready for what?"

"I'm trying to get her to go for a *walk*. There's room to breathe out at the old ash tree," Warren said, looking pointedly at Caraline.

Caraline's cheeks turned to a mottled pink, making Rowan wonder if "walk" was a euphemism for something else.

"A few more minutes," she told him. "Patience."

Rowan's gut hollowed in dismay. She wanted to tell her sisters about the letters under the floorboards and Biddy's letter to Paddy, but she wouldn't do that with a stranger in the house, no matter how smitten with him Caraline was, and she couldn't tell them if Caraline was out on a walk.

For the moment, she was stuck holding what she'd found close to her chest.

In the apothecary, Saoirse was deep into the creation of a topical cream, another distraction for her, just like attacking the winter creeper had been for Rowan. "Anything?" Saoirse asked.

"Not really. What are you making?"

"It's for Mr. Floyd. I'm using *Althaea officinalis*—" When Rowan stared at her blankly, she clarified. "Marsh mallow. It's a flower. Usually, I use a powder from the mallow root, but the leaves and flowers help with irritation and inflammation."

"Marsh mallow . . . like marshmallows?"

"Yes . . . but no. The plant *was* used to make them but not anymore. Now they're just gelatin. Originally the mallow root was the thickening agent. What I'm doing is making a cream with it for Mr. Floyd to put on his scars."

"Does it grow around here?" Rowan asked, marveling at Saoirse's knowledge.

Saoirse smiled at the collection of flowers scattered on her worktable. "It does if I need it to."

Of course, because that was part of Saoirse's magic. She could conjure up whatever she needed, whenever she needed it.

Rowan left Saoirse, retracing her steps back through the kitchen. Caraline and Warren were gone, out for their walk, Rowan guessed. She didn't move for a long time, just stood in the open space of the kitchen breathing in the dill and lemon from the soup, and catching a hint of something different. Something she couldn't identify.

The house was still. Almost too still.

Her gaze pulled to the wax-wrapped bundles still on the table and the little cellophane pouch. She picked them up, putting the dried leaves and blossoms to her nose and breathing in. They were neat and perfectly preserved, but the scent turned her stomach. Unceremoniously, she dropped it all into the waste bin.

Chapter Seventeen

Outside, the swallows had grown restless. She could hear their scattered song, hear some of them nesting, and the flapping wings of others. Dark clouds loomed and like Rowan, like the house, they were out of sorts.

Caraline was back, along with Warren. She brushed her hair back—as dark and luminescent as the black obsidian pendant Rowan wore. The flecks of gold in her eyes sparkled with energy. She rolled her hand, gesturing that Rowan should go ahead and say what she needed to say. Rowan shook her head. "The three of us." Rowan leaned in and hissed in her sister's ear. "*Without Warren.*"

Caraline looked conflicted. She wanted him to stay, but did she? Rowan could see the emotions warring on her face. "He shouldn't have to lea—" Caraline started, but she stopped when Rowan squeezed her hand and she registered the tense expression on her face. "Okay," she said, resigned.

It was dusk by the time Warren finally sauntered across the footbridge. Once he was out of sight, Rowan sat with her sisters in a circle on the floor of the gathering room, legs crisscrossed, knees touching. Hazel curled up, her body pressed against Rowan's back. Outside, the wind kicked up, blowing the blanket of leaves on the ground into frenzied cyclones.

Caraline's eyes were wide as she stared out the window. "It's going to storm. He'll be caught in it."

"He'll be fine," Saoirse said.

Caraline nodded. From her forlorn expression, you'd have thought they'd been together forever and couldn't stand a single minute apart. She shook it off but a visible quaver ran through her body.

The sky turned dark and rain started again, tapping on the skylights, lightly at first, then with sharp pings. Something crackled, loud and buzzing. A second later they were pitched into utter darkness. Before Rowan could even formulate the thought that she should light some of the candles scattered around, they flickered to life, one by one, the flames casting shadows on the uneven walls of the room.

"I found something," Rowan started, telling them about the letters.

She kept her voice low, though the storm outside had begun to rattle the windows again. "They were under the floorboards, hidden away."

Saoirse leaned in, her brow furrowed. "Letters from who?"

"From someone signed S, to Bridget," Rowan said.

"So Bridget hid them?"

"I think so," Rowan said, "except for the last one. It was written after she left the island. They used to hide them in a hollow in a specific tree. I think maybe Everly found that one and added it to the others."

Caraline straightened, arms folding tight across her chest. "Why would Bridget hide them?"

Rowan had given this some thought. "They weren't exactly love letters, but they were letters from someone who'd loved her. Those couldn't have been easily thrown away."

Saoirse glanced toward the window, silent, where lightning painted the woods in stark white light, and Caraline picked at a cuticle.

"I saw something else," Rowan said, then she told them about the vision in the puddle. "I'm not sure what it means yet. But if what I saw was real . . . Bridget didn't just trip and hit her head. She didn't accidentally drown."

Caraline's eyes widened, disbelief etched across her face. "No way."

"I saw someone push her . . . then hold her head under the water."

"You think she was killed," Saoirse said quietly, her voice barely carrying.

Caraline shot to her feet and started pacing, twisting her hands together. "Why?"

Rowan exhaled, her chest tight with the weight of it. "I've been thinking about that. The note on the back of the photo, Bridget left that before she . . ." Her voice faltered. "Before she died. She *wanted* us here."

"Then why would someone kill her?" Caraline asked, frowning.

Rowan's gaze drifted toward the crooked staircase as the house groaned softly, the sound rippling through the walls like an echo of memory. "Because she was supposed to be the next Keeper," Rowan said. "But not just any Keeper. Everly said she was Silverborn. The house listened to her—bent for her—in ways it didn't for anyone else."

Saoirse's brow creased. "If she was meant to protect the house, then why did she leave?"

Rowan shook her head slowly, the pieces shifting uneasily in her mind. "Think about it. When we were teenagers, our magic was a mess. It was unpredictable. Hers probably was too. Everly couldn't help her—not really. She's not Silverborn. Bridget must've felt it unraveling. Maybe that's part of why she left."

"But you think this guy—Cillian—could be our father? That she left with him, so she left for love," Caraline said.

"Maybe." Rowan's voice dipped, uncertainty drawing out the word. "But what if it wasn't *just* about him? What if staying made everything worse? If the house was reacting to her fear, her lack of control, and her emotions, maybe she thought leaving was the only option."

She glanced toward the walls, the crooked staircase. "Everly said things unraveled after Bridget left, but maybe . . . maybe they were already cracking."

The floor creaked beneath them, faint and uneven, like it was remembering.

Saoirse's gaze darkened, her arms crossing as the idea settled. "And if Paddy's descendants were already out there . . . looking for the book . . ."

Caraline shook her head, slicing the air with her hands. "No, if Bridget was Silverborn, her leaving made the house vulnerable. She would have known that! She wouldn't have risked it."

Rowan's pulse quickened. "Unless leaving wasn't about protecting the house. Maybe she thought she was buying time."

Saoirse's eyes narrowed, still watching the window. "But Everly never said anyone tried to get in."

Rowan gestured to the room, to the uneven walls, to the floorboards that groaned underfoot. "No, but look around. The house is falling apart. Everly didn't have enough control. What if that wasn't Swallow Hall just grieving? What if it was a reaction to them trying to . . . I don't know . . . *infiltrate.* Maybe Everly never realized it?"

Caraline's expression tightened. "The book's still hidden. Only a Silverborn—"

"—could take possession it," Rowan finished, her voice low.

"Right," Rowan said. "Biddy would never release it to anyone else."

Saoirse nodded slowly. "So Bridget thought leaving would protect it. No Silverborn, no access to the book."

"But then . . ." Caraline hesitated, shaking her head again. "Why would they kill her? They needed her."

Rowan's chest tightened. *One of you is Silverborn.* Everly's words echoed in her mind, each syllable sharp as glass. A chill prickled over her skin, the realization threading through her. "Bridget knew how to fight," Rowan said quietly. "She wasn't here, but she was still the Keeper. Still Silverborn. She wasn't going to let them drag her back and force her to help them."

She exhaled, the final piece falling into place. "One of *us* is Silverborn." Her pulse kicked up. "What if they suspected that? What if they killed her because they thought that would bring us back here? That us being here would open the gate for them?"

Caraline's frown deepened. "But why would Bridget *tell* us to come back? She had to know it would put us in danger."

Rowan's jaw clenched. "Because we were only meant to find the photo if something bad happened to her." She looked between her sisters, the truth pressing against her ribs. "The three of us. The triptych. Maybe we were always meant to come back. Meant to finish what she couldn't."

Overhead, the wooden beams groaned, the walls settling like they were listening in. "They couldn't let her come back. Couldn't risk her passing down what she knew to us, or waking the house properly." She looked through the shimmering glass panes of the old windows at the vines creeping along the brick. "Bridget was always a threat to them, even when she wasn't on this island."

The house groaned softly overhead, the sound threading through the beams like a warning. Saoirse's expression twisted, her eyes shining with realization. "And now Everly's gone and we're here . . . completely untrained, yet one of us is Silverborn. Exactly how they want us."

Rowan nodded, the truth lodging in her gut like a stone. "The house is vulnerable. Whoever it is, they've been waiting for exactly this moment." She paused, steadying her voice. "We can try to do what Everly did—"

"Like be the Keeper?" Caraline interrupted, one brow arched, skepticism sharp in her voice.

Rowan hesitated, because the word felt too heavy on her tongue.

"There might be more to it than just hacking down the winter creeper and talking in a soothing voice," Saoirse said, her arms crossed tight over her chest.

She was right. They didn't really know what it meant to be Keeper. It wasn't a title passed like a crown. It was legacy, magic, responsibility tangled with secrets Bridget had never shared with them and Everly hadn't explained.

A whisper of cold drifted through the room again, curling around Rowan's ankles, brushing along her skin. They might not understand the full weight of the role. But ready or not, it was already waiting for them.

Silence settled between them. Instead of words, the crackle of wind and rain filled the space.

Then Caraline stepped closer. "Show us the letters."

"They're upstairs," Rowan said.

Caraline headed toward the stairs. She paused, turning when neither of them followed.

Saoirse pointed.

"Oh God, what now?" Caraline said, slinking back.

Rowan's gaze followed Saoirse's outstretched arm to one of the windows. It was large and upside-down and overlooked the edge of the beach and the woods. Had it grown bigger since Rowan last noticed it? Her breath caught. A beam of moonlight broke through the cloud cover, and through the wispy fog, a shadow moved.

"Someone's definitely here," Caraline whispered with a hiss.

"Warren?" Rowan said. But no, he had no reason to come back. In a split second, she was on her feet and sprinting through the house to the kitchen door, Hazel on her heels yapping. She could hear the beat of Saoirse's boots and the light thud of Caraline in her Keds behind her.

The letters forgotten, she flew down the steps and into the misty rain, onto the spongy earth. Her arms windmilled as she lost purchase on the ground. Her knees started to buckle, but she righted herself and ran down the path, stopping when she got to the clearing where the shadow had been. Saoirse and Caraline skidded to a stop next to her, both doubled over catching their breath.

Caraline spun around, eyes wide. "Are they gone?"

"Everly?" she called, then louder. "Everly!"

She listened for the crunch of leaves to give her a direction to follow, but it was hauntingly, eerily silent. Above, the dark shapes of the birds circled frenetically. The song of the red-breasted swallow broke the silence. Rowan followed its trajectory as it swooped low. Her gaze landed on the bubbling earth. From above, the moon shone brightly, shooting a spotlight down on a gurgling puddle above the moon circle and the still high tide. She gasped. Pressed her hand to her mouth. Beside her, Caraline caught her breath. Only Saoirse didn't react. She lifted her arm and flicked her wrist. In an instant, the swallows arced low and circled her. Her voice dropped low and took on an ominous tone. "By the pricking of my thumbs," she murmured, "something wicked this way comes."

They watched as the swallows slipped into formation and disappeared. Finally, Rowan brought her attention back to the area just outside of the moon circle where water pooled and bubbled like a pot of boiling water. As they stared, the puddling water slowly seeped into the ground, absorbed by the earth. One swallow dipped low before rejoining the others.

Behind them, the birds erupted into a cacophony, cutting through the quiet of the night. They turned to see the house ablaze with light, every fixture lit. Every window—straight, crooked, or upside-down—glowed. The eaves creaked and the swallows squawked as a mud nest hurtled toward the bay.

Rowan grabbed for Saoirse's hand, forgetting for a moment the discomfort Saoirse would feel. When their fingers touched, Saoirse lurched back, eyes flashing, darting from window to window of the glowing house.

Rowan dropped her hand to her side, watching Saoirse, worried about how distressed she looked. Then she lifted her gaze to the house. What was happening?

Caraline stared. "What the hell?"

The earth gurgled again, loud and unsettled. Rowan looked back to the moon circle and froze. The taste of dirt on her tongue turned putrid and vile and evil. Before her eyes, the earth disappeared, forming a sinkhole before rising up again and belching.

An electric charge buzzed along Rowan's hairline. She pressed her fingers against the strip of crimson hair, trying to tamp down the feeling of a breaker short-circuiting. A drizzle started again, its fine mist coating every inch of her.

Suddenly, the earth disgorged a flat piece of stone. Caraline inched forward, crouching down, her white sneakers now dark with mud. "It looks like a grave marker," she said.

Saoirse bent down next to her and brushed away a layer of muck clinging to the stone. Letters had been etched into the surface, now worn almost to nothing. Saoirse traced them with one finger.

Rowan's breath hitched. The taste of mud filled her mouth again, wet and bitter. The stone read: *Patrick Ea—* The rest of the name smoothed away with time.

This was the gravesite of Patrick Early.

As the wind chased them all the way back to Swallow Hall, questions pressed into Rowan's mind: Why now? Why had the island finally spit him up, like a truth it could no longer stomach?

Rowan's muddy boots scraped softly over the floorboards as she stepped inside. They all peeled off their muddy shoes and socks, leaving them by the door, cleaning themselves up as best they could. Around them, the house creaked, and she began to understand. The island had been holding Patrick Early down, swallowing him whole for as long as it could. But the earth doesn't keep what it wants to forget forever.

The balance had cracked. Everly was gone. The house was faltering without her, and now, with an interloper from Paddy's other bloodline bringing darkness, everything was unraveling again. They weren't strong enough. They didn't understand their magic, or what the house needed, and without Everly, Rowan feared it would all spiral beyond their control.

And the island—the land itself—had finally spit Patrick Early back to the surface, like a splinter it had finally worked out of its skin. Rowan's gut twisted. She was sure his grave rising was a warning. The island was trying to purge him, but the poison he'd brought was still here, buried far deeper than his bones.

And now, someone else was here. Someone who wanted Everly gone. Someone who had waited for the island to falter and for a new Silverborn to rise.

Chapter Eighteen

Exhaustion had settled into the sisters, but none could sleep. Saoirse retreated to her apothecary and Caraline to the kitchen. Rowan was restless. She could feel the frayed thread of the Keepers who'd come before stretched thin. The house wasn't just waiting for them to pick up where their ancestors left off. It *needed* them to. They had to set things right.

She exhaled, her hands curling into fists at her sides. Ready or not, it was up to them to quell the chaos until Everly returned. But what if Everly never came back? How could any of them take over Everly's role when they didn't even know what that meant? What else was there to being the Keeper of Swallow Hall? Everly had lain her hands on the undulating wallpaper to calm the house. Rowan had done the same to the winter creeper once with her words. *Irish* words. Now she walked to the wall and pressed her palm against it. Nothing happened. There was no sizzling sensation shooting from her flesh to the house. No subtle vibrations shot up her arm. No zings or jolts flooded her. *There was no connection.*

At this rate the house would sink. And whatever it meant to be a Sky Girl would be swallowed up by the Chesapeake Bay right along with it.

She couldn't sit still for another minute. She stared out one of the gathering room's window into the inky darkness toward the place where the grave marker surfaced, then paced as she fought against the chill spreading through her body.

After she made one pass around the room, three candles sparked to life. After the second pass, flames crackled in the fireplace sending warmth into the room. When she'd made a third pass, the study door released a long, deliberate sigh as it swung open. Rowan's heart slid up to her throat. She knew by now that the door opening meant Swallow Hall wanted to show her something. She also knew from experience that if she didn't go of her own volition, some invisible force in the house would push her there. Resistance was futile. She strode to the doorway and peered inside. Pixelated squares flickered in and out along the far wall, slowly forming the clerestory windows. Moonlight that didn't shine brightly outside seeped into the room giving Rowan enough light to see by. The shelves looked just as crooked as they had the day before. The secretary was in place. Everything was the same. Except . . . her gaze fell on the armchair and the little table next to it.

A book lay there.

A book that hadn't been there before.

The book?

Each beat of Rowan's heart sent a reverberation through her body that alighted her nerves and tightened her chest. She might not have Everly's connection to the house, but Swallow Hall *was* communicating with her. Had it just given her what it had kept hidden all these decades?

She clutched the two sides of her shawl with one hand as her feet moved slowly, taking her across the room. She reached to pick up the book, but it didn't move. It was as if its back cover was glued to the table.

The old oil lamp that had lain on one of the shelves now also sat on the side table. Before her eyes, it flickered to life, sending an incandescent glow radiating from its center. She got the picture. She had to stay here. "Fine," she said, knowing she couldn't fight it. Still, she exhaled a shaky breath as she sat down. She'd accepted the level of magic coursing through Swallow Hall, but it still sucked the breath from her sometimes. She tucked her legs under her, then reached for the book again. This time it lifted with ease, no oppositional force holding it down. The second she took hold of it, her hands tingled, the feeling creeping up her arms, centimeter by centimeter.

The book was two inches thick with a hard cover, the corners frayed. It was nondescript, and yet she knew its importance. She turned it around so she could see the title and drew in a sharp breath.

The Keeper's Journal

It was not Biddy Early's grimoire or book of shadows, as she'd described it in the letter to Paddy. Of course. That would have been too easy.

The letters shimmered for a moment, then the glow faded and became black. Her mouth filled with the taste of old paper, musty and damp. Without warning, it released three words, speaking them into her mind: *Scryer, Synesthesia, and Psychometry.* She leapt up, dropping the book. It was one thing for her and Caraline and Saoirse to play the whisper game, but this was different. These words had come from the energy of the book and it unsettled her.

She shook her hands out, took a breath, and sat down again. This time, when she picked up the book, she expected the jolt that coursed through her and the words, formed through its energy.

It wasn't as strong this time, merely an echo of what it had been moments before. *That* she could handle. She opened the book to the first page. The writing was hard to decipher. It was masculine with unusual spellings and Irish words interspersed.

Similar to the letter Biddy had written to Paddy. She had to concentrate, working through what each word meant, piecing together the meaning. It had to do with sailing from Ireland. Building the house. Something stolen. Rowan couldn't decipher any more from the writing, but she understood enough to know it was Paddy's story.

She turned to the next page and the next, each written by the same hand. With each line, each piece of handwriting became more erratic until it looked more like jagged scribbles scrawled haphazardly across the page. With the blotches of ink spattered on the paper, feelings of betrayal and anger flooded her, her mouth ripe with Paddy's rancor. She smacked her tongue against the roof of her mouth. This was new. She'd never looked at or held another person's journal before. The letters she'd found in the hole in the stairs were the closest thing. They had also filled her with a haunting sense of betrayal, but the anger from those was different. Less volatile. Less . . . destructive. More emotionally personal.

She quickly flipped through until she came to a break. The next page was written by someone new. The writing was neater, more controlled, and had a heavy slant to the right. It was still difficult to read, the letters made in what looked like continuous strokes as if the pen never left the page. A signature ended each section. Maeve. Paddy had built the house and started this journal, but Maeve, Rowan's great-great-great-grandmother, she'd been the first true Keeper, sent by Biddy. The awful taste and the uneasiness that had filled her when she read Paddy's words shifted to puzzlement and frustration. These were Maeve's emotions.

She fanned the pages looking for something more legible. The second half of the book was blank so she turned to the last page that had writing on it. A feeling of familiarity wafted through her. She'd seen the half cursive, half printing of notes, the notebook Saoirse had found with directions on making ginger reishi tea, scented soaps, and other tinctures, and the client list kept in the delivery basket.

But it wasn't only the handwriting that confirmed who had written these pages. It was the combination of sweet, tart, and tang that settled on Rowan's tongue. It was the taste of blackberries. The last entries in the Keeper's Journal were written by Everly.

Was this experience meant to show Rowan the journal itself, or was it about reading the words and feeling what the Keeper who'd written them had experienced? She closed her eyes and ran her fingertips over the ink on the open pages. The pads of her fingers tingled, sending a shock up her arms and into her core. A deep sorrow permeated her. Not her own, but Everly's. "Because of Bridget?"

The pages rustled under her touch. "We brought your daughter back to you, Everly, to rest in peace here," Rowan said aloud. The sweetness of blackberries magnified. She spoke as if her grandmother was right here in the room with her and could hear her words.

The competing tastes in her mouth subsided and the sense of sorrow faded. Rowan exhaled her surprise. She was communicating with the book just as she had with the house. She flipped through the pages until she found the beginning of Everly's section, adjusted the lamp, and started to read.

I found this journal today. I guess that means I'm the new Keeper. It must, since my mother is gone. My grandmother is gone. It's just me now. I'm not Silverborn, but I'll do my best . . .

An instant feeling of the loneliness Everly must have felt sliced through Rowan, stinging like a cut exposed to alcohol. She read between the lines. Everly had found this book when there was no one else to take over as the Keeper of Swallow Hall. Now Rowan and her sisters were in the same boat. The book had appeared to Rowan. Did that mean—?

"No!" She slammed the book shut and bolted out of the chair. Her eyes welled. She bit her lip to stop her chin from quivering. "Nooo." The word stretched into a sob. "She's not gone. She's not gone. She. Is. Not. Gone. She has to come back." She swiped the back of her hands under her eyes, whisking away the hot tears. She shot lasers at the walls of the room as if they were the ears of the house and spoke through gritted teeth. "Everly is *not* gone and I'm *not* the Keeper. Do you hear me? She is. Not. Gone."

Chapter Nineteen

The rain continued, harsh and steady, like it wanted to make itself known. Rowan went to her attic room, bleary-eyed, but sleep escaped her. She returned to the gathering room and minutes later, Saoirse and Caroline were there too. They had gathered not because they had answers or even because they'd planned to, but because the house had gently nudged them there by doors creaking open, lanterns lighting on their own, and a quiet hush settling over the hallways like Swallow Hall was holding its breath.

Saoirse had brought a posy of flowers and her herbal journals.

Caraline had a tray with three mismatched teacups and a pot of brambleberry tea, just like Bridget had taught them to brew, along with a basket of hand pies still warm from the oven. The scent of rosemary and lemon balm trailed behind her as she moved.

Rowan had debated telling her sisters about the Keeper's Journal. It was physically impossible for her to take it out of the study, and she was the only one, so far, the house had allowed into the room. To her, that meant the book was a secret she wasn't yet meant to share.

But she had brought down the letters she'd found in the floorboards. Now she held them on her lap, lifting the first one. The paper gave a delicate sigh as she unfolded it, reading from it aloud.

"So this man, Cillian Tully . . . *he's* our father?" Caraline said. She stood suddenly, the chair scraping. She threw up her hands in frustration. "What are we supposed to do with that?"

All Rowan knew was that the time had come to listen to the past, before it became their future.

They didn't speak for a while, instead just moving in their own orbits, quietly passing each other things—tea, a blanket, a hand pie, a knowing look. The rain ticked gently against the windows. The swallows tittered outside before settling in their nests.

Finally, Caraline broke the silence. "So the house is listening to us, right now," she said, glancing around as if she were looking for a pair of ears to explain how that could possibly be.

"To every word," Rowan said, knowing it was true.

Caraline looked at Saoirse, then Rowan. "Can you hear it? Is it supposed to be like a voice? Because I don't hear anything."

Saoirse shook her head. "Not a voice. Not exactly. It's more like . . . a feeling. A change in the air, like when someone walks into a room and you *feel* it. You just *know* they're there before they speak."

Rowan nodded slowly, pulling her shawl more tightly around her. "Sometimes it's a scent. Sometimes it's a breeze in a hallway with no windows open. Or the lights flickering only when you're thinking something you don't want to say out loud."

Caraline leaned back on her elbows, the lantern light casting a soft glow over her face. "So we're being haunted by a polite ghost that waits for the perfect dramatic pause."

A squeak behind one of the walls repeated over and over, sounding an awful lot like a chortle. And that made them all laugh—just a little. Just enough.

A long silence followed. For once, it didn't feel heavy or sad—just full.

Finally, Caraline broke it. "Do you think we'd be like this if we weren't triplets?"

Rowan knew just what she was talking about. They were tethered to one another. Knotted together almost like a . . . spell.

"I used to wish I was born first," Saoirse said, breaking into Rowan's thoughts. "Just by a second. Just enough to claim something. To know I came before anything else."

"What do you mean? You were born second," Rowan said. "By four minutes."

"Exactly," Saoirse said. "Caraline was first. You were last. I was just . . . in between."

Rowan blinked. "You thought that mattered?"

Saoirse shrugged a little, pulling the petals off a flower. "When we were younger, it did."

Caraline leaned forward, pressed an open palm to her chest. "I hated being first. So much pressure. I swear Bridget looked at me like I was supposed to know better. Be the example."

Rowan held her teacup to her lips. "She knew it was hard for you. She just wanted you to try."

Caraline made a face and threw a blanket over her head in protest, like she had when she was a kid.

Saoirse turned to Rowan, her voice gentle but sure. "What about you?"

Rowan blinked. "What about me?"

"You were always the one who remembered things—packing the bags, checking the locks, keeping track of everything we forgot. You made us feel safe, but . . . I think you lost yourself sometimes."

Rowan set her cup down slowly, the soft clink louder than it should have been. "I don't think that's true," she said, feeling her defenses come up.

"It is, Row," Saoirse said, her tone quiet, steady. "But now . . . here? It's different." She glanced around the room, her gaze drifting to the beams above them, to the way the shadows pooled in the corners like memories waiting to surface. "I feel like you're hearing the echoes of the house. Things the rest of us can't. Like it's speaking to you in ways only you can understand."

Rowan opened her mouth to respond, but nothing came out. Because Saoirse was right. She *had* heard things. Felt them. The whispered name carried on the wind. The warmth that pulsed beneath her fingertips when she touched the attic wall. The scent of blueberries that had no source, but reminded her of something—or someone—long gone.

Saoirse leaned in, her voice low. "Maybe you've always been the one holding the memories, Rowan. Not just ours, but the ones that have been waiting in this house for years. Maybe it's not about protecting us anymore. Maybe it's about listening."

Rowan's throat tightened. Everly understood the house. So had Bridget. But of the three sisters, did she want to be the one the house was whispering to?

Did she have a choice?

The silence that followed felt heavier than any argument. Rowan looked away, but the questions lingered, subtle and refusing to fade.

The house creaked gently, wood shifting beneath the weight of time, as if it too were waiting. Listening. Holding its breath.

Rowan swallowed hard. Lately, it *had* felt like the house was filled with echoes—memories trapped in the walls, voices that surfaced only for her. She was searching for her mother here. For the echo of Bridget's presence.

Caraline pulled the blanket off her head and rested her chin on her knees, her voice quiet but sure. "We all lost Bridget. But I think you lost her in a different way."

Rowan blinked hard, willing the tears not to fall. She hadn't said it out loud, not to them, not even to herself, but she *did* feel that . . . like she *had* lost her differently. They'd shared an inexplicable unspoken bond. Maybe it had to do with Swallow Hall.

"But we all loved her. And we have each other," Caraline said gently. "We'll do this with you, Row. We'll find the truth."

Rowan nodded slowly, her throat tight. The house might be whispering, but she didn't have to face it alone.

Saoirse nodded. "By bloom."

"By flame," Caraline said.

They swung their gazes to Rowan. It started as a childhood promise they shared only with each other. But as they grew—and the magic in them deepened—it became something more. A vow. A bond. A spell spoken not with power but with love.

Now, in the gathering room of Swallow Hall, Rowan whispered her part of the chant, feeling the words settle into her bones like truth. "By moonlight."

Together, they spoke the last line. "We are one."

Just as they finished speaking, the rain ticked harder against the windows, wind curling around the house like it wanted in. The chandelier flickered once. The house felt them. Felt their bond. It always did.

And then, the gathering room wall began to shift. Not dramatically. Just a soft pulling back of the ivy wallpaper, the sound of tearing cutting through the rain. Rowan stood. Walked to the wall. She peeled back pieces of the torn paper. Underneath was what looked like an old hand-painted mural.

Saoirse and Caraline were by her side in an instant, staring at it. It was faded with time, but the images were clear: three women, back to back, surrounded by vines and swallows. One held an open book. One held a wooden bowl. One held a lantern, its flame flickering.

Caraline reached out first. "Is that . . . us?"

"Maybe?" Rowan said quietly, but she didn't understand *how* it could be them when the painting looked very old.

Saoirse traced the edges of the twining vines. "Is the house showing us who we are or what we can become?"

Rowan nodded slowly. "Or what it remembers."

A slice of moonlight broke through the dark clouds, slanting across the wall, illuminating the mural like it had been waiting for them all along.

Caraline tilted her head, studying the woman with the lantern. Her face was half in shadow with one arm raised, the flame inside lighting the path ahead. "She looks determined. like she'd walk straight into the dark if it meant protecting the others."

Saoirse glanced at the one with the bowl, surrounded by tiny painted herbs and roots winding up her arms. "And this one . . . she's the healer. The one who makes things whole again."

Rowan's gaze lingered on the woman with the book, its pages worn, her arm reaching up. Around her, the painted air rippled, and moonlight shone down like an echo in the dark.

"She holds the memories," she said softly.

Rowan looked at the mural again. At her sisters. She felt the house, humming quietly in her bones. Her fingertips brushed the surface of the wall, feeling the faded paint, the old magic woven into it. The silence around them pulsed. The house knew them. Had long ago known they were coming.

It hadn't been waiting in despair. It had been waiting in *preparation*.

Not just to be remembered.

To be *understood*.

To be *heard*.

Rowan turned to her sisters, her voice low. Reverent. "We're part of it. Whatever this place holds—whatever it's becoming—we're part of it."

Caraline swallowed, her usual contrariness gone, replaced with something respectful. Knowing. "We're written into it, aren't we?"

Saoirse nodded. "Did Bridget know that we're part of this place, even though we'd never been here? Does Everly?"

Behind them, the wallpaper gave a soft sigh, another edge curling free.

The sigh turned into a sound. Into some semblance of words. *Of course. Of course. Of course.*

Rowan's skin pricked. That was definite communication. She looked at her sisters, but neither one looked like they'd heard it.

Chapter Twenty

Somewhere deep inside Swallow Hall, a door clicked open.

"Did you hear that?" Caraline looked at Saoirse, then Rowan. They both nodded, the sound echoing softly in Rowan's mind.

The house had done something. It had turned the key in a lock that had been long forgotten. It was beckoning them.

The air shifted. The walls themselves seemed to hum again, not loudly but low and steady, like something new, just beneath the surface, had stirred awake.

Caraline stood. Trailed her fingers along the paneled wall near the dining room. "Is it just me, or is this wood . . . glowing?"

As Rowan joined her, one of the sconces flickered, pulsing in sync with the grain of the wall. Her breath caught. "It's reacting to us."

"Probably Saoirse," Caraline said, giving her a side-eye glance. "You've always been the spookiest one."

Saoirse rolled her eyes, but she moved forward and put her hand on the wall. Nothing changed. Then Rowan took a step closer and the glow sharpened.

All of them froze.

"Okay," Caraline said, half laughing. "So now Rowan's the spooky one."

Rowan crouched, running her hand just above the floorboards. "It's inviting us . . ."

"Inviting us to do what?" Saoirse asked, her eyes gleaming.

Rowan didn't know how she knew, but she did. Something readjusted itself inside her, like a closed door nudged open an inch.

The words came out before she had time to think. "To remember."

They didn't discuss what to do next—they simply moved. Drifted. It was as if the house had tugged loose a thread in each of them, unwinding the braid that held them together, and now it was gently reeling them in different directions.

Rowan wandered through the various corridors, touching the walls, opening doors, examining anything that looked unusual. Eventually, she ended up in the west corridor, fingers brushing the edge of a crooked frame. She paused before a tilted portrait she didn't remember seeing before. Behind it was a hollow in the wall. She reached in and pulled out a thick piece of parchment rolled up like a scroll. She untied the thin twine and let the paper unfurl. It was faded with age, layered with ink and ghosted pencil lines. It was a floorplan . . . of Swallow Hall. The original one Paddy had used? She traced the lines of the house as she knew it, then blinked, quickly dismissing that idea.

There was a staircase that didn't exist anymore.

Walls where rooms once were.

Paths deliberately severed.

Saoirse appeared at the end of the hallway, gripped something in one hand. "Look!" She held up a bundle of brittle muslin. "It was tucked in the corner of my closet," she said. "It's filled with yarrow, mugwort, and goldenrod. But Row, listen." She looked toward Rowan, talking briefly to the blank space over her shoulder before looking back at the object in her hand. "It's not old. I mean it is, but it's not. The herbs are too well preserved. I think the house kept them. But look. When I unwrapped it, I found this." She held open the muslin and held up a small rusted key with a crescent moon etched into its head. "And this." She palmed the key, then moved the herbs aside. Beneath the bundle, someone had drawn a crescent moon in wax with a swallow in midflight at the bottom point. At the top was a Celtic knot with a circle running through it. And inside the triquetra was an herb. Four arrows marked the cardinal directions, like a compass guarding its center.

"What is it?" Rowan asked.

"I think it's a sigil. A mark of Biddy's magic. The house. Her bloodline. All of it."

A shiver coiled around Rowan's spine. Had the bundle of herbs with the wax-drawn sigil inside belonged to Bridget? And why did the house guide Saoirse to find it?

Together they backtracked down the corridor to rejoin Caraline in the gathering room. She had four unlit candles lined up on the mantel and she stood facing them.

"This time," she said, holding her hand over one, "I ask, not tell."

She exhaled slowly. "I am the flame. Burn bright."

One wick flickered briefly before dying out.

"I am the flame. Burn bright," she repeated, more forcefully this time. The first candle flared to life, then the next, then the final two. It happened without her even touching them.

Rowan and Saoirse both stopped in their tracks. Caraline had never used magic like that before. None of them had. The flickering light cast dancing shadows on the wall, climbing to the ceiling. She turned to them. "Not bad for a first attempt," she said with a satisfied grin. "Well, third attempt, but who's counting? I'm liking this place more and more."

At that, a gust of wind materialized out of nowhere, snuffing out the flames in an instant.

Caraline frowned, not at the candles but at the walls of the house. "Hey. I said I'm liking you. Geez."

Just as quickly as the candles had gone out, the flames sputtered to life again. A creaking came from deep in the walls. Rowan smiled. She had come to associate that particular sound as laughter.

Saoirse showed Caraline the muslin bundle filled with herbs and the wax sigil drawn inside.

"It's like our family crest," Caraline said.

Rowan agreed. Every element seemed to represent something connected with the Earlys and their magic.

"What's that?" Saoirse asked, eyeing the rolled parchment in Rowan's hand.

She knelt on the floor and spread the paper flat. "I think it's a floorplan of Swallow Hall."

Caraline and Saoirse crouched next to her. "Are you sure? It looks a lot bigger on paper," Caraline said.

Rowan nodded. "That's what I thought too."

Saoirse sat back on her heels, adjusting her glasses. "Like, enchanted bigger?"

"Maybe?" Rowan shrugged uncertainly.

"Probably," Caraline said dryly. "This house uses magic for everything. Why would more secret spaces hidden away be any different?"

"True," Rowan said. "Look. It's like whole sections have been sealed off."

Saoirse leaned over her shoulder. "Strange."

The storm had finally stopped, only intermittent raindrops dripping from the eaves.

Rowan studied the floorplan. "I think we're supposed to explore."

"What about Everly? And Bridget, and all the rest of it?" Caraline said.

Rowan felt her heart beat with anxiety of all that was unfinished, but the house was leading them somewhere. If it didn't want them to search, it would have locked doors rather than open them. It would have guided them somewhere else. No, she knew they had to find what it wanted to show them. Her fingertips traced the faded inked lines on the parchment. Before her eyes, some of the markings grew bolder. Easier to see. "We have to follow the map."

They walked down one corridor, Caraline holding a lantern, its flame casting flickering light in front of them. They turned into another hallway that Rowan could have sworn wasn't there the day before. The plan led them to the west wing again, past the hollowed-out wall where she'd found the floorplan. They passed a dusty linen closet and a narrow hallway with stairs leading up. They stopped when the corridor ended at a blank stretch of wall covered in wide lengths of a floral wallpaper.

"Classic. A hallway that goes nowhere, and there's no door."

"Not anymore," Rowan replied. She tapped the map. "But look. There *was* a staircase here. Going down."

Saoirse stepped forward and pressed her palm against the wall.

Nothing.

Rowan did the same, and this time, beneath her touch, the wall shivered. Then pulsed.

Caraline stepped back.

"Look." Saoirse pointed to the wall where Rowan's palm still lay. To one side, the wallpaper peeled like it was exhaling.

The baseboards groaned softly.

And then, bit by bit, the outline of something began to materialize. Rowan stepped back, staring. It was an archway.

"And here we go again," Caraline snorted. "A door with no handle."

The wall undulated again and as if in response, right where a handle should be, a mark appeared.

The light from the lantern made shadows dance on the blank wall. One took shape, looking like . . . "Oh!" Rowan remembered what Saoirse had found. "The key!"

Saoirse and Caraline both jumped at the volume of Rowan's voice in the quiet house, but Saoirse reached into her pocket and handed Rowan the little rusted key with a crescent etched into its head. They probably didn't need it—the house could have just let them in—but it was a nice touch, giving them some agency in what they chose to see.

Rowan closed her fingers around it and touched the wall again. She fitted the key into the keyhole and turned. Instantly, the outline became an actual door, which swung inward. The air that drifted out was cool and dry, as if untouched by time. How long had it been sealed up, and what was inside?

The sisters stood side by side, staring at the dark space beyond the arch. Rowan could just make out a narrow staircase spiraling downward. It looked to be carved from rough, mottled stone. This was the place the house had decided they needed to see.

Rowan's pulse thudded in her throat. She looked at her sisters, each of them lit by the soft gold of Caraline's lantern, the magic, the moment.

Rowan glanced sideways at them. "Ready?"

Saoirse shook her head. "Not really, but we have to stay together."

"Damn straight we do." Caraline held up the lantern. It cast an eerie glow on the curved wall beyond the archway. "Let's go see what else this house is hiding."

Together, the three of them stepped into the dark.

Chapter Twenty-One

Caraline handed the lantern to Rowan, who led the way down the spiraling stone stairs, leading her sisters into a cool, unknown silence. Her socked feet were quiet on the old steps. Saoirse was next, with Caraline last. The three of them moved almost as one at a steady pace. They were quiet and reverent. The deeper they went, the more the air changed. It wasn't stale or damp, both things she'd expected from a dungeon. It was fresh. Clean. It seemed to Rowan that maybe it had been waiting for them.

At the bottom, they reached another door, this one made of oak and grayed with age. Carved into the wood were vines and roots, and . . . Rowan drew in a sharp breath . . . the sigil Saoirse had discovered on the muslin bundle.

"Do you think Everly knows about this place?" Caraline asked.

"She's not Silverborn so . . . I think it was hidden to her."

They held each other's gazes for a beat as Rowan reached for the old brass handle. The door swung open, smooth and fluid, without a single creak.

The room beyond could have come straight from a story about King Arthur. It was round, the walls covered by something Rowan couldn't quite make out. There were no windows. No obvious source of light, yet they could see just enough to walk to the center of the room where a pedestal stood. It was waist-high and carved with the same vines as the door, the sigil in the center. Suspended above it, untouched by gravity, hovered a shallow silver bowl of water. A spiral circled the floor, beginning at the pedestal and rotating out and around.

Rowan reached forward toward the pedestal but drew back before touching it.

Saoirse's eyes swept the perimeter of the room. "Oh!" She exhaled. "They're tapestries."

Rowan and Caraline turned. The walls had been dark when they'd entered, but now they emitted a soft, pulsing glow. On them hung what looked to be four ancient, handwoven banners. Each was faded, but they looked completely intact. One was plain, devoid of design. The other three had symbols woven throughout: flowers, flames, moons.

Three symbols.

Three elements.

Three women.

Once again, Rowan felt as if the women depicted in the mural upstairs were the three of them. By bloom. By flame. By moonlight.

They walked slowly, taking in the details of each one.

Saoirse stopped and crouched beside a raised stone along the wall and brushed her hand across a circle of carvings. Rowan knew it meant something, she just didn't know what. Everly's voice came to her: *Another thing Bridget didn't teach you.*

Caraline folded her arms over her chest as if she was warding off the cold. It was all so overwhelming. Rowan felt it too. She walked back to the pedestal. The water in the bowl shimmered faintly. The entire room seemed to breathe—the heartbeat mirroring her own.

"Why did you lead us here?" Rowan spoke aloud, talking to the empty room that pulsed with energy. To all the women in Biddy's line who had come before. To the memories the house held.

She waited for the answer, knowing it would come.

"Look." Caraline pointed at the fourth tapestry. It had been a solid dark color with nothing on it, but now a long thread hung in the center, glimmering. They walked up to the tapestry. Rowan's fingers itched to pull the thread. "Should I?"

She mouthed the question, no sound coming out, but Saoirse answered her, the words carried through the air. "Do it."

"If you don't, I will," Caraline said.

Rowan exhaled a shaky breath. She grasped the end of it with her thumb and middle finger, then tugged. Instantly, the solid color of the cloth silently exploded, like glass shattering into dust, the particles spraying outward, vanishing into thin air.

Beneath, the tapestry still existed, but it was now a pale, dusty rose. Before their eyes, words materialized.

"Oh. My. God." Caraline folded her arms more tightly and took a step back. "Is that a . . . a . . ."

She trailed off, staring.

Rowan scanned the words once, then read them aloud:

When the Loom is stilled and the threads lie frayed,
they shall gather once more, as it was written:

One of Bloom, whose hands stir life from root and ash.
One of Flame, whose fire guards the way.
One of Moonlight, who bears the memory of the dark.

And one more still—
The Shadow-Tethered,

the Unseen Heir,
the one who walks with ruin close behind.

The House shall call them by names not yet spoken.
The Land shall brace them in stone and soil.
The Magic shall test what they hold—and what they hide.

Only in joining shall the Old Weave be renewed.
Only in truth shall the Binding hold.
But beware the fourth—
for if they supplant, the threads shall unravel again.

Behind them, from the center of the room came the trickling sound of water. They turned. The water in the bowl shimmered more brightly than before. A single droplet rose—hovered—then fell onto the spiral below.

It hissed softly, before lighting up, the spiral glowing. A whisper drifted through the room: *You are the thread restored.*

Caraline jumped. "Did something just speak?"

Saoirse blinked, pushing her glasses up. "And what does it mean?"

Silence filled the room, heavy and ominous. The three sisters stood shoulder to shoulder, and as the light from the quartz walls flickered, Rowan felt something click into place in her mind. "It's saying we're not here to *inherit* Biddy's legacy," she said. "We're here to *reclaim* it. Together."

Chapter Twenty-Two

Rowan slammed the door of her room shut. Hazel lifted her head and cracked open her eyes. She didn't appreciate being awakened in the dead of night. "Sorry, girl," Rowan said, running her hand down her back. Hazel laid her head down and settled back to sleep. If only it was that easy. Rowan dropped her shawl over the back of the chair and curled up under her covers, pulling the quilt to her chin. She squeezed her eyes shut. Counted sheep and bottles of beer and the crooked windows of Swallow Hall. Still, sleep wouldn't come.

The secret room the house had revealed and the message in the tapestry circled in her mind. The last lines played over and over in her head.

Was the truth their mother wanted them to find the same as the truth the house warned them about? And who was the unseen heir, the one who the tapestry mentioned walked with ruin close behind?

A tap on her window startled her from her thoughts. Hazel popped her head up.

Tap, tap, tap. Hazel's ears perked.

Tap, tap, tap. Hazel barked.

In a split second, the dog was up and charging to the window.

Tap, tap, tap.

Rowan's stomach roiled as she crept from her bed and pressed her back against the wall as she slid closer to the window. Not that that made any sense. She was high up in the house and her room was dark. Even if someone was out there, they wouldn't be able to see her.

Still. Another *tap, tap, tap.* She braced herself as she turned her head and peered out, jumping back when she came face to face with the dark beady eyes of a swallow pecking its beak against the pane of glass. She doubled over, hands on her knees, shooting out a ragged breath. "You scared me!" she hissed, but of course the bird couldn't hear her. It tapped again, insistent, over and over and over.

"Fine!" Rowan stood and moved to face the window, her heart back in place. The bird hovered, its wings flapping like arms in a pool treading water. It met her gaze and then turned and glided toward the barren tree line. A layer of fog had settled low over the island, blocking out the base of the trees. Only their branches, like skeletal fingers, reached into the sky. She watched as the bird landed on one. And then . . .

She blinked. Looked again and saw them all. The entire flight of swallows perched on branches, all of them facing in her direction, silhouetted in the moonlight. Her breath lodged in her throat.

The bird that had woken her took flight again, gliding to the window. Straight at her. "Stop!" Rowan shouted, her voice reverberating in the room. She jumped back, sure it was going to plow right through it. At the last second, it made a sharp turn, angling sideways, barely avoiding a collision with the glass. Rowan locked her gaze on it, following its trajectory.

Behind her, the door flew open, banging against the wall. "Row? What happened?" Saoirse's voice. "Are you okay?"

Rowan beckoned her sister over, never breaking her focus on the red-breasted swallow as it soared upward, circling the tree where the rest of the birds still perched. For a moment, she lost track of it. Searched the dark sky. She hissed. "Where'd it go?"

She heard Saoirse's shallow breath beside her as she registered the birds. With her peripheral vision, she saw her leaning close to the window. "There," Saoirse said, pointing above the trees.

The red-breasted swallow swooped down, arcing as it sped toward them. Before Saoirse could react, the bird made another hard turn, careening into a nosedive. Rowan wanted to grab hold of Saoirse's hand and squeeze. Instead, she gripped the window-sill. "What's it doing?"

"I don't know."

Too many times to count, Rowan had seen her sister flick her wrist and make the birds slip into formation. She could blink and they'd fly away. "Can you stop it?"

"It's trying to tell us something," Saoirse whispered.

Rowan lost sight of the swallow again as it dipped into the fog layer.

"There!" Saoirse pointed as it emerged from the mist like a phoenix rising from the ashes. Rowan stared, willing herself not to blink, staying completely focused on the bird's flight so she didn't lose it again. It made another circle above the trees, then plummeted toward the ground, once again disappearing into the fog. It emerged, but this time it flew in a broad circle. It let out a warble, followed by a blast of mechanical whirrs, repeating over and over and over. The call roused the flight from the tree where they'd been perching. The sky rumbled with the maelstrom of flapping wings as they stirred the air, creating a storm. And then, perfectly choreographed, they fell into a line, following the first bird where it flew in a circle above the fog layer near the moon circle and

Paddy Early's grave. Around and around, faster and faster. The force of their flapping wings created a funnel that cleared the mist.

Rowan's head felt fuzzy, like she was outside herself as she watched the circle grow bigger with each rotation they made. And then they were done. One by one, the birds flew off, the moon circle now clearly visible.

Rowan reached for Saoirse's hand. She wanted to feel her sister's warmth. To let it seep into her. Saoirse sensed Rowan's need and slid away. Rowan dropped her hand. They didn't speak as they watched cloudy tufts appear in the center of the clearing. The wisps began circling as the birds had and a shape formed.

Saoirse lay her palm against the glass. "What do you think it is?" she murmured.

They didn't have to wonder long. The form became more defined. It turned to face the window where they stood, one arm outstretched, beckoning to them. It looked like a person, but what could it really be, appearing out of thin air on a magical island?

Rowan and Saoirse launched into motion without talking, practically flying out of the attic room, a current in the house carrying them. Rowan shouted for Caraline. No answer. Saoirse cut away for a few seconds and threw open the door to Caraline's room. "She's not there," Saoirse announced.

After the tapestry room, Rowan and Saoirse had gone up to bed, lost in their own thoughts, but Caraline had gone to the kitchen. Rowan's insides seized and now the darkness of anxiety filled her mouth. She knew instinctively that Caraline wasn't in the kitchen anymore. Wasn't anywhere here in Swallow Hall. Had the hidden room and the message in the tapestry spooked her more than she'd let on? Had the island let her pass the footbridge? Was she out somewhere with Warren seeking comfort? It was better to think that than believe she'd disappeared like Everly had. She shoved that fear out of her mind.

Rowan and Saoirse plowed out the kitchen door. Raced down the path leading to the shoreline. They stumbled on the spongy earth, pushing through the fog. The closer they got, the more Rowan expected to taste something dark and ominous, but as they approached the clearing, it was expectation that filled her mouth. They broke through the mist and into the open space. Rowan was first, stopping short. Saoirse darted to the side, grabbing Rowan's arm to stop herself, letting go an instant later, as if she'd been burned. They stared. Because the apparition—and that's definitely what it was—tilted its head to one side. No, not *it*. Rowan detected a woman's form. The shape of a dress. And she clutched something bulky, holding it to her chest.

There were no facial features, nothing identifiable about the figure. Then the wisps started to break apart, as if the wraith was undoing itself, moving backward in time. The pieces of mist that had formed a shape seconds ago swirled into a vortex that hovered above the object. Before their eyes, the center of it opened like a black hole, and the bits of air, gossamer fine, were sucked into it. Rowan blinked and it was all gone, vanished.

Chapter Twenty-Three

Rowan didn't know how long she and Saoirse stood in the darkness, staring at the space in the moon circle that, moments ago, was occupied by a figure made of mist. She stepped forward, reaching her arm out, then swinging her arm wide, trying to detect . . . what? A change in the temperature? Air that felt heavier to the touch? "What *was* that? Or *who*," she whispered, voicing the question she knew Saoirse was thinking too.

She caught a glimpse of Paddy's grave. For a split second she wondered if she could have been mistaken and it had been his ghost, but no, the shape of the dress had clearly been that of a woman.

"Everly?" Saoirse said slowly, her voice trembling. "If she's dead . . ."

She trailed off, leaving the thought hanging between them, but Rowan dismissed the suggestion. They had never seen Everly wear dresses. She had overalls and jeans. Plus, she wanted to believe her grandmother wasn't dead. She had to hold on to her hope. It was a deep-seated feeling she had, the lingering taste of blackberries that told her Everly was out there somewhere, alive.

That and something blue and sweet . . . like a bilberry. It was a taste she'd never experienced before, and it disappeared the moment the figure had.

For the hundredth time, she thought how much they needed Everly here with them. How *she* would probably understand what had just happened. Slowly, as the fog seeped back into the clearing, Rowan and Saoirse retraced their steps to the house. There was no way either of them would be able to sleep after that experience. They didn't even try. Saoirse went straight to the apothecary, which streamed with light despite the darkness outside. Rowan followed, perching on the edge of a stool. She watched as her sister milled around, picking up this flower, moving that one, holding a vial of liquid up to the light like she was checking for clarity.

"Caraline," Saoirse said.

"Caraline," Rowan repeated, and that was enough to know that they were thinking the same thing. Where was their sister? "She must be—" Rowan started.

"—with Warren," Saoirse finished.

Rowan wanted to go find her, but she had no idea where Warren was staying, and no idea if he and Caraline had some secret meeting place. As Saoirse worked, Rowan retreated to the gathering room to think about Bridget and Everly and the wraith that had appeared. She slouched in one of the stuffed chairs. She hadn't planned to, but she fell into a fitful slumber.

She woke with a start when the clocks scattered around the room began to strike, one at a time, overlapping each other. They'd never done that before—struck when the hour hand had made a full rotation, but they did now, asynchronously and loud. So loud. She rubbed the sleep away and peered at the biggest one, the pendulum swinging back and forth in a steady rhythm. Eight o'clock.

In an instant, Rowan's tastebuds exploded with sweet berries mixed with the soft roundness of hope. She inhaled sharply and clasped her hand over her mouth. It was exactly what she'd tasted outside during the night. She stood abruptly and looked around. She expected to see the apparition, but the room was dim, only the flames of the candles casting shadows on the walls.

She heard the sigh of a door opening behind her and turned again, icy fingertips crawling up her back. The door to the study was open. She felt the air around her change. Just like the current that had hurried her and Saoirse down the stairs and outside, it pushed her gently toward the room and to the Keeper's Journal.

* * *

She walked in just as the shiplap high above dissolved into the clerestory windows. Like the sunroom, light streamed in, bathing the room in a warm glow. She quickly glanced around. The Keeper's Journal was right where she'd left it on the table next to the overstuffed chair. The oil lamp, she realized, was no longer next to the book. She looked at the shelf where she'd first seen it on its side. There it was. Not because Everly was dead, she thought, but because they needed it.

She sat in the chair and picked up the journal. It pulsed in her hands emitting the energy of her ancestors, the life force of the people who'd taken pen to paper and put their words down on the pages inside. When she closed her eyes, she could almost hear their voices echoing in the room, the ghosts in the walls of Swallow Hall.

She fanned through the pages, then propped the spine on her lap, letting the book fall open. "What do you want to show me?" The energy vibrating from the book unleashed, blasting into the room like a roll of thunder. Like Pandora's box. The book had opened to pages toward the end, with writing she hadn't noticed last time. She held her breath as she read.

I know it's Biddy. She showed me the book. I touched it. I felt its energy, but I couldn't take it. I have to go. He's just waiting. Leaving is the only way.

It was Bridget's writing. Rowan read it three times, her hands shaking. Tiny needles pricked her eyelids.

She blinked and read the lines again. *I know it's Biddy.*

Bridget had *seen* Biddy Early, but how was that even possib—

The apparition. The realization slammed into her. Had their oldest ancestor, the original Sky Girl, shown herself to Bridget before she'd left Bird Island? Is *that* who had shown herself to Rowan and Saoirse?

Rowan summoned an image of the bulky thing the figure—Biddy—had held. It had floated up and faded into the mist. Was *that* what Bridget was talking about? Was that the book?

Another question clawed its way to the surface. Why couldn't Bridget take the book, and was it the person who signed off as S who was there, just waiting for her? Did she feel that she had to get away from him?

Rowan's pulse spiked, her gaze darting to the windows, the corners where the walls leaned just slightly wrong. If it was S, where was he now?

The floorboards shifted beneath her feet, the faintest vibration curling through the wood, like the house bracing itself for something it remembered too well.

The threat wasn't coming.

It was already here.

Chapter Twenty-Four

Rowan mentally shuffled what she thought she knew. The letters from S had made one thing clear—he'd loved Bridget, and she betrayed him. At least, that's how *he* saw it. The taste of him lingered faintly in Rowan's memory—sharp with heartbreak, brittle with resentment, but hollow beneath it all. It wasn't the taste of malice.

Was S the true threat to Swallow Hall? Was he tied to Biddy Early's bloodline or the legacy the house protected? It was possible, but the pieces didn't fit. She reordered them, thinking about Bridget's message in the Keeper's Journal:

I have to go. He's just waiting. Leaving is the only way.

S had seen Bridget leave with Cillian Tully. He'd assumed it was an affair. He'd assumed she'd chosen someone else over him. But what if that hadn't been betrayal? What if it was *strategy*? Rowan could taste the faintest trace of it now, tucked beneath the bitterness: distraction. Sacrifice.

What if the one who was waiting was Cillian Tully? And what if he wasn't waiting for her, but for his opportunity to get his hands on Biddy's book?

It felt so crystal clear. Bridget had drawn Cillian away from the island because, without her, he couldn't get the book.

If Cillian Tully was the hidden heir—the fourth thread in Biddy's bloodline—that changed everything.

It wasn't S Bridget had been running from. It had always been Cillian.

And the sour, acrid taste Cillian left behind . . . that wasn't heartbreak. That was danger.

She worked to rein in her spiraling thoughts. S might have been hurt and angry. But Cillian . . . he was something else entirely. Dangerous. If Bridget believed he was a threat to the island and if she risked everything to lure him away, then whatever S thought he saw wasn't the full story.

But still . . . something gnawed at the edges of her mind, a frayed thread she couldn't follow.

She exhaled. She didn't know who S was, but he wasn't the one they had to worry about. At least, not yet.

It was Cillian. He was the one Bridget had been running from all along.

People had said Cillian had never come back to New Bethel. But what if he *had*?

Chapter Twenty-Five

By late morning, Caraline still wasn't back and Rowan couldn't simply sit around waiting. As she started to holler to Saoirse that she was going to town, a shriek came from the sunroom followed by a forceful "Damn it!"

For Saoirse to swear, something serious had to have happened. In seconds, Rowan stood on the threshold of the apothecary. Saoirse stood in the center of the room, her hands pressed to her head, fingernails clawing at her scalp. Everything in the room was scattered. Dried herbs and flowers were strewn haphazardly across the tables. Jars were overturned, a few broken, their contents spilled among shards of glass. "What happened?"

Saoirse looked toward Rowan but not quite at her. She stopped, spinning around, eyes wide as if she couldn't believe it. "Wind. It just suddenly blew through here like a *gale*." She flung her arms wide. "And look!"

The air was perfectly still now, all the windows closed and latched. Rowan felt Swallow Hall's unrest deep in her bones.

"Go," Saoirse said.

"What?"

"Get Caraline."

Of course Rowan's thoughts about finding Caraline had slipped into Saoirse's mind. "You'll be okay?" she asked as Saoirse crouched down on her haunches, carefully picking up the shattered glass.

"Of course I'm okay."

"Can I help?"

"No. Go."

Rowan hesitated for a few seconds, but Saoirse was already fully absorbed in her new task. Rowan wanted to scurry to her and brush a kiss against her cheek, but she didn't. The gesture would have been for Rowan's sake, but it was not what Saoirse needed or wanted. "Okay. I'll be back soon."

Saoirse moved on to the dried flowers scattered across the floor and Rowan left her to it, heading to the front door. She slowed when she felt the pressure of two hands on her back trying to push her toward the stairs. She didn't fight it—what was the point? And a minute later, she stood in her bedroom on the third floor. "What?" she demanded.

Across the room, on the dresser, the camera she'd found in the floorboards of the stairs moved. Just barely, but it definitely had. She grabbed the old camera and turned to leave. For a split second, she paused. "I'm trying to find the truth," she said aloud, quickly kissing her fingertips and tapping them lightly on the ceramic container with Bridget's ashes. Back downstairs, she grabbed one of Everly's handwoven baskets and set the camera inside, covering it with an embroidered tea towel. Then she was out the door, over the bridge, and through the woods to New Bethel.

The town was bustling, busier than she'd seen on her past visits. She found herself tensing, her gaze sweeping the streets as Everly had. She'd been so single-minded about getting out of Swallow Hall and off the island that she hadn't prepared herself for the assault on her senses. She hurried on, trying to block out the barrage of tastes dodging in and out of her mouth, there and gone before she could get a handle on any of them. It might be called clear-tasting, but at the moment it was a muddled mess of mud in her mouth.

She crossed to the other side of the street to avoid a group of teenage girls and the onslaught of angst that would flood her mouth if she got too close. She felt their eyes on her as they stared, whispering behind the backs of their hands. The pungent tartness she'd experienced when she'd first seen Louise Janson and Lorna McNicol surfaced. She picked up her pace, glancing at the church she was now in front of. As if she'd sensed Rowan coming, Lorna, in an old-fashioned black dress, stood in the open doorway, her beakish nose turned up, her beady eyes on her as Rowan wrapped her hand around Everly's obsidian pendant—something she found herself doing more and more—and crossed the street at a diagonal.

With the tabernacle behind her, the number of pedestrians dissipated, but the acrid taste in her mouth lingered. She thought about crossing the road again to avoid another group of walkers but stopped when she saw Esther Canvey and Macy Davis strolling in her direction, arms laden with shopping bags. A minute later, they were in front of her. Instantly, her tastebuds were alight with the zestiness of citrus, with undertones of vanilla and chocolate. She welcomed the more pleasant tastes and the lack of emotional weight that usually came with the onslaught of flavors.

"Rowan, my dear, so lovely to see you," Esther said.

Macy spread one arm wide. "Beautiful day to be out and about."

"Everly has a stone just like that," Esther said, catching sight of the pendant strung around Rowan's neck.

She just nodded, not wanting to tell them that it *was* Everly's.

"Oh!" Macy's age-worn face lit up. "The lavender soap your sister made with the peppermint? It works wonders! I woke up with such a headache this morning. I usually do, but whatever she put in that soap was a miracle. I rinsed my face with it and it stopped it cold. I still love the one Everly makes for me, but your sister—what's her name?"

"Saoirse," Rowan said.

"Lovely Irish name. I'll save the one Saoirse made for when my headaches are especially bad."

"She has a gift," Rowan said. "She'll love knowing you're happy with it. I'm looking for my other sister. Caraline. Dark hair. Maybe hanging out with a tall guy—"

Macy snapped her fingers. "Yes! We passed them, what? Ten minutes ago?"

"Maybe fifteen," Esther agreed. "They were going on a picnic. So romantic."

Rowan's anxiety ratcheted up. How could her sister just ignore Everly's disappearance and the prophecy from the tapestry room to go on a picnic? She tried to tamp down her frustration. "Any idea where?"

They both frowned. "No, my dear. In the woods somewhere, no doubt," Macy said.

Esther and Macy tried to make more small talk, but Rowan excused herself and walked on. A few minutes later, she pushed through the door of Chesapeake Camera Hut. The store was compact inside, more like a closet than a decent sized shop. No one was in the front, but she heard movement behind the dark curtain that separated the front of the shop from the back area. The acridness of development chemicals coated the inside of her nose. Oddly, it wasn't unpleasant. It simply . . . was.

"Hello?" she called.

"Coming." A second later the curtain was shoved aside and the man who went with the voice appeared. He looked to be mid-forties with ruddy cheeks and a pronounced dimple in his chin. A dead ringer for Kirk Douglas. "Help you?"

He was tall, filling so much of the space in the shop that Rowan almost felt claustrophobic. She set her basket on the counter and pulled back the tea towel. He let out an appreciative whistle. "That's a beauty," he said.

"Is it?"

"For a camera buff, it is," he said. "Are you selling it?"

She shook her head more vehemently than she'd intended. "No. I found it and—"

A deep vertical line carved into the space between his eyebrows as he frowned. "I'm sorry, did you say you *found* it?"

"In my house, I mean," she said quickly. How easily she identified Swallow Hall as hers.

"Ah. Got it." He nodded at the camera. "May I?"

"Sure." She pushed the basket toward him, and he lifted the camera out, handling it with care as he turned it over in his hands. He took his time, studying every centimeter of it. "Where did you find it?" he asked, finally done with his inspection.

"Stored away in a box," she said, omitting that the box was a cubby in a hollowed space in the stairs.

"That explains it. It hasn't been cared for. See here? The bellows are pretty brittle." He used his hand as a platform and pointed at an area where they were flaking.

"I don't know how long it was in there."

He released something with a faint click. "There's a roll of film here."

"I was wondering if there might be," she said with a flare of excitement. Whether the camera had belonged to Bridget or Everly, there could be photos of her mother from her childhood. "Is it still good, do you think?"

"Hard to say. Depends how old it is and what condition it's in. I can develop it for you."

"That'd be great."

"I'll put it in the queue. Probably a week or so."

Her face fell. "A week?"

"Maybe sooner. We'll see."

She gave him her name. Right away, he narrowed his eyes at her. "Connors, huh? You look like an Early."

"I'm both. Everly's my grandmother."

"Yup, I see the resemblance."

She gave him the phone number to Swallow Hall and started toward the door.

"I'll get to it sooner if I can. Whatever's on here is probably way more interesting than the normal stuff that comes in."

"Thank you," Rowan said. At the door, she stopped and turned back to him. "Where's the library?"

He pointed absently, his attention on the camera. "Make a right at the next corner. It's two blocks down. Bay Hollow. Can't miss it."

Outside, the cloud cover had cleared again, the sky cerulean blue and dotted with cartoon clouds. She breathed in the crisp air, letting it spread through her body, fortifying her. The warm glow of autumn painted everything with a golden hue. A few of the shops along the street had decorated their storefronts with garlands of colorful autumn leaves and had arranged pumpkins in their front windows. She stood back as pedestrians passed her by, controlling her breath, trying to keep her so-called magic in check. When she prepared herself, had time to focus, and wasn't distracted, it worked better. Everly's absence remained present, and the appearance of the apparition the night before stayed on the edges of her mind, but Caraline was safe on her picnic and the camera was in good hands. It felt like progress.

She turned left at the next street, and less than ten minutes later she was at the corner of Bay Hollow and Pinewood looking at an old building painted maritime blue. Like everything else in New Bethel, the structure had been built in a different era and brought lovingly into the twentieth century while maintaining its historical charm.

Inside, the renovations had been more about function, which meant much of the appeal was gone. The circulation desk had a beige Formica counter. A brown metal cart held books to be reshelved. A low-looped navy carpet covered what were probably hardwood floors. Like all libraries, the stacks of books were differentiated by genre. A walnut card catalog cabinet sat next to the circulation desk with row after row of five-inch drawers. Thirty in all. Affixed to each drawer was a brushed metal finger pull, and inside, she knew, were the cards that held the biographical information for every book in the building denoted by its Dewey decimal number, as well as whether it was in the stacks, lost, stolen, or moved into storage.

A man rounded the corner heading for the circulation desk. The second he spotted her, he changed course and walked up to her. He had intense blue eyes that made you think he really saw you. He nodded at her with the faint trace of a smile. "Hello there."

"Hi," she said, immediately noting the woody, earthy sweet flavors commingling on her tongue. They were grounded and rustic and reminded her of the woods on the island.

He looked at her, zeroing in on the sprout of red hair at her temple. "Can I help you find something?"

She hadn't thought about what to say, other than she needed information on scrying, synesthesia, and psychometry. She had a guess about synesthesia but not the others. What if they were something so strange that the man standing in front of her with a puzzled half smile kicked her right out of the library? Of course, she didn't think that would be the case.

"Hello? Are you okay?"

She noticed the way he stood, his legs apart, his arms folded over his chest, his open hands tucked against his sides just below his armpits. He looked to be a few years older than Rowan, somewhere in his early thirties, if she had to guess, with a few shallow lines starting to mark his face. It was a good face, she thought, then quickly pushed that thought away. "Sorry. Yes, I'm fine. I'm looking for a book on . . . um, scrying?"

His mouth pulled to the side as he considered her. "That sounded like a question. Are you not sure if that's what you're looking for?"

She felt a blush creep up her neck. "No, no. I'm sure. I need a book on scrying."

"Got it. Let's see what we can find," he said. A minute later he was rifling through stacks of cards he'd pulled from the card catalog. "Scrying, scrying, scrying," he muttered to himself, then turned to her. "What is it?"

She gave him a sheepish grin and a one-shoulder shrug. "I don't know."

His lips quirked. "But you want a book about it?"

"Yes, so I can learn about it." She'd perused the shelves of books in the Swallow Hall study, but hadn't seen anything that looked helpful. She wasn't optimistic that she'd have better luck here, but it was worth a try.

"How do you know you want to learn about it if you don't know what it is?"

That was a great question, but she didn't have a great answer. Not one she could share, anyway. She hiked her now empty basket, save for the tea towel, up on her forearm. As casually as she could, she said, "It has to do with magic."

"Magic," he repeated. "Like Houdini?"

"Magic like witches and fortune telling. Stuff like that."

"Okay, that helps. I think. Why don't you have a look around while I do a little research? It's going to take me a couple of minutes."

She thanked him and walked toward the fiction section, then changed her mind and turned back to him. "Also, is there anything on witchcraft in Ireland? Maybe in the eighteen hundreds?"

"Really interested in the occult, eh?" His gaze skimmed over her for a quick second. "Funny, you don't *look* like a witch."

"What does a witch look like?" she asked, a slightly playful note in her voice. The second the question was out, she bit her lower lip. Was she flirting?

A little twinkle sparkled in his blue eyes. "Pointy hats and black clothes?"

She rolled her eyes. "So typical," she said with a laugh.

"So not pointy hats and black clothes?"

She glanced down at her brown sweater, bell-bottom jeans, and rust-colored boots, then looked up at him through her lashes. "I guess not."

"Okay then. Well, we've got plenty on the Salem witch trials," he said. "Not sure about Ireland in the eighteen hundreds, but I'll look."

"Thank you . . ." She paused, wanting to say his name.

"Ryan," he said, filling in the blank. "Ryan Winchester."

"Thank you, Ryan."

She started to turn back to the stacks but stopped when he cleared his throat. "And you are?"

"Oh. Rowan." She didn't give her last name because saying she was a Connors was starting to feel wrong. Incomplete. It was the name she'd grown up with, yes, but she'd only just learned about its connection to Biddy. Up until now, it had held no meaning. Not like Early did. But she didn't quite feel like an Early, either.

"I'll find you, Rowan," he said, and this time he walked away.

She headed straight for the geography section, perusing books on Ireland. Being a direct descendant of Biddy Early had drawn a heavy black line between her and the emerald isle. Other than St. Patrick's Day, shamrocks, and leprechauns, she didn't know much about it.

She spent the next twenty minutes reading snippets about Dublin, the IRA, and the Tuatha dé Danann. She tasted that pleasant woodsiness again before she saw that Ryan was heading her way.

"There you are."

She frowned at his empty hands. "No luck?"

"I found one title: *Crystal Gazing: A Study in the History, Distribution, Theory, and Practice of Scrying* by Theodore Besterman, first published in nineteen twenty-four, but we don't have it anymore. Long gone."

"Crystal gazing?" So was scrying something to do with crystals then? Was that why she'd been drawn to making necklaces from the gems she found?

"I'm not giving up yet," he said. "We can check the encyclopedia. Come on."

She followed him to the reference section and a row of hardbound books. Encyclopedia Brittanica. He pulled out the S volume and flipped through it until he found the page for "sc," then ran the pad of one finger down it, stopping when he found what he was looking for. He turned the book to face her.

As she took it from him, her fingers brushed his. A jolt shot through her, the sweet earthiness in her mouth intensifying. "You okay?" he asked her for the second time.

She shook her mind clear. "Fine," she said again, thinking he probably thought she was a little unhinged. She scanned the page until she found the entry for scrying and read the brief entry, which led to information on the divination of crystal gazing and its history dating back to the fifth-century medieval Christian church's condemnation of it as devil's work, and its popularity as a pastime in Victorian England.

So she hadn't been far off the mark when she'd compared it to fortune-telling. A scryer saw visions through things like crystals, mirrors, water, or even fire or smoke.

The vision of someone holding Bridget's head down in the fountain had been in the reflection of water. Had it been a vision of the past or a message telling her what really happened? Her blood ran cold. She had to get home. Back to Swallow Hall to . . . to what? Look in that puddle again, if it was still there? It probably wouldn't be, but then maybe any liquid or mirror would work.

"Thank you!" She hurried toward the exit, realizing she still held the encyclopedia. She turned to go back and—"Oh!" She bumped right into Ryan, who'd followed her. She shoved the book at him, thanked him again, and started for the door again.

"What about the Irish—?" he said, but his voice trailed off as she fled the library and raced back to Bird Island.

Chapter Twenty-Six

Back at Swallow Hall, Rowan looked for Saoirse, expecting her to be in the sunroom, but the apothecary was oddly silent. "Saoirse?" she hollered, walking through the house.

No answer. She checked the bedrooms. Empty.

In her attic room, she looked out the window and saw Hazel chasing rogue leaves and racing around barren trees in the woods, leaping over a few of the fallen trunks. The shadow in the woods hovered in the back of her mind, as well as something Warren had said about Swallow Hall and Bird Island. *It's a little creepy, like someone's always watching.*

A vice gripped her insides, growing tighter and tighter with each passing minute. The idea that Cillian Tully was the fourth thread had permeated her brain. Everly was gone. Caraline was off with Warren, but she hadn't seen her since the day before. And now she couldn't find Saoirse. The blood inside her skull pulsed with worry. If Everly had been taken, it could happen to any of them.

She paced, looking at the clock on the wall. The second hand crept around the face at a snail's pace. She pressed her hands to the sides of her head. She needed her sisters! She hadn't realized it, but she also needed Everly.

Her gaze strayed to her mother's ashes. She needed Bridget, but someone had taken her mother from her. Her gaze shifted to the coal-black bowl and oily liquid in the tiny jar she'd found in the stair hollow, still sitting behind the ceramic jar. What were they for? Why had they been hidden away?

The thought struck her suddenly. The bowl and the contents of that jar could have been her mother's divination tools, left behind when she'd run from Swallow Hall. She remembered her mother slipping into a trance-like state when the sisters had been bathing or at the pool. Bridget had been a scryer.

She picked up the black bowl, cradling it in two hands as she carried it with her to the center of the room. She sat on the floor, cross-legged, and placed it in front of her just as she had the letters the day she'd found them. She ran her fingers along the inside of the bowl, feeling the slick polished surface. Before she could think too hard about it, she uncorked the little bottle filled with oil and sniffed. It didn't smell like anything. She tilted it, pouring out the slippery liquid, which barely covered the bottom. She stared into the bowl, but it wasn't reflective enough. She hurried to the bathroom, filling a cup with water, and ran back to pour it into the bowl.

She didn't know how this worked. Without a better idea, she closed her eyes and counted to five, opening them again and focusing on the glassy surface.

She waited for a flash or a jolt of energy. For *something.*

The water stayed completely still. Not even her reflection showed in the dark fluid.

Maybe she'd misunderstood the whispered voice in the study. Maybe the vision in the puddle had been a fluke. Maybe this wasn't her magic at all.

But then why did the house lead her to it? And to the letters and the camera?

She was missing something. Her gaze ticked to the bottle. It had been with the bowl. *With the bowl.*

Oil and water didn't mix. Oil sat on *top* of water. She hadn't needed anything extra when she'd seen the vision in the puddle, but maybe this would help. Maybe she was supposed to pour the oil in *after* the water was in the bowl. But she'd used all the oil and now it sat coating the bottom of the bowl.

She didn't know how to do this! She snatched it up in frustration, lifting her arm, wanting to hurl it across the room and watch it shatter. She stopped abruptly as oil streamed out of the upside-down bottle.

She stared at it, puzzled. She'd emptied the bottle into the bowl, hadn't she?

Yes, she definitely had. She looked at it now, still upside-down and empty. She righted it. Held it up to the light. Let out a screech. It was full again!

Without thinking, she turned it upside-down over the black bowl—the scrying bowl—and watched as a steady stream of thick liquid flowed out, settling on top of the water.

The bottle slipped from her grasp. "No, no, no!" She grabbed for it but missed. She braced herself as it hit the floor, but it didn't shatter. It bounced.

She snatched it up and held it to the light. Inside, it was filled with liquid. Now the jolt of energy she'd felt outside at the puddle shot through her. Her magic.

She sucked in a breath and held it, counting to five again, and then she peered into the inky liquid.

Chapter Twenty-Seven

Bridget's face appeared, grainy and distorted, but it was definitely her. Rowan closed her eyes and just like before, when she opened them she saw the same scene playing out before her. Her mother walking. Her head hitting the edge of the fountain. Someone holding her face in the water.

Bile skulked up her throat, turning to acid in her mouth. She couldn't dismiss it as a fluke this time. She'd seen a vision in the inky, oily water. She'd *scried.*

Scried. *Skried.* Her skin pricked with a memory. Biddy's letter to Paddy, the one Macy Davis and Esther Canvey had shown her popped into her mind. In it, she'd said she'd *-kried.* Rowan thought she'd meant *cried*, misspelled, but had Biddy written *skried*, the S faded from time?

Had *Biddy* been a scryer? Was Rowan following in the footsteps of the original Sky Girl?

She looked back to the scrying bowl. The same scene played out again. If she'd questioned it before, she couldn't this time. There was no doubt in her mind. Someone had killed Bridget.

Her body stiffened. What was she supposed to do with this information? "Everly, where are you?" she muttered, choking back renewed grief for her mother and wishing her grandmother was here.

Her gaze flicked to the scrying bowl again, and she nearly jumped out of her skin. Another scene played like a silent movie—a figure, rough and twisted, walking. Arms suddenly flailed as she was swallowed into a black hole, disappearing. Rowan blinked. Her eyes burned. She wanted to reach in and pull her out. To go back in time and save the figure from her fate.

Over and over, the new scene replayed. She tried to pick out details, but unlike when she saw Bridget's face, clear as day, this time the figure was blurry. And then the figure's blank face angled toward her as if it could see Rowan watching. Rowan sucked in a sharp breath. It was something dark. Something that turned her blood to ice in her veins.

She knew it was just a vision, but if she had scried it, then surely she could figure out what it meant. Had it already happened, or was it a vision of something yet to be? She blinked, but when she peered into the dark liquid again, the images were gone. "No, no, no!" She spoke aloud hoping that would trigger something, but the water and oil were just water and oil. She sat back on her heels. Why wasn't it working? She tried again, speaking the question into the room. Nothing.

What was different about the times it worked? She'd focused and concentrated. She'd spoken her question aloud. Neither had worked. It was only when she had almost given up that the vision appeared. She hadn't tried, she realized. Maybe *that* was the trick. Maybe she had to just let it happen.

She tried to relax, to let go of the tension coiling through her, but she couldn't unsee someone holding Bridget's head down or a figure being sucked into a black hole of nothingness. A thought struck her with such power she lost her breath. Could this be a vision of Everly being sucked into a pool of water? Surely she hadn't gone into the bay and drowned, had she?

She squeezed her eyes shut and pressed her palms against her ears as if that would block out the very idea. No, Everly couldn't be dead. It was too cruel to lose the grandmother she and her sisters had just met on the heels of losing their mother. She refused to believe it. "She's alive," she said, as if speaking it could make it true.

There was a quick knock on the door of her room. It flew open before she could respond. Caraline strode in, followed by Saoirse. "Hey, baby sister," Caraline said.

"You're back!" Relief flooded through her.

"Of course I am."

"We didn't know where you were—"

"I was with Warren," Caraline said. "He wanted to have a picnic, but then . . ." Her mouth twisted and she gave a small shrug. "I thought you might need me, that I should come home."

Rowan's brows lifted—at her sister choosing them over Warren, and at her calling Swallow Hall home. "I'm glad," she said. "And where were you?" Rowan said to Saoirse.

"Collecting," Saoirse said.

Rowan wanted to smack her forehead. Of course Saoirse had been collecting.

Caraline peered at Rowan. At the scrying bowl. "What're you doing?"

Rowan beckoned them forward. "Come here."

Saoirse crouched down, looking at the stone bowl. She reached her hand out, letting it hover, tracing its edges in the air. "What is this?"

"I'm calling it a scrying bowl. I think it was Bridget's."

Caraline tensed even more. "You think that was Bridget's? Why?"

Apprehension fisted in Rowan's gut. They'd seen the letters, but now she thought it was time to come clean about everything. "Sit down."

Saoirse dropped to the floor right where she was, sitting cross-legged like Rowan, pulling the hem of her dress around her knees.

Caraline's folded arms were like a brick wall between them. "Why?"

"Because I have some things to tell you," Rowan said.

Caraline crooked a brow, but she sat. "Spill it," she said.

The second they were knee to knee, a disquieting rumble sounded from the depths of the house, like something was trapped beneath the floorboards. It moved on its foundation and not for the first time, Rowan felt as if the ground had awakened after a long sleep, stretching and shifting beneath them. The scrying bowl rocked as the tremors built, growing and gaining momentum. It felt as if Swallow Hall was splitting in half, a fissure forming in the center of the structure.

Rowan's mouth turned dry, all the moisture suddenly sucked out. The next second, it burned, as if she'd taken a bite of a fiery habanero pepper. She buckled over, trying to awaken her salivary glands, to chase away the burning.

Saoirse reached for Caraline's hand. For Rowan's. Rowan stared at Saoirse. She couldn't remember the last time they'd had physical contact like this. Caraline caught her eye, her expression telling her she thought the same thing.

Rowan squeezed before pulling free and scurrying to stand. She focused on the discoloration on the walls. The bubbling of the wallpaper. The buckling of some of the floor planks under her feet. Her heart battered in her chest, but she took deep breaths. She laid her hand on the wall like she'd seen Everly do. Summoned up the image from the photograph that had led them here: Bridget and Everly in happier days, the house tranquil in its halcyon days. She closed her eyes, letting that sense of peace seep from her palm into the walls. "*Stad a chur le*," she said quietly, repeating the words Everly had said when the house had been in distress.

Nothing happened. "*Stad a chur le*," she said, trying again.

The planks beneath her feet settled.

"*Stad a chur le*," she repeated.

This time, after a few seconds, the tremors subsided, the intensity of the shaking waning. And then, finally, it stopped. It was as if the house had vented its emotions, and now, spent, it had retreated into a state of uneasy rest.

Rowan drew her hand away, rubbing her fingers together. They were wet. Bits of the wallpaper flecked her palm. As she brought her hand back to the wall, her eyes welled, as much for Swallow Hall as for Everly, wherever she was, because with her, its Keeper, gone, Swallow Hall wept. Her eyes flicked over Saoirse and Caraline, both ghostly white.

"How did you do that?" Caraline's voice came out hoarse. Strained.

Rowan didn't know how. Instinct, she guessed. "It's what Everly does. She talks to the house. Treats it with respect."

Caraline's eyes flashed, the color returning to her cheeks. She started to speak, but Rowan's hand shot up to stop her. Whatever she'd been about to say froze on her lips. Rowan put one finger vertically to her lips, a silent message to her sister to be quiet.

Caraline blew out a shaky breath, but she kept her mouth shut.

Rowan sat, once again knee to knee with her sisters. Saoirse's hands were folded in her lap. Caraline picked at a cuticle. Rowan took a deep breath and began, telling Caraline about the apparition she and Saoirse had seen, then both of them about the camera, the Keeper's Journal, and then, finally, about the scrying bowl and what she'd seen in it, both a repeat of their mother and a figure being swallowed up by the water.

They took it all in, simply accepting the magic that surrounded them. "How does it work?" Saoirse asked about the scrying.

"I don't know. It's happened three times—"

She broke off when she looked at the bowl sitting between them, the liquid still again after the rumbling of the house. Without warning, images flashed across the still liquid, one after the other, like a highlight reel. Air caught in her lungs, weighty and thick. Heaviness pressed down on her as if she was being held underwater. She shuddered. Like Bridget.

"Row?"

The three girls as infants.
Bridget when she was much younger, stepping onto a bus.
A man, dark-haired, from the back.
A man with an ax.
An apparition.
Rowan in the study.
She and her sisters walking over the footbridge onto Bird Island.

She felt her heartbeat pulsing in her temples.

"Rowan."

A cliff.
A figure sucked into the water.
A man in a doorway, the features of his face blurred.
The girls as toddlers behind Bridget like ducklings trailing after their mother.
The wheels of a car rolling down the highway.
Bridget looking over her shoulder.
A thick book.
Bridget, her head being held down.

Rowan shuddered.

Rowan carrying Everly's basket on her arm.
Bridget with a suitcase.
Swallow Hall transformed from an ordinary house into the nonsensical one it was now.
A man running.

They played over and over, each time in a different order. She tried to make sense of them, but they felt disconnected. It was like trying to fit the puzzle pieces of a Jackson Pollock painting together, matching the paint spatters to one another. Her neck felt tight. Swollen. She tried to swallow. Gasped for air.

"Rowan!"

She jerked, her head shooting up as a hand came down on her knee. Saoirse's hand, touching her again. "Did you see something just now?"

Rowan took a shuddering breath. She managed to nod and then described what she'd seen.

"Jesus," Caraline muttered.

Saoirse jumped up and ran out of the room, returning a moment later with a small notepad and pencil. "Tell me again," she said.

As Rowan went through each image, Saoirse wrote them down on separate sheets of paper, tearing each one off, and making a small stack. When Rowan was done, the two of them scooted back, creating more space between them. Saoirse spread the papers out, like cards from a memory game, only instead of finding pairs, they worked to rearrange them, putting them in some sort of order.

"They're like parts of the same story," Caraline said. She scooted around until she was next to Rowan, who moved closer to Saoirse. They tried different configurations, but none were cohesive.

Caraline tapped one of the papers. "This one is Bridget leaving Bird Island," she said, and she moved that piece of paper far to the left as a starting point.

Rowan reached for the paper that had the wheels of a car rolling down the highway. "Another one of her leaving," she said, putting it next to the one of Bridget leaving the island. She created a second row beginning with the three sisters crossing the footbridge, moving Everly disappearing next to it. She tapped the first row. "Before us—" she started.

Caraline placed her open palm on the second row. "—and after," she finished.

They worked silently, moving the papers around until they held the semblance of a story.

Bridget with a suitcase.
Bridget when she was much younger in a car.
The wheels rolling down the highway.

"These are Bridget before she had us," Saoirse said, sitting on her heels.

They moved to the ones after their birth.

The three girls as infants.
The three of them as toddlers following Bridget like ducklings.

"Then it skips," Caraline said.

Bridget, her head being held down.
The sisters walking over the footbridge onto Bird Island.
Rowan carrying Everly's basket on her arm.
A figure—Everly?—being sucked into the water.
An apparition, the woman Rowan and Saoirse had seen.

They sat back to survey the sequence, looking at the ones they hadn't yet placed. "A man with an ax," Rowan said. "Oh!" She grabbed that paper and put it at the very beginning. "Everly said Paddy Early took an ax to the house, and that's when the house started to transform." She moved the paper about Swallow Hall right after it.

Saoirse tapped the pad of her index finger against her lower lip. "Then it skips ahead to Bridget leaving with her suitcase. So where do the men fit in, and the cliff and book?"

Bridget's message in the Keeper's Journal rose up. She said Biddy had shown her the book. "The apparition looked like she was holding a book."

Saoirse's eyes lit up. "Right!" She placed the paper that said *A thick book* at the end of the sequence.

"If we don't know who the man—or men—are," Rowan said, "then we have no idea where they fit." She looked at the letters. "But maybe one of them is S."

"There aren't cliffs around here," Caraline said.

No, there weren't.

They spent the next thirty minutes reading and rereading the letters from S to Bridget. "Is Cillian Tully our father, or is it this man, this S?" Saoirse said, echoing what they all wondered.

"God, I hope it's not creepy Cillian Tully. But whichever one this is, maybe he's the one running," Caraline said. "Running after Bridget, trying to get her to stay." She placed that piece of paper after Bridget with her suitcase. "So Bridget is leaving. This man runs after her."

Saoirse put the dark-haired man from the back after the one about the wheels of the car. "Maybe this is him watching her go."

"And maybe Bridget is looking over her shoulder, looking at him."

That sounded like a romantic notion . . . and not right to Rowan. In the visions she'd seen, there had been enough detail to know that Bridget had been scared but determined. She'd left, not out of love, but out of necessity. "I don't think the dark-haired man is S." She moved the papers around, looking at them in their new order.

A man, dark-haired, from the back.
Bridget looking over her shoulder.
Bridget with a suitcase.
A man running.
Bridget in a car.
Wheels rolling down the highway.

The three girls as infants.
The three of them as toddlers following Bridget like ducklings.

Bridget, her head being held down.
The sisters walking over the footbridge onto Bird Island.
Rowan carrying Everly's basket on her arm.
Everly being sucked into the water.
An apparition, the woman Rowan and Saoirse had seen.
Rowan in the study.

Something didn't feel quite right, but she couldn't put her finger on it. And the one with the cliff and the man in the doorway were still on their own, not fitting in anywhere.

She let it go because, at the moment, there was no way to figure out how or where they fit in the sequence. More than that, Rowan had no idea what they were supposed to do with the information she'd seen in the scrying bowl. Everything was just as much a mystery as it had been before—more, even—and she felt no closer to any sort of truth than when they'd started their journey from Arkansas.

But the house and the island had a way of revealing things in their own time.

Outside, the wind shifted, brushing past the house with a faint whisper, the leaves trembling like they'd heard something Rowan hadn't yet. Somewhere deep within the walls of Swallow Hall, the wood creaked. It wasn't the usual settling groan that had become familiar. It was sharper and more deliberate. Rowan held her breath, sensing the house was doing the same, because all they could do now was hope that Biddy would come again.

Chapter Twenty-Eight

The sky bled with streaks of lavender and rust as the sun slipped behind the tree line. Rowan's stomach twisted with nerves. Caraline pulled back, her arms crossing tight over her chest. "What, we're just supposed to wait for the ghost of Biddy Early?" she asked, her voice low and sharp. "I'd rather stay inside, thanks."

"We have to be together," Saoirse reminded her, her gaze drifting toward the fading light. "Remember? That's what the tapestry said."

Caraline's mouth pulled downward, her frown deepening. "I don't like this."

Neither did Rowan, but it wasn't like they had options. She ushered her sisters toward the moon circle, every step heavy with the gnawing frustration that they had nothing else—no plan, no answers . . . just this.

An hour passed. Then another. The shadows thickened, the sky smudged in mauve. The moon climbed higher, pale, mottled, and almost watchful, but there was no sign of Biddy's apparition. Not a single swallow glided through the gloaming sky. The air hung heavy and still. There were no whispers of magic.

Rowan's gaze roamed from the mud nests beneath the eaves to the branches where the swallows had gathered the last time, right before Biddy appeared.

Tonight, the birds were gone. The house was still. The sky was empty.

Her pulse thrummed with the quiet certainty that something was coming. Her chest tightened with frustration. They were just standing here, waiting, while Everly was missing and the house felt like it was moments away from splitting apart at the seams.

They should be *doing* something. But there was nothing left to do. They couldn't force the island to reveal its secrets any faster than it wanted to. Until then they waited, helpless.

Caraline broke the silence. "What were you doing when you saw her?"

"We weren't doing anything—" Saoirse started, but Rowan interrupted. "A swallow woke me up. It tapped on my window."

"Right! They were stirred up," Saoirse said. "It was like they knew . . ."

Rowan's gaze swept the bruise-colored sky again, devoid of movement. Her thoughts wandered. What if Biddy didn't come to them? What then? Or . . . what if she *did*? What were they supposed to *do*?

Another ten minutes passed, then suddenly Saoirse pointed toward the distance. "They're here," she said, her voice low and haunting. Rowan saw nothing but the bony fingers of barren tree branches reaching into the darkening sky.

And then there they were, the flock of swallows appearing out of nowhere, gliding toward them until they circled overhead.

In one choreographed movement, the birds changed directions, flying off, reappearing a second later, diving toward the earth at a breakneck speed.

Caraline gasped. "What are they doing?"

A mere inches from hitting the ground, the birds turned as one, shooting upward, turning at a forty-five-degree angle before flying off.

Rowan whispered hoarsely. "This is what happened before. Just like this, only we were inside."

The words were scarcely out of her mouth when the flight of swallows reappeared, scattering around them. Rowan's nose pricked. Her eyes burned. Time seemed to slow. The sound of their flapping wings magnified in her ears. Their haunting song echoed around them.

They swooped low. Caraline screeched. Ducked her head. "Jesus!"

The scene felt straight out of Hitchcock's *The Birds*. She and Caraline both had their arms thrown overhead to protect themselves. Only Saoirse seemed unfazed. As Rowan had seen her do so many times before, her sister whispered under her breath, talking to the birds. She gave a quick flick of her wrist. Instantly, they flew into formation and were off, disappearing above the bare branches of the trees in the woods.

Slowly, Rowan and Caroline uncovered their heads. "What. Just. Happened?" Caraline ground out, her teeth clenched, but before Rowan or Saoirse could answer, the swallows reappeared above the trees. Caraline scurried backward, grabbing Rowan's arm.

This time, instead of feverish flight, they slipped into a long line, plunging toward the water. So fast. It looked like they were going to plummet right into the bay, but at the last second, they changed direction, each bird nearly hitting the water before abruptly turning. They began circling like the funnel of a tornado, the channel growing bigger as more birds turned away from the water and joined the whirlwind. Round and round and round they flew at a breakneck speed.

Rowan stared. Barely dared to blink. And then she saw it. Her head turned wooly. She lifted one arm and pointed. "She's here."

She watched as the birds flew off, the flock separating, their job done. The water of the bay had spun into a whirlpool. From the center of it, a loose form appeared, taking shape before their eyes.

Caraline sucked in a ragged breath. "Is that . . . ?"

Rowan had wanted this, but still, it felt like her insides were twisting until her breath turned shallow.

Saoirse stood and walked toward the shoreline, her attention focused on the figure hovering over the water. "Biddy," she said, and walking up next to her, Rowan nodded. She knew it was Biddy just as sure as knew Bridget had always been trying to protect Swallow Hall and Bird Island.

The wraith floated forward toward Saoirse. Toward the shore. Saoirse stepped aside as it moved past her, a translucent form made of a filmy web, delicate and wispy. The face was featureless, just like the first time Rowan and Saoirse had seen it. The wisps gave the illusion of a dress.

It came to an undulating stillness in the center of the moon circle. Saoirse and Rowan came back, and, with Caraline, they stood side by side staring. For a moment, Rowan could feel her heartbeat in her throat, but she swallowed. She forced herself to be calm and steady. The form before them was their great-great-great-great-grandmother, the woman who had been accused of witchcraft, who'd been tried and exonerated. She'd been a scryer, like Rowan and Bridget, and a healer like Saoirse, Caraline, and Everly. She was the woman who had enchanted Swallow Hall to protect her book of curses and cures. Her grimoire.

Rowan's gaze slipped to Biddy's arms, clutching something close to her chest. *The Good Book.*

Biddy's visage had no discernible eyes, yet Rowan felt them bore into her. Felt a silent plea pass between them, ghost and woman, ancestor and descendant, witch and witch. Before Rowan knew what she was doing, she took a step toward Biddy.

Caraline hissed at her. "What are you doing?"

"It's okay," Saoirse whispered, patting the air.

"Oh my God, no, it's not! What if that thing took Everly? What if that's what happened to her? What if it takes—"

The roar between Rowan's ears blocked Caraline's frantic whispering and Saoirse's efforts to settle her. Rowan focused only on Biddy, taking another step closer. The wisps that formed Biddy's figure were like tufts of clouds that had been stretched out like sugary threads of cotton candy pulled into long strands.

She reached out her hand, palm up, supplicant. "Is that your spell book?" she asked, letting her gaze drop to the object Biddy held close. "The Good Book?"

Rowan heard the words leave her own mouth, but they didn't sound like they came from her. They were low and slow, deep and haunting like what happened to a record when you dragged your finger on the spinning vinyl, slowing it down, changing the sound of the music to something deep and cavernous. She could almost see them, filaments stretching through the night air, reaching Biddy's form and seeping into her.

A thunderous roar came from behind them. Rowan nearly jumped out of her skin. She spun around, gaping at Swallow Hall. Its windows were illuminated, the house fully lit just as it had been the night the island spit up Paddy Early's grave. It looked as if every lamp in the house was switched on, their light pooling together, shooting like laser beams and forming a spotlight in the woods.

The woods, not the moon circle. Rowan stared. Was that . . . had something moved? She saw it again. A shadow dodging out of the light. "Someone's there," she hissed.

Saoirse and Caraline spun to look. Blood crashed through Rowan's head. Both she and Caraline had seen someone in the woods. She'd felt it from the first day they arrived on Bird Island, and now here it was again, a presence, a shadow, someone watching.

One second it was just darkness, the next a cloud of fireflies danced, their light flickering, calling to her. A dozen . . . two dozen . . . a hundred maybe. They flitted around her, blinking, then flew off toward the woods.

Chase the fireflies, Everly had said.

She didn't want to leave the moon circle, her sisters, or Biddy, but she had to follow Everly's instructions. She raced up the path and across the footbridge, following the lightning bugs. She knew the way to town by heart and could find it in the dark, but the fireflies lit the way deeper into the woods, away from the path.

Her conversation with Ryan Winchester from the library shot through her mind. She didn't look like a witch, he'd said, but she was one. She came from a long line of them. That wasn't the truth Bridget had compelled her to discover, but it *was* the truth. More of Everly's words found their way into her thoughts. *You'll find your truest self here.*

She was a descendant of an Irish witch. An Early.

A pungent sourness filled her mouth. It was the same sensation she experienced when she'd seen Louise Janson and Lorna McNicol the first time in New Bethel, and stronger still when she'd seen Lorna staring at her from the threshold of the church. Could it be her lurking in the woods, looking for proof that Everly wasn't an ordinary woman? A proper witch hunt, she thought, and a shiver wound through her.

She wove around the trees, her boot crunching on the dry leaves underfoot, her skirt wrapping itself around her legs. Suddenly, the fireflies stopped. They hovered in place, flitting around her, the old ash tree in the clearing ahead. But all was quiet. Whoever had been here was gone now.

She hadn't been fast enough.

She hitched at the waist, panting. She spit, clearing her mouth of the acidity, the mixture of other flavors that mashed together into a putrid mess she couldn't pull apart.

She pushed her worry away as she made her way back to the moon circle. Just in time, it seemed. Saoirse and Caraline hadn't budged. Around them, the air was charged. Rowan gasped when she saw energy shooting from Biddy's core like the sun's rays.

Behind her, she sensed the light from the house fading back into darkness, the threat to Swallow Hall passed. Rowan couldn't tear her eyes away from Biddy, though. Didn't dare look away for fear her ancestor would swirl into a vortex and vanish before her eyes.

As she watched, mesmerized, the loose forms of Biddy's arms lifted overhead releasing the object she held. The swallows materialized from nothing, gliding beneath the object. It was as if their flapping wings created a cradle of air in which to carry it. Rowan and her sisters watched as the birds slowly glided toward Swallow Hall, the wispy object—the Good Book, she was sure—buoyed by the channel of air they generated. The diaphanous ghost of the book grew closer to the house, but Rowan didn't fear they'd ram into it. Not after seeing the birds' own magic bringing Biddy to them. They were close to colliding with the walls, but they stopped and hovered in place just as the fireflies had. It was as if they'd hit an invisible force field. The object they'd been ushering, however, didn't stop. Rowan stared as a section of the wall turned black, spreading like a stain, rippling across the surface.

And then the object was gone, sucked through the black hole. Caraline slapped her hands over her mouth, and Saoirse stood frozen. The whooshing in Rowan's head sounded like crashing waves beating against her skull. She blinked as the space in the wall closed up again. It was gone.

Biddy! Rowan spun around, but she was too late. The ethereal form was pixelating, the strands of mist that had formed her shape swirling, swirling, swirling in a maelstrom until it turned dark. A word emanated from the figure. *Pishogue.*

The darkness opened up, wide and sudden just like the house had done moments ago, as if some unseen force had pulled back a veil. The air rippled, charged with ancient magic, Rowan thought, and for one suspended breath, everything was still.

Then, like smoke pulled into a void, the last traces of the Irish witch unraveled. Her presence, her power, her tether to this world were swept away into the chasm and she was gone.

Chapter Twenty-Nine

Pishogue. Was it even a real word? Once again, Rowan searched the study in the house, but she found nothing. Which left the New Bethel library. Rowan watched the clock on the wall and as soon as the minute hand clicked into place and it was 8:45, she was out the front door and across the foot bridge. The moment she stepped onto the sidewalk in New Bethel, the island's energy evaporated like a balloon pricked by a needle. The hum beneath her skin stilled, the whispers fell silent, and the invisible tether between her and Swallow Hall went slack. It was like surfacing from deep underwater—her body felt lighter but hollow somehow. Untethered. The absence of magic left a strange ache in her chest, like something essential had been left behind.

She exhaled, trying to shake it off, focusing only on the task at hand. She walked briskly, rounding the corner before she got to the Chesapeake Camera Hut. Just ahead, the outline of the library came into view, and Rowan picked up her pace.

Ryan Winchester was just turning the deadbolt, unlocking the doors, when she arrived. He reached for the handle to open the door, a collection of books and papers teetering in his arms.

Rowan hurried forward, brushing past him. Instantly, an earthy nuttiness filled her mouth, and the urgency that had been pushing her settled. "I'll get it," she said, opening the door.

He gave a sheepish smile. "Thanks. I got all this from an estate sale. I should have put it in a box. Rowan, right?" he said, those impossibly blue eyes intense and searching.

"Right."

"You're out and about early today."

She nodded to the haphazard heap he still held. "You too."

"Ah, just part of the job. Now, what can I do for you?"

She'd wanted to ask more, to keep talking to him, but he'd gotten right down to business. It was probably better that way. "I need to do a little research."

A faint dimple carved into one cheek as one side of his mouth lifted. "More scrying?"

"Nooo," she said, hoping he wouldn't ask her about that. "It's just a word I came across that I want to look up."

He let the door close behind him. "So you need a dictionary?"

She said yes, and he managed to point to the reference section. "There are several over there. Let me put this stuff down and finish opening up, then I'll come check on you."

They headed off in opposite directions. The farther away she got from him, the more the woodsy, rustic flavors in her mouth dissipated, the more her heart ratcheted up again and she tensed. That man had a reassuring presence about him. It reminded her of the warmth she felt when Everly was around. It was a new experience coming from a man . . . and she liked it, immediately missing it when it was gone.

She let the thought drift away as she pulled out a dictionary, flipping to the P section, and letting her finger trail down the words. She hadn't expected it to be there—and it wasn't. Even thinking the word filled her with trepidation, anxiety building like a gathering tempest.

Her mouth suddenly filled with that earthy, woodsy taste again. Ryan. Her tastebuds were as effective as a butler from an English manor in the nineteenth century announcing a guest. She looked up as he approached her, his brow knitted with concern. "Hey. Are you okay?"

"Yeah—" she started, but her voice caught in her throat. She let out a small cough. "Yeah, I'm fine."

The way he looked at her—head tilted to one side, worry lines creasing his forehead—made it clear he didn't buy it. "You don't look fine. Here, sit down."

The truth was, she did feel a little woozy, so she sat. "I'll be right back," he said—and he was, reappearing and handing her a glass of water.

She sipped it, then tilted her head back and drained the glass.

He'd crouched in front of her, taking the glass from her hand and setting it on the table behind him. "Better?" he asked.

Rowan pressed the heel of her hand against her forehead. "Yes. Thank you."

He stood and took a step back to lean against the table. He tucked his hands in the pockets of his brown khakis as he considered her. "Did you eat today?"

Had she? She walked through her morning. She'd had a fitful night after the encounter with Biddy and the shadow in the woods. She didn't remember getting dressed or brushing her teeth, but here she was, mouth clean, in jeans and a plain white T-shirt under her oversized sweater.

"Rowan?"

She blinked at him. "I don't think I did," she said. Or the night before, for that matter.

"Come with me," he said, pushing himself off the table. He held out his hand to help her up. Normally she wouldn't have taken it. Would have made an excuse and left. But being near him was like being around Saoirse and Caraline. Easy. She took his hand. Once she was standing, he pushed in her chair, grabbed the dictionary, and guided her into the office behind the circulation desk. Three ordinary desks rimmed the room, each with a mounds of catalogs and stacks of books. A small refrigerator stood in one corner. Large glass windows divided the two areas, giving a full view of the library's entrance.

He pulled out a chair for her, which she sank into, before filling another glass of water and taking a bowl from the refrigerator, handing them both to her. "Have some grapes."

"I'm really not hungry," she said, not at all sure she could keep anything down in her tumultuous stomach.

In the quiet of the room, an audible rumble sounded from her gut. Ryan cracked a smile. "Seems your stomach says otherwise."

She shook her head and gave a sheepish grin. "Maybe just a little bit," she said and popped a grape in her mouth.

Ryan plucked a handful of grapes from the bowl. He leaned against the desk opposite her, munching them while she ate hers. "Better?" he asked after she'd had several.

"Definitely. Thanks."

Ryan struck her as the exact opposite of Warren or any other guy Caraline had ever dated. He was attentive and had a sincerity about him that most of her sister's beaus didn't. He was solid, like the trunk of an old tree, rooted and strong. "So. You're a librarian," Rowan said.

"Yup."

"How does that work?"

He looked at her, amused. "What, being a librarian?"

She forced a smile. She was terrible at small talk. She'd intentionally found a job after high school where she'd thought she'd have minimal person-to-person interaction—a law office where all she did was file paperwork, reshelve law books, and deliver mail. It had been a disaster. Every day her senses were overwhelmed. Although she'd had zero contact with clients, handling the files that contained notes about their stories had set her mouth ablaze or turned it ice cold or filled it with some other sensory blast. Next, she tried an accounting firm, but the same thing happened. The files she worked with contained the financial information of people who struggled with debt or didn't earn enough so were barely getting by. She constantly battled the despair. She'd been working as a florist when Bridget died. The flowers had no history and little human contact before she got them. She worked in a backroom where it was just her and the roses and carnations and lilies, all of which left her with a pleasant botanical flavor, like chewing lavender gum all day long. She could never work in a library or bookshop where every volume told a story, not only the one written in the pages but also the echoes of the people who'd held them. She could read books she bought, ones with no history to them, but she'd never once checked one out from a library. She envied people who could, who had such vast collections of knowledge and entertainment at their fingertips. "I mean, did you go to college for it?"

"I did."

She would have loved to go to college, but that was another thing that was simply out of the question. The books. The professors. The students. All of it blended together would have been a disaster of flooding senses.

"I have a master's degree in library science. I specialize in archiving and historical research," he said.

Ah, the haul he'd gotten from that estate sale made more sense now. She nodded to it, now teetering on the desk beside her. "So all this is for your research?"

"Yup."

He smiled as he pushed his fingers through his hair, brushing it to the side. Whatever his intent, he'd only succeeded in making it more tousled and . . . appealing. She swallowed. Yes, Ryan Winchester was an attractive man.

She inched backward in her chair. She hadn't let herself feel attraction for anyone in so long she'd forgotten what it felt like. The tingle in her stomach caught her off guard—light and sharp. She couldn't let herself explore that attraction. It would only open her up to vulnerability. And vulnerability meant risk. Not just of heartbreak but of distraction. Of letting someone in when everything around her was already on the verge of unraveling. She couldn't afford it—not with Everly missing, the house fraying at the seams, and old graves rising from the earth like a warning.

Still, she couldn't deny the flicker. The quiet whir in her chest she had never felt.

She folded her hands in her lap, anchoring herself. She focused instead on the pile of books again, letting her fingers trace the spine of the one closest to her. "What's in here that's so interesting?"

His face brightened. "It all belonged to a woman born and raised here in New Bethel. Her family goes back generations." Either he was oblivious to the electrical pulses coursing through her or he was politely ignoring her fluster. She didn't know if she felt relieved or disappointed. "She was a bit of a town historian," he went on. "She kept everything. Photos, letters, journals, even receipts. I've been cataloguing what's relevant for the library's local archive."

He reached for a battered manila envelope from the top of the stack. "Some of it's junk, but there are always a few treasures."

Rowan tilted her head. "Like what?"

He shrugged. "Sometimes it's an old newspaper clipping with a forgotten story. Sometimes it's a photo. You just never know. That's the fun of it."

"And you live here?"

She cringed at how it came out, as if New Bethel was a terrible place to end up, which it wasn't. She had grown to love it, and now that she'd found it, she never wanted to leave.

He chuckled. "If you mean do I live in the library, then no. If you mean New Bethel, then yes. I could have gone to a bigger city with a bigger library with research departments. DC or Philly, but I'm more of a small-town kind of guy. I like being near the water and being able to walk to the ice cream shop if I want a sundae, go to the hardware store for a lightbulb. The slow pace fits me." He paused for a split second. "You're Everly's granddaughter, right?"

She wondered how long he'd been waiting for an opening to ask *that* question. Everyone seemed to know Everly, and Rowan and her sisters' presence had been hot gossip. "One of them."

"And? Are you a city girl?"

A shudder passed through her at the thought of city sidewalks and downtowns. Too many people. "Definitely *not* a city girl."

"So you like New Bethel?"

"I do."

"Are you here visiting, or here to stay?" It was a nonchalant question, but her mouth was laced with the rustic taste of bark, suddenly commingled with the zestiness of his curiosity.

"To stay, I hope. We love Bird Island."

"And Swallow Hall?" he asked, brows raised. "I've only seen it from a distance. It seems like an . . . mmm, interesting place."

That it was. She thought about his question. Her feelings were complex. She loved the house and its history, but a niggling apprehension was layered into it too. "It's home now."

"So you plan to stay here? Not just a visit?"

She had a fleeting thought that if he got to know her better, he might *want* her to stay. For a second she let herself imagine what it would be like to do some of the things Caraline did—go on picnics and walks, dates at the movies, and dinner. She never let herself imagine this because of the intensity of others' emotions grating on her. She always imagined she and Saoirse would grow old together.

But was her future written? After all, she'd also thought she'd keep moving like Bridget always had. But here she was, wanting to never leave New Bethel or Bird Island. She blinked, slipping back into the moment. "I hope to . . ."

She stopped. She wasn't going to run away like Bridget had. She didn't want to live her life wandering from one place to the next, never putting down roots. She could change her stars. "I'm staying," she said, decisively. "Yeah, I'm staying."

His lips ticked up in a small smile, and her heart did a little dance. Maybe those dreams she had—the picnics and the dinner dates—maybe they could become a reality with the right person. With someone like Ryan who didn't saturate her tastebuds or overwhelm her senses.

And maybe she and her sisters could realize their childhood dream of a café. It seemed possible in a place like New Bethel.

"So," he said. "What's the deal with that word you wanted to look up?"

The question snapped her back to the reason she'd come to the library. She'd thought about this question, and how to answer it. She'd planned to brush it off, chalking it up to random curiosity. "It's Pishogue," she said. "I heard it last night, Everly doesn't have encyclopedias or even a dictionary, so that's why I came. To look it up."

"Where'd you hear it? Maybe there are some context clues?"

She shook her head. "No context."

He frowned. "Who said it? What were they talking about?"

Her words fumbled on her tongue. "It wasn't a . . . It was, I mean, it was just . . . the word."

If her explanation seemed strange to him, he didn't say. Still, he seemed to sense there was more to the story. "Pishogue isn't the kind of word dropped in everyday conversation."

No, it wasn't. It was a word whispered by the spirit of her dead ancestor. She stood, straightening her sweater. "Thanks for the snack. I better go," she said. At the door, she stopped and turned. "One more thing. Have you heard of a man called Cillian Tully?"

Whatever Ryan thought she might have said, it was clear from the surprise on his face that it wasn't this. "No," he said slowly. "Who is he?"

A name from Biddy's letter to Paddy had stuck with her. She conjured it up now, and instead of answering his question, she asked him one. "What about the name Ó Ruadháin?" She pronounced it phonetically and probably butchered it.

He drew his brows together, clearly puzzled—and maybe intrigued—by her. "First Pishogue. Then Cillian Tully. And now an old Gaelic name." He cracked a smile. "You, Rowan, are a very interesting woman."

She had no idea what to say to that. She tried to force a smile in return, but she could feel how tight it was on her face. "Yep, well, all we Connors girls are."

"Not Early then?"

"Both," she said. "Definitely both." And before he could say anything else, she was outside and heading back to Swallow Hall.

Chapter Thirty

Saoirse and Caraline were already in the gathering room when Rowan returned. She was grateful for the flames crackling in the fireplace casting dancing shadows on the walls. She shook off the cold, as well as the lingering heat of Ryan Winchester. Her sisters sat on the floor like they'd done around the scrying bowl in Rowan's room, three orchids on the floor in front of Saoirse. "What's happening?" she asked.

"The house swallowed it," Saoirse said, not looking up.

Rowan stopped short. "What did you say?"

"Not me," Caraline said. "That's what Saoirse thinks the *ghost* was trying to tell us."

She emphasized the word as if she hadn't been there. Hadn't seen it with her own eyes, and now that she'd put some distance between the night before and this moment, she could reason it away.

"We saw her twice," Saoirse said. "And last night, she was showing us what happened to her book after Paddy built the house. It *swallowed* it to keep it from Paddy."

"Gives new meaning to the name *Swallow* Hall," Caraline sniped. She sat with her knees pulled up against her chest like a barrier, then looked at Saoirse again. "Okay, Edgar Cayce, explain."

"First of all, Edgar Cayce was a clairvoyant, not a healer," Saoirse said matter-of-factly. "I can't read Biddy's mind or speak for her through my higher self. What I *can* tell you is that, as a fellow healer, I know she was telling us something specific."

"We already know Paddy stole the spell book from his mother and really? The house swallowed it so he couldn't have it," Caraline said.

"It makes sense."

Caraline frowned. "Does it, though?"

Saoirse looked up, leaning forward and leveling her gaze at Caraline's lips rather than her eyes. It was focused and intentional, something Saoirse rarely did. Caraline noticed it too and sat up straighter. "You saw it, Cara. You saw Biddy and the swallows and the book. You saw the wall sucking it in. It's in here. That's what Biddy was trying to tell us. This house has the book—"

A realization struck Rowan. "And I think she wants us to find it. Why else would she be showing it to us?"

Saoirse was back to plucking the petals from the black orchids she held. They scented the air with the aroma of a chocolate cake baking in the oven. "The fourth thread," she said softly, her brow furrowed as the words from the tapestry echoed between them. "Maybe, at first, it was Paddy—"

"And then Cillian Tully," Rowan finished, the name twisting uneasily in her mouth. The thought clicked into place too easily, like a puzzle piece that fit, but at the same time didn't belong.

Saoirse muttered under her breath, repeating what Rowan had been thinking. "The Shadow-Tethered. The Unseen Heir."

Rowan's pulse rasped in her ears. *The Unseen Heir.* If Cillian was descended from Biddy, through Paddy and Siobhan—if his bloodline was hidden, buried beneath years of secrets—then it made sense.

But . . . it also felt like a trap. Like they were only seeing what they were meant to see.

She folded her arms across her chest, unease prickling beneath her skin. "Maybe it *is* him," Rowan admitted quietly. "But maybe that's exactly what we're supposed to believe."

A breeze snaked across the floorboards, but it wasn't cool. It carried a faint static charge, raising the hairs on the back of her neck. The light in the corner of the room flickered, just once, like the island itself was caught between wanting to reveal the truth and keeping it hidden.

"*The one who walks with ruin close behind.* Jesus, I would have left too if I was Bridget," Caraline muttered, her eyes flicking toward the window as the light steadied again.

Once again, lines from Biddy's letter to Paddy surfaced in Rowan's mind. What if the Good Book was the proof that could have convicted her when she'd been tried for witchcraft? She said in the letter that Paddy had saved her. A chill danced over Rowan's skin. He'd saved her because he'd taken the book that could have proved her witchcraft.

"She sent the swallows. Harbingers of the truth," Saoirse said thoughtfully. "I think she enchanted them so they'd protect her magic."

Harbingers. Another word Biddy had used in her letter.

At that moment, something tapped against one of the large windows facing the bay. They all jumped and spun around. The red-breasted swallow hovered. The same bird who'd tapped against Rowan's attic window the night Biddy first appeared. Then suddenly the planks of the hardwood floor in the center of their little circle creaked, sounding as if they were splitting apart. Rowan, Saoirse, and Caraline scuttled backward as the wood buckled. The middle of each piece bulged up, up, up until they each split in half with a cascade of booming cracks. The ragged ends shot toward the ceiling.

It felt like a resounding confirmation. The house wanted them to have Biddy's book. But why reveal it after all this time? The answer curled through Rowan like an instinct. Everything about this place—the island, the house, the tapestry, the sigil, even the tangled bloodlines—wound back to the same truth. The triad. The three threads. The knot that bound them together, tighter than they'd ever understood. It was about the three of them here together.

She dropped to her knees, inching toward the jagged opening in the floor.

Saoirse's breath hitched. "Be careful."

"I will." Rowan's voice was quiet and steady, but her heartbeat fluttered unevenly in her chest. The house wasn't resisting. No, she felt it *relenting*. Letting go, like it had been *waiting* to, but only when the three of them understood what was at stake, and when they were side by side, all there to receive what it was offering.

She leaned forward, peering into the dark space beneath the floorboards. The faint outline of something rectangular hovered in the shadows. *The Good Book.* She curved her arm to avoid the sharp edges of the upright slats, reaching for it. As her fingers came near to it, the object rippled as if it were nothing more than a mirage, and for a moment, she wondered if it was even real. "I can't quite reach it." She inched closer to the planks of wood the house had torn apart. As she bent over them, the spiky points grazed her arm through her shirt, then the floorboards shifted beneath her, slow and deliberate. The jagged edges softened and the shadows pulled back. The house eased its magical grip. The book shimmered just out of reach.

Rowan's fingers hovered just above it, her pulse ratcheting up. Biddy had wrapped her book in spells, and Swallow Hall had hidden it away. In the marrow of her bones, Rowan knew that it had been waiting for this exact moment, for the triad returned, for the three of them bound like the knot on the tapestry.

And now . . . it was finally ready to let them have it.

Beneath her, the loose planks of the floor gave, creaking under her weight and her upper body slid deeper into the hole.

Suddenly hands came around her middle and she felt a body against her back. "I have you."

Caraline. She was holding on to her so Rowan could reach further down. The edges of the wood were sharp, digging into her, but not with enough force to impale her. This time, as she reached, her fingers grazed the object the house had swallowed so long ago. It was solid. Real. She torqued her body, thrusting her left arm toward Caraline. "Hold on to me," she said. Caraline released her torso and wrapped her hands around Rowan's forearm instead, allowing her to reach her right arm further into the abyss.

"A little more," she said, and Caraline let her hands slip down to Rowan's wrist, giving her more slack. Finally, she was able to grab hold of the book, just barely.

"Pull me up," she said, and Caraline tightened her hold and yanked. A ragged piece of the flooring scraped Rowan's stomach. She curved her back as Caraline gave a final tug, heaving her up and away from the torn-up planks. Caraline let her go and she fell back, clutching the book like Biddy had done, afraid that if she didn't, it would disappear. The loud creaking sound came again, and they all lurched backward as the planks moved back into place, covering the gaping hole, the jagged ends fitting together like puzzle pieces until the floor was whole again.

The house had swallowed the book more than a hundred years ago, but now here it was clasped in Rowan's hands. Bridget had seen the book. Biddy had shown it to her. Rowan remembered what her mother had written in the Keeper's Journal. *She showed me the book. I touched it. I felt its energy, but I couldn't take it.*

Or, Rowan thought, maybe Biddy had never intended to give it to Bridget, but instead planted the seed of its existence. She couldn't shake the idea that everything came back to her and her sisters. The triad.

As if in response, the book trembled in Rowan's hands, turning warm to the touch. Threads of gold shimmered along its binding. The sigil on the cover glowed faintly, a line of fire burning the outline of the swallow, the crescent moon, the Celtic knot, along with the name—*Spells—Coehrses—Cures.*

Saoirse stood and crossed the room, crouching near the hearth, lost in thought. Caraline moved to the edge of the velvet chair, elbows propped on knees, her eyes locked on the book. Rowan sat on her heels, the hush pulling tight around them, energy pulsing from the book.

The book was heavier than it should've been, humming faintly against her thighs and the palms of her hands where she held it. She stood and carried it to the center of the gathering room. Saoirse and Caraline joined her. Together they formed a quiet triangle, just as they had when they were girls whispering spells into the wind. The only light came from the flickering candles and from the quivering flames in the fireplace.

Rowan brushed her fingers over the book's cover. "Remember the tapestry . . . *The House shall call them by names not yet spoken.*"

Caraline crossed her arms, more guarded. "I thought that meant titles because it couldn't know *our* names."

"Right," Rowan said. She'd thought it meant calling her as a scryer, Saoirse a healer, and Caraline a kitchen witch. Now she wasn't so sure. "What if they're names from before?"

"From before what?" Caraline asked, still wary.

Rowan held the book between them on her open palms. "Something ancestral," she said, knowing she was right the second the word left her lips.

The book shuddered once in her hands, then opened itself, as if confirming the notion. They stared, watching the pages flutter and then stop somewhere near the center. Ink spread across the parchment, as though some unseen hand was writing just for them.

A name appeared, with an ancient calling, magical and mysterious.

Greenmother: *She who heals, who binds earth to body and soul to soil.*

Saoirse stepped closer, drawn to the page like a moth. "Greenmother," she breathed. "It knows me."

Another name materialized.

Brightwill: *She who burns bright enough to reveal the truth.*

Caraline's eyes shimmered with something unreadable. She didn't speak the word aloud, but Rowan saw the way her spine straightened, the firelight dancing across her hair. Brightwill.

The third name appeared, and Rowan froze.

Silverborn: *She who remembers, who hears the memory of what was lost.*

Her throat tightened as the truth settled low in her chest. She traced the name with her fingertip, the letters carved sharp and certain. "Silverborn," she whispered, the word curling over her tongue like it had always been inside her ready to surface.

She knew it from the way the house had been calling, from how the walls bent and the whispers threaded through the floorboards, from the way the island breathed beneath her feet.

She was the next true Keeper, the one meant to remember, the one the house would rise for, or fall to ruin with.

The house creaked overhead, another soft exhalation, this one of agreement.

"This is who we *are*," Rowan said, understanding rooting deep in her bones. "This is Biddy's blood in us."

"But why now?" Caraline's eyes swept over them, then back to the book. "Why us?"

The fire popped again, a sharp spark fluttering out, landing on the floor before extinguishing. "It's been waiting for us—" Rowan said.

"—like a prophecy." Saoirse nodded, clarity written on her face. And then she recited from the tapestry. "*When the loom is stilled and the threads lie frayed, they shall gather once more, as it was written. One of bloom, whose hands stir life from root and ash, one of flame, whose fire guards the way, and one of moonlight, who bears the memory of the dark.*"

Gooseflesh prickled along Rowan's skin. Their magic wasn't happenstance—it was inherited, a legacy rooted deep in blood and bone, traced back to Biddy. Holding the book now, she didn't just believe it. She felt how real and potent it was. She felt it alive within her veins.

The pages of the book fluttered again, then a fourth name took shape, appearing not in ink but in shadow. They stared at it. It felt too dangerous to speak aloud but also impossible to ignore. She read it to herself, just as she knew her sisters had.

Ashborne—*Of burned lineage. A child of ruin and survival.*

Rowan blinked, her breath stuck in her throat. Her fingers reached for the name, but the book closed, and the moment passed. Still, she couldn't unsee it.

Chapter Thirty-One

Hazel had taken to slipping under the covers, her warm body like a heater against Rowan's side.

Pine.

Rowan turned onto her belly, the movement pushing Hazel out of the way.

Earthy.

She threw her arms over her head to block out the light.

Nutty.

Hazel yelped and Rowan cracked an eyelid. Was it morning? She'd tossed and turned all night with Biddy's book under her pillow, and didn't think she'd gotten any sleep at all.

Citrus. Iron. Nutty. Grains.

She grabbed the glass of water on her nightstand and gulped it down to chase away the flavors clashing in her mouth. She was dressed in minutes and taking the stairs two at a time, book in hand. It felt like déjà vu when she saw Caraline grabbing the handle of the front door and yanking at it. Swearing at it. Throwing her arms up in frustration.

Rowan stopped. "What's happening?"

Caraline grabbed the handle and gave it another go. It didn't budge. "I can't. Open. The. Door."

"Where are you go—"

She broke off, jumping when someone pounded on the other side. "Come on, Caraline!"

"Is that Warren?" Rowan said.

"Yes." She smelled of lemon. "I made some tea with the lemon balm," Caraline said, knowing Rowan's thoughts.

"Let me try," Rowan said. She looked around for a safe place to set the book, finally landing on a console in the corner. She dropped her shawl on top of it. Back at the door, she grabbed the handle just like Caraline had. She gave it a good yank, but it didn't open. "It's stuck."

"It's not stuck," Caraline said, not sounding as angry as Rowan would have expected. Still, she swept her gaze up and around, then slapped the door with the palm of her hand, yanking it back and rubbing the sting away. "Come on. Just let me out."

The house was utterly silent.

"Warren?" Caraline called, but it was quiet on the other side of the door. It seemed Warren had given up.

Once again, Caraline stepped up to the door, took the handle, and turned. This time it opened to a screen of winter creeper crisscrossed over the opening, the branches of the espalier tree completely covered with the vine. All new growth from overnight.

Caraline clawed through the vines, straining as she tore them apart enough to crawl through. Warren stood there, stone-still and fuming, a canvas bag slung over his shoulder. He glared at the vines. At the door. He glared at Rowan through the vines too, the scent of lemon permeating her senses. Then quick as a flash, he threw up his hands and turned on his heel and strode toward the footbridge.

Caraline scurried after him. "Warren, wait!"

"Caraline!" Rowan hollered, willing her sister to stay here. They had too much to do, too much to think about for her to disappear with Warren right now.

Caraline needed her. Rowan could feel the pull deep inside, a tether that held the sisters together lightly fraying yet struggling to stay connected. Rowan grabbed the Good Book, along with her shawl, and started out the door but plowed into an invisible wall. It stopped her in her tracks. She understood instantly. She couldn't take Biddy's spell book outside. "Okay," she said, backing up.

She heard snippets of Warren's frustration as he and Caraline walked toward the footbridge. ". . . doesn't like me."

Was he talking about her? She had glared right back at him and had made no secret that she didn't want him intruding.

Caraline's placating voice replied. ". . . the three of us . . . to stay here, together."

Their voices faded away as Rowan ran to the sunroom and handed the grimoire to Saoirse so she could get to Caraline. After the night before, she didn't think her sister would leave with Warren, but she didn't want to take any chances. The prophecy, if that's what it was, was clear. It was about the three of them. "Keep it safe."

Saoirse nodded solemnly and hugged it to her chest.

Seconds later, Rowan was back at the front door. She put her hand out in front of her in case the invisible barrier was there, but the coast was clear. She climbed through the hole Caraline had made. Her sister stood alone, her skirt caught in the wind, arms folded tightly across her chest. Rowan slowed her pace, watching as Warren stopped a few feet away from Caraline, frustration rolling off him in waves.

"You don't have to stay," he was saying, his voice low but urgent. "Whatever's going on with the creaky floors and flickering lights, it's not normal, Caraline. It's not *safe*."

Caraline shook her head, breathing out a sharp sigh. "Swallow Hall has its quirks, but you don't understand. It's more than an old house."

Warren clenched and unclenched his fists, clearly trying to keep calm. "I'm not trying to be the bad guy here, okay? But from the outside, it looks like your grandmother has you wrapped up in . . . something weird."

As she approached, the acidity of citrus filled her mouth, magnified with Warren and Caraline together. She saw a cascade of emotions cross Caraline's face. She knew her sister liked Warren. She liked his company. Hell, she liked *male* company. And now Rowan prayed she wouldn't be swayed by the man's charm and his romantic picnics in the woods. She prayed that Caraline wouldn't leave with him.

Her sister leveled her gaze at him. "You don't even know me." She gestured wide, encompassing Swallow Hall and Bird Island. "You don't know anything about my grandmother or this place."

Rowan arched her brows. She hadn't expected that response. She reached her sister's side, staying quiet, watching with wonder as Caraline made her choice.

Warren's expression changed. He looked shocked, as if he couldn't believe Caraline was resisting his charm. His voice came out with a hiss. "The lights go out for no reason. The doors open and shut on their own. It's like that place is . . . alive or something."

Rowan arched a brow, finally speaking up. "It's an old house. Sometimes old things act up."

He shook his head. "You think I haven't heard the talk around town? People think your grandma is . . . you know. Strange."

"Beautifully strange," Caraline said.

Warren looked at her like he didn't know what to say. "So that's it?"

Caraline nodded. "I guess it is."

He hesitated, then stepped back, looking at Caraline with disbelief. "Your loss," he said, giving a short, breathy laugh, sharp at the edges. His gaze lingered on her, then he lifted the canvas bag. "I was gonna take you to the old ash tree for a quiet picnic. Just us, away from all . . . this." His eyes flicked to Swallow Hall, then back to Caraline. He gave her a baffled shake of his head. "We could've been good together, you and me, but I guess some people prefer holding on to what's already broken."

Caraline stood staring at him. He threw a final disappointed look at them both, then, without another word, he turned and walked away, disappearing into the mist.

Rowan looked sideways at her sister. "You alright?"

Caraline let out a breath she'd clearly been holding. "Yeah. It's his loss."

There was her Caraline, the heartbreaker. Warren would get over her, and she'd eventually find love with someone else, hopefully one day a love that would last. Rowan linked arms with her. "Definitely his loss."

They turned back toward Swallow Hall, the glow from the windows casting long shadows behind them, two sisters walking into a story too old for the uninvited, and far too real for those who refused to believe.

Chapter Thirty-Two

Rowan, Caraline, and Saoirse sat around the kitchen table, Biddy's book between them. Rowan pulled the grimoire toward her and placed it on its spine. She let the front and back covers fall open. The pages in between drew her attention. The words were written out like a recipe with ingredients and instructions. The book fell open, settling on a page. "This one's a cure for 'inflammation due to crystals in de joints. toes. ankles. knees.'" She turned it so they could see. "Do you think she meant arthritis?"

Saoirse scooted her chair next to Rowan's and read. "Maybe. Lemon and coffee," she murmured. "Interesting. Could be gout."

Rowan started to flip through the discolored pages, but they took over, fluttering then stopping on their own.

"It's definitely enchanted," Caraline said in awe as Rowan read, sounding out the words. "'Boehrsts o' 'eat. Dampness aha de skin. Loack o' sleep.'" They hadn't spoken about Warren again, and for the first time since they'd come to Swallow Hall, Caraline seemed completely present and accepting.

Saoirse took over, reading it again, sounding out the words with more ease than Rowan had. "'Treated wit soehlfoehr. Ahr a derivative made farm de ink sac o' coehttlefesh.'"

Rowan pulled a face. "That sounds gross."

Saoirse shrugged. "Nature is powerful."

The page on the left held what looked like an incantation.

Rowan had to read it several times to make sense of it. She pieced together that it was about a woman going through menopause and the beauty of the next phase of life. She ran her fingers over the words on the page.

Saoirse placed her fingertips alongside Rowan's, dancing over the letters. "Biddy helped people."

"What about the curses, though?" The grimoire, after all, was called Spells—Coerses—Cures. That meant there had to be some darkness inside. Maybe it was that darkness that couldn't fall into the wrong hands.

The book seemed to have heard Rowan's question. The pages whipped until they settled again.

Another incantation. Rowan read aloud this time, "The hurt someone causes coming back to them and spreading like a deadly mold." For a brief second, Warren came to mind because he'd hurt Caraline, Something about him still felt . . . unsettled. Just slightly off, like the edges didn't quite line up. Like he was already overrun with mold.

She shook the thought away and sat back, folding her arms over her chest. "That's intense. How do you think Biddy figured all this out? How to cure people, and how to curse them?"

"It's who she was, I think, just like we're who we are. I just know about flora. Caraline just knows about herbs and food. You just intuit and now scry. It all just *is*."

Once again, the pages fluttered, then settled. Rowan felt that familiar pricking of needles inside her body, poking her like they were trying to cut through the skin and break free. She swallowed the mixture of flavors trying to find purchase in her mouth. Not now, she said, taking a deep breath in and exhaling slowly. They leaned over to read. This passage was short—not an incantation or a curse, but a message with similarities to what Biddy had put in her letter to Paddy.

Siobhan is wit cheld. I fear a peshahgue.

"'I write this to *you*. *You* have the power,'" Rowan read aloud. Gooseflesh rose on her skin. "She wrote this *to* the book."

They were quiet for a few seconds, letting this sink in. The book, Rowan realized, was more than just enchanted. She ran her fingers over the slanted script, the faded ink catching the light. "It's like the book remembers. Like it carries her voice. Her magic." It was a vessel for Biddy. It *was* a Keeper of her magic.

Chapter Thirty-Three

They'd moved to the gathering room and had been there for two hours, reading and trying to decipher the muddled words Biddy had scrawled in the grimoire. They were part English, part Irish, part something else entirely. Caraline had made a pot of brambleberry tea and raspberry scones with clotted cream. Saoirse carried a stunning Black Dracula orchid, its roots curling in the small pot, setting it next to the book. Flower petals—violet, chamomile, and sage—were scattered across her lap, a trail left from her spellwork.

Caraline's countenance had changed again. She shot looks at the front door, as if she'd changed her mind, wishing she could go after Warren. The tea and the scones were comforting for Rowan, but the tastes were muted compared to the deeper tastes moving across her tongue. She closed her eyes and swallowed, grounding herself in the energy of her sisters as she processed them. First was a flicker of something sharp and coppery, like hurt. Then something soft and floral. Grief laced with longing, she thought. And beneath it all was the tang of old magic. It felt wild and untethered. It was like tasting a storm just before it hit.

They weren't flavors, not really. They were memories, bright and shimmering. They were echoes left behind by the woman who'd written in this book before them. Like moonlight, they illuminated what had been hidden for more than a century, casting silver light across the shadows of the past. Rowan let them settle on her tongue, quiet and powerful, each one like the whisper of something that had been lost but was now returning.

Saoirse flipped a page carefully, her fingers stained faintly from her work in the apothecary. "So before any of Paddy's children or descendants were able, the swallows were the Keepers," she said thoughtfully. Then she looked up. "So what is a Pishogue?"

They all started when a knock came at the front door. Rowan raised her brows, looking at Caraline. Her face lit up like she was hoping it was Warren, back to apologize.

Rowan hoped it wasn't. She stood, going to the door, yanking it open. She opened her mouth, ready to send Warren on his way, but froze when she saw it was Ryan Winchester standing outside the crisscrossed vines of the winter creeper, a worn brown leather messenger bag slung across his body.

He looked a little shell-shocked, his eyes searching the property behind him, the espalier above him, and whatever was visible inside the house through the narrow opening of the vines.

"Oh," Rowan said, any other words tangling on her tongue.

It was midafternoon, but he had a good coating of stubble on his face and windblown hair from his walk from town. "Good way to keep out the riffraff," he quipped, gesturing to the winter creeper.

"I have to stay on it or it'll take over the whole house," she said. "Of course, we don't get many visitors."

She clamped her mouth shut, hoping he wouldn't ask why, because what could she say? That the house was magical and protected a grimoire so strangers weren't really welcome?

"Right."

They stood there awkwardly on opposite sides of the threshold. She thought about the taste of rustic earthiness she'd experienced earlier, stronger now that he was in front of her. If she'd paid attention, she'd have known he was coming.

Finally, he cleared his throat and gestured toward the inside of the house. "Could I, uh, come in? I did a little research after you left yesterday and I want to show you something."

"Oh." She looked over her shoulder at the wonky windows and overlapping area rugs. At the door high up on the wall that had no stairs leading to it and that went nowhere. The house had let Warren in, so why not Ryan? Assuming the winter creeper didn't block his entrance. "Um . . . yeah."

He hesitated for a second before feeding one leg through the opening in the vines, then hitching at the waist so he could drag the rest of his body through. The fabric of his pant leg snagged on one of the vines. He turned and kicked, breaking free. Was that a sign that he shouldn't enter? But no, she was able to open the door and the house let him in. She led him to the gathering room, relieved to see her sisters had covered Biddy's book with one of Everly's knitted shawls. They stared at Ryan, openly intrigued by this man who'd come for Rowan. She saw him look around, his eyes wide, his forehead creased. But he didn't say anything. He just blew out a breath and sat down in Everly's rocking chair, his messenger bag on the floor at his feet.

Rowan hesitated, unsure of herself. Having a man she knew come to see her, even if it was for research, was a new situation for her. "Uh, Ryan, these are my sisters, Saoirse and Caraline." She looked at them. "This is Ryan. He's the librarian at the . . . library." Obviously.

As she sat again in her velvet chair, she felt her sisters' gazes on her, burning with their curiosity, but ignored them, trying her best to chase away the bloom heating her cheeks.

Caraline grinned, nodding at him. "Hello there, Ryan."

Saoirse looked past him. "Hi."

He smiled. "Nice to meet you both."

Rowan saw him notice the scones and tea set out in front of them. The roots at her red streak of hair sizzled with energy. She pressed her fingers to the spot, willing it to be calm, to not start glowing. "Can I get you some, uh . . . tea?" she managed.

He looked at her, narrowing one eye just a bit. "I'm good," he said, "but thanks."

"You have something for us," Saoirse said, looking at his bag.

He blinked, coming back to his purpose. "I do. See, I love a good puzzle and figuring out that word you came to ask about, Pishogue," he glanced at Rowan. "It lit a fire, so I called a friend of mine—"

"Another librarian?" Caraline asked.

He swung his gaze to her. "Historian, actually," he said, then looked back to Rowan. "We weren't far off the mark when we were talking about the Salem witch trials—"

"*Were* we talking about that?" she asked. Because other than a cursory mention, they hadn't had a conversation about them.

He shrugged. "You know, tangentially. Because you were asking about scrying."

Scrying. That seemed so long ago. "Right."

He carried on, excitement rippling off him. "So. Pishogue is an Irish word. A noun. It means charm or incantation or spell."

She frowned. Was it something to do with the grimoire? But why would Biddy have feared a spell? The book was full of charms and incantations.

Ryan seemed to register her knitted brows. "It has a second meaning, though," he said. His blue eyes sparkled. "It also means witchcraft or—" He paused—for effect, she thought. "*Sorcery*."

The word hit her hard. Sorcery was about black magic, not the type of healing Biddy had done, or that Everly or her sisters did. And scrying and tasting emotions certainly wasn't dark magic.

The darkness deep inside Paddy was what Everly feared. What every Keeper before her feared.

"What's the context?"

She snapped her attention back to Ryan. "What?"

"The context. For the word." He paused, then added, "Pishogue."

She blinked. He's asked her that at the library. She couldn't give him the context. The word, written in Biddy's hand, shot into her mind. It was in the grimoire, but almost the exact words were written about it in her letter to Paddy. *Siobhan is wit cheld. I fear a peshahgue because you left her.*

She feared a *Pishogue.* Not dark magic itself, but one who wielded it. The ruin that would come if a Pishogue was able to harness Biddy's magic. If a Pishogue got hold of the grimoire. The fourth thread.

Her head snapped to Ryan. He was practically a stranger, yet here he was sitting in the room with her and her sisters, the grimoire barely hidden beneath the knitted yarn. Could *he* be the fourth thread? A sorcerer would be able to mask his identity, wouldn't he?

She cleared her throat, wishing he would just leave. "My great-great-great . . . uh, great-grandmother used it in a letter she wrote to her son."

His face lit up. "Really? You have letters from, what is it, a hundred and thirty, forty years ago?"

She clapped her palm to her chest. "*I* don't have it. It's on display at the Historic Society."

He grinned, knowingly. "Ah. Esther and Macy. Of course. I haven't been in there for years. I never underestimate those two and their ability to ferret out the history of New Bethel."

"Well," she said, standing. "Thanks for stopping by."

"Oh." His face fell. "I found out some other things . . ." He trailed off, one hand on his messenger bag, waiting.

Caraline frowned at her, whispering in the air, "What are you doing?"

She whispered back, "What if *he's* the Pishogue?"

Caraline's eyes widened. They both turned to him. He looked like a kid who'd just seen eight magical reindeer pulling Santa's sleigh across the sky. There wasn't a bit of darkness in him.

"He's not," Saoirse said so only they could hear. She frowned, as if puzzling through something she couldn't yet name. "There's nothing masking him."

Oblivious to their silent communication, Ryan reached one of his hands into his bag again.

"What kind of things?" Rowan asked, finally looking back at him.

"I found out a little bit about Cillian Tully."

Rowan's back went ramrod straight.

"There isn't much about him. From my calculations, he lived here in town about thirty years ago. No family. And then he just disappeared."

"He left with Bridget," Rowan said.

"Bridget?"

"Our mother," she said.

He looked at her, processing. "Your mom's probably, what, late forties? From what I gathered, he's got to be quite a bit older than her."

She'd felt the color drain from her face at the mention of Bridget's age. "Forty-four. My—*our*—mom would have been forty-four . . . if she was alive."

He looked ready to say something else but stopped, registering what she'd said. "Oh. Um. I didn't know that—"

"Research will only get you so far," Caraline said.

Ryan nodded his agreement. "Very true. I'm really sorry."

If he paid attention to the gossip in town, he'd have known, but maybe he didn't buy into that sort of thing. Or maybe Saoirse was wrong and he was playing them.

"He's not," Saoirse said, her words going straight to Rowan's mind.

"We know they left together," Rowan said, wanting to learn what else he'd discovered about Cillian Tully. They might never find him, but they were supposed to. She knew that just as surely as she knew that Bird Island and Swallow Hall possessed Biddy's magic. The wind had carried his name to her. So had Biddy herself. The manifestation of her, anyway. It meant something. *He* meant something.

Hazel meandered into the room and Rowan absently scratched her head. Somewhere deep in the house, a door slammed. Ryan's head whipped around as he tried to place where the sound had come from.

"Old house," Caraline said nonchalantly.

He turned back, his gaze snagging on Everly's shawl. The one that had been covering the Good Book but that was now pooled on the floor.

Rowan's blood ran cold. She saw Ryan notice the book with its aged leather binding and gilded-edged, timeworn pages. The air in the room thickened, like it had turned to fog. Every instinct in her body snapped to attention. She followed Ryan's gaze to the book, then back to his face. His eyes were wide, almost reverent, but she couldn't tell if it was simple curiosity or something else entirely. Something more dangerous.

He gave a low whistle. "That looks—" he said, voice strained. He cleared his throat and tried again, more casually, "—pretty old."

Rowan's hand shot out, snatching up the shawl and draping it back over the book. "It's a family heirloom."

Ryan blinked, his expression neutral, but was there more behind it. He nodded slowly. "From your grandmother?"

Rowan hesitated. Her heartbeat was thunderous in her ears. He could be a friend. He could be nothing more than a helpful librarian with a knack for finding old records. But he could also be the sorcerer . . . the Pishogue who was of burned lineage. A child of ruin and survival, *Ashborne*, the ancient name they'd seen written in the grimoire.

She didn't know what a Pishogue looked like, but she now knew it was connected to darkness and secrets.

"Something like that," she said.

He smiled, but it didn't reach his eyes this time. "I'd love to take a closer look sometime. Old books are kind of my thing."

Rowan forced a smile in return, her hand tightening around the shawl. "Maybe."

Ryan rocked in his chair a few times, hesitating like he was deciding whether to say more. Rowan watched him carefully. Her gut churned, her magic buzzing just beneath the surface because she wasn't sure if she could trust him.

Finally, he reached into his messenger bag. "There's one more thing," he said, glancing at Rowan. He carefully pulled out a clear archival sleeve. "I found this tucked into a folio of church council documents from the late thirties, maybe early forties. It says *B&C* on the back. It was just . . . there."

He handed the photo to Rowan. She took it gingerly, holding it by the worn edges. It was old and faded, but the figures were still clear. A young woman and a slightly older man side by side. The girl wore a summer dress and an uncertain smile. The man's arm was on her shoulder. The sun caught something baleful in his eyes.

Rowan's breath hitched. "That's Bridget," she said slowly, her thumb brushing over the girl's face. "That's our mother."

Caraline and Saoirse were by her side in an instant. Ryan nodded. "Do you recognize the man?"

Rowan stared, pulse thundering in her ears. She felt Caraline stiffen behind her. She felt her bewilderment first, then fear reared up. The man's hair was a little longer, the face a little older, but it was him. It was Warren.

"I thought it might be the one you were asking about. Cillian," Ryan said, oblivious to the way the floor seemed to tilt under their feet.

Rowan said nothing. She couldn't break her stare so she just kept looking. At Warren—who was also . . . Cillian Tully? Warren, who shouldn't be in a decades-old photo. Who shouldn't have been with Bridget at all.

But he was.

And now, she finally understood why the house had never trusted him.

Chapter Thirty-Four

As Ryan looked from Rowan to Caraline to Saoirse and back, Rowan tasted the cool wash of his confusion, sharp and bracing, flowing over her tongue like rainwater. But beneath that, something steadier flourished. It was earthy, familiar, grounding. She detected a faint trace of cedar and stone, solid and honest in a way that settled in her chest.

She could trust him, there was no deception clinging to him.

She knew he wanted to stay, to learn more about the book and the photo and what they'd seen, but he also clearly sensed that something was happening and he should go. He flicked his wrist to look at his watch, then cleared his throat self-consciously. "I better head out. I got someone to cover for me, but I need to get back."

"Right." Rowan shot her sisters a look that said she'd be right back and walked Ryan out.

"That book on the table," he said once they'd climbed through the winter creeper and were clear of the espalier. "It's beautiful." His tone was reverent.

"It is. Saoirse makes teas and soaps and things. The book has some information about salves our great-times-four-grandmother used to make. I'm sure she'll try them." She tried to sound casual, as if her insides weren't churning like the ocean roiling in a rocky whirlpool. She hadn't meant to share that much, but this man brought something out in her, something she didn't understand. She was comfortable around him.

"So it's an old recipe book?" he asked as they stopped at the footbridge.

She thought about how to answer his question. She couldn't come out and tell him it held the spells and curses and cures the Irish witch Biddy Early had used. That it was a grimoire. She went with a vague, "Kind of."

She liked talking to him. She didn't want to stop, but she had to before she said something else she shouldn't. Because figuring out the truth about Warren . . . *Cillian* . . . was most important. She started walking across the footbridge and he fell into step beside her. She'd walk as far as the sidewalk on High Street, then turn back.

"Swallow Hall is an unusual house," Ryan said, pivoting the conversation away from the book, thankfully, but onto equally unsettling ground.

"It is. But, you know, it's home," she said, trying to speak brightly.

"Are you okay?" he asked.

She batted away the question with a flutter of her hand. "It's just, that photo, and you know, with Everly missing and—"

He stopped short. "Everly's *missing*?"

Rowan hadn't meant to blurt that out. But with everything going on, it had slipped. She backtracked. "No, no. I mean visiting . . . with an old friend."

Ryan looked skeptical, like he didn't believe her and wanted to say something more but thought better of it.

They reached the edge of the woods. "Thank you for the information," she said.

He was taller than her five feet eight inches. He dipped his chin, looking at her. "Come visit the library any time," he said, offering her that crooked smile.

She wanted to say that she would. She liked being around him. But she wasn't like Caraline, in it for a good time and okay keeping one of the most important facts about herself to herself. If Rowan was in a relationship, she'd want to share that secret. She'd want to be honest and let that person know who she really was. But that was too scary of a thought. What if he didn't believe her and thought she was crazy? Or what if he rejected her and then shared what she'd told him? And what about the pact she and Bridget and her sisters made each year?

This was why she'd always imagined herself alone. "Yeah, I will," she said.

If he heard her uncertainty, he didn't let on. "I'll be seeing you, then," he said.

"Yep. See you. And thanks again."

"I hope it helps. If there's anything I can do . . ."

He left the offer hanging there, because really, there was nothing. It was up to the sisters to find Everly, protect the grimoire, and stop Ashborne.

They stood awkwardly for a few seconds. Finally, he ran his fingers through his hair, making it stand on end in an endearingly tousled way. "Okay. See you," he said again, and this time he walked away.

A swallow dipped low and glided by, its wings so close to the ground that they stirred the leaves. She couldn't visit him or the library again, could she?

"Hey." She looked up, startled to see Ryan in front of her again. "I almost forgot the other thing I wanted to tell you."

She didn't remember asking him anything else.

"About the name. Ó Ruadháin."

"Oh. Right." She pressed her palm to her forehead, feeling like her head might explode. "It's a name my great-gre—Biddy—" she amended. "Anyway, she mentioned it in the letter Esther and Macy have. The one she wrote to her son." Whose bones had been buried for decades on Bird Island. Who'd stolen the grimoire and somehow unleashed the darkness of the Pishogue that now threatened Swallow Hall and Bird Island.

He explained how it had taken some time to figure out what the actual name was since she'd only said it once. "I tracked it down, though. It *is* Gaelic."

Like he'd said when she first brought it up. "Okay?"

"There's always an evolution of names, especially surnames. It wasn't until the birth of the Roman Empire that they became a thing in Europe. From there, the use of what's called bynames came into practice."

She couldn't help a small smile to herself at how animated he was again. "What's that?" she asked.

"It's when someone's job or where they lived evolved into their surnames. Like Baker or Cook or Lake. Then there are cognominal names. Names based on appearance, like White, Armstrong, or Short. And ornamental names based on something more poetic or regional like Windsor—from the English House of Windsor, or de la Cruz—of the cross, or Rosenberg—rose mountain."

"So where would Connors have come from?" she asked, thinking of the family Biddy had come from.

"I actually looked it up. It's from the Ireland. They were originally the O'Connors. The O with the apostrophe means *descended from*, and it's usually someone royal. The O'Connors descended from the ancient Irish king, Conchobar mac Nessa. Eventually, the O was dropped."

She tried to get her head around this. Biddy Early had descended from Irish royalty, which mean Everly and Bridget and

Rowan and her sisters all did too, albeit centuries ago. "And Early?"

"A little less impressive. It was probably an ornamental name. From early riser, for example."

She stared at him. "You researched all this since I saw you at the library? And you remembered it all."

He gave a self-effacing shrug. "It's what I do."

"Right. You do it very well."

His mouth curved into a slight smile, but she could tell her bombshell about Everly had tempered his mood. "So did you find something about Ó Ruadháin?" Again, she was sure she butchered the name.

"Yes. Like I said, it's Gaelic. There's a progression of the name through pre-medieval clans. The O was eventually dropped too. But here's the interesting thing. It's *your* name."

She thought she felt her heart skip a beat. "What?"

"When you look at the evolution of names, it's about finding the earliest records of those names. So Ó Ruadháin became Ruane—R-U-A-N-E. From there it's been recorded as O'Ruan, Rogan, O'Rogan, Raine, Ryan," he gave a little chuckle at that connection to his name, "and O'Rowan and Rowan."

Rowan felt heavy, her feet rooted to the ground like the roots of a tree, yet she swayed unsteadily as if a windstorm was blowing through. *She* was Ó Ruadháin? Ó Ruadháin was her?

Ryan's hand encircled her arm. "Are you okay? Do you need to sit down?"

God, but he had to ask her that a lot. He had to think she was a mess, always flustered and unsettled. She *did* need to sit down, although she couldn't move.

What did this mean, that she was Ó Ruadháin? She thought of what Biddy had written in her spell book and the line in the tapestry: *The House shall call them by names not yet spoken.*

Scryer. Silverborn. Ó Ruadháin. They were all names now spoken. All her. And Biddy had written her name more than a century ago.

Everything was starting to make sense, like the cogs in a wheel suddenly fitting into place. She focused on the letter Biddy wrote to Paddy, going through the lines one by one. *Siobhan is with child. I fear a Pishogue.* The Earlys had magic in them. Everly. Bridget. Rowan, Saoirse, and Caraline. Their magic was all good. Helpful.

But she feared a Pishogue. She feared a sorcerer. Someone with black magic. Someone descended from Paddy and Siobhan.

Paddy took the grimoire. The swallows, sent by Biddy, had protected it. They were the Keepers—and then Maeve. They kept the book safe until the last of the Sky Girls came, and *until the light shines again through Ó Ruadháin.*

Rowan caught her breath. It *was* a prophecy. Biddy had foretold the future. Someone named Ó Ruadháin would be the one to, what? Defeat the Pishogue? Not the original one. Not the child of Siobhan, but the descendants of Siobhan and Paddy.

And that someone—if Ryan was correct—was her.

Chapter Thirty-Five

Rowan made a hasty retreat, leaving Ryan, whose eyes she felt watching her as she slipped back into the woods. At Swallow Hall, she told her sisters everything he'd said. The memory of a conversation she'd had with Bridget pushed through into her consciousness. Her mother had given her the name Rowan. She'd called her a leader and said she'd grow into her name, as well as her magic. Had Bridget known of the prophecy?

Rowan was learning about scrying. She was learning how to manage her clear-tasting ability. And now, there was an old Gaelic version of her name in Biddy's letter. "It's not a coincidence, is it?" she asked, after telling them everything she was thinking.

Saoirse turned to the page in the book with the message, looking circumspect. She read and reread the three lines. "I don't think so. And I think you're right," she said finally. "I think you must be Ó Ruadháin. Biddy was a witch. We know that. So she prophesied the defeat of the Pishogues. The defeat of the sorcerers who came from Paddy's betrayal of Siobhan, that betrayal that resulted in the dark bloodline."

Rowan switched gears, thinking of Warren and the house. Warren trying to get *in* the house. Something else pricked at the edges of her brain. It came to her finally: whenever he was near, she had the distinct sensation of citrus, but there were other things too. Vanilla. An underlying spiciness. Chocolate. And something metallic. The taste of blood. That taste of iron always faded, though, overtaken by the tartness of the lemon.

"Saoirse, why do you think Warren always chews lemon balm?"

"I asked him that," Caraline said. "He said it was better than smoking."

But Rowan thought it was more than that. "I always taste a little iron when he's around. Sometimes hints of other things too. Then the lemon and mint take over."

Saoirse looked up, her focus just past Rowan. "I smelled vanilla." She frowned at the black orchid she'd put on the table.

Rowan waved her hand in front of her sister's face. Saoirse blinked and refocused. "What is it?" Rowan asked.

"I rescued a little packet of orchid seeds," she said slowly. "They're not easy to tend and keep flourishing, even for me. Especially that one." She pointed to the black orchid. "All flowers have meanings," she continued. "Like the little white flowers on the rowan tree. They protect. They mean strength and power and psychic intuition. The magnolia represents wisdom. The amaryllis is about beauty and pride."

Rowan's stomach tightened. She could already feel where this was going. She nodded at the Dracula flower. "What about that one?"

"It smells amazing. Vanilla and spicy chocolate, but not like the normal kind." Saoirse looked at Rowan, their eyes locking for a split second before Saoirse's gaze slipped past. "It's distinct. Almost . . . off. But the meaning . . ." Her voice dropped lower. "Absolute authority. Submission. Control."

A cold shudder swept over Rowan. "You rescued the seeds?" she asked carefully.

Saoirse nodded. "From the kitchen trash next to some dried valerian and foxglove."

Heat pulsed behind Rowan's eyes. Warren had brought those seeds for Saoirse, expecting her to grow them here, at Swallow Hall. Rowan had thrown them away, but Saoirse had found them, nurtured them, unknowingly planting exactly what Warren wanted rooted in this house. She exhaled, slow and loud, realization clicking into place. "Is that who he really is inside? A black orchid?" Her voice came out rough. "Dark and controlling? But the lemon balm—"

"It masks it," Saoirse finished. "And probably his true age. It hides from the outside what's really underneath."

Rowan's blood turned to ice. Warren hadn't just been hiding his scent. He'd been hiding himself. She thought about how fluid his edges always seemed at first, until they settled into his form. He used magic to keep himself hidden in plain sight. Cillian Tully had been right in front of them the whole time.

Caraline drew in a sharp breath. "At the footbridge with him, I felt different. Like I could resist him."

She took Caraline's hand, steady and sure now. "He was manipulating you . . . but it didn't take hold."

Caraline frowned. "Why not? Before . . . I couldn't see it."

Rowan exhaled, the answer rising like instinct, sharp and certain. "Because you don't want to leave. You called Swallow Hall home. And we're together now. All three of us. The house feels that—or the island does—"

"Both," Saoirse said.

"It's stronger when we're here together, all of us."

Her thumb brushed over Caraline's wrist, grounding them both. "And so are you."

The color drained from Caraline's face. She sank into a chair, pulling her legs up under her, wrapping a blanket around her. "I was so stupid," she said. "How could I be so stupid?"

"You couldn't have known," Saoirse said, patting the air behind Caraline, not quite touching her back.

Rowan had been asking herself why the house was so intent on keeping Warren out. But, of course, the answer was obvious. Warren was one of Siobhan's and Paddy's descendants. *He* was the Pishogue.

"So Warren is a *sorcerer*?" Caraline said after Rowan said it aloud, her eyes wide.

"That's too literal." Saoirse plucked a curled petal from the Black Dracula plant and crushed it in her fist. "But if he's a descendant of Biddy Early, he could be like us. He has some kind of magic. And he's had decades to understand it. To grow it."

Siobhan and Paddy's descendants had Biddy's blood in them, and Paddy had left them in Ireland with untamed and untested magic, magic that had twisted down his line. Had Biddy known they were Pishogues? Had she rejected them? It made sense that they needed the book to harness their magic, to grow it into something they could control. Or weaponize.

Another realization struck. Rowan's eyes locked on the black orchid. "If his essence is rooted in that flower, all that control, all that submission, it's not just symbolic, right? He wanted it seeping it into the house. Into *us*."

The room pulsed, the floor groaning beneath them. She kept going, the ideas forming quickly, the words tumbling out. "It has to be how he got to Everly. Twisting her, weakening her. It's probably what he was doing to you, Caraline—making you see him the way he wanted to be seen. That scent. It's the essence of the black orchid—the chocolate and spice and vanilla, masked with the lemon balm he always chews."

Caraline let out a wretched cry, her hands pressed to her mouth. "You think he has Everly?"

"Maybe that's his magic. Using those things on other people to get what he wants."

Without warning, the hearth flared to life on its own. Flames licked up the brick as if the house had been listening, waiting.

Rowan's gaze snapped to the fire, heat radiating out. She understood. "That flower—it's him. His magic creeping into this place, into us," she said, her voice steady now, eyes shifting to the black orchid. "We have to burn it."

Saoirse stood and strode to the fireplace, tossing the black orchid into the flames without ceremony. As it sizzled and burned, Rowan's hand slipped around the obsidian stone. A protection. Was that why Everly had yanked it from her own neck and left it behind? So Rowan would be protected? Or was she meant to give it to Caraline? If only she'd known!

A sickening feeling flooded her. The way Warren had looked when he couldn't get into the house. His anger. His frustration. Rowan stood, walking to the window and pressing her hand to the glass. What if they didn't get to Everly in time? Now that the house had freed the book, what if Warren managed to get his hands on it?

The question slithered beneath her skin. The Good Book wasn't just written words. She felt the grimoire's power radiating outward. It was a living thing. It was an archive of their bloodline, their stories, their power. It responded to them because it *remembered* them through Biddy. They were the prophecy, which meant they were part of Biddy's memory. It had to be part of the solution too, but if Warren got hold of it, if his magic sank into its pages and corrupted its spells . . .

He wouldn't need to destroy the sisters.

He'd erase them.

Their names would fade from the tapestry. Their sigil would vanish from the house. Swallow Hall would sink into the bay, its magic silenced. The forest might no longer answer when they called. The prophecy could be twisted into something dark and false. Something that crowned *him* as the rightful heir.

The thought made her dizzy. A cold thread of fear wound around her ribs.

He could summon what Biddy had sealed away. And once that door opened, it wouldn't close again.

Rowan turned from the window, her hand brushing the leather cover of the grimoire. She couldn't let that happen. She *wouldn't.* Not while she still had breath. Not while the house still knew her name. She was Silverborn. And with that came more than just power. It came with memory. The house, the island, the bloodline. They carried every truth like whispers.

She jerked upright, urgency rising in her chest. "I'm going to find Everly," she told them, voice steady now. "Guard that book."

Saoirse nodded solemnly.

Caraline stood, tossing aside the blanket. "But . . . you don't know where she is."

Rowan hesitated for only a breath. It wasn't a thought so much as a thread connected to a memory that she pulled out of the darkness. The house itself had stitched the knowledge beneath her skin. The shadows in the woods, she thought, but then she remembered. She'd chased the fireflies the night Biddy had come, ending outside the clearing with the ash tree. Warren had mentioned the ash tree twice. Taunting, Rowan now realized. It was almost like he wanted her to find it. Like he wanted her to be a worthy adversary. Her Holmes to his Moriarty. A picnic under the ash, he'd said. Room to breathe under the old ash tree. The detail had seemed innocuous at the time. Harmless. But now she realized that nothing about Warren was harmless.

And then there was his name: Ashborne. If he was a descendant of Siobhan and Paddy, he *was* a child of ruin and survival.

As she moved toward the door, it swung open before she could reach for it, the vines of the winter creeper curling back, parting to let her pass. The house agreed.

Caraline was on her heels.

Chapter Thirty-Six

Dusk was approaching, the light from the sky dimming, the moon barely visible above them. Rowan and Caraline crossed the footbridge and raced into the woods. The trees were like old sentinels standing at the edge of the bridge, their limbs arched overhead. They'd been through these woods so many times since arriving on Bird Island, but right now the path felt different. The air was thicker. It felt energized with something ancient, like something on the island had awakened and the plant life was responding.

As Rowan's boots hit the ground, she felt the trees, felt their joined heartbeat. She could sense their roots intertwined underground like veins, like memory, the mycelia indisputably connecting them. The trees were a living network. Rowan wondered what they'd seen over the past century. What they knew. Because the trees were listening.

Caraline stayed close behind, her shoes crunching leaves as they ran. Rowan didn't speak. She couldn't. Everything around them had gone quiet. She glanced up and caught a thread of red feathers caught in a breeze that didn't reach the trees. The red-breasted swallow, ready to guide them, and around it were the blinking lights of the lightning bugs.

Everly's words came to Rowan. "*Chase the fireflies.*"

They did.

* * *

They reached the clearing. It was as if the glade had appeared out of nowhere. Silverleaf trees stood warped at its edges, their shimmer dulled like moonlight through smoke. Moss blanketed the earth.

Rowan stopped short behind a wide pine outside the circle, Caraline pulling up short behind her. They froze. Caraline's hand clenched Rowan's arm, her fingernails digging into the flesh. At the center of the clearing were two figures. One was Warren. Rowan blinked as the edges blurred and the figure shifted before her eyes. It was no longer Warren. It was an older version of him with graying hair and aging skin. It was the man from the photo Ryan had shown them. It was Cillian Tully.

The other figure flickered in the light, sitting on a flat stone, completely still, her arms wrapped around her knees. Her face was turned away, but Rowan recognized the curve of her shoulders and the thick braid of hair hanging down her back.

Rowan could hardly breathe. It was Everly. She was alive.

Warren—*no, Cillian*—paced around the stone, slow and deliberate. His figure was dappled with the waning light, his voice quiet, almost reverent. They shouldn't have been able to hear, but like the sisters' whispers carried in the air, so did his. "It's finally time."

The trees around them pulsed. Rowan could taste it in the back of her throat. Ash. Smoke. Rot blooming beneath moss in the ash glade. The woods knew what Cillian was. It remembered.

She pressed her palm to the damp bark of a nearby tree. The roughness bit into her skin. Ahead, Cillian stalked around Everly's flickering form, relentless as a shadow that refused to break apart.

"You shouldn't have come back," Everly rasped, her voice weak but laced with defiance.

"I never really left," he said smoothly, his words curling through the space, sinking under their skin. His eyes gleamed, sharp with that insipidly false charm. "Not entirely."

Rowan's pulse surged. The taste of him filled the air now—burnt sugar, clove, iron. That bitter, metallic tangle of bad intent, the fading lemon balm no longer masking his true self.

Bridget had lured him away once. It had been the only way to protect the house, to buy time. But he'd never given up. He'd spent years unraveling the threads of Swallow Hall, chasing the pieces he didn't yet understand, waiting for his moment.

He'd fractured his identity, hidden behind spells. Warren had been a carefully constructed mask to slip back inside the walls of Swallow Hall unnoticed. Cillian's magic was raw and incomplete but still dangerous, and now the house was weakened thanks to the black orchid. The quiet, creeping roots of control he'd planted here, his belief that Rowan, Caraline, and Saoirse's presence with their untapped, untrained magic would only unravel it further. He didn't know that Biddy had prophesied their coming. He'd trusted that one of them was Silverborn and could release Biddy's book, but he hadn't counted on the house holding the memory of them through Biddy's magic. It had been waiting for them. It had chosen them.

"You'll never get inside," Everly snarled.

"It's already let me in," Cillian continued, his gaze cutting toward the trees where Rowan and Caraline hid. "The house faltered, didn't it? It always does, when the bloodline is fractured. When the Keeper's too weak. Bridget ran. You were never strong enough, and your granddaughters don't even know all they are yet."

Everly straightened "You think the house won't fight back?"

"It's already crumbling," Cillian said calmly. "They're don't know how to hold it together. And then, of course, there's the black orchid." His voice dropped lower. "Once the book is mine, it's over."

Rowan felt the earth stirring beneath her as her magic sparked, alive in her veins. Cillian thought they were still weak. He was wrong.

Everly drew in a deep breath. "I won't help you."

"Oh, but you came when I called. You followed the birds. The fireflies. The trees opened for you."

"I thought they were . . . calling me," she said, faltering.

"They weren't. It was me," he said darkly.

Rowan had heard enough. As he moved inside the circle of ash and feather at the clearing's center, she stepped from the tree line, jaw set. Caraline followed.

Cillian turned, then smiled, almost as if he had known they were there. "Perfect," he said. His gaze searching over their shoulders, amused. "But where's the third sister?"

"What do you want?" Rowan asked, her voice tight, every nerve in her body coiled.

"The Good Book, of course," Cillian replied, exhaling like it should have been obvious. "I've been waiting for it to reveal itself since the day I met Bridget." His smile curled at the edges. "For a while, I thought Everly would claim it. The house would weaken, the magic would fade, and it would fall to her. But I was wrong. She's not Silverborn."

His eyes gleamed with quiet satisfaction as they landed on Rowan, then Caraline. "It's been waiting for you." His smile darkened, edged with quiet contempt. "The house thinks you're ready, but we all know you're not. You've barely scratched the surface of what's in your blood."

"You don't know what you're talking about," Caraline snapped, stepping forward. "You don't understand the first thing about this house. About Swallow Hall."

"Oh, but I *do*," he said. "I've studied every word Biddy ever left behind. Every false trail. Every buried truth. The line of Keepers should never have remained unbroken. It should have evolved. It should have made room for the Pishogues. For Siobhan's other descendants."

Rowan stepped closer, feeling the magic in the clearing shift. It tasted like copper and ozone, like the air before a storm. She could *feel* the threads beneath the earth, the trees whispering. Warning. Watching.

"You think *you're* evolution?" Rowan said. "You're nothing but decay. Mold and fungus."

Warren flinched. His mask cracked. "I waited decades for this. For the book. For the Sky Girl who could open the door to Biddy's magic. And now I have her."

"She's not the door," Caraline snapped, gesturing to Everly.

"I know that. But one of you is."

"You don't have any of us," Rowan said as she stepped into the circle. The moment her foot crossed the line of ash, the ground moved, quaking beneath the soles of her boots. A soft hiss filled the air and the black feathers floated up, scattered by a wind no one could feel.

"The magic needs balance," Cillian said. "I can give it that."

Caraline scoffed. "You don't want balance. You want control."

"And you want the illusion of safety," Warren countered. "You think because the house let you in, that it trusts you? That you have any power? It doesn't. And you don't. It's testing you."

Rowan stepped closer. "No, it's not. It's protecting us because we're Sky Girls. It's protecting Biddy's magic."

In response, Cillian lifted his hand, summoning something. A pulse of dark energy radiated outward, sharp and bitter like gas laced with blood. Rowan flinched, the taste of it hitting the back of her throat. Burnt sugar and scorched pine.

For a moment, she hesitated. How could she counter his magic, magic he'd had decades to learn and harness?

Before she could give in to her doubts, Bridget's voice rose from somewhere deep inside her, soft and steady, like it had all those years ago when Rowan was just a girl.

"I feel it in you, *a leanbh*," she'd said. "You have to trust me. You will grow into your gifts and your name. You, Rowan, are important. You will protect them."

She heard something else, the echo of words Bridget hadn't spoken aloud. *You will fight the darkness.*

Cillian was the darkness.

She closed her eyes, letting the magic course through her body. She didn't need to counter it with fire or light. She didn't have an incantation, but she didn't need one.

That wasn't her way.

Her magic ran deeper. It flowed over her bones, through skin. It was in her breath and instinct. She was ready, her senses alive with memory and meaning. She was a protector, just like the house itself. She understood that now. She was Ó Ruadháin. She was Silverborn.

She dropped to her knees, her palms pressing into the mossy earth, not like Saoirse consorting with the plant life, but to anchor herself, to connect with something deeper, something older. She felt the heartbeat of the land moving beneath her skin and in time with her own. She wasn't connecting with it through petals or roots, but through the echo of memory, sound, scent. Her magic wasn't in the growing, it was in the remembering. In the protection. In the knowing.

She didn't ask for help.

The forest answered anyway.

The vines came first, moving like tentacles creeping up, slowly at first, then faster. Before Cillian even registered what was happening, they coiled around his legs. He shouted, twisted, but the earth cracked beneath him. From above, swallows descended, aimed straight at him like silent arrows.

"This won't stop me," he laughed.

Rowan flashed a beatific smile. "Oh, of course it will."

The ground opened.

He looked at the circling swallows, then back at Rowan, his eyes locking with hers. "Buried things always find a way back," he said with a smirk.

And then he fell.

Beneath the ground, the moss still pulsed faintly. An erratic heartbeat. Faint. Distant. Ashborne's life force fading away.

The gaping chasm sealed behind him, the moss smoothing over the break like skin healing a wound.

Silence dropped over the clearing. He was gone.

Rowan didn't wait. She rushed to Everly, wrapped her arms around her. Her body was cold and insubstantial. The ordeal had taken a toll on her.

"I couldn't stop him," Everly whispered, her voice frayed. "I couldn't fight back."

"You didn't have to," Rowan said, tears catching in her throat. "You held on. That's enough."

Caraline joined them, her touch grounding. Together, they sat in the dirt and moonlight, the three of them tangled in magic and breath. Above them, the swallows circled once . . . twice . . .

three times. They moved in synchronicity, the flight led by the red-breasted swallow.

Then they turned abruptly, gliding toward Swallow Hall, vanishing in the darkening sky. Only one swallow lingered, orbiting them as if was keeping sentry over the ash glade.

Around them the forest exhaled.

Chapter Thirty-Seven

Caraline guided Everly from the clearing, Everly leaning heavily on her oldest granddaughter. Rowan walked behind them, her palm pressed to her heart until it didn't feel like it was going to thrash its way out of her chest. Now that they were all safe, the revelations came at her fast, carrying the power of Muhammad Ali hitting a speed bag over and over and over.

Everything was about Biddy's grimoire. The house Paddy built swallowed it, keeping it hidden from him. Biddy's female descendants from Paddy and Maeve were the Sky Girls. The Keepers had kept the house calm, had kept the Good Book safe from the Pishogue. Biddy had warned Paddy of the consequences of his actions. The consequences of him stealing her book of spells, curses, and cures. The consequences of leaving Siobhan behind, pregnant.

Rowan slowed, her thoughts rolling breakers on the beach. Biddy said in her letter to Paddy that Siobhan was Pandora, but Rowan thought Paddy was Pandora. He'd cracked open the box when he'd taken his mother's grimoire. He'd opened it wider when he left Siobhan. He'd opened it fully when he left Ireland. Biddy had known the magic in him had turned dark.

Cillian was one of the evils that could not be put back in the box.

Why had his children with Siobhan turned evil? Was it Paddy's betrayal of Siobhan on the heels of his betrayal of Biddy? A line from Biddy's letter struck her again.

Look fahr de swallow wit de red feathers . . . de first speirbhean. de first keeper. Throoehgh 'er, o ruadhain'll shine de light again.

Biddy hadn't been able to stop Paddy, or the magic in his offspring with Siobhan, but she had been able to make a countermove. Maeve was born of the red-breasted swallow. She was the first *Spéirbhean.* She was the first Sky Girl, because she'd come from the sky.Through Maeve, Biddy had protected her book and her descendants on this side of the Atlantic.

"We came from the swallows," Rowan said aloud.

She slowed as Caraline led Everly through the winter creeper. It opened up for her, welcoming the Keeper home. Rowan stopped at the far side of the footbridge. Looked up at the swallows who were in chaos above her. As if they'd heard her voice, the frenzy in the sky stopped and the birds slipped into a choreographed dance, moving together toward her like they were darts and she was the bull's eye. Had their swallows gone mad? Rowan raised her arms, draping them over her head. She watched, heaving a relieved sigh when they made a hard turn, then flapped their wings, flying toward their mud nests.

She chased her fear away, chiding herself for doubting that the swallows were their protectors. They'd always guided them.

But then her breath stuck in her throat. They hadn't gone to roost in their mud nests. They moved chaotically above the house, their normal song discordant and haunting. Something was wrong.

She broke into a run, sprinting over the footbridge, careening toward the front door. The vines of the winter creeper that had opened for Everly and Caraline now covered the entire front of the house. The canopy of the espalier tree was weighed down with the heaviness of new growth. These were its defensive moves. But what were they defending against now?

It couldn't be Cillian. He was gone.

And then she froze. She tasted him, that bitter chocolate, the bite of vanilla, the slap of citrus. It was so sharp and cloying . . . and wrong.

She looked over her shoulder, half expecting to see him flying toward her out of the trees.

The woods beyond the bridge were quiet.

Now the barren trees shivered. Their branches trembled, though no wind stirred.

A single swallow, its feathers raven black, soared slowly above the trees, its path too precise, too controlled. Rowan's breath caught. This one was different. It had lingered in the ash glade after Cillian vanished. She'd thought it was there protecting them until they returned to Swallow Hall, just like the swallow Biddy had sent from Ireland, the first Sky Girl.

How wrong she'd been about this one. It wasn't one of Biddy's swallows. It wasn't there for the Sky Girls. It was there for *him*. The lone swallow was no ally. It belonged to the Pishogue.

At the house, a flight of true swallows burst upward in a sudden, frantic spiral—scattered, disoriented, like they'd been spooked from within.

As the island inhaled, then held its breath, Warren's words came back to Rowan. *This won't stop me. Buried things always find a way back.*

Cillian Tully was not finished.

Not yet.

Chapter Thirty-Eight

With every footstep she took, the bitterness in her mouth expanded until all she could taste was malignancy spreading like a cancer. She searched the darkening sky for the lone swallow, but it was gone. Cillian had to be here, somewhere. She had to stop him.

Biddy had warned of the darkness that was coming. She had created Maeve and the Sky Girls. And Rowan was Ó Ruadháin. *Throoehgh 'er, o ruadhain'll shine de light again.*

So why hadn't Rowan's magic in the clearing vanquished Cillian?

Then it hit her. The sigil. The three points of the Celtic knot. The prophecy. The bloom, the flame, and the moonlight.

The three sisters had to be *together* . . . and Saoirse hadn't been there. She was guarding the Good Book. *That's* why Cillian had smirked when he'd realized Saoirse wasn't with them.

Rowan jagged to the left, snatching the pruning shears from where she'd left them. It felt like so long ago when she'd worked to keep the winter creeper at bay that day she'd seen her first vision in the water . . . the first time she'd scried.

Without breaking stride, she flew to the porch and attacked the vines. With each slice of the blades, another piece of woody stem fell away, but with each cut, the ground shook beneath her feet. The island pitched to one side and she stumbled, lurching as it dipped. The fear that Warren would get his hands on Biddy's grimoire, that the house would stop communicating with her, that she, Caraline, Saoirse, and Everly would be erased gripped her. With the help of Biddy's spells, could he replace her—Ó Ruadháin—naming himself the rightful heir? Could he manipulate Bird Island, stopping it from sinking into the bay and the house from destroying itself, severing it from Biddy's Sky Girl bloodline and binding it to his own? She panicked. Could he turn himself into the very fulcrum of future magic?

Questions threw themselves at her as she tore away at the winter creeper, cut back the espalier. Could Cillian have gotten here before her? Was he inside the house at this very moment? Was Saoirse okay? And Caraline and Everly? They'd be blindsided if he showed up. Saoirse was not equipped to fight against the evil that Cillian embodied.

"Come on!" she yelled, slicing faster and faster, combatting the new growth that sprouted. With each snap of her blades, they multiplied at a dizzying rate. It was like a Hydra, two heads growing with each one she lobbed off. Finally, she created a space barely big enough to crawl through. She grabbed the doorknob. It stuck.

"Come on," she growled. "Let me in."

The ground beneath her feet jerked again. She lost her balance, falling against the trunk of the espalier, grabbing hold of it to keep herself upright.

Everly's words on the morning of the autumn equinox exploded in her mind. If the darkness comes, the house will destroy itself, the island will sink, and whatever it is protecting will be gone forever. She didn't want that any more than she wanted Cillian to find the grimoire. The only option was to defeat the Pishogue once and for all.

The island shook again, the earth beneath the house—beneath her—roiling. She grabbed the knob with both hands and roared. "Let me in!"

The house exhaled, as if it had been in a trance but now suddenly realized it was Rowan trying to get in, not Cillian. The knob turned suddenly and the door flew open, taking her by surprise. The invisible force the house exerted pulled her in. The door slammed shut behind her.

She waited for the bitter chocolate taste to hit her, but it didn't. She didn't sense him. Her hope lifted. The lone swallow had been above the woods, guiding Cillian. She breathed out her relief. He wasn't here yet. Her gaze swept the gathering room. An energy pulsed. The wallpaper moved as if something was trapped between it and the wall. She started when a section of it pushed out like two hands pressing against it from the inside, stretching it outward. The house had swallowed the book when Paddy brought it from Ireland. Could it do the same with a person? A shudder coursed through her at the thought. She blinked and the section that was pushed out was gone, as if the hands had never been there at all.

There was no sign of Caraline and Everly but at the staircase, Rowan gripped the balustrade, hearing her sister's voice whispered in the air. Caraline had taken Everly upstairs to tend to her. Relief flooded her. They were safe.

Something imperceptible propelled her toward the kitchen. Toward the apothecary where she knew Saoirse was with Biddy's spell book. They had to stop the house from swallowing it up again.

Legacy, Rowan realized, was never enough. Without choice, the magic would become a burden. After Bridget left, Everly began to see her role as the Keeper of Swallow Hall as a obligation born of legacy rather than a choice to carry on the birthright. Although Biddy had offered the book to Bridget, she had refused it. But now

Rowan, Caraline, and Saoirse had come to Bird Island. They'd chosen to step into the unknown. They didn't want the grimoire for the power embedded in it. No, through it, they had found their birthright. They had found their family and their connection and the truth Bridget had sought. With the Good Book, they could rewrite what the magic of their bloodline meant.

She hurried through the breezeway. Worry for her sisters and for her grandmother consumed her. They had to live by the magic the way Biddy intended. They had to stop Cillian—for good. This was going to be a fight for their lives.

She jerked when she heard the unmistakable sound of glass shattering in the apothecary. She opened the door slowly, freezing when she was hit with a blast of mint, chocolate, and cinnamon. The flavors exploded, ricocheting like pinballs on her tastebuds. Her mouth went dry, every bit of moisture sucked away. She'd been wrong. Cillian was already here.

She steeled her nerves and pushed the door open an inch at a time until she saw Saoirse standing in the far corner, her hands firmly on her hips. Cillian stood about ten feet away from her, his back to Rowan. Defiance burned in Saoirse's eyes, sharper than Rowan had ever seen. It was anger, yes, but it was also a fierce and unshakable resolve. It was as if something inside her sister had finally caught fire. "You shouldn't be here," Saoirse said to Cillian, her voice low but unwavering.

Cillian turned slightly, the corner of his mouth curling into a mock smile. "And yet, here I am. Lovely setup you have—potions, petals . . . the illusion of power."

"I work in remedies and protection, not power," she snapped. "Things you know nothing about."

"I know enough," he said, stepping toward the long table in the center of the room that separated them. "I know you're not the fighter. That's not your role, is it? You heal. You hide. You hope the others will do the hard things."

Saoirse didn't move, but flames blazed behind her eyes. "You are *so* wrong." She pressed her pointer finger to her chest, then at him. "I'm the one who puts things back together after people like you break them."

He hesitated, just slightly. Just enough for Rowan to feel him faltering. "You're just playing dress-up in Biddy's shadow."

Saoirse blinked, her face clouding briefly, and then Rowan saw the slight flicker of recognition when she registered Rowan's presence. Before Cillian noticed, Saoirse met his gaze head-on. "No. I'm picking up the mantle with my sisters. We're stepping into the light she left for us. We're choosing Biddy's magic, the way she intended for it to be used."

Rowan's mind raced, thinking, strategizing. She looked at Saoirse again, whose eyes flicked up and around, not meeting Cillian's. Not meeting hers. For a split second, Saoirse's gaze passed over her and Rowan nodded, looking pointedly at the dried flowers and petals. Saoirse gave the slightest nod.

"You're like the rot that grows in whatever is left behind," Saoirse said, baiting Cillian, giving Rowan time.

Rowan crept forward, as stealthy as a panther hunting its prey. If they had any chance of saving Biddy's book, Swallow Hall, Bird Island, and themselves, it was now or never. Saoirse used flora to make her soaps and tinctures in small doses, but in a larger dose and with her magic, it could be enough to debilitate Cillian. Rowan needed to distract Cillian long enough for Saoirse to do what she did best.

Rowan picked up one of Saoirse's fluted beakers. She crouched down and cocked her arm, aiming for the cabinet a few feet from where Saoirse stood. She held her breath and hurled the glass through the open space of the center table.

Cillian jerked and turned. Rowan could see him trying to figure out what had caused the crash. She and Saoirse and Caraline had grown up finishing each other's sentences, anticipating each other's thoughts. Now, as he stared at the broken glass, Rowan stood and held out her hands. *The grimoire!*

Saoirse heard her words in her mind. Instantly, she grabbed Biddy's book from the counter behind her and hurled it across the room. It flew toward Rowan with dizzying speed. The second she released the book, Saoirse snatched a jar of something from her collection of dried flora. Cillian had caught sight of the book flying and spun to face Rowan just as she snatched it from midair. He launched toward her, stopping short and whirling around when Saoirse let out a banshee cry.

Saoirse flew at him and hurled a fistful of dust at his face. He sputtered and wiped at his eyes. "What did you—" he started, but he couldn't finish. Confusion crossed his face. His lids fluttered and he collapsed, his limp body sprawled on the ground

"Let's go!" Rowan yelled. She waited until Saoirse had leaped over Cillian before turning to run from the apothecary, stumbling as the house shook under their feet. Rowan turned to see the door to the sunroom ripple, and like the clerestory windows in the study, it disappeared, turning into solid wall. She silently thanked the house. "It'll keep him in there as long as it can," she told Saoirse, then she grabbed her sister's wrist and ran through the kitchen and into the gathering room. "Wait here," she said, thrusting the book at her.

The color drained from Saoirse's face. "Where are you—" she started, but Rowan was already heading up the first set of stairs. It felt like déjà vu from the very first day she climbed these steps. The pin nails popped and the carpet pulled up, moving like a wave under her feet, carrying her up faster than she could have made it on her own. In her attic room, she grabbed the scrying bowl and the vial of viscous liquid. "I know the truth," she said aloud, hoping that somewhere, her mother could hear her. She turned and in a flash, she was crashing back down the stairs.

At that same moment, Everly's bedroom door flew open and Caraline appeared . . . alone. One look at her sister's face was all Rowan needed. Everly wasn't here.

A chill slid up Rowan's spine as the pieces clicked together. The flickering form in the woods. The shifting shadows. The hands behind the wallpaper.

None of it had been real. Cillian's trick to scatter them, to lure them out.

The floorboards groaned beneath Rowan's feet, low and strained, as though the house had finally seen through the lie too. The walls seemed to lean in, old wood creaking with unease, the bitter scent of burnt herbs threading faintly through the air.

Swallow Hall knew they'd all been deceived.

"She was here with me and then she . . . she . . ." Caraline pulled her fingers together, then let them splay open. "Poof, she was gone. Where is the son of a bitch?"

As if he'd heard her, Cillian's muted voice echoed through the house. "It's all an illusion. Know this. I'm coming."

Tears pricked behind Rowan's eyes. Her heart plummeted to the pit of her stomach. She'd failed. They hadn't saved Everly like they had thought.

"No!" Caraline said. "You didn't fail. We can find her. We can still save her."

Rowan dragged in a breath. When had Caraline become the voice of reason? She wrapped her purple amethyst crystal in her hand, letting it infuse her with calm energy. Her sister was right. It couldn't be too late. Back downstairs, she turned to Saoirse. "It wore off already?"

Saoirse shrugged helplessly. "I was rushed and I've never . . . never . . ."

Rowan held up her hand, stopping her. Saoirse used her magic for good, not to debilitate someone. This was new territory, for all of them. "It's okay."

Clarity slid over Caraline's face. "What did you use on him?"

"Belladonna dust," Saoirse said.

"It knocked him out for a few minutes," Rowan added.

Saoirse saw the scrying bowl in Rowan's hands. She disappeared into the kitchen, returning a few seconds later with a cup of water.

Rowan dragged a hip-height table from the wall to the center of the gathering room. She placed the scrying bowl on it, glancing at the place the floor had opened up, revealing the book to them. She poured the water in the bowl, uncorking the vial. Holding it over the obsidian vessel, she poured a steady stream of the oily liquid into the water.

Caraline eyed the scrying bowl. "Will it work?"

Rowan didn't know what it would do. She only knew she had to tap into the ancestral magic coursing inside her.

As Cillian's voice grew angrier, shouting unintelligibly. she closed her eyes. "Show me what to do," she said, then opened them again. The image appeared instantly, the same one she'd seen in her room. A dark faceless figure looking up at her. This time arms flailed up and the form stretched and elongated, a gaping hole appearing in its face like Edvard Munch's famous painting of a screaming man. She held her breath as she watched the figure disappear into the black hole. Watched as the hole closed up and seemed to turn solid again. It was a replay of what had happened in the ash tree glade, but the sisters hadn't been together, and without the triad born of legacy and choice, the magic hadn't held.

She remembered the wallpaper moving and what looked like hands trying to claw their way through from the inside. The house had shown her. She looked at the spot where the floor had dissolved into a hiding space where Biddy's book had been. She turned to her sisters. "I know what to do."

* * *

Rowan pressed her forehead to the wall, her palms flat against the warm plaster. “Please help us,” she whispered to Swallow Hall.

A hum shivered through the walls. The lights of one of the chandeliers above flickered once, twice, then glowed steady. Somewhere upstairs, a door clicked shut on its own. Swallow Hall had heard her.

From the pantry, Caraline emerged with an armful of jars—dried yarrow, bay, thyme, cedar tips, and bloodroot. At the table next to the book, she arranged them by purpose—protection, clarity, warding, binding.

Saoirse pulled a cluster of blooms from her small satchel—honeysuckle and lemon verbena, then added the single petal she'd kept from the Black Dracula orchid she'd been gripping in her fist. Her fingers moved quickly, weaving them into a loose braid. “For clarity,” she murmured. “For truth.”

Rowan joined her, brushing her fingers along the stem of a rosemary sprig until it warmed in her hand. “We'll do this together.”

Caraline was still a whirlwind. She grabbed the iron tongs from the hearth, tied them with twine and sprinkled them with sea salt. She pushed chairs out of the way, leaving only the two velvet chairs and the tall table all pulled to the center of the gathering room. She chalked a protective circle on the floor, encircling the chairs, the table, leaving room for all of them to be enclosed. She stacked three white stones she pulled from the windowsill within the circle, laying out lemon balm like she was preparing an altar. “It's a perimeter,” she said when Rowan raised a brow at her. “He's not getting through without knowing we're ready.”

Rowan stood within the circle, her gaze sweeping over her sisters. She placed the grimoire on the table next to the scrying bowl. It fluttered open, pages rippling even though there was no breeze within the walls of Swallow Hall. Rowan's fingertips touched the edge of the paper, and she felt the old and powerful pulse of it, waiting.

"This is for you, Bridget," she said quietly. "For Everly. For us. And for everyone who came before and everyone who will come after."

A low rumble echoed beneath their feet . . . the house shifting, settling, readying.

From the windows, Rowan registered the change in the wind outside, how it carried a ribbon of smoke in the moonlight.

And then the air inside turned cloying. The three women looked at one another as the scent of scorched earth and sour lemon filled their nostrils. The sharp bite of chocolate and vanilla twisted into it. The time was now. Cillian was coming.

And this time, they'd meet him as one.

Chapter Thirty-Nine

Rowan heard the distant sound of a door creaking, then slamming, creaking, then slamming, creaking, then slamming, as if it was saying, "*Now, now, now.*"

The next second, another door thwacked closed, then another. Soon it was a cacophony of banging doors. The hands on the clocks spun round and round and round, forward, then backward. The phone rang, shrill and loud. Above them, the candelabras began to spin in slow circles, picking up speed until Rowan thought they might come crashing down. In the fireplace, flames exploded, the flickering light casting shadows on the wall.

Her breath stuck, the taste of bitter chocolate clawing at her throat. The sharp bite of vanilla. Lemon rind curled into something rotten. The flavors exploded on her tongue and vanished just as quickly, leaving the air dry, brittle, dangerous.

Cillian.

He was almost free.

She touched the grimoire on the table. It lay open, the scrying bowl beside it shimmering faintly. The candle flames along the mantle flickered sideways, not from wind but from energy. The kind that moved through the walls. Through the bones of the house. Her gaze strayed to the grimoire. Rowan moved to one of the chairs, taking the book with her, balancing it on her lap. She started to flip through it but let go of the pages when they began moving on their own.

"We don't have much time," she said, her voice low and tight.

Caraline and Saoirse looked up sharply.

"He's coming now?" Caraline asked.

Rowan nodded. "The taste of him's all wrong. Too sharp. Too fast. He's not hiding anymore. No more mask."

Saoirse's fingers hovered over the edge of the chalk circle, her magic humming just beneath her skin. "Then we finish this."

The chaos of the house had stilled. Now the room responded with a quiet exhalation through the rafters. A sigh in the floorboards.

The three of them began to move again. Rowan felt no hesitation. No fear. They were tethered together by blood and by purpose. Caraline grabbed the candles, repositioning them at the four points of the circle—north, south, east, west. She traced the lines of the ward again in chalk, firmer this time, as if the weight of her hand could reinforce the boundary between what they were protecting and the ruin that lay beyond.

Saoirse scattered dried rosemary, yarrow, and apple blossom along the rim of the table, whispering their names like a prayer, then uncorked a dark vial and let a drop of perfume—a piquant blend of lilac and myrrh—fall into the water of the scrying bowl.

Rowan took Everly's obsidian and topaz pendants, holding them in her palm for a long moment, feeling the hum of their burden and of their protection. She placed them next to the grimoire, but kept the purple amethyst she'd made for herself, letting it continue to infuse her with calm. She looked to her sisters. "Ready?"

Caraline answered by stepping carefully across the chalked line. She removed the yellow agate necklace Rowan had made for her, a stone for protection, for grounding, and laid it next to Everly's.

Saoirse was next. Her fingers drifted to the carnelian crystal at her breastbone, but she left it there, its energy still needed. Instead, she picked up a small ceramic bowl from the mantle and scooped up some of the smoldering ashes of the Black Dracula orchid from the fireplace. She let it pour onto the table, the remnants of Cillian's twisted magic, burned clean, stripped of its power.

The sisters tightened their stance around the table, shoulder to shoulder, their small offerings laid bare. Without speaking, they'd chosen symbols of protection, resistance, and the fight still ahead.

Each item shimmered, absorbed into the magic within the circle. The silver thread inside the scrying bowl rose, spiraling between them, weaving into a braid made of shimmering moonlight. Rowan felt power in the beat of her pulse. "The Spell of Three," she whispered.

The grimoire glowed. Words appeared scrawled across the open pages, written in translucent ink that was fully legible, the letters forming as if they'd been written on glass, materializing with the heat of breath. They read Biddy's aged language silently.

Rowan didn't have to try to decipher it. She heard Biddy say the words as if she was here, in this room, speaking directly to her. Her own voice rang out as she began reading, not what was written, but her own version of it. Caraline and Saoirse instantly joined, and together they recited the incantation:

What was kept in shadow, we now claim.
What was broken, we now mend.
As three, we choose. As one, we rise.
Let the thread of Biddy's magic become our own.
Let the bond lead us forward—into all that was lost, and all that is yet to be found.

The circle responded. The scrying bowl brightened, and the vision returned of Everly in the water, standing waist-deep in a place that was not of this world but tethered to it. Her eyes were closed, her arms wrapped around herself.

But this time, Rowan didn't hesitate.

She pressed her hips against the table, reaching into the bowl just as she'd done when the floor opened up and she'd reached into the abyss, retrieving the grimoire.

Her fingers met resistance—not water, not glass, but memory. And then something gave way, and she felt skin—cold, solid, familiar.

"Now!" Rowan cried, her voice cracking.

Caraline and Saoirse rushed in, each grabbing Rowan's arms.

Together, they summoned every ounce of energy they had, pooling it together and they pulled. A wind whipped through the gathering room. The silver braid of light spun once, then burst outward with a crackling burst in a shockwave of magic.

The scrying bowl stretched and morphed into something alive, and then Everly gasped—real and wet and alive—in Rowan's arms. In the glade, she'd felt cold and weak, almost ethereal. Now she was solid. She was flesh and bone. She collapsed forward, coughing, clinging.

"Is it you?" Rowan asked, holding her at arm's length.

Everly trembled, her voice raw. "I couldn't stop him. I couldn't fight back."

They were the very words she'd said to her in the clearing in the woods. They'd sounded hollow then, but now they were solid. Everly and Cillian had never been in the glade. It had all been an illusion. The earth had never swallowed Cillian. But Everly was here, now, and so was Ashborne. They'd saved the former. Now they had to destroy the latter.

"You didn't have to," Rowan whispered. "We brought you home."

Caraline wrapped her arms around Everly and Rowan, crying openly now. Saoirse stayed behind them, grounding them with her breath and her presence.

For one brief moment, all was still.

The chalk circle held and the grimoire glowed with a soft, satisfied light. And then Rowan's mouth turned dry again. The smack of bitterness returned, the burnt citrus, the false sweetness, the taste of a lie clothed in power. Her eyes flicked toward the windows.

Everly stiffened in her arms. "He's not finished, is he?"

Rowan stood slowly, her body trembling from the spell, from the effort of pulling someone across worlds. But her magic flared again—her own, uniquely hers.

"No," she whispered. "He isn't."

As if in response, the flames flickered and a single door creaked. A split second later, they heard Cillian's footsteps banging against the floor, growing louder and louder. A cacophony of tastes accosted Rowan as he rounded the corner. Her hands fisted and she breathed deeply, forcing the acerbity away. Cillian's gaze landed on Everly.

"Nice of you to join us," Everly said dryly.

He gaped at her. "How did you . . . ?"

Caraline gave him a hateful smile. "You're not as smart as you think you are."

He darted a look at Rowan, at Saoirse and Caraline, then at the tall table with the scrying bowl and the grimoire, open, its pages fluttering. He stopped, his legs rooted to the floor, and his expression slowly changed. He looked victorious, as if he'd already won.

Rowan worked quickly to deflate his ego. "I have a question for you, Cillian," she said, her voice steady, low. Up close she could see the lines framing his fiery eyes and the thirty years he'd wiped away with the mask he'd been wearing. "Did you kill our mother?"

Cillian tilted his head, feigning surprise. "Why would I do that?" he drawled.

Rowan folded her arms across her chest, one hand finding her purple amethyst. "I think you found her all those years after she ran, after she tried to bury the past. Revenge is a powerful motivator. You knew Everly wasn't the only key. When you realized who *we* were, what *we* could unlock, you saw your second chance. You didn't think we'd fight. So you made sure she couldn't stop you this time."

Cillian clapped, slowly, mockingly. "Well done, Rowan."

Caraline's breath hitched. She stepped forward, rage rippling off her. "You cowardly bastard," she spat. "You murdered her and thought we'd be your pawns? You are *so* done."

Cillian laughed again, sharp and humorless. "Oh no, Caraline. That book belongs to me. Her death gave you purpose. How nice. But me?" He pointed to the grimoire. "It gave me the path forward, at long last."

The grimoire twitched, the pages flipping back and forth, back and forth until they fell open. Rowan glanced at the book, registering what was written on the page. They were getting a little help from Biddy.

"No," Rowan said. Just one word. But it landed like a punch. "You don't get to twist this. Her death doesn't justify you. The book isn't yours. It never was."

He eyed the bowl on the table, the one that had just helped them rescue Everly. "What are you going to do, scry me to death?"

"We have a better plan," Rowan said, stepping forward.

Her eyes were drawn again to the open page of the Good Book, the spell already shimmering on the parchment, waiting for them.

Rowan didn't hesitate.

Her voice rang out, steady and sure, each word pulled from blood, memory, and bone:

What was hidden, we reveal.
What was broken, we reclaim.
By line and bond, by route and name.
We cast you out. You hold no claim.

Cillian flinched. His smile faltered. His eyes, already too dark, turned bottomless. Black as pitch. They flicked from Rowan to Caraline to Saoirse, and back again. For the first time, the mask of arrogance he wore so well cracked.

Rowan knew he felt it. The shift in the room. The power gathering—not just from the spell but from them. From the triad. The Celtic knot. The bloom, the flame, the moonlight. Greenmother, Brightwill, and Silverborn. They were the Sky Girls.

Fear flickered behind his eyes, brief but unmistakable.

"You don't know what you're doing," he growled, but his voice had lost its bite.

"We do," Saoirse said quietly, stepping beside her sisters. "And it's too late for you."

As she had in the apothecary, Saoirse raised her fisted hand, cocked back like a pitcher mid-windup. Cillian flinched, lunging toward her—just as Caraline let out a sharp whistle behind him.

He spun, startled.

She stood only a few feet away, just outside the chalk circle, her stance mirroring Saoirse's. Cillian hadn't realized she'd moved into position. He hadn't expected the raw, grounded power in her eyes.

Caraline didn't give him time to think. With a guttural cry, she hurled the contents of her clenched fist, a mix of crushed lemon balm, salt, and ashroot powder, straight into his face.

Cillian recoiled with a shriek, hands clawing at his eyes. He surged forward, stumbling directly toward Rowan.

But his body hit an invisible wall—the barrier of the chalk circle. He rebounded, violently flung away, landing on his back.

The protective ward flared, a ring of white light sparking along the line.

Inside the circle, Rowan gathered her power like storm clouds. It was intuitive, rooted in protection. Rooted in the echoes of memory. Her palms pressed to the air between where she stood and where Cillian lay, sprawled out. Her fingers splayed. The circle held.

Cillian writhed. His expression morphed from confused to enraged. He was blinded by the powder Caraline had thrown at him and trapped outside the protective ward she'd drawn.

As the floor beneath him trembled, Rowan's eyes locked with Everly's and she shouted, "Now!"

Saoirse leapt over the ward, inside the perimeter of the circle. Together she and Rowan chanted the banishment verse. Caraline raised her voice in unison with them. Their words braided together, growing louder: "Be undone. Be gone. Be nothing."

Cillian howled. The floorboards beneath him cracked, splintering wide with a thunderous clap. A viscous blackness bloomed from the seams, shimmering like oil. It curled upward and out, reaching for him.

He tried to slide back, but there was no ground left to find.

His eyes met Rowan's.

"You don't know what you've done," he spat.

Rowan's voice was calm, final. "Oh, but we do, *Cillian*. We've vindicated our mother. We've righted the balance Paddy stole from *his* mother. We've chosen Biddy's magic and this house full of spells and secrets."

Everly and Caraline, who was back in the circle, grabbed her just as the blackness surged. They yanked her back as the abyss hauled Cillian downward. His scream echoed for a moment longer, and then silence.

The circle dimmed and the floor sealed behind him, whole again, but scorched from the pyre.

The four Early women stood together in the center of the chalk circle, their breathing ragged, their bodies spent. But they were bonded and unbroken.

A sigh, deep in the house made Rowan turn. The wallpaper undulated, then pulled outward. A shape formed beneath it, hands clawing at it, then a face, its mouth open in an endless scream.

She drew in a sharp breath. The air whispered and the wallpaper settled back into place. Cillian Tully existed somewhere within the walls of Swallow Hall, now nothing but the echo of a memory.

Chapter Forty

Rowan had shown up at the Chesapeake Camera Hut at ten o'clock to reclaim the photos from the old bellowed camera she'd found under the stairs. The town felt different to her this morning. Fresher and brighter. The sun cast the kind of light that made everything look warm and welcoming.

Now she stood at the entrance to the library facing Ryan Winchester. One of the swallows had followed her from Swallow Hall. It perched on the railing next to her like a protector.

Ryan handed her a mug and poured a stream of steaming tea from his green metal thermos. She cradled the mug, letting the warmth permeate her skin. Neither of them spoke for a moment.

Even from here, blocks away from the entrance to the woods, she could feel the magic. It hummed under her skin, ever-present.

"I'm glad you're here."

"I was passing by," she said, holding up the sealed envelope with the developed photos inside. She didn't say that she'd gone back and forth, finally deciding that maybe she'd stop by another time. She'd been heading back toward Bird Island when the swallow showed up, circling her until she changed course toward the library.

The swallow sang, its tune sounding like *You're welcome.*

Ryan tilted his head, looking at the bird almost as if he'd heard it too. He leaned back against the railing. "What's kept you so busy over there on the island?

She gave him a sidelong look. "I can't tell you all my secrets," she said, going for coy.

He smiled. "You could tell me some."

They stood in the quiet for a moment. Rowan sipped her tea, her eyes fixed on the horizon where the woods pressed against the edge of the sky. "I'm not going to pretend you didn't notice that Swallow Hall is . . . different," she said at last, her voice low.

Ryan didn't answer right away. "You know I specialize in historical records, right? I've read a lot of old things. Weird things. Places that show up in footnotes and folklore, and don't always make sense."

Rowan smiled faintly. "So Swallow Hall doesn't scare you off?"

"It makes me curious." He shrugged. "And I've learned that sometimes history lives in the walls, not the books."

She looked at him, surprised. "That sounds like something my sister would say."

He gave her a half smile. "Then she's probably right." A moment passed before he added, "You always carry everything on your own?"

"Not alone. I have my sisters," she said, then added, "and my grandmother."

"I see your walls, Rowan Connors Early, but they're not made of stone. More like . . . stubborn hedges."

Rowan gave a little laugh. "With thorns."

He shrugged. "As so many hedges are wont to have."

"They're thorny thorns."

"Good thing I like a challenge."

Rowan picked at a loose thread on her sleeve. "I'm not saying anything more. Not yet. But . . . maybe eventually."

He nodded, quiet and understanding. "Fair."

"I've spent most of my life moving. Kind of . . . hiding. From people. From feelings. My sisters are all heart-first, you know? I'm the 'get-it-done' one. The fix-it person. The one who doesn't fall apart."

"You say that like it's a bad thing."

She raised her gaze to his. "It can be . . . when it's armor. It keeps the world out, but I've realized recently that it keeps you out of the world too."

Ryan shifted closer. "So what changed?"

"I don't know. The house, maybe. My sisters. Even . . . you." Her voice caught. "It's like everything here pulls at me. And for the first time, I don't want to run. I'm tired of bracing for the next bad thing."

Ryan reached out, his fingers brushing hers, tentative but warm. "Then don't run."

She didn't pull away. She closed her eyes, letting the earthy, woodsy taste she experienced anytime he was near sink into her. She could get used to it. She felt the air between them shimmer. It was the kind of moment you could miss if you blinked. Rowan had missed too many of them already.

"I've never been the person who stays," she said.

Ryan turned his hand so their palms pressed together. "You don't have to know how. You just have to want to try."

Rowan closed her eyes. For the first time, she wasn't holding her breath. "I think the house likes you," she said.

He cracked a smile, surprised. "Was there a chance it wouldn't?"

She couldn't explain, but she knew there'd come a day when he'd understand Swallow Hall . . . and her. "Definitely. It's very particular."

"And how do you know it liked me?" he asked.

"Because it let you in."

"Not sure that's reassuring."

"It is, though. I've seen it closed off to everyone, but it's started to breathe again. I think it sees you as part of that."

Rowan leaned her head back, breathing in the autumn breeze. She let herself exhale the doubts she'd lived with for so long. She let the walls start to crumble. Her sisters would be wondering where she was. Or maybe they'd know. Maybe the magic told them. She was beginning to understand it worked that way sometimes, like intuition with roots.

She glanced at Ryan. "You hungry?"

"I will be."

"There's leftover chicken and dumplings at the house."

He gestured to the library behind him. "I'm off at four."

She smiled. "See you then."

She left him, walking back through the woods and across the footbridge to the house waiting with its wild magic and its weathered bones. The espalier tree canopied the entrance with a welcoming arch. The winter creeper bloomed out of season, contained and happy. Walking through the front door into Swallow Hall, Rowan didn't feel like a visitor. She felt like a thread being woven back into something ancient and warm and waiting.

Chapter Forty-One

Back on the island, Rowan felt the house breathe behind her, its heartbeat syncing with hers. She turned toward the water and that's when she saw it. The tide had receded—but not in the ordinary, predictable way of coastal rhythms. The entire shoreline had shifted, and the island, once precariously close to sinking into the bay, had exhaled, its mass now lifted out of the water. The spongy earth had turned solid again, the ground dry. Even the house's foundation was dry and balanced, untouched by seawater for the first time in decades.

The sea had pulled back, revealing more of the rocky causeway that linked the island to the mainland when the tide was at its lowest. But it wasn't just exposed. It was anchored. The shifting sands had settled, the stones no longer loose and sliding but firm beneath wild sea grass. The mudflats were gone. Even the spot where Paddy's bones had been unearthed had become an actual burial site. The placard, once lodged far underground, marked the grave.

The island had righted itself.

Swallow Hall was no longer on the brink of disappearing into the sea.

It had reclaimed its place.

* * *

Rowan waited until she was in the moon circle to peel back the sticky flap that sealed the picture envelope she'd picked up from the camera shop. She sat in one of the Adirondack chairs and slid the stack of glossy photos out, laying the envelope on her lap. The first few looked like black smudges. Damaged, she guessed, or shots from the end of the roll that hadn't been used.

She slid them to the back of the pile then drew in a deep breath when she looked at the next photo. It was Bridget as a teenager. Younger, yes, but still just as beautiful and carefree as she was in Rowan's mind. She stood at the shoreline, her back to the ocean. She had her arms spread wide, the tails of the scarf on her head billowing in the wind, the long strands of her hair right along with it. Rowan kissed the pad of her finger and touched the image before moving on.

The next several were of Bridget in the passenger seat of a convertible; the top down, leaning against the hood of the old car; running toward the woods, throwing a flirtatious look over her shoulder at whoever was taking the photo. In one, she sat in the center of the moon circle where Rowan now sat, the woods in the background, swallows perched on the branches watching over her. Another showed her waving goodbye from the threshold of Swallow Hall, a soft smile curving her lips. Rowan knew that smile. The sadness that hid underneath it. Every photo was of Bridget, each one capturing a familiar element of her mother's personality. A blanket of melancholy settled over Rowan. Bridget had been so lovely. The photographer had loved her mother.

S.

Her boyfriend.

The man who'd written her letter after letter, hoping she'd come back to him.

The man she'd left behind so she could save Swallow Hall. So she could protect Biddy's magic.

Rowan turned at the sound of leaves crunching underfoot. Everly walked toward her cradling a mug of tea, steam ribboning up. "You kept the winter creeper cut back," she said, joining Rowan in the moon circle.

Mostly, Rowan thought, but it had done its job in protecting Biddy's book by keeping Cillian Tully out. "It grows fast when it wants to."

Everly settled in the chair next to Rowan. "That it does. And the fireflies?"

"They guided us to the clearing. To you."

Everly's expression darkened with understanding. "He was always watching. I see that now. He knew the book wouldn't reveal itself to him. He couldn't take it by force. He had to wait for the magic in the house to weaken and he had to wait for a Silverborn."

Because Bridget had refused to take the book from Biddy. She might not have known about Paddy and Siobhan's lineage or the Pishogues, but she'd known enough that she had to lure Cillian away from Swallow Hall and that she, as a Silverborn, couldn't return.

Rowan's pulse thrummed in her ears, the weight of that knowledge and of being Silverborn settling into her chest. "The lemon balm . . . it masked him."

"He was clever," Everly said bitterly. "It kept you from seeing who he really was. From tasting the truth of his magic. But even that couldn't change his blood." Everly leaned over and laid her hand on Rowan's knee. "You did it, my dear. You did what no one else could have. You brought the light back to Swallow Hall."

Rowan shook her head, the memory of Everly trapped, of the gathering room floor collapsing, of Warren—*Cillian*—being swallowed by the black hole still raw in her mind. The lights inside Swallow Hall flickered. The windows rattled, the wood shingles on the roof jouncing with the movement. Rowan held up her hand. "You're right. We did it together," she called to the house.

Everly studied Rowan. "It communicates with you more than it ever did with Bridget. Certainly more than with me. I have no doubt. You are Ó Ruadháin."

"You know about that?"

"Biddy's letter? Of course. Esther and Macy are nothing if not persistent when it comes to that museum. They wore me down until I gave them a box of old books. The letter they have displayed at the Historic Society was tucked inside one of them." She shook her head. "I didn't know about it, of course. Once they had it, it was near impossible for me to take it back. They live and breathe New Bethel history."

"They've taken good care of it. If they hadn't shown it to me . . ." Rowan reached under her chair and pulled out the stack of letters. Everly peered at them. "What are those?"

"Letters to Bridget."

"Letters *to* Bridget?" she repeated.

Rowan nodded. "From someone named S." She leaned forward and propped her elbows on her knees. "She never told us who our father was. I thought . . . worried that it was Cillian Tully, but these—" She waved the letters. "The man who wrote the letters clearly loved Bridget. I don't think he knew about us, but it's the timing. He wrote to her before she left, and after—" A thought occurred to her. The last one. "Did *you* hide them?"

She balked. "No, my dear. I didn't *know* about them, so how could I hide them?"

Everly looked sincere. She hadn't hesitated. "Bridget couldn't have. At least not the last one. It came after she left."

Like a few minutes ago, the lights flickered in the house, every window illuminating. The house had led Rowan to Bridget's hiding place. If the last letter came after Bridget left, the house had somehow added it to the collection.

Rowan took the last letter from the bottom of the stack, the one that mentioned Bridget's pregnancy. She slipped it from its envelope and handed it to her grandmother. Rowan had memorized it.

Everly read it, then looked up at the sky, tears pooling in her eyes. "Oh, my Bridget. You sacrificed so much, *a leanbh*."

Rowan flipped through the stack of photos again, rifling through them, seeing her mother in her youth. She came to the ones with the vintage car. She pictured the convertible with its ragtop up. She could tell from the black-and-white photo that it was a light color. Rowan cleared her throat. "Do you know who wrote the letters?" she asked, because she saw in Everly's eyes that she held the truth.

Slowly, Everly nodded. "I've never seen two people more in love," Everly said quietly. "I used to say they were fierce with it."

Deep down, Rowan realized she already knew. The truth had been creeping in for days. It had coated her mouth with bitterness and grief, the taste of self-reproach, frustration, sorrow. At the time, she thought it belonged to Bridget—or maybe to herself. But now, the pieces fell into place. It wasn't just her grief she'd been tasting. It was *his*.

S.

He had lingered in their story like a shadow. She'd seen the emotionally laden interaction between him and Everly. Everly had even said he sometimes came to Bird Island. And he'd known Bridget. He'd ached when he heard she'd died.

Rowan had tasted his anger and resentment. His sadness. The melancholy he carried with him. She just hadn't understood the reason behind it all. Her voice came out low, certain now. "It's . . . Moody," she said quietly. "Simon Moody is our father?"

Everly's expression was answer enough. Her gaze softened. "He always hoped Bridget would come back to him. That she'd come home."

Rowan's fingers curled into her palms, the truth settling low and heavy in her chest. Bridget had wanted to come home. Rowan remembered the faint, aching sweetness she had sometimes sensed in her mother, buried deep. There had always been a hint of sorrow. Bridget had stayed away to protect them. But she had never stopped wanting to find her way back. "She knew she couldn't," Rowan said softly. Bitter traces of heartbreak and unfinished love curled on her tongue. She ached for everything Bridget had given up to protect Biddy's magic.

"No." Everly's gaze drifted toward the house, the glass of the windows fogged. "She stayed away to protect you, but even the strongest magic frays under longing."

Rowan considered her grandmother's words. Bridget had longed to come home, for Simon, and for what she left behind. That longing pulled at the edges of her magic, weakening it over time. "That's how Cillian found her, isn't it? Her longing frayed her magic."

"Yearning is human and messy, and . . . unavoidable. Even magic, as powerful as it is, isn't immune to the quiet unraveling that comes from deep, unresolved emotion.

Rowan's eyes traced the outline of Swallow Hall, knowing that the walls still held Bridget's absence, cradled like a lonely shadow. But beneath that ache, she could taste something new now. It was faint and unfinished, but it was real.

Hope.

Bridget had left Simon Moody behind to protect everything and everyone she loved, but maybe—just maybe—there was space now to reclaim what had been lost. To forge something new with their father. It might not be simple. But it was a beginning.

* * *

Later, Rowan filled the scrying bowl with water. The surface rippled as she added a few drops of Biddy's oil and waited.

She peered into the bowl, focusing on the reflection. Finally, the vision came. A cliffside road above the Atlantic. Bridget stood there, her hair loose and tangled by the sea air. Behind her, parked at an angle on the shoulder, was the turquoise and white Nash.

Bridget wasn't crying. She wasn't scared. She was focused. Sharp. Determination clear on her face.

Rowan blinked, and the image shifted.

A man appeared behind her. It was Cillian, who Rowan and her sisters had known as Warren. His stance was tense, predatory, like he thought he was still in control. He reached for Bridget's arm.

Bridget didn't flinch. She stepped back, just enough. She said something, her mouth forming deliberate words Rowan understood: *It will never be yours.*

Then she tossed something over the cliff's edge. A book.

Cillian lunged for it, but pulled up short at the edge, watching in horror.

Bridget ducked low, spun, and sprinted for the car. Tires squealed. Dust rose.

The final image was Cillian on the rocks below holding the book Bridget had thrown over the edge. It had been a decoy. A false trail. Not Biddy's grimoire. He was furious. He'd been beaten not by strength, but by Bridget's cunning.

Rowan gasped, clutching the edge of the table as the vision snapped away.

This was the proof that their mother had run not to escape Bird Island or Swallow Hall or Everly. She had run to protect all she held dear. All she loved. She had outsmarted the man who'd hunted her, and disappeared, leaving behind a trail only her daughters would one day be able to follow.

Rowan closed her eyes. Counted to five. Reeled back when she opened them again and looked into the scrying bowl. Bridget stared right at her. Her mouth moved, but no sound came out. Rowan bent closer. "Say it again," she said, wrapping the palms of her hands around the outside of the stone bowl.

Bridget's mouth moved again, slow and deliberate, as if she knew this moment would come and that Rowan would one day be watching.

The image blurred, then sharpened, Bridget's face filling the surface of the scrying bowl until there was nothing else. Her expression was calm and loving but fierce.

She repeated the words, again and again.

Rowan blinked, focused, and watched until she finally understood.

I didn't just leave to save the magic. I left to save you.

Through teary eyes, Rowan saw her mother speak again. This time, she could almost hear it, like words whispered on the wind. *All of it was for you.*

Rowan carried those words with her when the fireflies came out and the four Early women stood in the moon circle.

"Are you sure?" Everly asked.

All three of them nodded. They'd never been more certain of anything. This was where they belonged, where they'd make their dreams come true, and it was where Bridget's ashes belonged, part of the sand and earth, part of Bird Island, an ever-present protector of them all.

A Sky Girl, forever.

Author's Note

House of Spells and Secrets was born the moment I discovered the nineteenth-century healer Biddy Early (born Bridget Ellen Connors).

She lived in County Clare, Ireland, during a time in history that was shaped by poverty, superstition, and colonial pressure. Despite the odds, Biddy carved out a life that defied every expectation and societal norm (she was married four times and often to younger men!). She was a healer and herbalist, known for her remedies made from plants and roots, her deep spiritual intuition, and the infamous blue bottle she carried with her always. It was a vessel many believed to hold otherworldly knowledge or power . . . and it was the inspiration for the vial Rowan finds in my story.

Biddy's book of curses and cures is my own invention, as she never learned to read or write. Her wisdom came from older places. It was passed through generations, whispered from the land, and carried in her bones. People came to her when no one else could help. When doctors failed, when priests could offer no comfort, or when illness, grief, or bad luck took root, people turned to Biddy.

Despite her gift of healing, the Church and the authorities feared her. In 1865, she was one of the few women in Ireland ever to be tried under the Witchcraft Act of 1586. Crazy! The case was dismissed (thankfully), but the message was pretty clear: women like Biddy, who healed and who didn't follow the rules, were dangerous.

There was, and still is, something incredibly powerful about Biddy's presence in Irish history. To me, she exists at the crossroads of myth and reality. When I first read about her, something inside me stirred to life. I couldn't stop thinking about how fiercely she lived and how unapologetically she took up space in a world that didn't quite know what to do with women like her. She was admired but also feared.

Biddy Early is remembered as a wise woman, a healer, a rebel. She was a *spéirmhná*, which is a poetic Irish term that can be translated as "sky woman or sky girl." I love this! To me, it speaks of someone untethered by the rules of the world, someone who listens to the sky and walks in two realms at once.

This book is not Biddy's story, but it is absolutely inspired by her essence. Her spirit is woven into these pages, and her legacy echoes in every word. I see *House of Spells and Secrets* as a spell of remembrance. It's a small act of honoring a woman that history almost forgot and a way to keep her story alive.

House of Spells and Secrets is my way of saying *Biddy, I see you and I carry your magic. Within me and this story, you live on.*

Acknowledgments

This book may have my name on the cover, but it's stitched together with the love, support, and encouragement of so many people. I have been held through every step of this journey by the most incredible circle of humans.

To my dad—this is the hardest part to write. You have always been my biggest cheerleader, the one who never once questioned whether I could do this writing thing, and who always knew I'd be successful. You believed in me so fully and so fiercely that sometimes, when I didn't have enough belief of my own, I leaned on yours. Losing you this year has left an empty space in my life that nothing else can fill. I wish, more than anything, that you could be here to hold this book in your hands. I hope, wherever you are, you know how much of your belief in me, your love, your steady, grounding presence lives in these pages. This one's for you.

To my mom—my first and forever best friend. Your love has always been such a steadying force. You listen without judgment, encourage without hesitation, and remind me of my worth when I forget. I carry so much of your quiet strength and unshakable grace in everything I do, and I'm endlessly grateful that I get to call you mine.

To Carlos, my partner in everything—thank you for being the unwavering support and ever-present love in my life. From the very beginning, you've been beside me, through messy drafts, last-minute edits, looming deadlines, and late-night bursts of creativity. Your patience, your positive energy, and your belief that I could achieve my dream mean more than I can ever put into words. I'm lucky beyond measure to do life with you.

To my kids—Caleb, Sophia, Jared, Sam, and Alex—you've grown up with a mom chasing stories and deadlines. You never once made me feel like this dream was selfish or out of reach. You are kind, brilliant, compassionate humans, and I'm so proud of each of you. Thank you for the patience, the hugs, the curiosity, and the understanding when I needed space and time to write. You've always believed in me, and that means more than I can say.

To Theresa Pastoriza-Tan, my grimoire sister—thank you for bringing magic in my life. Dreaming up this project has been one of the most joy-filled and meaningful creative experiences I've had. And to Theresa and Amy Whitney, my entrepreneurial partners, you have helped me tap into a playful and wondrous side of myself. You reminded me why I love this work, even on the hard days. Our shared world is a kind of magic all its own, and I'm so grateful we get to live it together.

To Diane Kelly and Kelly Rose Whitney—my fellow creatives and kindred spirits. You remind me every time we talk that this writing life is better when it's shared. Thank you for the friendship, the wisdom, and the laughter, and for reminding me that perfection isn't the goal but that connection is.

To Margaret Danko, my agent and partner in this crazy publishing business—thank you for believing in my stories from day one and for loving them with such fierceness and conviction. Your insight, advocacy, and unwavering support have made all the difference. What a wonderful thing it is to have an ally like you. What we have feels like a true partnership, and I'm beyond grateful to be walking this path with you.

To my publishing team at Alcove Press—Melissa Rechter, Holly Ingraham, Rebecca Nelson, Thai Fantauzzi Pérez, Dulce Botello, Mikaela Bender, Bethany Pullen, Lunaea Weatherstone, and Stephanie Manova—and to Colin Verdi for the phenomenally stunning cover: thank you, thank you, thank you! I can't tell you how much I appreciate your trust in me as a storyteller and your belief in this book. Melissa, your guidance and insight helped make *House of Spells and Secrets* shine brighter. I'm incredibly grateful for the care, talent, and enthusiasm you've all poured into this story.

There were moments while writing this book when time seemed to bend a little. It was as if the words came from some powerful liminal space, somewhere just beyond the veil. It was during these times when I felt closest to the heart of this story, to Biddy Early, and to the magic that I believe pulses beneath everything. That feeling, and those threads of wonder, memory, and something unseen, are embedded in every word. I hope you feel it too.

Finally, to you, lovely reader—whether this is your first book of mine or your tenth (or thirtieth!)—thank you. Thank you for returning to the worlds I create, for loving these characters, for trusting me to take you on what I hope has been a magical journey. Every story I write is, in a manner, a love letter to you.

There's no single path to finishing a book, but if I've learned anything during my writing career (and I've learned a lot), it's that stories don't come to life in isolation. They're built on a foundation of memory, love, friendship, and hope.

And yes—always a little magic too.

Ivy Cassidy/Melissa Bourbon